COMPANION

FIRST OF THE NINE BLOODLINES

K. R. BADY

TANGLEWOOD PRESS

To Frank and Nate
For their endless support in becoming the person and creator
I was meant to be.

To Nayya
For making me a significantly better writer.

CONTENTS

*E*arth was a dumpster fire, as far as planets were concerned. It started running out of resources centuries ago when humanity was still on top of the food chain and had yet to completely fuck Mother Nature over. The American Port was one of the few that maintained its legacy as a stubborn stronghold against the elements.

The Guards responsible for keeping interspecies violence to a minimum were likewise immovable. They had to be, because there wasn't enough money, time, or blind optimism in the universe to make their jobs easier. At least their endless list of problems no longer included the antiquated communication system. Again.

"Thank God," one of the watching Guards muttered as the station's intercom system buzzed to life.

Sly closed the control panel with a cheeky grin. "That's not my name, but you're welcome anyway."

A chorus of long-suffering groans and reluctant chuckles answered him from the surrounding Guards. Sly's dad, John Spurgeon, rolled his eyes as he chuckled.

The communications center was tiny. Gray walls framed

the setup, and there were just two cracked monitors, an array of controls, a microphone for announcements, and a switchboard. Sly's dad sat in the sole rickety seat, the center's dispatch headset on his head. The control panel was tucked under the desktop, no matter how many times Sly had complained about the inconvenience over the years. He had to back out on his hands and knees before popping to his feet.

"Since I don't actually work here," he said, dusting off his knees, "how about you pay me with some of that premium moon-made chocolate you confiscated yesterday?"

John's expression cooled. "No."

Someone else scoffed. "A bit late to ask for special favors, Sly."

"Come on!" Sly whined. "You wouldn't have an intercom if it weren't for me! I think single-handedly keeping this trash operating for over a decade with my free child-labor more than earns me a treat." He held up his fingers in a pinching gesture. "Just a little one."

"No," several voices chortled.

A Guard clapped him on the back fondly. "Thanks again, kid. For real."

Another waved, saying, "You're a good one, Spurgeon."

As the assembled Guards began to disperse, Sly was jostled out of the way till he and his old man were alone. Without the audience, relief began to spread across John's face, the creases between his brows easing, the bags under his eyes sagging. He wasn't bad looking, but plain, with limp brown hair and dull brown eyes, with too much gray in his hair. There were too many lines on his forehead and craters on his cheeks.

John Spurgeon was young at forty-seven years old. On a different planet, he would be at the prime of his life.

Unfortunately, John was too enamored with the used-up Earth beneath his feet to trade it in for greener pastures.

Sly had a touch of red in his short brown hair, but otherwise, he was the spitting image of his dad at twenty-three: brown hair and eyes, fair skin, and long, gangly limbs. Sly hoped he didn't look as bone-weary and aged as John within a couple decades.

Sly clapped his hands together, rubbing excitedly. "Since my plan to get at the good stuff failed, let's move on to the real reason I stopped by."

John's eyes brightened. "You quit your job?"

"Nope."

John slumped back into his chair.

Sly whipped out a canister from his pocket and checked that the weather seal was intact. He smacked it on the smooth section of the switchboard that masqueraded as a desk.

John grimaced. "Oh, kid. You shouldn't have."

Sly grinned. "You're welcome!"

"I mean it. You really shouldn't have—"

"Don't hate! Nutrient packets might feel like sawdust, but they do the job and go down smooth if you mix them with enough liquid."

"If you say so."

"I do," Sly insisted, tossing the meal to him. "Ungrateful brat. Eat your damn lunch."

"You have a remarkable gift for reminding me why I avoid HEPP with more diligence than I do vamp territory."

The only thing John distrusted more than the Nocturni was the Human Existence and Preservation Project. The organization that ensured their species' survival shouldn't logically be on any man's shit list, but logic didn't hold much sway for conservative folks like John when it came to anything too different from themselves.

Sly and his dad didn't see eye-to-eye on a lot of things, though, and neither of them was good at biting their tongues.

But Sly tried, even as he sassed, "Yes, you're inordinately lucky to have someone looking after your sorry ass."

John lifted the thermos unenthusiastically. "It's not your job to take care of me."

"Not my job to keep your ancient tech up and running either." Sly perched his hip on the corner of the console and patted it. "But here we are."

"Here we are," John mocked, bringing the sustenance toward his mouth. He caught Sly's eye and paused. "You know… The Guard would be happy to have you."

Sly's jaw tensed. "Don't start."

"We don't need the money that bad—"

"We do."

"If my job's not glamorous enough for you—"

Sly cut him off with a high, terse laugh.

"I'm trying to have a serious discussion here, Sylvester! You have other options!"

"Yeah? How well do they pay?"

John looked away. A clenched fist covered his frown as he scowled down at his meager meal.

Sly glared at the ceiling and counted the cracks in the overhead cement. Words clipped, he said, "We need the money."

Sly hoped they could just leave it at that.

John said, "I called the bank this morning."

Sly closed his eyes and groaned.

"I know exactly how much we have stashed away, boy. We have more than enough to cover taxes and necessary home repairs for a few years at least."

Sly groaned. "It's not about the house, Dad."

John leaned forward, his chair squeaking. "No. It's about you being unreasonable."

Sly guffawed.

John flushed, his voice dripping with accusation. "We could have replaced the airlocks on the windows ten times over by now with that money, Sylvester!"

Sly laughed mirthlessly. "With the shit rejects available at Earthly warehouses? They'd need to be replaced again within a year."

"Which we can apparently afford!" John waved his hand dismissively. "I'll deal with it when the time comes. I always have—"

"No!" Sly shoved off the desk. His wrist snapped as he gestured between them. "*We* will always be dealing with it! We can't keep running paycheck-to-paycheck patching things as we go or I will still be fucking *dealing* with it after you've worked yourself into an early grave, and in twenty years, I'll be right behind you!"

There was no pretending to be calm anymore, not once he lost control of his volume and his jaw ached from grinding his teeth too long. He should have cut the conversation there, but the words kept flying off his tongue with zero regard for familial peace.

"But, sure, let's keep wasting away on this rock. Mom would be so happy for us."

"Shut your damn mouth!" John lurched to his feet, sending his chair crashing into the wall as he shook his fist in Sly's face. The red on his cheeks flared, and the color emphasized the lines in his skin.

Sly hated red. He saw so much of it on this stupid, toxic planet. A familiar spike of unpleasantness raced down his spine as he watched the splotches on his father's face shift with shadows, mortal flesh mimicking the rolling smoke and devastating fires outside.

"Hit me if it'll make you feel better," Sly said, chin up and arms spread wide, "but you know I'm right. This isn't what she wanted, and it's not what I want."

John's temper infused his cheeks with a tinge of purple as he hissed, "You don't get to disrespect me in my own office."

"Stars above." Sly huffed, pulling up his sleeve to tap at the busted comms unit wrapped around his wrist. It whined at him then flickered a halfhearted projection of the time. "I'm not doing this right now. I have to get to work."

He turned to leave and John shouted after him, "There are other ways to earn money, Sly."

"Not fast enough," Sly shot over his shoulder.

John grumbled as the door slammed closed between them. "So impatient, Sly…"

"'*SO IMPATIENT, SLY,*'" SLY MOCKED AN HOUR LATER AS HE ripped his mask off. "Damn right. I hate it here."

He jammed his mask into his locker. One filter's heavy casing hit the back wall and clanked to the floor, leaving a noticeable dent behind. The mask was unscathed. Naturally. It wouldn't protect him from the inhospitable atmosphere if it couldn't take a casual beating.

At least part of the universe had its priorities in order.

"It's what he knows," Blythe replied as she finished applying her makeup in the locker beside his. "Besides, he has a point."

"Which one? The part where we should replace the bad airlocks with different bad airlocks? Or the part where I should be grateful to be alive and just suck it up like everyone else?"

"It's a fair question." She flipped dark curls over her shoulder, plush lips pouting as if she were an up-and-coming Moon Diva. Her voice deepened with a comic grumble, "Why can't you live and die on this rock like every other nobody, Sylvester?"

Sly gaped at her. "You sound just like him!"

She winked saucily. How she managed it without looking ridiculous was beyond him. It probably had to do with her effortless confidence and well-proportioned face. Ever since childhood, Sly always knew Blythe Ramos to strut about with an innate acceptance of her place in the world. She was born an Earthling in the same shabby hospital in the same grimy port as Sly but, unlike him, it never seemed to bother her. She owned her misfortune and wore it well.

It was no wonder Blythe was a much happier person than Sly.

Sly bent down to replace his outdoor boots with a pair of sleek dress shoes that would never see the harsh light of day. When he looked back up, Blythe was watching him with a somber glower.

He sighed. "All right. Give it to me."

"Give you what?"

He beckoned for her to be forthcoming. "You know, the scolding. The talking-to. The sage advice making me question how much makeup you're wearing to hide such deep lines of wisdom-granting life experience."

She rolled her eyes; the gesture was like looking in a mirror despite her drastically darker coloring. She grinned despite herself. "You're such a spaz."

"Tell me something I don't know."

They knew each other too well. They were two of a

measly hundred-or-so people born to their generation of Americans, after all. Sly couldn't recall the last time he saw another of their classmates; they probably had the sense to leave while the planet was still intact enough to launch from.

While he was thinking, Blythe's attitude eased into a sad smile.

He glared at her. "What?"

"You're smart, Sly."

"Pretty sure I specified 'something I don't know,' but okay." He raised his chin expectantly. "Go on."

"Your dad's never leaving this port."

It might have been less chilling if she'd dumped ice water over his head.

She sighed as she approached and rubbed his shoulders. "Even if you manage to afford two passes off-world, you'll never convince him to go."

Sly said nothing. He unfolded his arms to ease the tightness in his chest. He tried to relax the muscles in his jaw and shoulders. As usual, it did no good.

Blythe squeezed him gently. "This is what he knows."

He nodded, throat tight and eyes burning. "The Guard cut his hours again. He talks like it irritates him, but sticking him behind a desk last year wasn't enough. He can barely keep up with the workload, and with the vamp on-human crime rate growing like it is, it's only a matter of time before they have to put him back on patrols."

Sly paused to clear his throat. He kept clearing it. He was stuck in the moment, a lump blocking his airway, and a monstrous weight pressed him into the floor.

Blythe hugged him. "Sly?"

He nudged her away. "Sorry, it's just…"

"I know. Law enforcement is a rough career for anyone,

even in the strictly human sectors." Her tone was sympathetic.

John tended to avoid areas of town where Nocturni gathered, but that meant less and less every year. Most of the species preferred the safety and comforts of life beyond the reach of Earth's vengeance, but it didn't take many of them to overwhelm the planet's lingering humans.

"He's nearing retirement, right?"

Sly winced. "Not for another sixteen years. He enlisted later than most."

John used to be a communications electrician, but that was before his wife died. Blythe was well aware. She'd been there the day it happened.

"Damn."

"Yep." Sly scrubbed his palms over his face till his cheeks burned. "Okay. Enough of that."

Like the good friend she was, Blythe let it go. They were less than five minutes late to their posts as a result. Apparently, that was long enough.

Sly found their boss pacing a hole in the carpet of the employee-only hallway, blocking the door to Sly's parlor. The sight made him grin.

Phink was secretly one of Sly's favorite people. He'd been splicing for longer than Sly had been alive, and enough bear DNA made it into his system to have a pronounced effect on his appearance. With long, haphazard fur of various browns, Phink looked like a bedraggled teddy bear who'd grown a beard and gotten himself zapped by an electrical short a few too many times. His finely pressed suit, complete with a golden tie and belt, did nothing to contain the fuzziness.

"Time is money, Earthling!" Phink snapped from Sly to the door.

"I know! Relax, Phinkly."

"We have three vamps in there tonight, Sly, and they're getting tetchy."

"I'm hardly late!"

"And that," Phink poked him in the chest, "is exactly what makes this business so problematic."

Sly quirked his head in confusion. "My characteristic tardiness has that much effect on your business? I think I'm flattered, Phinkerton."

"You're an idiot."

Phink's general disdain was a comfortable pretense. Originally from Luna, Phink hadn't been to the moon in decades. Earth was his home. He was an honorary Earthling, just with a better wardrobe.

Sly rolled his eyes. "I'll make it up to them, Phinkle. Promise."

"You do that." As Sly opened the door, Phink gave a halfhearted mutter, "Quit fucking with my name!"

"Sure thing, Phinkster!"

"Spurgeon!"

Phink cut himself off as Sly opened the door. Sly shot his disgruntled boss a wink before vanishing into the dim lounge.

Showtime.

"Good evening, lovelies!"

Sly twirled to face his guests with enough gusto to forgive his gracelessness. Thanks to years of practice, he didn't fall on his ass, but he doubted it would matter either way. His long, gangly limbs could flail about with all the coordination of a brain damaged rodent, and he would still have a job.

The room erupted with noise as he stumbled into view.

"You're late!" someone shouted from the crowd.

"We missed you!" Another pouted as she leered at him. Glancing over, all he saw were boobs and fangs.

That was all he could make out from the cacophony. The sound used to be startling, disturbing even. Now, he recognized the cheers for what they were.

"My sincerest apologies!" Sly yelled, his grin shameless.

There were enough humanoid vocals in the crowd that night to make the sound almost pleasant, though it remained alien as ever. The majority of his audience were Nocturni, according to the chittering, gurgling calls, and lusty growls. It took excessive and painful treatment to warp a human's vocal chords, but the Nocturni borrowed animal attributes with ease.

Odds were good that Sly was the only unmodified person in the room, maybe the whole building. America didn't have Europe's sterling reputation for top-tier human eye-candy, and expectations of finding a bona fide pureblood in the port were kept at a lukewarm rumor.

It was a narrow point at the intersection of a lucrative career and mortal danger. After five years, Sly knew how to keep his balance.

The volume lowered as attention focused on him. Sly gave his eyes a moment to adjust to the theater lighting, shooting smiles and gestures at his regulars as he moseyed through the tables toward the raised platform at the center of the room.

"Believe me, I wish I were here earlier collecting overtime and flirting with you beauties. Sadly, it couldn't be helped!" With a dramatic sigh, Sly's grin turned impish. "Daddy issues, you know?"

They chuckled and clucked appropriately, tickled as always by his easy humor.

That was why they came to Centrism: to see him. To feel his presence, breathe his air, know his scent and, if they were lucky, feel his skin. They wanted a reminder of their humanity.

The more Earth degraded, the more the human race fought to redefine themselves and adapt to the wider universe. At some point over the centuries, people gave up on the planet and turned their collective attention toward cleaner, starrier horizons. Eventually, some rich bastards decided it was easier to alter their own genetics than to keep terraforming new planets into something habitable. So, *Homo nocturni* were created, and the rest of humanity was busy playing catch up with their evolved cousins by injecting themselves with additives and creature DNA.

Fortunately, that worked out for Sly. Mostly.

He reached the stage, and the crowd erupted with renewed cheers. He spun to survey the room, another packed House, and sidled over to Phink's prized antique keyboard. He was no pianist, but Phink taught him a few jingles after Sly fixed up the keys and made the relic operable. He reached over from the far side to tap out a little tune, and the promise of a melody was enough to rally the crowd into a hush.

He waited for complete silence.

Then, Sly teased, "How about a song?"

The answering cheer was deafening.

Sly's spirits lifted. The exhausting argument with his dad faded into nothingness, and the ever-present threat of sunstorms and unbreathable air fell to the wayside.

Sly opened his mouth and sang.

It was as if he were casting a spell. As if he were magic itself, hypnotizing them just by being. As far as Sly was concerned, he could barely carry tune and he had no formal training to speak of, but that meant nothing to the raw power he wielded from that stage. He was one man among outlandishly intimidating and powerful beings. Most of them could squash him more easily than Sly could breathe the air of his native planet.

People like John saw it as a risk, his paycheck earned in vulnerability and degradation. Sly knew better. Centrism was the best thing in the whole, wide, wasting-away world.

He was the smallest and weakest of them by far, but he commanded the room's attention just by existing. So, he sang and, for the briefest moment, the world stopped crashing down around him.

CHAPTER 2

*W*orking at Centrism was a heady thing. It was a shining diamond in the grimy muck of Earth-bound life.

Was it a legitimate business? Absolutely.

Was it good money? Hell yes.

Was it fun? Usually.

Did it make him feel sleazy on occasion? Yes.

No job was perfect.

"Charming as always, Sylvester."

Sly stiffened as he descended the stage at the end of his Saturday night shift. Like all humans on staff, Sly knew a predator's attention when he had it.

"Le Vau." Sly kept his tone professional as he stepped aside.

He avoided the hand chasing after his ass. Quin Le Vau never attended a performance without a casual groping attempt. With his other regulars, Sly sometimes allowed contact, but Le Vau was a loner Nocturnus, the sort of entitled personality that earned a bad reputation. A real vampire.

Sly discreetly put some distance between them. "Show's over."

Le Vau chuckled. "Yes. One of these days, you'll have to give me a private encore."

"Not likely."

It was ironic, really; Le Vau wasn't the only regular Sly refused to be alone with, but he was one of the few that Sly found unfairly attractive. Lean and tall, dark-haired with bronzed skin, and a strong, smooth jaw, Le Vau had the look of a galactically renowned celebrity despite the unusually large fangs sprouting from his mouth. Looking like that, he should have been on Luna, beloved by his Harem, the extended family unit the Nocturni formed from a shared bloodline. It was anyone's guess how he ended up on Earth, divorced from his Harem and living among remnants of Earthly society. Sometimes, Sly thought he preferred solitude; other times, he was convinced Le Vau wasn't there by choice.

Sly wasn't the only one with suspicions.

"Move along, bloodsucker."

A large mass of golden skin planted itself between him and Le Vau.

Le Vau's flirtatiousness vanished as he glared up at the newcomer. "Watch your tone, Earthling."

Tilla was another of Sly's regulars. If any human could beat the crap out of a Nocturnus, it would be them. At nearly six feet tall and built like a curvy tank with killer boobs, they were large by human standards. Tilla's skin and hair were golden as a lion, their demeanor easily as proud and tough. Their clothing was tight and high-quality, and it did nothing to hide their muscle.

As Tilla stared down the vampire, Sly thought he heard a low, warning purr and, not for the first time, he wondered how much lion DNA was in their veins.

Le Vau studied Tilla, clearly weighing his chances in a fair fight. The vamp's fingers, dressed in fine leather gloves, curled into a fist, and he began to growl. Sly reconsidered whether fairness would be a factor; there was no telling what advantages Le Vau might have digested lately.

Tilla was a good person and a great tipper. Sly didn't want to see them thrown through a wall tonight.

"Alrighty, then." Sly peered around Tilla's bulk with forced cheer. "How about we all put our dicks away and—"

"You have your dick out?" Tilla glanced at him, hopeful.

Le Vau laughed. Sly nearly did too. Tilla stood between them, completely serious and perplexed, and the threat of violence passed.

Le Vau's chuckle turned mean, and Tilla's gaze narrowed on him again. "Unless you're leaving a tip, I suggest you walk away now."

"You'll have to forgive me." Le Vau's smile had as much charm as it did fang. "I had my heart set on taking Sly for a drink this evening."

"No thanks," Sly interjected.

Le Vau turned that false pleasantness toward him. "You'll have to give me a chance eventually."

"I don't, actually."

"I've been telling you for years now—"

"And I've been saying no for years."

Le Vau's smile was sharp, heated. "Yes. I do love a good chase."

"Wow." Sly took a step back into the safety of Tilla's shadow. "Your creepiness has successfully wowed me into changing my mind. Let me slip into something more comfortable and grab refreshments from the bar. What would you like? A shot of holy water? Some garlic bread, maybe?"

"Sly," no less than three voices said his name with pronounced exasperation.

Sly peeked around Tilla to find his bodyguard had doubled. Le Vau was still eyeing him like a piece of meat, but now Phink was there, nearly shoulder-to-shoulder with the leonine human. His expression was thunderously unhappy.

Sly scooted into their combined shadows like the little mortal he was. "Shutting up now."

"You do that." Phink focused his glare on Le Vau. "If you want a private session, you can fill out the paperwork like everybody else. I make no promises you'll get approved."

Le Vau graced Sly with a chilling smirk as he strode away. "Until your next show, Sylvester."

The moment he was well and gone, Phink turned on Sly with his teddy-bear muzzle pinched like something smelled bad. He flicked a finger at Sly's face.

"Ow!" Sly grabbed the stinging tip of his nose. "What was that for?"

"You have a smart mouth, Earthling."

"Indeed." Tilla crossed their arms, frowning at Sly.

For his part, Phink seemed only mildly judgmental. "You know that superstitious nonsense has no effect on Nocturni, right?"

"No shit. You actually think I'm an idiot, huh?"

They stared at him, unimpressed.

"Yes," Sly reassured dryly, "I know real vampires are not demonic entities. No more than the rest of us, anyway."

Tilla nodded, satisfied.

Phink sighed and walked away, grumbling, "I swear, Sly, keep taunting him, and one of these days, he's going to back you into a dark corner and take a bite out of your ass."

In his wake, Tilla added, "The Nocturni are dangerous. Especially for you."

"I'm aware," Sly agreed snidely.

"Earthly ports are unfunded and ill-equipped to keep the peace. It'd be safer for you off-planet."

"I know that, too."

"You could always take me up on my offer."

"And there it is!" Sly sang, exasperated.

Tilla was a successful interplanetary trader. They had their own state-of-the-art ship and everything, including a peculiar fetish for skinny, pale boys with more sarcasm than sense.

"I only come here for you, Sly."

After all this time, Tilla still made him blush. Sly had a hard time seeing what all the fuss was about. Tilla was as close to organically human as any of Sly's guests. Sure, they undoubtedly spliced so their mortal body could withstand indefinite space travel, but to the naked eye, they could almost pass as pure-blooded. Almost. Sly was sure a decade of splicing with giraffe molecules wouldn't give him Tilla's height.

"You have shit timing," he told them. "I'm off for the weekend. Unless you're planning to stick around a few days, you won't see much of me."

Tilla gave him a slow once-over. "You could still make the trip worth my while."

He laughed. If there was as much resignation in his voice as there was in Tilla's, no one commented on it.

Earth was far from a grand tourist attraction. Between the unstable atmosphere, hostile weather, and most of its originating species either fleeing or dying off, resources were rare, viable opportunities even more so. Humans too stubborn and stupid to leave were the only remaining commodity.

Sly was plenty stubborn, but he wasn't stupid.

"My crew would love to have you," Tilla reminded him. "Come with us?"

Sly's heart seized before plummeting toward the ground. "Thanks, but you're not my type. Besides, I can't leave my dad."

~

SLY DID NOT WAKE UP AT SIX IN THE MORNING ON HIS DAY OFF for just anyone. Blythe was special. He got her back to her tiny apartment in one piece, but he wasn't thrilled about it.

"Remind me why you do this again?" Sly teased, yanking her coat from her arms.

Normally, Blythe carried the heavy protective layers necessary to survive outdoors with ease. Normally, she wasn't hours fresh out of a splicing session.

"Fuck you." She scowled as he pried off her mask. She looked miserable, even a little green under her dark complexion.

"Rude." Sly shoved her.

Blythe flopped onto the futon just inside the doorway. It doubled as her bed, so she would likely stay put for the night.

"Son of a bitch," she grumbled, boneless and splayed out where she landed.

"Excuse you," Sly snipped as he hopped over to the kitchenette. "I'm not the one with animal DNA coursing through my veins."

"It's feline, not canine. Keep your facts straight if you're going to insult people."

"Yes, ma'am."

"I changed my mind. You're not the son. You're the bitch."

"Aw! You say the nicest things!"

She gagged, possibly for show, but maybe not.

"You need to eat." Sly began hunting through her fridge for something mild.

"I'll puke."

"You won't."

It was a casual, emotionless exchange, their words dulled by repetition. Blythe started elective splicing when they were kids, and Sly was always the one to care for her during recovery. She might not trust anyone else to be there for her; sure as sun's fire, Sly didn't.

"How about...?" Sly whistled, perusing the shelves. "Dry cereal? Is it still breakfast if it's nearly noon? It's technically still morning, and you haven't eaten yet."

Blythe wasn't allowed to eat for eight hours leading up to the procedure. She was no Nocturna with the born ability to integrate foreign genes simply by drinking a donor's blood. For humans, a full stomach made the process worse. She was usually ravenous by the time he got her home, but sometimes—

She gagged again, heaving violently.

"Maybe later then," Sly quipped, peeking over to ensure she wasn't choking on vomit.

He returned to the futon with a bottle of water. The moment he sat down, her head landed on his thigh.

"Ugh," she groaned. "You're so bony. Worst cuddle buddy ever."

Sly rolled his eyes as he stroked hair from her face. He glanced down, rebuttal ready, but it died on his tongue. Her beautiful brown skin was discolored beneath his fingertips.

Blythe made a discontented noise when the petting was interrupted. "Don't stop. Please?"

Sly resumed stroking. The hint of wrongness was directly over her temple, creeping toward her hairline. If his fingers repeatedly passed over the mark to confirm the texture of smooth, plain flesh, she didn't notice.

"What splice was it this time?"

She closed her eyes as she snuggled into him. "A little jaguar. It's a wild cat from ancient times."

Sly leaned closer. The mark seemed less like a blossoming bruise and more like a yellowing circle ringed in black. "You don't say."

"Don't judge," she chided without heat. "It's an investment in my career."

He snorted. "Right. Your ultimate goal in life is to retire early from Centrism at the ripe age of forty by making bank off all the humanity fetishists you can find. Look, it's not the splicing I have an issue with—"

"Yeah? You're sounding an awful lot like your old man."

"No," he squawked with affront. "I don't care about splicing, but I do care about you, and yes, I do judge you for setting your standards so abysmally low. You won't be young and pretty forever, you know, and Phink doesn't have stellar retirement plans."

Centrism was like all HEPP's Houses, it was the best money a mortal could make on Earth, but it was no more than the money-making entertainment that funded HEPP. Not everyone was cut out for show business, so the organization funneled every coin they could justify into off-world programs. There were few ports still struggling on Earth's surface, but HEPP had a House in each of them.

Centrism was rolling in unaccustomed riches since Sly joined the payroll, but everyone knew Europe was where real opportunity lay. When the Nocturni took on a Companion, the walking blood bag always seemed to originate from Europe's Port.

Sly studied the faint blemish on Blythe's head with a

scowl, "I don't follow the logic here, Blythe. Further altering your genetic makeup will help achieve your lofty career goals... how, exactly?"

She sighed. "Sorry I don't have any of your alluring sass and adorable charm, Sly. Most of my tips come from dancing, and there are limits to what this mortal ass can do."

"They don't come for your masterful choreography."

"No," she agreed, "but the more impressive the show, the better the pay. So long as I look pure."

The spot on her temple seemed darker than it was moments ago.

"Let me guess, wild cats are natural athletes?"

She started counting traits on her fingers. "Agility. Stamina. Reflexes. Strength. This splice will get me going faster and better for the rest of my years on that stage. In the end, I'll have enough to move to Europe and languish in relative comfort and serenity."

"Assuming sun fire doesn't burn the entire continent to ash first." His reply dripped with condemnation. "Or you could do the smart thing, and trade in those tips tomorrow for a one-way ticket off this rock."

Admittedly, he was envious. She'd been in this game longer, and what she lacked in so-called charm, she more than made up for with sex appeal. Fresh out of a splicing session, she still was gorgeous in tight leggings and a skimpy top.

"I could say the same thing to you, boy,"

They were well-matched when it came to sass.

Sly laugh humorlessly. "I'm years away from affording interplanetary passage for two, and you know it."

Blythe blinked up at him imploringly.

"Don't," he warned.

"You should do it."

"I said don't."

"Half a dozen folks from Centrism would give you a ride out of here tomorrow, if you asked."

"Their charity doesn't extend to my family."

Blythe rolled onto her back and stared at him till he twitched.

"I'm not leaving without him."

It sounded pathetic even in his head, but out loud? Sly wanted to bash his skull against the wall. He knew where that line of thought could lead him though, so he cut it off at the start.

Blythe let out a breath, soft and sad.

"Can we not do this right now?" Sly's face warmed as he looked away. "I'm supposed to be having a break from the papa-drama here."

She frowned. "Only you would call this 'a break.' Stars above, Sly, you need a life."

"Hey!" He slapped her exposed belly. "You're way less work to look after! This is a vacation by comparison."

He gestured around her studio apartment. Blythe's place was a quarter the size but four times the value of his dad's house. There were cracks in her countertops and the bathroom door was missing, but the window was solid, inches thicker than what awaited him at home. Blythe's entire building was sturdy and impervious to the elements.

"Someday," she said, "I'm going to drag you on a real vacation, and then you will know the error of your ways, Sylvester Spurgeon."

"Sure," Sly agreed cheekily, "but you'll have to find someone to keep Dad out of trouble while I'm gone."

She stuck her tongue out at him, then snuggled closer. In doing so, her shirt slipped off her shoulder to reveal not one, but three faint circles. One of them had a distinctly golden hue at its center.

Sly's heart plummeted.

"Was this your first taste of jaguar?" he asked, voice neutral.

It wasn't a big deal, he told himself. People exhibited phenotypes of the foreign species all the time as a side effect.

But most people didn't rely on their mundane, homogeneous looks to keep food in stock and a roof overhead. The further a human ventured from Earth, the more unrecognizable they tended to be due to splicing, and the smartest and most successful were getting as far as they could. Centrism was supposed to provide the illusion that pure humanity was still possible.

Sly was the only person at Centrism more in-demand than Blythe. It wasn't a coincidence.

Blythe shrugged that spotted shoulder. "Maybe? It's hard to tell with the big cats, they get used in splicing cocktails so often. I've definitely done feline before, though. Luna has this preserve filled with Earth's ancient cats, so I know our splicing center gets plenty of stuff from them."

"…Cool." He kept stroking her hair, grazing the marks on her forehead.

They sat in silence for long moments. Just as Sly was beginning to relax, content that Blythe was resting well, she spoke.

"I don't blame John, you know." Her eyes remained closed, body lax and blissfully ignorant, "It's far from perfect, but Earth's not all bad. It's home."

Sly glanced awkwardly at her lone window, with its carefully opaque curtain hiding thick plexiglass. "It's a death trap."

"So is space." She yawned. "At least here, I'm comfortable, with a job I like."

"You could have that anywhere." A bemused smile

crossed his face. "You just like being the prettiest girl in the neighborhood."

"True."

They shared a friendly chuckle. It was a nice sound, familiar, small, and warm.

Blythe's mirth faded with sleepiness, but she managed to say, "It's a good life, Sly."

"Maybe," he whispered, "but don't we deserve better?"

Blythe didn't answer. She was asleep.

BLYTHE HAD JAGUAR SPOTS. LOTS OF THEM.

"It'll be okay," Sly tried to reassure her. "You just have to rebrand a little."

"I'm hideous," she told her bathroom ceiling without inflection. She wasn't avoiding the mirror, exactly, but she lay motionless and despondent in her bath, surrounded by bubbles.

Sly propped his hip against the counter, snorting. "Not even whiskers and enormous ears could make you hideous."

"True." She lifted a hand to frown thoughtfully at a gold and black spot on her wrist. "Maybe I could cover them with tattoos? Our coworkers have gotten away with that, right?"

Sly dubiously eyed the spattering of spots near her hairline. "Maybe."

Her hand dropped with a blunt splash. "Whatever."

Sly crouched beside the tub, his tone reassuring. "You take this risk with every splice, right? I'm surprised something like this didn't happen sooner."

"Thank you, voice of reason. I feel so much better now."

Sly rested his chin on the tub's ledge and grinned, "Don't sass the Sass Master, girl. Or should I call you pussy cat?"

She splashed water in his face.

He stood, blinking rapidly only to see her pouting up at him. His humor evaporated.

"Sly!" she whined, "I'm supposed to be back to work tonight!"

He nodded unsympathetically. "I know. I was supposed to be back yesterday. Instead, I called in sick so I could talk your sorry ass out of taking a walk in the garden."

"Spare me," she huffed, but her gaze softened with apology. "Cover for me tonight?"

Sly groaned and dropped his forehead onto her countertop.

She splashed him again. "No dramatics! Please? Buy me one more night?"

"Why?" He straightened, hands on his hips, so he could stare her down. "So you can try soaking the new phenotype out of your skin some more?"

"Don't be an ass."

"I have my own show tonight."

She sat up and poked his knee, too fast for him to flail out of range.

"Back, foul beast!"

"Get over here, asshole!"

They yelled nonsense over each other as Sly lurched out of the tiny bathroom. He poked his head back in and stuck his tongue out.

"It's a private meet-and-greet!"

He froze, tongue extended.

Blythe's bare breasts pushed together as she leaned out of the tub. She grinned like a cat with fresh prey in its claws.

Sly sucked his tongue back into his mouth. "How much?"

"Five."

He stepped back into the bathroom, leaning on the door frame.

She added, "It's just one guy."

And she had him. If nothing else, Sly was too curious for his own good. Possibly too desperate, but he refused to look at that too closely.

"Five?" he repeated. "For one guy? Vamp?"

"Obviously."

Only Nocturni were rich and wasteful enough to dish out that kind of money for an hour with a random Earthling. Even Le Vau couldn't afford it, so they were probably talking about someone mooching off their Harem's collective riches.

Sly slid further into the room and perched his ass on the tub's ledge.

"Five grand for an hour? That's a bit suspicious, don't you think?"

She shrugged and settled back into the bath. "Phink said the request came through HEPP, and the only demand was a conversation with a pure-blooded human. At first, Phink figured it was a Humans First purist or some shit, but then he got a look at the paperwork. The guy's Nocturnus. Either way, it overlaps with my audience best, so—"

Sly's jaw unhinged as he shot to his feet. "Blythe! You've been splicing since you were twelve!"

"Thirteen!"

"Same difference!" He flung his hands up in a wild gesture. "You are not *pure* anything! Never mind if the wrong vamp gets peeved at you for false advertising, If Phink's been marketing you to Humans First activists like that, he's going to get you killed. As in dead!"

"Yeah, well—" She pointed at the animal print marking her skin. "Obviously, that's not happening anymore—"

"Anymore? Blythe! How many of your regulars have

been coming to you specifically because they think you don't splice?"

She looked up at the ceiling, chewing her lip as she counted. "Maybe... four? Five?"

Sly stared, speechless.

"...What?"

He pressed his fists into his eyes. "You are not this stupid."

She sighed and slushed back into her bath. "I have bouncers and friends at Centrism, same as you."

"*Unlike* me, you don't live with someone who has standing poker nights with those prejudiced douchebags!"

Finally, Blythe began to squirm. They normally pretended John had no knowledge of Humans First circles. Worse than that, while she was used to him yelling, Sly rarely yelled *at* her.

He heaved a breath hard enough to rock him back on his heels, and his shoulders hit the wall.

"I'll take over your meet-and-greet," he gritted through his teeth. "I'll give the vamp what he asked for in the first place."

Blythe whined into a handful of soap bubbles.

"I'll fix things with Phink, and you will park your ass in this apartment until we handle the fallout."

"I only need today—"

"What you need is an insurance policy!" Sly glared her into silence. "What do you think those five fans of yours will do if they find out you've been conning them while you secretly—" he added air quotations. "—*Pollute your body with animal fecal matter and demon spunk?*"

She flinched. The frequent protesters outside the splicing center and HEPP's main offices were memorable like that.

Sly wasn't done making his point though.

"I told you the first time you brought me to Centrism, I would never host those bigots!" He was vibrating out of his skin, his stomach tying itself in knots. "Sure, their money's as good as anyone's. But it's not a matter of pride, Blythe. It's a matter of survival. You don't fuck around with crazy!"

With that, he stormed out of the apartment.

CHAPTER 3

S ly made it home in record time and was on and off comms with similar speed. Once the necessary people recognized Blythe's situation for the shitstorm it was, he finally paused long enough to breathe. It was a bad idea.

He was a wreck.

He was exhausted, and he stank. Three days cleaning up after Blythe in the throes of splicing backlash did him no favors. The stress of the past few hours didn't help. He had no time for a nap.

He was slumped in the shower when reality hit him. He was alone in the house. At midday.

"Dad?" Sly called as he stepped out of the bathroom, towel around his waist.

The house was motionless, just himself and the shower's steam. At least John's protective gear was still missing from its hook by the door.

One parent gone for a walk in the garden was enough.

That reminder did nothing to calm the anxious boiling in his gut. He tore his eyes from the hooks to glare at a box of beer bottles on the floor by his dad's favorite chair. He didn't notice the contraband earlier, too preoccupied with Blythe. Sick with tension, he crossed the room and snatched up the nearest bottle. It was empty.

"Fuck!"

Sly tossed the bottle onto the chair and kicked the remainders over. All empty.

He wished it was a surprise. John's reaction to the very minor fortune Sly had stashed away had been rough, and the only luxury John ever wasted expenses on was booze. Sly was lucky the old man stocked up at home instead of pouring hundreds into Mickey's bar again. It was the whole reason Sly took over micromanaging their accounts shortly after his mother died.

But the old man knew about the money now. Just in time for Sly to take off for a long weekend.

"Fantastic!" Sly grabbed at his hair with both fists. "Can this day get any worse?"

Someday, he needed to learn to keep his mouth shut.

THE FIRST TIME SLY AGREED TO A PRIVATE MEETING, HE WAS terrified he was about to be sold into sexual slavery. Instead, Sly spent an hour playing therapist, listening to a guy with tusks and more facial hair than he bargained for wax poetic about Sly's enviably smooth skin. After that, his private sessions became more predictable.

The Nocturni loved him, and they had the means to fill up Sly's schedule from now until forever. He often entertained small groups of vampires, usually visitors from the Lunar Harems, out for a weekend of slumming in the most convenient Earthly port. Local loners splurged for a one-on-one less often.

Sly wasn't marketed as pure-blooded out of a healthy sense of self-preservation, but there was something subliminal about it. Unmodified human blood was considered a delicacy, rare in the modern day of mainstream splicing. John raised him to guard that information with a jealousy bordering on militant, but sometimes he wondered if the vamps knew anyway. Depending on their diet, it was possible they could smell his raw humanity.

The Nocturnus waiting for him in the lounge was precisely that kind of vamp, with an obvious taste for canines. He sniffed the air as Sly opened the door.

His eyes were lupine yellow, the tips of his ears elongated beyond the standard practice for his kind. His tawny skin was completely covered in the finest fur, with the only exception being the long ebony hair on his head and the tasteful goatee growing through the fur. Beneath it all was an androgynous, sculpturesque face. He was dressed in a deep-purple suit of an expensive material Sly couldn't name and shiny black high heels.

As Sly opened the door to the cozy lounge, the vampire stood. He was tall even without the heels, but Sly found the way he raised his chin and sniffed the air a second time more intimidating.

The vampire's grin was decorated by dainty fangs. "You're perfect."

Even in Sly's line of work, that kind of immediate come-on was unusual.

"Uh... thanks?"

Before Sly could close the door behind him, a manicured hand was shoved in his face for a hopeful shake. "I'm Master Vauqeulin, but please, call me Kamari."

It was less an invitation and more of a command, Sly noticed.

"Oh… kay," Sly hesitated, watching as Kamari settled back into the corner of the large couch that predominated the room. "Nice to meet you, Kamari. Just to let you know up-front, I don't do bloodletting."

"If I wanted a bloodwhore, I wouldn't be here. Thank you for meeting with me, Mister…?"

"Smith," Sly answered, sitting on the farthest end of the couch. "Thank you for paying me."

"You're very welcome."

There was no pretense in the way Kamari surveyed him, none of the cloying charm vamps commonly used. There was nothing threatening in the way those yellow eyes studied him, like Sly was a challenging and alluring puzzle, but he didn't like it either way. His attitude was unusual. Concerning.

Sly stretched his arms along the back of the couch, sinking down with feigned ease. "What's up?"

He wasn't ready for the blunt conversation that followed.

"When was the last time you spliced, Mr. Smith?"

"Does it matter?"

"Yes."

"…Why?"

"If it's been too recent or too often, I won't waste my time."

Sly snickered. "Your loss. You already paid me, remember?"

"For this evening, yes." Vauqeulin leaned forward, golden eyes intent on Sly's face. "If I had to guess, I'd say it's been a few years. You're… what? Twenty-six? Twenty-seven?"

"Twenty-three."

"Really?" Vauqeulin froze, and his eyes narrowed. "You haven't spliced since childhood?"

Sly's spine stiffened. "Why do you care?"

"Depending on your answer, I might want to hire you."

33

Sly summoned his most professional smile. "I'm not telling you shit about my blood work, Kamari."

He didn't like where this was going. The allure he seemed to have with vamps was supposed to be subconscious, base, and excusable. Vauqeulin watched him with a sharpness that was too knowing.

Before the vampire could respond, the lounge door opened, and in walked Phink and a frail twig of a man with spliced bug-eyes predominating his face.

"Sorry for the intrusion, Master Vauqeulin," the unknown man simpered.

"Sly," Phink sighed, shoulders sagging. "We need to talk. It's about your dad."

"HELP KEEP THE HUMAN RACE CLEAN!" A MAN YELLED through his mask, his picket sign raised high. The poster wasn't particularly creative, just a messy red "X" painted over a poorly drawn caricature of a humanoid figure humping what could arguably be called a dog. It was probably open to interpretation.

"Sign the petition!" a second protester stepped into his path with a tablet in her gloved hand. "Force the American government to refuse breeding rights to the animal sodomites who disgrace our ancestors!"

Sly muttered a numb "no thanks" into his mask as Phink urged him past the crowd.

Once safely inside, Phink announced, "Welcome to the bureaucratic side of the business: The Human Existence and Preservation Project!"

Sly snorted.

The building was utilitarian and clean, white-washed and

bland. It was devoid of Centrism's pulsing atmosphere. There were no decorations, no sitting area, just a front desk, flyers, and a single overhanging sign proclaiming the organization in residence. The guy manning the desk was drooling in boredom.

Phink and the human-bug led him straight through the lobby without further comment. Down the hall. Into a conference room. Right up to the table where Phink pulled out a chair and motioned for him to sit next to the hung-over heap of a man he called father.

"Misters John and Sylvester Spurgeon," the bug-man said as he sat down across from of them with a folder of papers. "On HEPP's behalf, I'm happy to welcome—"

"Oh, shut up," John grumbled.

Sly glared at his old man. "Don't."

"Very well." Bug-eyes cleared his throat. "You may call me Myers. I'll be your liaison and legal aid regarding this incident."

"There was no in—"

Sly kicked him under the table, and John went quiet.

After a beat of awkward silence, Phink spoke from where he stood by Sly's shoulder. "Sly works at Centrism. I can vouch for him, and we can give him an advance to cover the debt."

"That's not necessary." John glowered over his son's shoulder at Phink. "We don't need anything from your kind."

"Shut up, Dad."

"Let's slow down a bit, sir," Myers said levelly, folding his hands together over his folder. "You dug yourself a rather deep hole with Nocturni from three different Harems. They are well within their rights to demand satisfaction."

"We have the money," John scoffed, cutting him off. He

patted Sly's shoulder. "Tell him, Sly. We can take care of ourselves."

Sly glared at him. "How much did you bet?"

John shrugged. "A bit."

Myers slid a page across the table. "This much."

Sly snatched it up right from under his dad's fingertips. One glance, and he had his answer.

"Phink," Sly said on an enraged exhale, "looks like I need an advance."

"Bullshit!" John spat.

"Shut up!" Sly shoved a trembling finger in his dad's face. "Zip it! Shush. Not one single, tiny, microscopic word!"

John didn't meet his glare.

Sly shook himself. He rolled his shoulders and jimmied his leg and tried to rally.

Phink stepped up to his side. "Sly?"

Sly closed his eyes. When he opened them, he did his damnedest to pretend no one was sitting beside him.

Myers cleared his throat. "The poker game was legal, I'm afraid. The Nocturni involved are entitled to compensation."

"I figured." Sly sighed, rubbing his temples as he threw the paper onto the table.

"Bloodsuckers," John muttered nastily.

"Let me get this straight." Sly pressed his thumbs into his temples till it hurt. "You willingly sat down in a shady bar—"

"Mickey's isn't shady!"

"—with shady people, despite all the time you've been harping on me for *fraternizing*—"

John cut him off with a huff. "Their money's as good as any man's, Sly. Just because I don't want to see you degrading yourself for them—"

"I'm not doing this right now!" Sly yelled, leaping to his feet.

"Please," Myers raised a cautioning hand, "sit down, Mr. Spurgeon."

"Just tell me it's enough," Sly demanded, dragging his hands through his hair. "I've worked for HEPP through the House for years. You know I'm good for it. With the advance, it's enough. Right?"

Myers's bulbous eyes blinked rapidly. He seemed frozen.

Phink picked up the paper from the table. His furry face scrunched into a frown as he read. A furry palm gripped his arm with uncharacteristic gentleness. "Damn, Sly…"

"Paws off!" John jumped up to slap Phink away. "You won't use this as a convenient excuse to ruin my son further!"

Sly rounded on him. "Don't you dare!"

"Sylvester!"

"No!" Sly steamrolled over his dad's booze-scented protests. "You sabotaged us into a corner with a species that is lightyears higher up the food chain! Now you have the nerve to try and make this about my imaginary job as a fetish escort? Are you shitting me right now?"

"Don't talk to me like that! I'm your goddamn father!"

"Yes!" Sly began counting on his fingers. "Father, Guard, alcoholic, racist, and now we can add thief to your impressive resume!"

"Those parasites cheated!"

"I don't care!" Sly yelled back. "How you feel about them doesn't matter!"

"It matters!"

"No! All that matters now is that they own you for more money than we have!" Wetness blurred his vision, but he didn't need to see, he just needed to make his father understand. "Whether you were conned or just genuinely reckless enough to take a bad bet, it doesn't matter! How do you think we ended up here?"

The tight expression on John's face as he turned away was more answer than he expected to get. At Phink's gentle urging, Sly left him like that and escaped into the hall.

"Don't worry about the vamps," Phink said when it was just the two of them. "HEPP paid them off before sending them on their way and letting the Guard take him into custody."

"Yay. So, his coworkers arrested him off the street."

Phink shrugged. "Could be worse. Those vamps weren't from The Nine Bloodlines; their pockets weren't deep enough to get away with taking payment via his jugular. That kind of shit's been happening more and more lately."

Phink had a point. Sly had never met a vampire descended from one of the original nine Nocturni, but he heard stories. More than one of those Harems were exiled from Earth and Luna because they were too inhuman and violent. Centuries later, those nine Harems had amassed more wealth than all of humanity combined.

"Look..." Phink hesitated, "maybe this is a good thing."

"Seriously?"

Phink held up his hands. "Listen. HEPP uses Indentured Service Contracts for precisely these situations: it ensures no loss of human life while ensuring punishment for the crime and satisfaction for the wronged parties."

Sly yanked at his hair. "I wouldn't call gambling into the hole a hard crime, but whatever."

Phink gave him another sympathetic pat. "He just needs to make up the difference to HEPP. You can sell the house, bunk with Blythe, and he'll do three, maybe four years on a cushy assignment that'll get him sober and off-world. You can recoup your losses and buy a one-way ticket to wherever he's at."

Sly considered that for all of five seconds then slumped in defeat. "He's never spliced."

Phink's jowls dropped. "Never? But… his medical history has bird DNA—?"

"Ostrich," Sly interjected tiredly. "Best immune systems of Earth's creatures. Public schools require it with vaccinations, so naturally, Humans First assholes made it the number one counterfeited splice record in the galaxy."

"Well, shit... Sly, he could probably walk out of here free and clear tomorrow if he sold a few pints—"

Sly interrupted with a high, sharp laugh. "And let the universe know he's a pure-blooded sitting duck? No way. He'll never bleed for a vamp. Not willingly."

"Well…" Phink turned in a wide circle, searching for an answer, "Shit."

SLY MARCHED BACK THROUGH THE PROTESTERS STRAIGHT TO Blythe's place. The idea of being home alone was nauseating. More than ready for the day to end, he let Blythe bundle him into a bubble bath with a glass of cheap wine. The reprieve lasted ten glorious minutes.

"Sly?" She sat down on the edge of the tub, twirling his dingy comms unit around her finger with forced levity. "Your dad called."

"I don't want to talk to him right now."

"I know." She bit her lip. "HEPP cut his deal down to a year."

"That's great," Sly snarked, gulping wine.

"They're sending him to a Harem."

Sly spewed wine and bubbles all over the bathroom wall,

flailing halfway out of the tub. "They can't! No way he agreed to this."

Blythe caught him before he could slip and concuss himself. "Sweetie, he doesn't have to agree. He has a debt to HEPP now, and this is the fastest way."

Sly splashed past her. "He'd sooner go to prison than bleed an ounce for a vamp. They're not supposed to bleed people involuntarily!"

Blythe winced.

"They can't do that to him." He dashed out of the bathroom in a towel. "Phink and I need to talk some sense into Myers."

He was dressed in record time, coat and boots on, mask in hand. He flew out the door and bypassed the elevator, taking the stairs two at a time. Blythe's apartment was only on the third floor; there was no need to pause, to wait on the world to catch up with him. He hit the exit of the stairwell and bounded into the building's lobby.

He crashed into a wall of solid muscle.

"Hello, Sylvester."

Sly stumbled back. "Le Vau?"

The vampire caught his arm and steadied him with a fang-heavy grin.

Sly pulled his arm free. "What are you doing here?"

Sly was never quite sure Le Vau existed outside of Centrism. He'd never seen him elsewhere in the port, despite the guy being a port feature for decades, generations longer than Sly had been alive. It was weird. Alarming. Definitely not good.

"I was here for you, actually," Le Vau simpered.

"So, *so* not appropriate!" Sly made to step around him, shaking his head. "I don't have time for this."

"You can make time. I heard about your father."

Sly froze. "Excuse me?"

Le Vau stood smugly not two feet away, at ease in the foyer of a mortal residence. His coat was off, tucked neatly over one forearm, but he'd forgotten to remove his gloves. Even with the overlarge fangs, he was too cool and composed.

"It's a small port, Sly. Word travels fast, and Mickey's is practically a cesspool of gossips. I came to find you, soon as I heard."

"...Why?"

"I just want to offer my help."

With eyes unusually soft, almost sympathetic, Le Vau was never more attractive. Sly didn't trust him one bit.

"I don't have time for this," Sly said, going for the door again.

The vampire stepped into his path. "Let me help you, Sly."

"No thanks." Sly raised his mask between them, stepping around the vamp. "I got it."

"Yes. You do," Le Vau agreed, sidestepping with him. "The thing is, maybe you shouldn't have to, Sylvester."

Dropping all pretense of friendliness, Sly snarled, "Back off."

"My apologies." Le Vau lifted his hands as he backed up. The rich leather on his palms was infuriating. "I only want to help."

"Bullshit."

"I could buy out his contract within the hour," Le Vau offered. "He could be home tonight. All it would cost you is one night in my bed."

Sly laughed. It was startled out of him like a punch to the gut.

The vampire's charming effect crackled into something dark and hungry. "I'll only offer once."

"Don't bother. I'm not a whore."

"I know." Le Vau's gray eyes dragged down his body with disgusting appreciation. "That's part of the appeal. Let me help your father, Sly, then I'll fly you off this rock, and we'll never come back."

"No thanks." Sly glowered as he yanked on his mask.

Le Vau's smirking voice persisted. "We both know your father won't survive with a Harem, Sly. He wouldn't tolerate it well, HEPP's precautions be damned."

"Fuck you."

Brandishing his coat like some uppity Moon Diva playing a folkloric villain, Le Vau was unfairly handsome, even with an ugly curl to his lip. "When they bleed him dry and you're left all alone and penniless, don't come crying to me."

CHAPTER 4

*S*ly burst into Phink's office before his shaking fingers could pry his mask off. "My blood's as pure as his is! Give me his contract, and I'll make it worth your while!"

"Your blood's pure?"

Said blood froze in his veins. He spun around to find Kamari Vauqeulin seated in Phink's best chair.

"Shit."

The vampire's eyes gleamed as he grinned. "Oh, I don't think so."

The office wasn't huge. There were two upholstered chairs in front of the desk, one behind it where Phink sat, and the rest of the space was reserved for filing cabinets. Sly measured the scant distance between the door and the chairs; it wasn't far, but there was no telling how inhumanly fast Vauqeulin might be.

Sly swiveled back to Phink, wide-eyed. "You were in a meeting? Why wasn't your door closed?"

"It was."

Sly's insides shriveled. "Fuck!"

43

Kamari stood. "What you just said, about your blood—"

"Forget it." Sly folded his arms, glaring. "You weren't supposed to hear that."

"You're John's son?"

Sly's muscles screamed as he tensed further.

"Let me guess, the only splicing I'll find on your record is ostrich? Allegedly." There was something greedy in the vamp's expression as he stepped closer. "Your surname's Spurgeon, isn't it?"

"Call him Sly," Phink chimed.

"Do you mind?" Sly glared at Phink as he backed up in step with the vampire.

Phink gestured to the remaining chair with a pointed look at Sly. "Have a seat, Sly. We should talk."

Thankfully, this seemed to jar Kamari into a semblance of restraint. He retook his seat in the better chair, folding one long leg over his knee. His eyes remained locked on Sly, his entire body tight like he was ready to pounce regardless of the pose.

Phink was also staring at Sly. Waiting.

Sly shifted his weight. Once. Twice. He'd be damned before he planted his ass in that chair. "Fine. What?"

Phink indicated the vampire. "Master Vauqeulin wanted a second meeting with you."

Sly studied the vampire shrewdly. "Why?"

If anything, Vauqeulin seemed pleased by his suspicion. His laugh was musical. "I like you."

"That's nice. What do you want? How do you know my dad?"

Kamari grinned at Phink. "Is he always this combative?"

"He's an acquired taste."

"He's perfect."

"*He* is right here," Sly snapped. "What do you want? Besides my blood. You can't afford it."

"Sly," Phink spoke stiltedly as Kamari chuckled. "He's a Harem Leader. One of The Nine."

Sly's jaw hurt, it went so tight. "Bullshit."

Kamari—no, Master Vauqeulin—folded his hands in his lap with satisfaction. "I can afford you, Mr. Spurgeon. And if you're as pure as you claim—"

"I'm not interested."

The room cooled.

Sly raised his chin, arms still locked across his chest. "I have nothing against the Nocturni, but whatever you're after, I'm not interested. My dad needs me here."

"Your father?" Vauqeulin's pretty head tilted to the side with curiosity. "You mean the one scheduled for delivery to my estate tomorrow morning? His record's as fictional as yours, isn't it?"

Sly jabbed a vicious finger in the guy's face. "Fuck you. He was coerced!"

Vauqeulin shrugged, smile fading. "HEPP agreed to it on his behalf."

"Sly?"

"Fuck you," Sly hissed at the vampire as Phink reached for his arm over the desk. He shrugged him off and, with a venomous glare, he shouted, "And fuck you, Phink! He was drunk, and he made a stupid mistake! You're taking advantage of him!"

"Yes."

Sly and Phink gaped at the vampire.

Vauqeulin smoothed imaginary wrinkles from his pant leg, remarkably calm for someone admitting dastardly deeds. "I'm taking blatant advantage of a terrible situation. Would you like to make it less terrible for everyone involved?"

Sly stared between the vampire and his boss, stuck on repeat. Phink's eyes were wide and dumbfounded. He gave Sly an unhelpful shrug.

Vauqeulin continued conversationally, "Gentlemen, one way or another, I am bringing a pure-blooded human to my Harem's estate to serve as a donor. This is nonnegotiable, but it's the only part that must be."

The vampire paused to level a challenging stare at Sly, one well-fashioned brow arching.

Sly's hands clenched into fists. "What do you want?"

"Never mind what I want." Vauqeulin waved the question aside with a flippant hand, but he was smiling. "There's a Nocturnus in my care who needs pure human blood. If I have to, I'll deliver your father to him under the constraints of an Indenture."

"Or?" Sly snapped.

Vauqeulin gave him an appreciative nod. "Or I could bring you. As his Companion."

Dread collected in Sly's gut like deadweight. He thought he might hurl.

Nearby, Phink choked on a gasp. "Companionship? With one of The Nine? Stars above, Sly! That's perfect!"

But it wasn't perfect at all. Companionships were as binding as marriage, arguably more so since the terms were written with the Nocturni's impressive lifespan in mind. Contracts were ironclad and tilted in the vampire partner's favor as a given.

It was a big fucking deal and far from perfect.

"I can't," Sly croaked over Phink's excited babbling. "I have people here who need me more than some entitled vamp looking for a tasty toy."

Vauqeulin's expression shifted to something sharp and determined. It was strangely scary on such a beautiful face.

Sly squirmed, looking anywhere else. "Are we done?"

"No."

"Then spit it out so we can move on with our lives."

Vauqeulin even scowled prettily. "I'm not looking for a toy, Mr. Spurgeon. I'm looking for a solution."

Sly's eyes stung. He was going to hurl.

"Sly?"

It was painful to tear his glare from the vampire. It felt like showing his back to an enemy.

Phink was watching him, concerned furrows on his fuzzy brow. "He's the scion of the entire Harem. Think about this, all right? You can negotiate!" He shot Vauqeulin a beseeching look. "Right?"

Vauqeulin nodded.

"Okay!" Phink rounded his desk and clapped Sly on the shoulder. "You came in here saying your blood was worthwhile? Well, this is how!"

Sly jerked away from Phink, grimacing. "We're not signing me into slavery, Phink!"

"Of course not!" Phink recoiled, appalled. "Let me talk to my guy at HEPP. Maybe we can make an agreement that's less permanent than a Companion Contract. You could go work for the Harem for a year, no more than your old man would have been indentured—"

"Six months," Vauqeulin interjected.

"Excuse me?" Sly asked, sure he must have misheard.

"Six months," Vauqeulin repeated as he got back to his feet. "We'll call a trial period."

Sly stared, feeling like his feet had been cemented in place. Maybe his heart too, now lodged in his throat. The ball of dread in his gut pulsed with warning.

The vampire held out his hand for Sly to shake. "I'll clear your father's debt, pay your missed wages from Centrism up-front and, in return, you give the idea of Companionship your full attention and open-minded consideration for the next six months. Deal?"

"That's an amazing deal, Sly," Phink murmured.

Sly was no stranger to the spotlight, but their combined attention was enough to make him twitch. He wanted to say no. He wanted to scream and cry and shove Vauqeulin's stupidly perfect face through a window.

Above all, he wanted to help his dad. He needed to.

"You won't keep me past six months," Sly vowed. "Not legally."

Vauqeulin laughed like soft, chiming bells. "We'll see."

THERE WAS NO TIME FOR SECOND-GUESSING. SLY MADE A hasty goodbye to Blythe and arranged for her to cart his dad home. He handed over his comms and gave her full access to their house's weather seal system. Then, he locked himself into a luxury land vehicle with Kamari Vauqeulin. With his wrist cold and bare, in the enclosed space with a sentient predator and no bouncers nearby, Sly was ready to hurl.

"I have questions," he snipped as he sat across from Vauqeulin on the plush seats that lined the cabin. The benches had royal-blue cushions, plusher than his bed at home.

Vauqeulin was already settled with a glass of something ruby red that smelled expensive. He pulled his gaze from the large window behind him with an encouraging gesture. "Ask."

Sly brandished his copy of HEPP's new Assessment Contract and read aloud. *"The Vauqeulin Harem hereby reserves the aforementioned six-month period to determine compatibility of personality, blood, sexuality, and circumstance*. I get the appeal of having a willing blood source at your beck and call, but is sex typically included on the menu?"

Vauqeulin bit his lip, attempting to mask a smile. "Direct feeding is often intimate, and arousal is common. Companionships are typically left open to possibilities."

Sly's face felt pinched, and there was a distinct headache building behind his temples. "Great."

"You're not obligated to sleep with anyone." Vauqeulin chuckled. "You simply have the option of engaging sexually if and when you're both interested."

Sly already knew this, of course. He wouldn't have signed the contract or boarded the craft without confirming the fine print himself. *Unwelcome advances on behalf of either party are grounds for immediate termination.* Paperwork or no paperwork, he didn't trust Vauqeulin.

"I'm not a whore. You get that, right? And so does your friend?"

"Brother."

Sly blinked. "I'm for your…?"

"My brother, yes." Vauqeulin sipped his drink, watching Sly over the rim. "His name is Kahled. He's well aware of your situation, and the only thing I have his leave to pay you for is your presence and the occasional blood draw."

Sly was still trying to wrap his head around the idea that he was solicited for vampire royalty. If the Vauqeulin Harem really was one of The Nine Bloodlines, then they would be one of the oldest and most powerful of the species. And this Kahled guy must be the younger brother to the freaking heir.

Holy shit.

"My presence and the occasional blood draw," Sly repeated in a daze, then shook himself. "Somehow, I still don't trust you."

"Smart. He'll appreciate that."

"Fuck you."

Vauqeulin laughed. "The two of you are going to love each other."

The fancy machine around them purred to life, lifting from the station floor without jostling, alarmingly smooth. As they began moving, Sly squirmed and eyed all the polished chrome and padded benches. The fabric felt smoother than anything he knew. He would melt into the softness if he wasn't careful.

Across the cabin, Vauqeulin watched him with silent consideration.

Sly shoved his twitchy fingers under his thighs to force them still. "This isn't what I expected."

"The accommodations? I can tell you right now, your standard of living is going to drastically improve while you're employed by my Harem."

"I meant the grounded transport." Sly tensed as he watched the scenery change from grimy port station to angry wilderness. "I thought all Harems made their homes off-world."

The vampire followed his wary gaze aimed over his shoulder. Sly wished he hadn't; now that Vauqeulin was paying attention to the smog outside the window with nothing but mild interest, it'd be pathetic to request closing the shutters. Seconds into the trip, and he was already regretting everything.

Sly murmured, "I thought getting off this rock would be the best part of this deal."

Sly shifted focus from the deadly clouds to the carpeted floor. He tried counting fabric fibers to distract himself from the vicious sunstorm and matching disappointment. The vehicle was sturdy, but it didn't have a prayer of sailing through Earth's decaying atmosphere.

If Vauqeulin noticed his discomfort, he didn't mention it.

"Are you familiar with Nosferatu's Curse?"

"Nope."

This was the closest Sly had been to exposure since his mother died. If he closed his eyes, he could still see her body blistering red and crumbling into ash.

Sly cleared his throat. "Nocturnus Curse, you said?"

"Nocturnus refers to a male of the Nocturni. *Nosferatu's* Curse is the disease Kahled inherited from our esteemed ancestors."

That nugget of information almost distracted Sly from his terrestrial anxieties. "Vampires have genetic diseases? Since when?"

"Since always. It's not common knowledge, of course, but the earliest splicing experiments were nowhere as balanced and precise as textbook history wants us to believe," Vauqeulin explained, swirling the final inch of liquid in his glass. "I suppose at the time, mankind was too busy reinforcing themselves to withstand Mother Nature's ire. They realized too late that certain genome cocktails were bound to react badly."

Sly felt a shiver race up his spine. "What do you mean?"

For the first time since they met, Vauqeulin wouldn't meet his eye. He set down his glass on his armrest with unnecessary care. "Certain animal instincts   certain traits, if you will—they compound each other sometimes. It can be a bit uncontrollable."

Sly's stomach churned, the knot in his belly blaring with alarms much too late. He thought about all the horror stories he'd grown up hearing about The Nine Bloodlines. The rumors.

"Your Harem's not rooted on Luna, is it?"

"No. We're the founding family of Ethos."

Sly gasped like he'd been sucker punched. Ethos was a dwarf planet on the outer rim of the Milky Way Galaxy. It was the most distant inhabited planet Sly knew of. A place far removed, intended for exile.

"Nosferatu's Curse was the whole reason we ended up there," the vampire continued with forced casualness. "Humans successfully created a species capable of enduring Earth's growing temper, only to decide some of them were too dangerous to keep around. So, our ancestors established Ethos and turned it into the thriving celestial oasis it is today. It was with that, or die."

"Bullshit."

"I wish, but no." Vauqeulin stroked his goatee, gaze distant. "We've adapted, fortunately. Just like we were designed to do. The Curse is still fatal, but it's slower now. Easier to hide."

Sly's heart constricted. "It's fatal?"

"That's what I said."

The great, terrible outdoors ceased to exist for a whole minute. Sly's priceless blood pounded fast enough to make him light-headed.

The vampire was too busy admiring the fucking scenery to notice. "That's why he's on Earth."

"Why he needs pure blood," Sly concluded, breathless.

"We're hoping you can cure him."

"Holy shit."

"Yes. The stakes are a bit higher than general Companionship would imply."

Sly clutched at his heart like he could do anything to calm it down. He was confused to find his chest warm and heaving when no air was making it to his lungs. He started feeling nauseous. Dizzy.

"Don't worry. He's a good guy. A real ass, on occasion, but I'm sure you can hold your own."

Sly didn't hear any of Vauqeulin's reassurances. For once, he felt stupid. He was young. Fit. He was likely to live decades longer than his dad. And now there was a rich, would-be immortal depending on him for survival.

He fainted.

SLY AWOKE ON A DIFFERENT PLANET. THAT WAS THE ONLY explanation.

He was tucked into a magnificent four-poster bed, the sheets sinful against his skin and the blanket thicker than anything in his memory. There was a chandelier. A rug that looked remarkably like real fur. No windows, just artwork on the walls.

Not one damn window.

Sly stumbled out of the bed and tried to shove a picture out of the way, bracing himself to reveal toxic red clouds and bars over plexiglass. The frame was too heavy to budge, bolted to solid wall. He dropped onto the bed, panting as he stared at a painting worth more than his childhood home.

"Vampires. Right."

Wherever he was, it was built for Nocturni. The species wasn't immortal in a true sense of the word, but they paid for their impressive longevity with a photosensitivity that didn't mean shit when nothing alive could breathe the planet's air anyway. The only difference that mattered was the Nocturni's penchant to afford lasting security and comfort. This place was a fortress, designed to last centuries without risking exposure to Earth's homicidal atmosphere.

"Fuck me," Sly whimpered, burying his face in his hands.

A sharp knock on the door made him jump.

Before he could recover, a tall aged woman marched into his bedroom. She was thin, and her skin was well-preserved, despite its lines. Her graying hair was neatly styled in an updo, and her dress was equally sharp. When she spoke, her attitude was as stiff as her impeccable posture, her voice crisp with a European accent.

"Mr. Spurgeon?"

"Yes?" he squeaked.

"Madam Walters." She extended her hand. Sly had no choice but to get off the bed to shake it. "I'm in charge of the Harem's Earthly estate and all its housekeeping," she explained. "Master Vauqeulin asked me to make sure you were comfortable, so feel free to address any requests to me directly."

"Sure," he trailed off, staring around at all the grandeur with wide eyes. "Where are we?"

She frowned. "The Vauqeulin Estate. It's a private property some distance from the European Port. Were you not given this information earlier?"

Sly's attention snapped back to the woman; she was watching him closely, her frown deepening with dignified alarm.

"Mr. Spurgeon, do you know why you're here?"

Sly's head bobbed in a vigorous nod, like it might jog his thoughts into order. "I remember the contract. Shit. Yeah. That contract."

He stopped nodding as his brain spun haphazard loops inside his skull.

"Who's dying again?" He peered around her toward the hall. "Someone's dying. Right?"

Madam Walters's face looked pinched. "Calm yourself."

"I'm calm!" Sly made a wild gesture, lurching toward the door. "Mildly headachy. Moderately embarrassed. Majorly concerned. You know that is the least calming advice in the history of humanity, right? Fuck!"

And he was on the floor. A tiny human on the floor of some fancy vampire lair with his heart clogging his airways.

Thin but strong fingers gripped his arms as the woman crouched in front of him. "Focus. Are you familiar with Three-Part Breathing?"

Sly shook his head.

"Close your eyes," she instructed, firm and kind. "Focus on the air entering and exiting your body. It will help you ground yourself in your body and reclaim control."

As Sly struggled not to hyperventilate, her palm patted his stomach, solid and insistent.

"Breathe in deep and slow. Fill your belly, then keep going till you've filled your diaphragm."

He pulled in more air, and her hand moved again, warm and steady on his chest.

"Good. Now fill your chest cavity completely, then exhale. From here first."

She tapped his chest, and he slipped into a reverse rhythm. He followed her gentle guidance, ending the breath with his abs squeezed tight.

He was calming down. It was working. Blythe wasn't there to slap the sense back into him, but it was working. Sly threw his head back, and his eyes landed on the open doorway.

There stood a Nocturnus unlike any Sly had ever heard of before.

Only part of his face and one arm were visible as he peered in from the hall. It was enough to give a solid impression of towering height, black hair, piercing gray eyes, and tawny skin. He was beautiful except for the scales mottling the skin on his hand. And the fangs.

Holy shit, the fangs. Those weren't Nocturni fangs. Those were full-length knives.

Sly whimpered, "I am so dead."

The Nocturnus yanked away from the doorway with a bestial growl and disappeared.

CHAPTER 5

"This must be heaven," Sly moaned as he sank into steaming water.

The bathroom was the size of Blythe's entire apartment. Marble pillars braced the walls, and the countertops were inlaid with gold flecks. There was no shower, but there was a glorious Jacuzzi. The steam filling his nose was earthy and sweet. Sly stretched his legs out fully without touching the tub walls and submerged everything but his face.

He groaned, sword-like fangs forgotten. "I could die happy right now."

"We'd rather you didn't," Walters announced.

Sly lifted his head from the water to see her close the door, a woven basket hanging from her arm.

"I should be bothered by a stranger barge in on me naked," Sly thought aloud, "but I'm not. Have I been drugged?"

"No." Her mouth thinned into a hard line as she sat on the bath's edge with the basket. "But you are exhausted, coming down from a considerable adrenaline spike, and soaking in more herbs than you can likely name. Are you familiar with the concept of self-care, Mr. Spurgeon? You're too thin, and you're sporting signs of chronic stress. You need to take better care of yourself to do this job properly."

She reached into the water and yanked his foot into her lap. He flailed, sputtering floral water. By the time he caught his breath, she was scrubbing something into his sole.

"What are you doing?"

"Pampering you. Try to enjoy it."

"I don't really need all this."

Walters dragged a steel tool up the length of his foot. It didn't hurt, but Sly's stomach rolled when she held up a strip of dead skin.

"Ew," he admitted.

She arched a brow and continued diligently shearing calluses from his foot. Eventually, she let him have his foot back and beckoned for the other. Reluctantly, he gave it to her, and his pedicured foot slipped on the tub's bottom like silk.

"Woah," he giggled, rubbing his heel. "That feels pretty nice!"

Her eyes never left her work. "Consider it one of the many benefits of Companionship."

Sly's eyes narrowed. "So, that's the plan? Get me nice and vulnerable, then guilt me into a lifelong commitment?"

She didn't blink. "Guilt is hardly an effective motivator, Mr. Spurgeon. If we aim to keep you, we'll have to do better than that."

"Good luck," he snarked.

"We don't need luck, Mr. Spurgeon." She set down the callus shaver to meet his eye. "We need you."

He shivered. "You have me for a few months. I can't give you more than that."

Her lips pursed in a distasteful response, but that was all.

She finished with his second foot. When she released his ankle, he scooted over to the far side of the tub, hugging himself. He watched her with a sinking feeling in his gut.

She reloaded the basket, tone cool and movements crisp. "You have the potential to bleed health and sanity back into Kahled's life, Mr. Spurgeon. I won't trivialize that. If you can't, the Curse will consume him within a few years, and we'll have to put him down before he kills us all like a rabid beast."

He couldn't meet her eye. "But that's not my fault."

When she looked at him, her eyes shined wet. Sly stared at the Jacuzzi bubbles like he hadn't noticed.

Walters sighed and set a bottle on the bath's edge before stepping toward the door. "Wash your hair with that. Twice. You may not want all that we have to offer, but so long as you're here, you'll reap the benefits anyway."

"OH, THAT'S MUCH BETTER." WALTERS NODDED APPROVINGLY when Sly stepped out of the bathroom a while later.

He scowled. "Where are my clothes?"

"Incinerated, I hope. Realistically? In the laundry."

The new clothes hanging off his frame were expensive. He wasn't familiar with the fabrics, but the pants were loose and silky, billowing around his legs before gathering at his ankles. They hung off his hips indecently, but the fitted top was long enough to keep him covered. So soft and wonderful on his skin, he almost mistook them for pajamas, but they were too solid, the subtle designs too fashionable. The material was meant to be shown off.

"These are beautiful." Sly gestured to his outfit. "But I'm going to need my stuff when I go home."

She answered with a strained smile. "You can take these clothes with you. They're yours now, a welcoming gift from Kahled. He's quite fond of Lunar textiles."

Sly gaped down at himself. "These are from Luna?"

Walters leaped on his astonishment like a hawk on an injured mouse.

"Your wardrobe is fully stocked. Kahled's accustomed to certain standards of presentation, you understand, so use it." Her voice went sharp as she added, "At least while you're here."

Sly stopped petting the luxuriant fabric. "Kamari told you I'm not a whore, right? It shouldn't matter how I dress."

She didn't answer. She was already heading down the hall as she announced, "Master Vauqeulin is waiting for you in the dining hall. Come along."

Sly scurried after her.

They came to a pair of intricately carved doors that shimmered with polish. The interior boasted a solid wood table spanning the length of the room and lined with at least two dozen upholstered chairs. There was matching artwork on the opposing walls, abstract splashed of purples and greens, and carpet runners along the edges of the space boasted delicate patterns.

Kamari Vauqeulin was indeed waiting, seated at the head end of the table with three silver platters splayed out in front of him. There were four place settings, each complete with shining cutlery, champagne flutes, and filigreed plates.

"Sylvester!" He grinned, rosy-cheeked and nursing another glass of something ruby red. He was splayed in his chair with the smell of alcohol wafting off him. "So good to see you conscious again!"

"That's debatable," Sly quipped as he studied the room.

"Come!" Vauqeulin sang, waving them over. "Sit! Eat!"

Sly frowned at the Nocturnus. "Are you drunk? I thought vampires had superhuman metabolisms or something."

"Rude," Walters interjected as she pulled out the nearest chair on Vauqeulin's right. "You realize the Nocturni are derived from humankind? They can do all that we can, including inebriation. It's more difficult," she shot a disapproving glance at the Harem Heir, "and more expensive."

Vauqeulin raised his glass. "It's a talent I excel at!"

Sly slid into the offered seat as Walters lifted the lid from a platter. A thick, savory scent hit him in the face, making him swoon.

"What." Sly gulped in the flavor. "Is. That?"

Vauqeulin wagged his fingers toward the dish with a proud grin and announced, *"Mansaf!"*

It was divine. With one glance, Sly knew there were no freeze-dried nutrient packets used in the recipe. Such a masterpiece wouldn't be possible back home. There were piles of hot seasoned meat and a creamy white sauce that smelled complex and delicious.

Sly drooled. "Is that real meat?"

"Mutton," Walters explained, cutting in without hesitation. "I don't suppose you've ever had lamb before?"

He had not, but nothing was going to stop him from trying it. The moment Walters set the food on his plate, he dug with a fork.

He moaned.

From behind him, a deep voice said, "You must be joking."

Sly choked on his mouthful.

He glanced around the table to see Walters shaking her head, clenched fist held over her frowning mouth. Vauqeulin was grinning like a drunken fool.

"Kahled!" the Harem Leader cheered, raising his glass to the newcomer. "You decided to join us after all! Wonderful! There's someone I want you to meet!"

Sly swallowed his mouthful, hyperaware of a heavy gaze on the back of his head. He cleared his throat and said, "We already met. Sort of."

Vauqeulin laughed and took everyone by surprise by patting Sly on the arm like an old friend. "You're hilarious! You know who else is hilarious?"

"Mari," came a warning growl from the doorway.

"My brother!" Vauqeulin cackled. He leaned into Sly, stage whispering, "He has the same sarcastic wit! I'm telling you, you'll love him—"

"Kamari!"

"Shh!" Vauqeulin swatted in his brother's direction. "I am *trying* to be your wingman, Kahled. If you must sabotage this, the least you can do is wait till I've left."

Sly frowned. "You're leaving?"

Walters sighed and began filling her plate.

From behind, Sly heard an ugly snarl. "He has a Harem to run. Stars above, Kamari, I thought you said he was smart."

"Excuse you!" Sly snapped, and he spun around in the chair.

He froze, all defense of his intelligence abandoned.

Kahled Vauqeulin stood before him, framed in the doorway. He was huge, taller and broader than Kamari, with significant muscle. While they did not share canine attributes, they had the same darkness to their hair, the same tawny gold to their skin, the same sculpted definition to their jawlines.

The resemblance ended there.

His fangs were terrifying. Before that day, Sly was sure Le Vau's were the most gruesome pair he would ever see.

Kahled's were so monstrous, Sly almost overlooked the other deformities.

Sly swallowed hard and whimpered, "Hi?"

There was no symmetry or reason to the splotches of silver-gray scales that randomly blemished Kahled's skin. His rich Lunar trousers had been cut to make way for his mismatched legs, where malformed bone and muscle had mutated to something bizarre, caught between the limbs of a land predator and the sinewy strength of a reptile. The distortions were likewise evident on his hands; the right was nearly proportionate, but the ring finger was swollen, the knuckle grotesquely warped, and its nail replaced by a lethal, glassy talon. Two of the fingers on his other hand were further mutated, inhuman and clawed.

Sly gawked. It was embarrassingly rude, but better than running for cover or throwing himself at the monster's feet in a plea for mercy. Sly wasn't sure which he was most likely to do if he dared move.

Kahled's full upper lip curled back from his fangs, and Sly's impulses leaned toward running.

"Well?" the vampire demanded, crossing thick arms over a powerful chest. His fancy Lunar shirt pulled taut over a solid build. He seemed far from ill. "Get a good look this time, Earthling. I'm sure you'll want to tell your friends back home all the wretched details."

Sly blanched. He'd never had a vampire address him with such open hostility before.

Sly closed his gaping mouth and rallied his brain cells. "I'm confused," he admitted. "I thought you wanted me here?"

"If I must rely on a random Earthling, I'd prefer someone with more sense." Kahled ran critical eyes over Sly's form and sneered. "And bed partners with more meat on their bones."

"Kahled!" Vauqeulin and Walters snapped in unison.

Sly kept his eyes trained on the monstrous visage in the doorway. He twisted backward on his chair onto his knees and let his mouth do the thinking for him.

"Is this normally how you greet someone you're trying to con into Companionship?"

Vauqeulin coughed, choking on surprised humor.

Walters sighed. "Stars above, I need a drink."

"In case no one's warned you," Kahled growled, "I have a slight homicidal streak when I'm irritated."

Sly paused, considering. He didn't know any details about Nosferatu's Curse. For all he knew, the threat was legitimate. The silence from the rest of the room had quite a bit of weight.

But Sly knew when he was being targeted by a predator. He worked at Centrism for years, mingling with all manner of Nocturni.

Kahled Vauqeulin had the means to do him harm, all right, but he wasn't poised for it. The heat in his eyes wasn't right, too full of challenge and a strange vigilance. He didn't loom over Sly, invade his space, or demand his attention; if anything, he leaned away. He was stiff, and as Sly watched, he shifted as if preparing to run.

"How's this supposed to work?" Sly pondered, bracing an elbow on the chairback, chin in his palm as he considered Kahled. "How do you expect those murderous tendencies to coincide with Companionship exactly?"

Vauqeulin burst into a fit of uncontrollable laughter.

His brother, however, turned a faint pink as he bared his teeth. "Do you think this is a game?"

A shiver of something that wasn't quite fear raced up

Sly's spine. He leaned back for his fork, spearing a mouthful with one eye on the vampire. He made sure to scrape the utensil's tines on the plate.

Kahled tried not to wince, but the pointed tips of his ears twitched in response to the grating sound.

Sly stuck the fork in his mouth and dragged his teeth along the metal.

Kahled's answer did not disappoint. He uncrossed his arms and released a threatening roar, but he didn't step into the room.

"All right." Vauqeulin gave an uneasy chuckle. "That's enough, Sly."

Sly ignored him, addressing Kahled around a mouthful of food. "You know I'm here on a temporary basis, right? Considering how valuable my blood is to you, you could probably stand to be a little nicer. It's just a thought. A suggestion. A little—"

"I could kill you," Kahled interrupted, his tone blunt, yet uncertain.

Sly pouted. "Was that a threat or a question? Honestly, I'm getting some mixed signals here."

Kahled's eyes went wide as he stared at Sly. He shot unreadable looks at the others but kept refocusing on Sly. It was bizarre behavior from a vamp. If Sly didn't know any better, he might think the guy was afraid of him.

"Look." Sly huffed, rising from his chair and stepping toward Kahled. All those muscles on the vampire's towering frame went taut with tension.

Sly stilled and raised his hands in placation. "Listen, all right? I'm not going to pretend to know what's going on with you, but you're literally the only reason I'm here."

They stared at each other for an eternity, but it might have been mere seconds. It was a long time for a staring contest without anyone making a peep.

Sly snapped. "The point is: I don't want to be here anymore than you apparently want me here, but you have a situation going on, so you're stuck with me for a while. We might as well be cool about it, right?"

Kahled stared at him.

Sly's shoulders sagged. "I'm just here to do a job, then I'm gone. Promise."

Kahled gave an animal grumble and shake of his head. For one wild moment, Sly thought he saw a flash of darkness obscure his eyes.

But then Kamari Vauqeulin was on his feet in front of him, blocking Sly's view with his tailored back.

"Breathe, brother."

Kahled did as ordered. Sly recognized the pattern from Walters's earlier guidance, and his appetite dissipated.

"Get rid of him, Mari," Kahled said with a mean, calm voice. "Or I will."

CHAPTER 6

*S*ly's second day working for the Vauqeulin Harem
went marginally better than his first.

He woke to Walters's insistence that he join the household
staff for breakfast, and he nearly cried at the sight of the
morning buffet. The other staff members fell out of his
awareness as he salivated over bowls of fresh cut fruit salad
and home-baked pastries. There were trays of steaming eggs
—the kind taken from a real, live animal's nest instead of
formulated in a lab—and more dishes he couldn't recognize.
He stuffed himself full.

Tummy pleasantly aching, Walters whisked him away for
a tour of the estate.

She shot him a reproachful look as they exited the dining
hall. "We should discuss your behavior last night."

Sly gave her an incredulous laugh. "*My* behavior? Toward
the giant asshole who insulted and threatened me? You know,
in hindsight, all those fancy clothes seem more like your idea
than his."

She didn't deny it. "Master Vauqeulin might find you
amusing, Mr. Spurgeon, but now he's gone, on his way back

to Ethos. That makes Kahled the Nocturnus in residence and master of this house. He's your boss and mine, yes?"

Sly nodded along. "Don't step on his scaly toes. Got it."

She sighed. "He is not pleased with your continued presence, Mr. Spurgeon."

"I noticed," Sly commented.

"He generally stays in his rooms and avoids interacting with the staff, but now he's in such a foul mood, I can't move him from his bed. You are meant to *alleviate* his symptoms, not exacerbate them."

Sly shied away from her reproachful side-eye. "I'm just here to bleed on occasion. Not sure how you expect me to do anything about his attitude."

He trailed off as Walters began marching faster down the hall.

"My staff is armed and trained with tranquilizers, Mr. Spurgeon." Her fists clenched at her sides as he rushed after her. "But we are human. There's only so much we can do if he attacks you. And he's no mere Nocturnus; he's descended from one of The Nine."

Sly interrupted, "And that might mean something in your circles, but to me, he's just another vampire."

It felt like a lie on his tongue, even as he said it. A full night's sleep wasn't enough to erase the impression Kahled had made of a wary critter prepped to flee. It sat on shaky ground next to the visual of a capable monster.

"Then you're a fool." Walters turned to glare at him. Sly stopped in his tracks before running into her. "If he hurts you, you'll have grounds to terminate the contract, but it will do you no good if the Harem chooses to make you regret it. Understand?"

Sly leaned away from her. "Understood."

Her eyes narrowed. She gave a brisk nod and resumed

strutting down the hall. "Besides, Mr. Spurgeon, there are no other vampires like Kahled. The last one to come close died nearly forty years ago."

Sly stumbled, gaping. "A Nocturnus died within my dad's lifetime, and nobody knows about it? Bullshit."

"Nocturna," Walters corrected, snippy as she turned a corner ahead of him. "She was Cursed. It was kept quiet."

His breakfast made a bid for escape. Sly choked it back. "Like Kahled? How old was she? Shit, how old is Kahled?"

Kahled appeared no older than a human in his early thirties, but the same could be said for any number of Nocturni. In Sly's experience, vampires aged with enviable grace; it went hand-in-hand with their superhuman healing and durability.

"Sixty-five. We hoped you might help him reach a century." Her voice went soft and sad as they entered a new wing of the manor. "We're going in here."

She led him through an archway, and it was like stepping into a different building. The stone walls and thick carpets of a traditional manor gave way to sterile metal and vast, empty passages in whites and grays. An automated sliding door admitted them to the most well-organized private doctor's office on Earth.

What was once a suite of rooms had been reconfigured into an open floor plan. The gray and white color scheme was joined by tasteful black and gold accents in the office space. There was a long desk stretching across the far wall with papers, textbooks, and medical equipment stationed on its surface and hanging from the wall. There were glass cabinets of labeled materials and specimens. A medical exam table was centrally located near various monitors and charts, and a hologram flickered in the corner, showcasing an anatomical model of Nocturnus musculature.

Walters called, "Doctor?"

"Right here, Emmeline."

Sly turned to see a middle-aged man enter from the back rooms, a modest door closing behind him. He was balding on the top of his head with round glasses and a cheerful, rosy-cheeked face. Despite the lines around his eyes, he might have looked disarmingly young without the gray in his groomed beard and mustache.

"Doctor Gorbon, at your service," Gorbon said with a breezy lilt to his voice that suggested a Lunar upbringing. "You must be Sylvester."

Sly smiled and accepted his offered hand, only to be tugged into a quick, one-armed hug. Sly hugged back on instinct. "Just call me Sly."

"Excellent! Welcome to my lair, Sly."

"I have to admit, this place doesn't really give off lair vibes," Sly commented, spinning to take in the room.

He balked when he spied the bedroom set up in the far corner. There was a grand bed decked out in deep navy blue and a large carved wood dresser beside it. A mere curtain, white and tied into the corner of its track, existed to separate it from the office. Sly's eyes narrowed on the steel manacles hanging off the metal headboard. It wasn't a bed, after all, but a large reinforced medical cot, cleverly beautified with the trappings of luxury and designed with violent Nocturni patients in mind. An IV stand was tucked beside the dresser.

Sly shuddered, nodding toward the setup, "That's for Kahled, huh?"

"Don't be alarmed," the doctor said as he waved Sly over to the exam table. "He's been here a year, and we haven't had to use it yet. The Cursed episodes are brief, and he's quite good at containing himself to his rooms." Under his breath, he added, "Too good, actually."

"He sounds great," Sly quipped as he hopped onto the exam table.

Gorbon chuckled. Even Walters managed an upward twitch of her lips.

"You'll do fine." Gorbon patted Sly's shoulder before guiding him to roll up his sleeve. "He said nearly the same thing about you, actually."

Unsure how to respond, Sly bit his tongue and rolled up his sleeve.

"Now..." Gorbon sat on a stool with a perky smack to his thigh. "I hope you know how to find my rooms, because all medicines are stored and all procedures are enacted here. Kahled's only excepted because I'm avoiding the day he destroys my space as thoroughly as he did his room."

Sly snorted. "He's that bad, huh?"

"He's not *bad*," Walters snapped. "He's ill. There's a difference."

"Don't listen to her," Gorbon teased as he beckoned for Sly's wrist so he could examine his veins. "Master Kahled is an ill-mannered brute with lingering delusions of entitlement and the emotional range of a human prepubescent."

Sly grinned. "You don't say?"

A new voice interjected, sharp as a whip, "He's also grieving."

Sly's heart sank at the reminder, but he turned to see a pair of human staff enter the suite. The speaker was a fit blond man, not much older than Sly, with nondescript glasses and no visible signs of splicing. The woman at his side had sharp-cornered eyes, the pupils slitted like a cat's, and pointed ears more common on a vampire, ebony hair framing her face. Neither wore a uniform, but the deep-purple fabric of the woman's knee-length skirt matched the quality of the man's black slacks and vest.

"Sly, meet Felix and Mae." Gorbon gestured toward the newcomers. "They're technically Emmeline's employees, but when I need an extra pair of steady hands, they're at my disposal."

"Hi!" Sly slipped off the exam table to hold out his hand.

Felix folded his arms and glared at the offered hand, but Mae smiled. "Hello," she said in a soft European accent. "Welcome to the Harem. We hope you like it here."

"For Master Kahled's sake," Felix interjected.

"On that note..." Gorbon urged Sly back to his seat on the table so he could press a sensor to his exposed forearm. "What do you know about Nosferatu's Curse, Sly?"

"Little," Sly admitted. He felt a small pinch as the sensor sneaked a speck of his blood, and the nearest computer beeped. "I know it's fatal, and it makes him dangerous. And it comes with some gnarly physical changes."

Gorbon smiled. "Noticed that, did you?"

"Hard to miss."

Felix scoffed, and Sly caught him glaring at him as he muttered in Mae's ear. Mae didn't seem to like whatever he said, based on the way she frowned and backed away.

Gorbon either didn't notice the exchange or didn't care. He turned to his computer screen and resumed addressing Sly. "The Curse doesn't always impose severe phenotype mutations, but given the state of Kahled's fangs, you'll have to visit me once a day for bloodletting."

Sly gave a relieved snicker. "Thank fuck. For a second, I thought he was planning on biting me."

Mae gasped, staring at him with a hand over her mouth in horror.

"My stars, he's an idiot," Felix huffed as he exited the room.

"We need you alive and well, Sly." Gorbon gave a stilted

chuckle. "Ideally, we'd like you to enjoy your time here enough to stay on beyond the current contract."

Sly scoffed. "How's His Majesty feel about that idea?"

Gorbon and Mae traded anxious looks, but Walters prevented them from giving a proper answer.

"Just remember, Mr. Spurgeon," she informed him, "Kahled may not be human, but he is an emotional and intelligent being. Try treating him as one, yes?"

Sly nodded, and there was an unpleasant clenching in his gut that felt eerily like shame. Years on Centrism's stage had never made him feel as judged as the stare Madam Walters leveled at him then.

"I'm sorry," he said, though he wasn't entirely sure what for. "I've never met a vampire like the Vauqeulins before. It's —" he stopped himself, reconsidering. "They're not what I'm used to. I'm a pretty open-minded person, I swear. I wasn't trying to upset anyone."

Over Walters's stiff shoulder, he saw Mae give a hesitant nod, her smile brittle.

"That's good," Gorbon said with forced cheer. "Fortunately, you have six months minimum to prove it."

"Max," Sly corrected halfheartedly, unable to meet anyone's eye.

"Regardless," Gorbon continued, "I'm faced with the daunting task of reintroducing raw humanity to a degrading vampire. I cannot stress enough how hopeful I am to have your assistance, Sly."

Sly believed him. He looked around the office, at all its Nocturni-specific details, and felt sick to his stomach.

He didn't have the luxury of investing himself in their fight. His father would never forgive him if he let a Nocturnus's sob story distract him.

Later, as Walters showed him from the impressive gymnasium in the cellar back toward the main house, she explained, "The rest of this level is reserved for storage, mostly. If you ever need spare linens or replacement parts for anything around the house, you can find it down here."

She kept tapping her foot as Sly opened doors at random to peek in at endless shelves of supplies. He expected her to swoop down on him for the delay, but she waited, stoic and still.

The cellar's main hallway was boring concrete. Sly opened another door halfway down to reveal a cluttered, dusty room stacked with disorganized shelves and equipment. Against the back wall was a masterpiece of smooth, outdated panels and intact controls, coated in a thick brownish layer of time and neglect.

Sly laughed as he admired the ancient communications system. "And I thought the Guard was behind the times."

"We don't use it," Walters insisted, reeling as if he'd slapped her. "It's a relic from when the estate was first built. I doubt it works anymore. The household has relied on personal comms units for centuries."

She presented her wrist to showcase the sleek gold band wrapped around the limb. It was a slender comms, the intricate controls so finely etched into the surface, they were invisible in the right light. It made the unit Sly left with Blythe look like bulky garbage.

"You know," Sly plucked at the lush fabric of his shirt, "this shit will get me mugged back home, but that's easy to hide, and I could seriously use a new comms. Trade you?"

"No." She spun on her heel and pranced off.

In her wake, Sly eyed the intercom. It was old, but not as

much as the American Guard's system, and far better maintained. Sly's fingers itched to play with it.

"Come along, Mr. Spurgeon."

Sly grinned as a wicked idea started to take shape.

THE FOLLOWING MORNING WAS MAGICAL. SYLVESTER Spurgeon woke early, and ten minutes later, he was in the cellar and happily fiddling with wires and buttons. Within the hour, the Harem's Earthly estate awoke as one to screeching feedback as he activated the outdated intercom.

Sly winced in sympathy for the staff, but he couldn't stop grinning. Half the labels were missing or polished off, so there was no telling which channel addressed which room. The entire household would just have to suffer until Sly figured out how to narrow the transmission to Kahled's private space. He imagined Kahled jumping and howling with a pillow over his ears and snickered. The vamp wouldn't know what hit him.

The control room was well-isolated from most of the manor; he couldn't picture a regal Nocturnus venturing down there. With any luck, Kahled wouldn't be able to track him down. If he did, Sly was counting on it taking long enough for the vampire to calm down first.

Maybe he'd get lucky, and Kahled would ship him back home by dinner time.

Sly pulled the microphone close and cleared his throat before putting on his best announcer's voice.

"Good morning, sunshine!" he began brightly. "I'm talking to you, Oh Great and Terrible Liege Lord. Time to put on your big boy pants and join the land of the living while you still can!"

He wasn't sure what his goal was until he started speaking. He knew Kahled Vauqeulin was a Nocturnus with more money than God, and he'd stuck his nose up the moment he laid eyes on Sylvester Spurgeon. Sly wanted to make him regret it.

"Today's forecast includes glorious sunstorms and copious amounts of toxic smog!" he chimed. "For those of you with fangs and nonexistent social skills, I recommend pulling the stick out of your ass and engaging in more than two syllables of conversation with someone, maybe even try venturing into the big wide mansion and enjoying the sauna or the indecently massive library."

At that point, Sly slipped up. The bubble of irritation in the back of his mind burst, flooding his voice.

"Seriously. I've been here two days and word is, I've seen more of this place than our esteemed evil overlord. You know, when people go around kidnapping hardworking mortals with other shit to do on your behalf, it is beyond rude to up and ghost them right out of the gate because you've got your panties in a twist!"

He stopped when he realized he was yelling. His hands shook, knuckles white around the mic. He took a cleansing breath.

"Sorry, everyone. Guess I've got some anger issues too. I'll work on that. You might try doing the same, boss."

He ended the broadcast, hands going to his hips as he nodded in satisfaction.

That was how Felix found him when he barged into the room, sweaty and dressed for physical exertion. "Are you insane?"

"Nope." Sly shrugged. "But I feel a lot better now."

HIS SPIRITS REMAINED LIFTED FOR TWENTY WHOLE MINUTES. That was how long it took for the vampire to find him.

Sly's stomach was already on board with the idea of regular satisfying meals, so he wheeled a begrudging Felix into directing him toward the kitchen. It was huge, designed to service the entire manor, with long counters and industrial appliances and a gleaming center island bigger than his entire kitchen at home. There was a gorgeous bowl of fresh fruit on the island, so he helped himself to a crispy golden apple.

He moaned around the mouthful, chewing slowly to savor it.

Kahled stomped in on the other side of the island counter.

It was better than Sly's imagination. Kahled's dark hair was a disorderly mop on his head, and the fine quality of his sleepwear was diminished by creases, the collar askew around his throat as if he'd yanked it on mid-hunt. He gaped at Sly around those enormous fangs.

Sly covered his full mouth before he spewed apple chunks with laughter.

"I'm going to murder you, Earthling."

Sly swallowed through the mirth and gestured to himself. "And waste such a fine blood bag?"

Kahled's expression darkened. It was no trick of the lightning, not Sly's imagination. The vampire's pupils expanded alarmingly, swallowing the gray of his irises. The whites of his eyes became shadowed.

Sly stopped laughing as the hair on the back of his neck prickled.

A low, rumbling growl vibrated through the air. That was the only warning Sly got before he was tackled. Kahled moved too fast to track. One moment, the island was between them, and the next, a heavy fist lifted him off the floor by the front of his shirt, and Sly's back met the fridge door. Pain from impact spread throughout his shoulders and back, the sharpness quick to fade to a dull and persistent ache. Fangs snapped inches from his face as the vampire's nostrils flared.

"Sorry!" Sly turned his head, squeezing his eyes shut. "Please don't kill me!"

Nothing happened.

Heart pounding, Sly unclenched one eyelid and braced for the sight of a seething vampire. Sure enough, Kahled's face was warped with an animal snarl, his brow furrowed and nose scrunched. His eyes were dark, fathomless pits.

"Okay. Okay! I fucked up!" Sly admitted as he gripped the arm holding him suspended off the floor. "I'm sorry! All right? I won't do it again!"

The flesh under his palm was uneven with scales. The formidable muscles flexed as Kahled's hold tightened, filling the kitchen with the sound of cloth tearing on claw.

The sound made Kahled flinch with a flick of his pointed ears. The shadows in his eyes began to recede, and the vicious expression melted as a touch of human awareness returned.

"Hey!" Sly said in a frenzied whisper. "There you are. How about putting the annoying little Earthling down now, yeah?"

Sly gave Kahled's forearm an earnest squeeze, and those dark eyes darted down to where their skin met. An unreadable expression crossed his face, his lower lip trembling between the bars of his fangs. His nostrils flared again with a hard, deliberate inhale. Kahled tilted his head as he studied Sly, the darkness in his eyes clearing as a confused expression replaced the danger.

The vampire's eyes were a soft gray—almost silver—as he grumbled, "Why would you do that?"

There was a note of accusation in his gruff voice, tempered by misery and awe.

"What?" Sly asked, breathless even as his fear began to fade.

Kahled frowned down at where their skin met, swallowing hard. "You're touching it."

Sly yanked his hands away from scaled flesh. "Oh shit! Did I hurt you? I didn't think— It's not— Are they sensitive?"

Kahled stared at him, his intense expression unreadable around those fangs.

Sly winced. "Shit. I'm sorry. They're freaking scales, for crying out loud. That's like nature's armor! If anything, they should be less sensitive!"

Kahled's dark brows drew closer together with each rapid word from Sly's mouth.

"I'm sorry. I already said that, but, yeah, I'm…" Sly bit his tongue, calming enough to squint at the vampire. "You don't look like you're in pain. Not physically anyway. Why are you looking at me like that?"

A shadow flickered in that silvery gaze as it trailed down Sly's cheek to his throat.

"Maybe you could put me down now?"

He did, but as Sly's feet hit the floor, the vampire's fist remained tangled in his clothes, trapping him against the fridge. Kahled leaned in, sniffing.

"Don't bite me," Sly warned, full of bravado. "Don't you dare!"

He braced for fresh pain, but it didn't come. Kahled didn't even bare his teeth as he drew close. Then, there was the hot press of warm skin and spiked stubble along Sly's neck and the hiss of an inhaling animal in his ear.

Then, it wasn't Kahled's hand pressing him to the fridge, it was his whole body.

"H-hello?" Sly squeaked.

Kahled released the fistful of his shirt, and there was a scratch of talon on metal as he caged Sly between muscled arms. A low, hungry growl vibrated against Sly's throat as Kahled nuzzled him.

"Okay." Sly gasped under the heavy body pinning him to the fridge. "Not that I'm not flattered—and really, I am, but— Ah!"

Sly's ass hit the floor. His front felt cold as Kahled jerked away, cursing. He backed into the island counter with pale eyes staring at Sly, wide with alarm. The Nocturnus was shaking.

It was painful to watch and confusing in the light of his own frantic heartbeat. Sly cast about for a distraction, an exit, something to say, anything that would get him out of this confrontation.

His eyes landed on the vampire's feet. The current lounge pants were absurdly long, pooling over him to hide the deformities. A single clawed toe was visible. It was grotesque and absurdly adorable.

Sly snickered and promptly slapped a hand over his mouth. He raised wary eyes back to Kahled's face as he fought the hysterical laugh. "Were you going to kill me?"

Kahled's eyes widened further as he gave a frantic shake of his head. "No. Maybe. I don't know."

Sly could still feel the phantom of heat and weight against him, a mouth on his neck. "What? Were you going to *fuck me*?" His voice cracked on the last two words.

A pink flush tinged the vampire's tanned skin.

Sly scrambled to his feet, shrieking, "Seriously?"

"I lost control," Kahled murmured, dropping his gaze. "It won't happen again."

"*It won't—?*" Sly lost it then. He burst out laughing, the adrenaline spiking through his veins, as he doubled over. His legs were shaking, his knees threatening to buckle.

For the second time, Kahled Vauqeulin ran from him.

He was three times Sly's size in pure muscle, with the most disturbing animal hardware of any Nocturni alive. Half-crazed with a rare disease, he could have ripped Sly's throat out at any moment. He had a Harem behind him, all the money and power in his favor.

And he ran.

Like Sly was his own personal demon. Like a vial's worth of Sly's blood wasn't already circulating in his deformed body.

By the time Sly managed to stop laughing and begin processing whatever had just happened, his face was a mess of tears and snot.

CHAPTER 7

*S*ly soon learned that the Vauqeulin brothers were Nocturni of their word. As Kamari promised, Walters and her staff expected nothing from him beyond his daily blood donation, and Kahled seemed set on ensuring Sly remained unmolested by making himself scarce. The first week passed with no sign of the mansion's master.

Gorbon and Mae insisted it wasn't personal. Kahled was careful to keep his distance from every mortal on the premises. Sly was quick to assure them how unbothered he was, but he wasn't entirely convincing.

The hefty ball of ugliness that his father's gambling had inspired was growing into a permanent feature. Sly refused to look too closely at how the knot pulsed in his gut with every passing day since he stared into Kahled's shadowed eyes.

He fell into a suspicious routine of casual comfort: three fantastic meals every day, unlimited access to the billiards room and it's endless array of holographic video games and intergalactic entertainment, and full control over his sleep schedule once again. Walters wasn't keen on his version of early morning wakeup calls, so she left him to wake up on his own time and grab his breakfast from the leftover plates left for him on the kitchen counter. Sly somehow talked himself into putting the gym and sauna to good use once or twice. The job was becoming one of Blythe's mythical vacations.

Within days, he was bored out of his mind.

One week down with twenty-five to go, and Sly resorted to camping out in the billiards room, watching nature documentaries about the wildlife preserves on Luna. It was ironic that so many Earthly species were thriving elsewhere while they were long extinct on their home planet. The sofa was honest leather, from hides harvested on distant planetary colonies, since cows hadn't graced Earth's surface in a millennium. He couldn't finish the second documentary. It felt wrong to gawk over the living miracles while he sat surrounded by animal remains that had seen more of the galaxy than he had.

The huge sectional created a tasteful partition between the voided space used for holographic video projects and the rest of the room. Between the display and the couch was a wide coffee table and two additional chairs. Stretching across the rear wall was an intimidating bar with lacquered shelves of fine crystal glasses and fully stocked bottles of rich liquids. The rest of the room was lined in shelves of media and games, including a modern, sleek-topped pool table and a virtual dart board.

Sly sat on the couch, glaring over his shoulder and reconsidering another solo dart game when Gorbon found him.

"Let's talk, Sly."

"…About?"

"You, for starters," the doctor said as he settled on the couch nearby. "Depending how that goes, maybe we'll discuss further options."

"Options?" Sly repeated with obvious doubt.

"Possibilities, if you will. Regarding Kahled's treatment plan."

Sly gave a strangled laugh. "I'm an entertainer, Doc, not a physician."

"True, but you're a living being with uniquely valuable physiological traits." Gorbon's smile turned fragile. "I'm the health official for the estate, Sly, not just for Kahled's sake. Your circumstances may be dictated somewhat by his condition, but your mental and emotional health needn't be."

"Is this a therapy session?" Sly squirmed. "Because if this is about that broadcast stunt, I already told Kahled I wouldn't touch it again. You don't need to worry about my mental well-being—"

"I'm worried about the mental well-being of everyone living under this roof, Sly. It's my job and my calling."

Sly's mouth pulled tight. "Fair point."

"I don't know the exact details, but I can sympathize with your position."

Sly barked a cold laugh. "Yeah?"

Gorbon sighed and nodded. "I know you're not here by choice, but since you are, you should at least consider the opportunity available to you."

Sly snorted.

"I've had time to study your blood work and its potential effect on Nocturni. Do you have any idea how rare it is to find a pure human adult in today's world? Specifically, one who doesn't pose a threat of suicide bombing a Harem if such a convenient opportunity presented itself?"

Sly couldn't meet Gorbon's eye then. He wasn't sure how the doctor would react if Sly admitted his father used to be pals with a guy who did exactly that.

"Kahled is the second in as many generations to develop

Nosferatu's Curse," Gorbon continued, shaking his clasped hands in a plea. "This disease is supposed to be rare, with only a dozen or so cases recorded in all Nocturni history. If the bloodline is devolving, the Harem at large is in trouble. More than that, imagine what they might do to the rest of us if this gets out of hand."

Sly winced. "Nothing good?"

"Exactly. If there is the slightest chance you and I could do something about it, isn't that a chance worth taking? For the future sake of humanity and Nocturni alike?"

Sly bit his lip, unsure how to answer.

"The Vauqeulins are good people," Gorbon pressed on. "Whatever prejudices you have, whatever you've been taught, it didn't stop Master Vauqeulin from contracting you. He believes you could be persuaded to save his brother's life, Sly."

Sly gave Gorbon's words the grave consideration they were due. He sat up straight, peering at the older man. "I get it, Doc. I really do. But everybody dies eventually, even the Nocturni. Is it fair to demand I sacrifice my life as I know it for a stranger? One who wants nothing to do with me, no less?"

Gorbon couldn't hold his gaze. He shook his head sadly. "And the greater ramifications?"

Sly looked away. "The survival of two sentient races doesn't rest on my skinny ass, Doc. Suggesting otherwise is absurd."

He gave a rough start when Gorbon's hand clasped his knee, giving him a warm jostle.

"We're both human, Sly. Our ability to sympathize and care for one another is one of our greatest strengths."

They lapsed into silence, staring past each other. Sly took a breath, trying to think of something to say that didn't make him sound like a callous ass while still making his position clear. He had family waiting for him back home, and that wasn't going to change.

Gorbon sparred him, clearing his throat as he pulled his hand away. "There's also the small matter that I've staked my career on the possibility of curing the only genetic disease known to Nocturni."

Sly laughed.

Gorbon shrugged. "It's a factor. Not the only one, but I'll own up to it."

"Weren't the Nocturni supposed to be the miracle cure for a homicidal planet?" Sly commented. "Since that didn't work out, seems to me, they're not the best choice for scientific breakthroughs and medical experimentation."

A slight smile crossed Gorbon's face. "Possibly, but there are accounts of unmodified human blood sending the Curse into remission before. A week's use of yours has already been promising."

Sly leaned forward again. "What do you mean?"

"By all rights, there is nothing remarkable about your blood, and yet..." Gorbon made an emphatic gesture. "The Nocturni's organic splicing capabilities respond to it like nothing I've ever seen. On a microbiological level, you're already impacting him, already stabilizing his moods! Give it a few years and medical intervention, and your blood might repair his physical mutations."

"Sure," Sly scoffed, deadpan. "It's so effective, which is why he's as unpleasant and antisocial today as he was on day one."

"No treatment can cure personality flaws." Gorbon offered a conspiratorial wink. "But a week ago, a Cursed episode would have resulted in thousands in property damage. Today, he shredded a pillow and threw a glass tumbler across a room. That's what we call distinct and quantifiable improvement."

"I'll have to take your word for it," Sly conceded. "Pretty sure he plans to avoid me right up until it's time for me to leave."

Gorbon sighed. "He's coping the best he can. Since you're here anyway, couldn't you try helping him?"

"He doesn't want my help, Doc," Sly grumbled. "Besides, I'm already doing my part."

His voice was damnably soft as he uttered that last bit. The ball of nastiness residing in Sly's stomach gave a vicious lurch.

Gorbon frowned at him over the rims of his glasses, as if he knew about the awful sensations Sly was so careful not to mention. "Perhaps. At least I asked."

The doctor stood, stretching with a hefty sigh.

"I'm sorry I can't be more help," Sly said, picking at the hem of his shirt as he avoided Gorbon's eye. "I can't stay beyond this contract, but if you need any help around the estate or whatever…"

Gorbon chuckled. "You're bored."

"Like you wouldn't believe."

"Maybe this will help."

Sly frowned as Gorbon retrieved something from his pocket and dropped it in Sly's lap. It was an elegant curve of smooth silver, thin but strong. Sly might have mistaken it for a bracelet if he hadn't watched Walters use her own gold-hued comms.

"It's from Kahled."

Sly frowned up at the doctor. "Another gift, huh? Should I thank Madam Walters?"

"No." Gorbon smiled patiently. "Emmeline mentioned you didn't have one during last night's progress exam, but it was Kahled's idea that we pull a unit from storage for you. It was a good idea. I'm sure you have people back home who'd like to hear how you're doing."

He gave Sly a pat on the shoulder. Then, he left him alone.

HE HOLED UP IN HIS ROOM, CURLED INTO A BALL AGAINST THE headboard of the guest bed. He bit his lip as he focused on the comms. He punched in the oldest code in his memory bank.

John Spurgeon didn't answer.

Sly's heart sank, but he shook himself and decided not to dwell on it. He moved on to the next name on his priority list.

"Hello?"

Blythe's voice hit him like a punch to the gut. He clutched at the metal on his arm as he murmured, "Blythe?"

"Holy shit. Sylvester!" she shrieked his name.

"Turn on your video feed. I miss your face."

He didn't have to wait long. The video features on his old unit hadn't worked cleanly in years, but Blythe's did, and the new one on his wrist alighted with ease. He got a detailed rendering of Blythe's face. Dark makeup lined her eyes, and the jaguar spots on her temples were stark, emphasized by the way her hair was pulled tight into a chaotic bundle.

The sight of her made him smile. He breathed easy for the first time all week.

"Sly!" She wailed, eyes wide and jaw unhinged. "You're still alive!"

Sly laughed. It was too loud, too sharp, but he didn't care. "Stars, I've missed you. Yeah, I'm alive. I'm fine."

"Phink said you would be." Blythe bit her lip as her wet eyes darted away. "I didn't believe him. Not really. Days went by, and no one heard from you and… Fuck. When are you coming home?"

"Soon," he vowed, lifting the comms closer to his face. "You and Dad can hold it together for a few measly months."

"Are you okay?" She blanched. "I mean, you look great. Seriously, are you wearing makeup? You're glowing. There's so much red in your hair!"

Sly snickered. "You would kill for a chance to use the bathtub in this place, Blythe. It's huge, and the water quality is something else. I doubt Luna has anything better."

"Lucky little bitch," she grumbled, but then her chin trembled. Her voice broke on the next few words, "They're treating you well, then? For real? No one's hurt you?"

Sly shook his head hard well before she stopped speaking. "No, I'm good. The vamp's hardly touched me, actually."

A baffled expression played across her face. "Seriously? What's wrong with him?"

Sly bit his lip. It was a joke, a rhetorical comment, really, but he never bothered to explain the full situation to her. Blythe knew how the contract impacted Sly, but she knew nothing about Kahled.

And now she was frowning at him, eyes soft and mouth pouty. "Sly?"

He sighed, shoulders slumping as he smacked his skull back against the headboard. Sly rubbed his fingers together, recalling the sense memory of mottled skin and malformed flesh.

"What's wrong, Sly?"

In his head, all he could see were black eyes snarling at him with the dangerous focus of an apex predator. Sly tried to reconcile it with the pale-eyed creature who shied away from his slightest touch and seemed to taunt him with every scant word uttered between them.

"I don't know what I'm doing here, Blythe," he admitted, tone dull and detached. "They want me to help this vampire, and I'm already bleeding for him, but it's apparently not enough."

"Hey." She scowled. "You only owe them six months of your time. You said so yourself; it's just a short-term gig with a big payout."

Sly kept nodding as her voice gave way to a tense quiet.

"Sly?"

Sly huffed, glaring around the room as if it held answers. "Any other vampire would pay a fortune to have exclusive access to me, and this guy… he's literally dying, but he's not interested!"

It wasn't until he said it out loud that Sly realized how unsettling that was. Whether they could recognize his blood as pure, or if it was subliminal or merely a suspicion, Nocturni always responded to Sly. Always. Some, like Le Vau, liked to cross the line between flirtation and harassment, but they were rarely mean with him.

What made Kahled so different?

Blythe was talking at him, her tone hot and snippy like it was whenever she tried to defend him from negative opinions. Sly didn't hear any of it.

"I think..." She hushed as he spoke. "I'm actually disappointed."

Her nose scrunched as she reared back. "...What?"

"He's a vampire," Sly stressed.

"Your point?"

"He's a *vampire*!" Sly repeated, bouncing on the bed as he shouted. "He's nothing like the vamps at Centrism; he doesn't want a reminder that humanity exists, he *needs* it. It's the only thing special about me, and he fucking needs it to survive, but this bloodsucker would rather avoid me like I'm here to make everything worse!"

Blythe stared at him from the comms. "Sly... you're not making any sense."

A shiver raced up his spine. Jumbled puzzle pieces were slipping into place in his brain, like he'd stumbled onto a golden cipher key.

Numb, he said, "It makes perfect sense."

And it did. It wasn't sane, but Sly understood anyhow. He wasn't conceited enough to think he deserved the Nocturni's attention based on personality or looks, but he knew damn well how a stable vampire responded to the mere presence of his blood.

But Kahled wasn't one of Centrism's lusty clients, not with those sad, tired eyes. And his wariness. His disinterest and borderline fear of one Sylvester Spurgeon.

He reminded Sly of his mother.

Comprehension dawned on Sly like a bag of bricks. Kamari Vauqeulin might have sent Kahled to Earth for treatment, but the knot in Sly's gut suggested Kahled had other reasons for cooperating.

Sly knew what it looked like when a person gave up on living.

HE STOOD BEFORE A SPACIOUS, DECORATED ELEVATOR DOWN the hall from Gorbon's medical suite. Its reflective doors slid open with a smooth, soundless glide, and he stepped in after a moment's hesitation. Sly barely noticed when it moved. It was nothing like the elevator in Blythe's building; the speed and effortless lift was almost eerie.

That concerning strangeness spiked as the doors opened into an empty stone entryway. Sly squinted while his eyes adjusted to the darkness. It was deathly quiet, the air heavy and thick, almost stifling. If Gorbon's rooms felt like a different building, than Kahled's qualified as a different planet altogether.

Sly weighed the slender vial of blood in his hand. His blood.

"You can leave it in the foyer," Gorbon had suggested when Sly offered to deliver the evening's dose himself. "I appreciate you stepping up, Sly, but if Kahled doesn't answer the door, don't test him."

Sly didn't plan to test anyone. He still had a tender spot on one shoulder from the last time he poked at the not-so-proverbial beast.

"I'm going to regret this," Sly muttered as he stepped out of the elevator.

Blood in hand, he crossed the foyer and followed Gorbon's directions down the righthand hall leading to Kahled's bedroom. The door was closed. Sly tucked the vial into his palm and knocked gently.

The door creaked open and Sly froze.

Nothing happened. Sly dared to breathe while waiting for an enraged vampire to start spitting at him to get out. The suspense went on for so long, Sly knocked again, harder, and the door swung inward.

Sly gaped.

The room was stunning, and not in a good way. It might have fared better after exposure to a violent sunstorm. There was broken furniture and shattered glass, books that had been torn in half and the pages scattered. There were expensive linens torn to rags on the floor, and more than one hole had been punched into the walls. The closet door hung off its final hinge. The only recognizable furnishing was a bedframe, but it was severely damaged, thick wooden supports snapped and discarded till the whole thing had collapsed.

At least the mattress and sheets seemed intact, smothered in pillows. It was the one spot untouched by brute strength and razor-sharp claws.

Kahled lay splayed on his front among so much silk and padding. His face was buried in bedding, and his lounge pants were exactly like the ones he wore last time Sly saw him. Now, though, there was an abundance of warm sepia skin on display, so much bronze stretched across a powerful back.

And scales.

From the doorway, Sly could plainly see the reptilian marks dotting Kahled's arms and shoulders. There was a single patch creeping up the broad expanse of his back.

Kahled didn't move as he growled, "What do you want?"

Sly jumped back from the doorway, Kahled's incredible form disappearing from his view.

He heard a noise like the inconvenienced huff of a wild cat, then, "Leave. I'm busy."

Sly coughed up a harsh laugh. "With what? Remodeling again?"

Silence answered him.

Sly shoved his hand into the room, the blood vial dangling between his fingers. "I brought a gift!"

Kahled responded with grumbling snarl. It sounded too tame for a real warning.

Sly peeked into the room to find the vampire unmoved on the bed. "Come on, Maestro," he taunted as he stepped inside. "You know you want it!"

"Enough."

Kahled moved way too fast for a creature so large. He rose from the bedding like an earthquake, shedding cushions

93

across the ravaged room as he rolled onto his knees to glower at Sly. His eyes were clear and gray.

"I'm no maestro," Kahled scowled, massive shoulders slumping as he perched himself at the foot of the mangled bed. "Do you have any clue what that title means?"

"Yeah," Sly said, defensive as he crossed the bedroom's threshold. "It's a pretentious way of saying Master. Obviously."

"It refers to a master of the arts," Kahled corrected with a snap of his teeth. He shook his head, rather like an animal, and gestured for the vial.

Sly toed his way through the debris cluttering the floor, willing his erratic heartbeat to stay calm. Soon, he was close enough to see the finer details to Kahled's spliced legs. The right foot was completely alien, closer to something prehistoric than to human biology. It made Sly's stomach churn.

Kahled didn't look at him as he drew near, holding out his hand with an expectant glower.

"You're not even going to offer me a seat?" Sly bristled. "How rude."

"Why should I bother? To impress you? I'd rather not. In case it slipped your notice, I'm busy dying a slow and uneventful death."

His fingers flexed, demanding the vial. It was his left hand where the middle and ring fingers were elongated and taloned. Warped and gnarled.

"Clearly." Sly frowned and crossed his arms with the blood solidly in his fist.

Kahled gave him an unimpressed look. "I'll bite you."

"Yeah? How would that work, exactly?"

Sly leaned in for a good look at those lengthy fangs. It was doubtful that Kahled could unhinge his jaw wide enough to fit Sly's wrist under them, not to mention his throat.

"I'm starting to think your bark is worse than your bite," Sly commented. He glanced down at the lethal talons and added, "Maybe."

Kahled dropped his hand in his lap, glancing away with supposed disinterest. "You haven't demonstrated any of the supposed intelligence Kamari has claimed you have. This conversation isn't helping your case."

"Then it's a good thing we're not trying to impress each other." Sly shoved the vial at him. "Drink."

Kahled glared at the offering, his jaw tense. Even seated on the leveled bed, he managed to loom somehow. "Remind me which of us is the master in this house again?"

Sly smiled, full of false sweetness. "You, Maestro."

Kahled glowered. "Do you have brain damage? We just established that title is not appropriate—"

"Drink!" Sly insisted. "That's premium human goodness there, I'd like to make sure you're not wasting it."

When Kahled kept glowering, Sly sighed and uncorked the vial himself.

The vampire stiffened, nostrils flaring with an inhale.

Sly palmed the cap and offered the blood with the other hand. He grinned ruthlessly. "Bleeding for you is the only job I have in this hellhole, and by the stars, I am going to do it. Now, drink."

Kahled didn't take the vial. His left hand, with the worse mutations, lifted with deliberate slowness. Sly had plenty of time to pull back, but he didn't, and then Kahled's fingers were wrapped around his wrist.

Sly's eyes narrowed. "What are you doing?"

"Drinking," Kahled snipped back, and he guided Sly's hand and the enclosed vial toward his mouth. Movements slow and smooth, he didn't spill a drop. All the while, he kept his eyes on Sly's face as if daring the human to pull away.

The cylinder of blood touched the vampire's lips, right between the bars of those terrible fangs, and Sly didn't back down. The danger flashing in Kahled's stare was familiar, heated and taunting, and blissfully free of darkness. Sly saw no reason not to, so he did what he did best and went with the flow of things, following his instincts.

Sly stepped closer, sliding his fingers up the vial and tipping his blood into Kahled's mouth. The edge of one finger settled on a full lower lip, his knuckle nudging a fang. There was wetness as Kahled's tongue swept out to taste him. His blood. His skin. Sly wasn't sure which. Maybe both.

Kahled's eyes were crystal clear the whole time, a lovely pale gray.

He finished drinking, red staining his lip. He kept Sly's wrist in his warm, manacle-like grip as he licked it clean.

"I can hear your heart racing," Kahled purred. "I can feel your pulse through the layers of Cursed skin on my fingertips. Under my claws."

Sly swallowed. He couldn't look away from those bright eyes.

"It doesn't disgust you?" Kahled whispered, a subtle croak lacing his words. "Truly? You smell like sin and heated blood, but not fear. Why?"

Sly blinked fast, trying to break out of whatever weird spell had fallen over him. "What's happening here? Are you threatening me or seducing me?"

Kahled dropped Sly's hand like it burned. He shifted backward on the bed, gaze averted. "Neither. I don't understand you."

"Well, that makes two of us."

Sly recorked the emptied vial without daring to look at

Kahled. He had the jarring impression that another staring contest might be catastrophic.

A low growl rumbled from Kahled's throat, but there was no other reaction.

"Anyway..." Sly sang, staring around the decimated room. "I was talking about you earlier, and I had this thought. An epiphany, if you will."

"Fascinating," Kahled muttered.

"That's not the word I would use, but okay." Sly shrugged. "See, here's the thing. I know about the Curse and all that, so I won't make things weird by asking if you're all right, but—"

"It's already weird."

"But!" Sly raised his voice, gesturing for Kahled to hush. "I wanted to stop by and make sure you were... not okay, obviously, but, you know... not dangerously depressed or something."

Kahled's dark brows lifted high on his ridiculously handsome face. He said nothing, only stared.

Sly fiddled with the hem of his shirt. "So? Are you?"

Kahled's stare was so heavy, it was impossible for Sly to stand still under it. He bounced his leg, fidgeted with his shirt, and existed as a bundle of nerves as he waited for a reply.

Eventually, Kahled uncrossed his arms with an unreadable expression. "Thank you for the concern, but no. I'm not depressed."

Sly gave a couple stiff nods, unable to hold his gaze. "Oh. Okay, then..."

"What do you want, Mr. Spurgeon?"

"It's Sly."

Kahled sighed. "What do you want?"

Sly hesitated. His eyes found Kahled's feet and stayed

there, locked on the bizarre mesh of convoluted flesh blending into a humanoid ankle on the one leg.

"I watched someone die once. From suicide. It wasn't a split second thing like people imagine it is. It took time. Weeks. Months, maybe, and…" Sly trailed off. He cleared his throat, harsh and grating, then said, "I can't just sit by and watch it happen again. Not like that."

He managed to lift his head, only to find Kahled staring at him with piercing, sad eyes. "I'm dying regardless, Sly."

Sly's gaze darted to the fangs without his permission, but he was quick to reclaim eye contact before speaking. "Just do your loved ones a favor and go out fighting, okay?"

Then, because it felt like the right thing to do, Sly gave Kahled's scaled shoulder a friendly pat. It was awkward and stiff, but he made solid contact.

It was too much for either of them. As Kahled shrank away from his touch, Sly's stomach twisted into knots. Taking pity on each of them, Sly took his turn to run away.

SLY HAD TROUBLE SLEEPING THAT NIGHT. EVERY TIME HE closed his eyes, he heard his dad shouting about parasites and humanity's extinction.

When he slept and was spared from the believable mindscape, he was plagued by flashes of memory. His parents fighting over his friendship with Blythe after her parents died and Phink took her in. His feet swinging inches from the floor while John drank and chortled with rough-looking men who praised Humans First and spat threats at HEPP. The time John slapped him for suggesting they donate blood for a Lunar Harem in need.

Mostly, he remembered his mom's weak smile as she set a

special treat of fabricated pancakes in front of him before stepping outside without her protective gear.

The Nocturni were designed to be indestructible in comparison to human standards. Sly wasn't even sure if they *could* kill themselves, but he knew he didn't want to find out.

CHAPTER 8

Four and a half months before the Assessment Contract ended, Sly found something to occupy his time. While Kahled was busy with Gorbon, he snuck into the Master's suite and snuck a look at the intercom panel in the sitting room. He'd put the direct line from the basement control center to good use every few waking hours since.

That lasted until Kahled put his fist through the center console with pale eyes and a perfectly sane grin on his face. It was going to take weeks to reconfigure everything so Sly could play with the system again.

Sly retaliated by delivering his daily blood donation himself from then on. He managed a full week of careful ribbing before the vampire finally caught on to his game and started locking his bedroom door. This only prompted Sly to hold his blood ransom while he wailed the most annoying songs in his repertoire until Kahled opened the door to admit him.

But then the vampire decided to be proactive.

"Kahled!" Sly shrieked as he stepped off the elevator. "What did you do to my comms?"

He barged into the bedroom to find the vampire lounging in his dilapidated bed, reclining on mounds of pillows with one grotesque ankle thrown over the other knee. A thin book was in his hand.

"Don't you mean *my* comms?" Kahled said without looking up from his reading. "It's my property, after all. Paid for by my Harem. To support my household."

"I can't call anyone outside the estate!" Sly flapped his hands as he shouted. "I keep getting error messages telling me to contact my system administrator! What did you do?"

Kahled wasn't reading, but writing. He set an old-fashioned stylus to the page, an intent expression on his face, and explained, "I revoked your permissions for outside communications."

Sly spluttered. "You can't do that!"

Finally, Kahled looked up from his book. He indicated himself with the stylus, "Evil Overlord." Then, he waved toward Sly. "Lowly Earthling. What's an appropriately immature term you'll understand? Checkmate? Yes. Checkmate." And he returned to his writing.

Bubbling with rage, Sly hissed through clenched teeth, "I need to talk to Blythe!"

Kahled shrugged. "That's your problem."

"Argh!" Sly ripped the comms off his wrist and chucked it at the vampire's face.

It bounced off Kahled's forehead with a satisfying thud. The vampire froze, blinking at him.

Sly took advantage of Kahled's stunned incredulity and launched himself at the bed. His only goal was to be as inconvenient and petty as possible. He ended up tumbling over the vampire, Kahled's knee forcing the air from his lungs along the way as he grabbed at random. His momentum carried him off the far side of the bed, and he flopped to the floor with Kahled's book.

Sly rolled onto his back and raised the book high with a victorious cry.

"What just happened?" Kahled murmured from the bed.

Sly opened his mouth to retort, but then he got a good look at the book in his hands. His mouth went dry.

It was a sketchbook. Staring back at him from the current page was an ink drawing, a startlingly life-like depiction of a young woman with shrewd eyes and dark curls crafted in a pile atop her head. There was something familiar in the shape of her eyes.

"Wow," Sly breathed. "You really are a maestro after all."

"Don't be ridiculous. It's just a sketch."

"It's amazing," Sly argued. He got to his knees and leaned his forearms on the bed, the sketchbook laid out on the blanket under his palm. "Fill it in a little more, and it's practically a photograph!"

He studied the drawing again, head quirked to the side. Her nose was slightly off center, a realistic flaw, but too imperfect for a celebrated Moon Diva, and yet…

"I've seen her before. Who is she?"

"Emmeline."

Sly looked up, startled. "As in… Walters?"

Kahled nodded and held out an expectant hand.

Sly had to climb onto the mattress and crawl to give him the sketchbook. Then, on a whim, he folded his legs under him and sat his butt among rumpled bedding fit for a king.

"You've known her since she was young?" Sly asked.

Kahled's face softened as he drawled, "She was my mother's Companion."

Something cold and slimy settled in the pit of Sly's stomach.

"Tahliah Vauqeulin," Kahled murmured as a slow, sad smile bloomed on his face. "She was Heir to the Harem before me. Kamari and I were so young when her Curse developed."

The lump of nastiness in Sly's gut rolled and twisted. "How long did she— Wait. Heir before you? But isn't your brother head of the Harem?"

Kahled released a breathy, humorless chuckle. His eyes flickered with shadows as he tossed the book aside like it was trash, and he said, "He is now. They can't have a Cursed vampire leading the family."

Sly's jaw dropped. "You're telling me *you* were in charge of one of the most legendary vampire bloodlines in existence?"

It was beyond rude of him to stare, but he couldn't help himself. He saw Kahled sitting there, slumped and alone on a broken bed, surrounded by the remains of useless wealth and so much violence. He tried to reconcile the sight in front of him with a Nocturnus at the pinnacle of known society.

Kahled shook his head, lost in thought as his jaw tensed. "It's been five years since my diagnosis. The Elders who helped me manage the Harem directed me to officially turn everything over to Kamari the very same day."

"That's fucked up."

Kahled didn't disagree. He turned his distant gaze more or less toward Sly. "Mari wasn't ready. He's still not ready. But after I…" he trailed off, swallowing hard. The lump in his throat was visible as his eyes gleamed with memories.

Sly held his breath, though he wasn't sure why.

Kahled continued after a hard moment of silence, "Once Nosferatu gets a firm hold of you, it's impossible to function around other Nocturni. Too much territorial aggression. After a certain point, exile became my only option. Now, here I am."

"Here we are," Sly corrected.

Kahled looked at him then. Properly. His eyes were bright and hard, still sad, but almost challenging.

"Leave. I'm not in the mood to entertain you today."

Sly should have backed off then. He should have scooted his ass off the bed and bid Kahled goodnight. If he were smart, he'd remember Blythe and Phink were still waiting for him, that his father probably still needed his help to keep the house intact.

Sly might have to admit that he wasn't that smart after all.

He shifted onto his knees. Stiff and awkward, he inched his way up the bed till he could sit beside the vampire. He meant it to be comforting, a show of solidarity, maybe, but the pillows heaped against the mangled headboard were too plush; they gave way immediately, and he slipped into Kahled's side till they were pressed together, from shoulder to hip.

Neither of them moved for many long, uncomfortable seconds.

"Sorry," Sly murmured.

Kahled said nothing. He didn't move away; he just sat there with Sly squished against his side. This close, Sly couldn't help noticing how weary his eyes were, the lids heavy, the skin beneath them purple and lined with exhaustion.

"You're irksome."

Sly didn't know how to respond to that statement, but Kahled seemed to be waiting for a response. "I can see why you would think that."

"You should leave."

"Probably, but I can't with you looking so pitiful." Sly

nudged him with his elbow. "Plus, you haven't reinstated my comms permissions yet."

Kahled gave a long-suffering sigh. "If I do, will you stop pestering me and go back to letting Gorbon deliver your *donations*?"

The way he sneered that final word made Sly straightened up, glowering. "What's wrong with my blood?"

"Nothing." Kahled met his eye, unimpressed. "It's does nothing but delay the inevitable."

Sly slumped with a confused frown. "You say that like…" Sly swallowed the lump in his throat. "Like that's the last thing you want."

"Obviously," Kahled drawled.

Sly went cold all over. The resignation in Kahled's expression had a disturbing familiarity to it.

Kahled noticed his reaction. How could he not, when they sat so close, staring so intently at one another? A thoughtful frown crossed the vampire's face, then he sighed again, louder, and lowered his hand to take hold of Sly's wrist.

Sly gave an awkward snicker. "We're holding hands now?"

Kahled huffed a small, primal sound that was caught between amusement and irritation. With deliberate, gentle pressure, he pulled Sly's limb to him, nearly hugging it to his chest. He caught Sly's eye with a look that was so fragile but so daring.

An unvoiced question blossomed between them.

Sly bit his lip.

He imagined what his father would do in this situation. Would he strike out and condemn a dying soul for being a parasite? Would he be the compassionate Guard, the peacekeeper who raised Sly and loved him his entire life, and make an exception for one needful vampire? Was there a universe where John Spurgeon would willingly give his vein to any Nocturni?

"Wait," Sly said, his soft voice exploding the quiet.

Kahled dropped his arm. He didn't push away or sneer, he just let go. It sent something sharp and poignant lancing through Sly's chest.

"Do you have a bloodletting kit nearby?" Sly suggested.

Kahled looked away, his tongue brushing over lethal fangs. "No."

Sly bit his lip and eyed the door. "I could go to Gorbon early, then come right back?"

Kahled prodded Sly in the side as his greater bulk shied away. An unsightly hand moved to hide the mutated teeth, and Sly's skin crawled with disgust that was entirely self-directed.

"Wait!" Sly cried, slapping Kahled's hand from his mouth.

With comical slowness, the vampire turned to stare at him.

"I'm not rejecting you or anything." Face flushed, Sly's gaze darted about the room. His voice faltered, and the childish fear of disappointing his father roared in the back of his mind, but it couldn't compete with his memories of distress and despondency so very, very similar to Kahled's. "You can't blame me for having a healthy concern about sharp things bigger than my pinky aiming for my veins. What about…? We could…"

His eyes landed on Kahled's hand where it had fallen, limp on the Nocturnus's thigh.

"How careful can you be with those claws?"

Kahled blinked at him, his face stoic.

Sly shoved at his shoulder to no effect. "You can manage a scratch that doesn't need stitches, right?"

Even as he pulled up his sleeve and held his arm out, Sly could hear his father's voice shrieking with panic in the back of his mind. *What the hell are you doing, boy? He'll kill you! He'll drain you dry like the leech he is!*

But Sly couldn't listen to such warnings, not with those sad eyes staring him down, glittering and crystalline with unshed tears. There was nothing malicious in those eyes, only raw human suffering.

It barely hurt when a lone claw drew a cut across his forearm. It probably should have. Sly went breathless as his skin parted in a clean line, an inch long at most. One second expanded into a small eternity before the blood rushed to meet exposed air.

Sly was shaking as Kahled pulled him closer. He wasn't the only one.

When Kahled hesitated, words stumbled off Sly's tongue. "You don't have to. I mean, if you'd rather, I could go get Gorbon? He might have some awkward questions, but that's no big— Ah!"

Sly's feeble humor failed him as a hot tongue swiped up his inner arm. Wet muscle dragged over the shallow cut and then some. It cleared away blood along with whatever thoughts were swimming around Sly's brain. All he could focus on was the solid grip on his wrist, the warm glide of the mouth on his skin, and the crystal-gray eyes boring into his own.

Sly's heart stopped. His breath caught, his body swayed, and time itself stilled. It didn't last long, but there wasn't a single part of him that escaped unaffected.

"Okay, Maestro," Sly breathed.

Kahled didn't look away, he didn't even blink as his other hand reached out for Sly's waist with glacially smooth movements.

Sly couldn't speak. He couldn't make a noise. He just nodded.

Kahled's eyes caught the light in a vivid flash as he yanked Sly onto his thigh. Stars above, but Kahled's leg was thick, nothing but solid muscle that didn't seem to notice his weight. Kahled's mouth smothered the open wound as his arm tightened around Sly's body. He wasn't exactly gentle, but his lips and the fronts of his fangs pressed against Sly with more heat than discomfort. Those concerning eyeteeth ceased to matter because the suction overrode Sly's better thinking like a state-of-the-art engine through meteor dust.

"Okay," Sly whispered as he grew warm and eager. For something. Anything. "This is fine."

Kahled's eyes clenched shut as he drew blood in long, achingly good pulls. His mouth worked, deliberate and hungry, as he cradled Sly's arm in his malformed hands. He let out a low, warbling moan.

"Good, that's… good," Sly breathed.

He wasn't aroused, not exactly. Half-hard at best. But there was anticipation zinging up and down his spine, growing stronger with every pass of Kahled's tongue on his skin. He brushed ebony hair from Kahled's face, and it was soft, startling compared to the stubble prickling his inner arm.

That wasn't all he felt. The cool wetness of tears pooled where his skin met the vampire's cheek.

Sly petted him with a trembling hand and soothed, "Shh. You're all right."

Except he wasn't.

Kahled's cries were quiet, more than stifled by his mouthful, but the low noise of distress coming from him was unbearable in the empty room. It was too eerie, too familiar.

Sly needed it to stop. It had to be stopped.

He did the only thing he could think of.

He sang.

He didn't think. He didn't make any conscious choice for the tune. He just opened his mouth and let the melody flow as if it had a life of its own. Familiar words rent the air with all the sharpness of painful memory, and he sang a song he hadn't dared sing in years.

He sang of stars and celestial forces beyond mortal comprehension. He sang about visions of galaxies and stardust. Comets and flares and angelic auras. The lyrics were full of a wonder and beauty that Sly couldn't begin to imagine.

He sang his mother's favorite song. "Starlight Daydreams."

By the time the last note faded away, Sly was crying too. Only a little. Silently.

Kahled knew anyway. He was motionless, his mouth still pressed to Sly's arm, but the mournful tension was lessened. It wasn't gone, not by half, but Sly could feel the huge body relaxing. He was held so close, he couldn't help but notice the slightest release of those considerable muscles. The vampire was no longer drinking from him.

After a moment's silence, Sly sighed and rested his head against Kahled's shoulder. He waited, quiet and still, until Kahled was ready to let go of his arm and push him off his lap.

Kahled released his wrist, but he didn't push him away.

"I don't want to die," Kahled admitted, voice numb, "but, then, there are days where it's all I think about, and it's the only thing that seems worth doing."

"I know."

Sly wrapped an arm around Kahled. He squeezed, not

gentle enough to avoid feeling the rough platelets of mutated flesh through the cloth covering Kahled's shoulder. They sat that way for a long time. Later, Sly would marvel how long he sat there, wordless and still, with nothing of note happening around him. He would question why it was so easy, so comfortable, and how anyone could possibly think the Nocturni were anything less than human. Much, much later, he would realize how relieved he was to finally give voice to a song that had haunted him half his life.

All of that would happen. Later. First, he needed rest.

CHAPTER 9

*S*ly wasn't sure when he started a game of chicken with the vampire. He wasn't even sure they were playing, exactly. They might have been flirting. They might have been baiting each other toward violence. It was anyone's guess, really.

Another week passed and nothing and everything had changed. The only people consciously aware of the shift were Sly and Kahled, but neither of them was willing to acknowledge it out loud. Nevertheless, a mounting tension was pervading the manor. The staff started noticing more and more each time Kahled prowled the halls beyond his private wing.

"Master Kahled's looking for you."

Sly glanced over his shoulder, tearing his attention from the box of spare parts in his lap to see Felix standing in the doorway of the comms center with his arms crossed and a scowl on his face. Sly wasn't going to give up on repairing the intercom, even if he knew better than to goad Kahled into a murderous rage with it. There was something familiar and soothing about the wires in his hands, a deep satisfaction in seeing the chaos of a broken machine coming together at his direction.

Felix's interruption was not appreciated.

"That's nice." Sly shrugged at the blond before returning to his goodie box. "I have a comms. He can summon me whenever he wants."

Felix huffed. "He's sniffing around the billiards room like a dog."

"Your point?"

Impatience weighed down each word as Felix said, "He's the master of this house. Give him what he wants so the rest of us can use the space in peace."

Sly tossed his head with a sharp laugh. "I've been here for weeks, and I've never seen you or anyone else use that room. Isn't that why all the long-term staff have personal lounges? Mae mentioned a personal library in hers—"

"Are you really that thick?" Felix snapped.

Jaw tight, Sly shoved the parts box onto the console before he spun in his chair to face Felix. "Excuse me?"

Felix's fists clenched at his sides as he said, "He doesn't like leaving his rooms, but he does because of you. I don't know what you've done or why, but he keeps seeking you out like a hunting hound, and you don't seem to care that he's making a fool of himself because of you!"

Sly's face grew warm as he glared back. "If Kahled wants to check out his own house, I'm not going to stop him. If your opinion matters so much, why don't you go tell him you're concerned about his reputation?"

Felix looked ready to throw a punch, fists shaking. "The only thing I'm concerned about is you. You're not fit to be anyone's Companion, least of all for a Nocturnus of The Nine Bloodlines. You're not interested in the job, so don't start acting like you give a damn now. You have no right to get his hopes up."

Sly's jaw dropped as he watched Felix spin on his heel and storm off.

HE WAS STILL SEATED AT THE CONSOLE, TRYING TO FORGET Felix's incomprehensible outburst, when Kahled found him.

"I thought we were done with this," Kahled mused as he ducked his head to invade the cozy control room. "Was smashing it to pieces with my bare hands somehow unclear?"

Sly shot the vampire a cheeky grin and held up a metal sheet that was two shades too dark, but otherwise a perfect replacement for the panel covered in Kahled's claw marks. "Thanks for the challenge, but I've dealt with worse."

Kahled's upper lift twitched. Before Sly could determine if it was done with disgust or amusement, the vampire reached up and ripped the overhead light fixture from the ceiling. With the cracking of glass and zapping sparks of electricity, the room went black.

Sly gasped, freezing in his chair. "Hey!"

Kahled's form blocked most of the light sneaking in from the hall, but Sly felt him moving. He could tell when the vampire was close, and then there was a huge, awkward hand latching onto his upper arm.

"This obsolete tech is nothing but trouble in your hands."

Kahled's voice was a soft, deep purr that made Sly shiver.

"And since I can't trust you to take a hint, I'll have to take more extreme measures to keep you away from here."

Sly squirmed, his mouth dry. "That sounds perfectly ominous."

It sounded dangerous. In the dark, in that wicked, alluring tone, it sounded exciting. It sounded like fun.

Kahled growled, and Sly had no time to decide whether it was the sound of a taunting Nocturnus or something more alarming.

In a rush of movement, he was pulled from the chair. His feet left the floor. The breath was knocked out of him as he was hauled over a powerful shoulder.

"What the fuck?" Sly squeaked on principle. He flailed for stability before he broke his nose against Kahled's back.

The vampire ignored him.

The dark room swirled as Kahled turned around and carried him back down the hall with impressive ease and little patience. A low, continuous noise thrummed through his chest and shoulders in a way Sly really couldn't help but notice.

"Holy shit!" Sly squealed, his eyes enormous as he watched the basement's cement floor fly by. He was not proud of how long it took him to find anything more to say. "What— Kahled? What are you doing? Put me down!"

"No. I can't have you irritating my servants with more inane announcements."

"It's not even operational yet!"

Kahled acted as if Sly hadn't spoken. His strides remained smooth and brisk. His tone was unbothered as he kept Sly flung over his shoulder with one arm, "I've been told you have a worrisomely low tolerance for boredom. If you're left unoccupied for too long, you'll end up ushering Emmeline into an early retirement."

Sly drummed his palms on Kahled's back to no effect as he argued, "That justifies treating me like a sack of laundry, how?"

"My laundry doesn't require babysitting."

"Asshole." Sly scowled. He set his chin in his palm as he dug his elbow into Kahled's back.

The vampire didn't respond with words. He kept walking as a hand clamped down on Sly's thigh, pinning the leg to his chest with a warm, firm grip.

Sly froze. Kahled was an inch away from cupping his ass.

"Huh," Sly wondered aloud, "you know, manhandling might be a new kink of mine."

Again, Kahled showed no sign of hearing him. He stalked off with his Sly-shaped bounty like a refined caveman rather than the evolved creature he supposedly was.

As it turned out, Kahled's idea of keeping Sly occupied left much to be desired.

"I'm confused," Sly said, staring at the parcels stacked against the wall of Kahled's bedroom.

"Of course you are," Kahled muttered as he sat on the foot of his bed.

The room was still an eyesore, but it was far neater than the last time Sly saw it. There were still holes in the walls and claw marks galore, but the damaged closet door had been cleanly removed along with the unsalvageable furniture and ambiguous debris. The bed frame was still collapsed, but at least the floor around it was clear, the stone washed and polished.

There were no new furnishings. Judging by the size of the parcels, he doubted that would change anytime soon.

"Emmeline's people cleaned up while I was with Gorbon," Kahled said with pronounced disapproval. "They delivered my personal items from the Harem's latest supply shipment, but…"

When Kahled's voice trailed off, Sly shifted focus from the packages to the vampire. Kahled sat with his posture relaxed, shoulders slumped as he gave a distracted shake of his head. His pale eyes looked unsettled as he frowned at the packages.

Sly cleared his throat and imbued his voice with some levity. "So, what am I doing here, Maestro?"

Kahled didn't buy into his attempt at easing the mood. He spoke with a numbness that made Sly's chest ache. "I don't want them in here. Touching my things. Leaving their scents behind."

Sly stared about the empty room. "What about me?"

Kahled shrugged. "You smell fine. And I may need help, preferably from someone who doesn't gag when they touch me."

"Okay." Sly heaved a breath and refocused on the packages. "What now? Should I just start opening boxes?"

Kahled stood with a grace and speed that was far removed from the dull look in his eyes and the numbness in his voice. He crossed the room and scooped up a parcel, shredding it open with a claw.

A river of lustrous red fabric spilled onto the floor, pooling at Kahled's feet.

The vampire stared down at it without expression. "I don't know why I bothered. It won't fit me."

Kahled didn't react as Sly approached. "What is it?"

"A day robe."

At Sly's blank look, Kahled sighed. "Think of it as a wearable blanket."

"Ah."

When Kahled continued to just stare down at it, Sly bent to collect the material. It was insanely soft in his hands, thin but warm, and with a subtle pattern woven in a darker shade of red. Sly was surprised to find he recognized the weaving as Lunar design. There was a lot of it; some remained folded on the floor even as Sly raised it to shoulder height.

"It's pretty," Sly commented.

Kahled snorted and stepped forward for another package. "It's the sort of thing I might have worn to entertain foreign Harem leaders or business partners at home."

Sly dropped his arms, letting the fine fabric fall as he watched Kahled tear open another box. The vampire glanced inside, then tossed it over his shoulder without a word. Another slip of fabric poked out.

"I have to ask." Sly bit his lip and glanced from the red robe to Kahled. "What's the point of decking out your closet when no one's going to see it? Hell, Maestro, your live-in servants rarely see you."

"I suppose it reminds me of home." Kahled opened and discarded another box with continued apathy. "I always liked fashion. It's a pointless and borderline masochistic habit to indulge in now, but old habits persist. Catch."

Kahled barely peeked into the next box before tossing it with a lazy flick of his wrist.

Sly caught it. As the vampire crouched to continue picking through the delivery, Sly peeled back packaging to find layers of blue. When he pulled the material free, it was small. Very small. Sly suspected Kahled's condition included an unwanted growth spurt, but he couldn't imagine the guy was ever small enough to fit into the blue top.

Trying to stifle a chuckle, Sly asked, "When did you order this?"

Kahled glanced up, and the blankness in his face gave way to a hint of liveliness. He abandoned the latest parcel and stood tall. "Two months ago."

Sly choked on his laugh. "Seriously? What was the logic behind that decision?"

Kahled strode over and lifted a corner of fabric so it was spread between them. Sly's breath caught as he got a good look at interlocking blues in too many shades to count. It was almost hypnotic, the longer he stared, the more the design seemed to flow without ever changing.

"No logic," Kahled commented, watching Sly. "More like a momentary bout of insanity."

"It's gorgeous."

"Good. It's yours."

Sly startled, and all that blue was flung in his face. He spluttered, pulling cloth off his head in a fit of flying limbs.

"Don't thank me," Kahled warned. "I ordered it before Kamari ever heard your name."

"But— But!" Sly freed himself from the fabric and clutched it in both fists as he gaped at Kahled. "You said you didn't want a Companion!"

Kahled was already snagging another package, his back to Sly. "I don't. It was nothing more than a passing whim, and it was well before I knew Kamari was bringing me such a disrespectful nuisance."

Sly shook out the garment and studied the shape better. He glared daggers at Kahled's back. "Is this a dress? Were you hoping I'd be a woman?"

"Don't be ridiculous." Kahled huffed, setting the package aside unopened. "The Nocturni haven't gendered clothing in centuries. Last I checked, most humans don't either."

Sly held the dress at arm's length and reconsidered it. He tried to recall the last time he saw anyone wear a dress or skirt. Before meeting Walters and Mae, he only remembered a few instances of someone changing into one within the context Centrism's locker room.

Sly winced as he realized the obvious. "Yeah, clothing that exposes your legs isn't the most popular thing on Earth. Makes sense."

Kahled laughed. It was quiet and brief, but real. It shook his shoulders a little.

"Should I try it on?" Sly suggested as he watched Kahled rifle through items. "Since you don't seem to need my help anyway?"

Kahled responded by chucking another parcel at him. Sly jumped out of its way. "Help me open them. Anything that fits can go in the closet, and the rest, you and the staff can pick through or send back to Luna. I don't care."

BUT KAHLED DID CARE, AND QUITE A LOT. THEY SPENT three days sorting and resorting clothing, from brand new packages as well as the depths of Kahled's closet. The undertaking was interspersed with minor anxiety attacks whenever Sly considered how many times Kahled's wardrobe could have paid off his father's debt to HEPP. The extravagance of it all threatened to overwhelm him at times, so Sly leaped on every chance for distraction. It inevitably dragged the whole process out.

Kahled was successful at keeping Sly away from the intercom, but it came with a cost.

"Put it back," Kahled growled, pointing at the closet.

Sly held his gaze as he set the top of a loungewear outfit in the junk pile by the door.

Kahled snarled at him, but his eyes were bright.

"They don't fit!" Sly insisted, kicking the pile. "You can't get half this shit on without ripping it on a scale or a claw or uncontainable muscle mass! Quit being a Moon Diva, and let it go!"

"Those pajamas are worth more than your life!"

Sly snorted. "Says the guy living off borrowed time with my blood."

Cross comments like that would have earned him a smack upside the head back home and a stern talking-to if Walters or her people overheard it. Kahled didn't so much as flinch.

"Put it back," Kahled repeated with hot insistence, "before you piss me off and I give into the growing urge to maul you."

It was a convincing bluff. Sly might have believed it if he hadn't spent so much recent time admiring the side effects his blood was having on the vampire. After three days with Kahled's presence more or less forced on him, Sly knew it would take a lot more than a disagreement over clothes to push the vampire into an episode. Monstrous posturing and threats aside, Sly hadn't seen Kahled's eyes go dark since their kitchen encounter.

Turning his back on Kahled, Sly grabbed the matching trousers from the closet. As he carried them toward the door, he met Kahled's glare with a grin and waved.

Kahled's eyes, so pale and clear they seemed silver, gleamed as they narrowed on him. "I will hurt you, Sylvester."

"Doubtful." Sly draped the bottoms over the matching top with a flourish. "If you haven't murdered me yet, you're not going to."

Kahled made a rumbling sound that started as a growl and ended closer to a bark.

Sly rolled his eyes.

A large feverishly hot mass tackled him. He landed in a plush mound of luxury fabric and jeweled buttons with a vampire crouched over him, crystalline eyes and snapping fangs inches from his face.

Sly blinked up at him.

Kahled shoved a hand into the laundry by Sly's head and yanked the controversial pajamas free as he snarled, "Mine."

Neither moved.

Kahled's eyes were so very bright. They sparkled, contrasting with the ebony hair that fell into his face like Sly imagined starlight would against a clear night sky. For a moment, Sly thought he saw tiny streaks of brilliant stark white lance through the gray of his irises.

Sly's mouth formed words faster than his brain could think to stop it.

"I would totally be into it if you wanted to kiss me right now," he said.

Those starlight eyes widened, dark brows shooting up in surprise.

"Just an idea," Sly added.

Those heavy brows lowered again in a severe frown. There was none of the possessive temper that had sparked the current situation when he spoke, "You're serious?"

"Honestly? I kind of said that without thinking it through." Sly shrugged and caught sight of a crumpled sleeve, which proved a much more comfortable place to stare at than Kahled's furrowed brows. "But now that it's out there, it seems a little silly."

Kahled blinked once. "Silly?"

"Well yeah." Sly glanced at Kahled's fangs and flushed. "No offense, but sword-teeth don't seem all that conducive to adequate lip-action."

Kahled's cheeks pinkened the slightest bit as he repeated the words "adequate lip-action" as if he were testing their flavor.

Under the vampire's bulk and encased in silks, Sly was getting too warm. He worried he might start sweating. Clearing his throat, Sly poked Kahled in the ribs.

Kahled swatted his finger away and kept staring down at him.

"If we're not going to make out, could you at least get off me? Otherwise, this is going to get twenty times more awkward when I pop a—"

The weight atop him vanished with a strangled mewl Sly had no hope of interpreting.

"…Kahled?"

Sly sat up to find himself alone. The master bedroom door was still waving in the wake of Kahled's exit. Sly stared around the barren room, at the unfortunate bed standing against the wall and the mess of designer cast-offs littering the floor. He thought he heard the ping of the elevator doors opening.

Sly huffed to himself, "Smooth, Sylvester."

CHAPTER 10

*A*nd so Sly was left to his own devices for a few hours. At first, he considered wandering down to the basement to pursue his pet project, but then he remembered the stricken look on Kahled's face before he recoiled from the obvious existence of Sly's attraction. He had aggravated the vampire enough for one night. Besides, the discarded clothes blanketing the room made Sly's heart sink, like the limp finery was embodying loneliness in their master's absence.

It didn't seem right to leave Kahled's bedroom in that state, not when it was on the cusp of becoming livable again.

By the time Walters realized he was unsupervised in Kahled's room, it was too late for her to stop him. He was deep into a project, repurposing Kahled's unwearable items.

She stepped through the doorway and balked.

"No judging," Sly ordered before she could speak.

Walters's mouth tightened into a thin line as she stepped into the room. Her wide eyes were locked on the cloth concoction he'd erected over the grounded mattress.

It was a masterpiece. More than a few of Kahled's ritzy Lunar outfits were stretched or ripped, but Sly salvaged the pieces by knotting them together. First, he made a series of ropes that crossed the ceiling, anchored to everything from long unused light and décor fixtures to pieces of stone walls jutting from holes the size of Kahled's fists. After that, he had to get creative, raiding the closet and even making one or two trips to the basement's storage shelves.

If he were a betting man, he'd say someone must have seen him and reported it to Walters. Probably Felix.

"Is that—" Walters brought a hand to her mouth as she stepped closer. "My stars. Mr. Spurgeon, is this why Kahled's hiding in the hospital wing?"

"Nope," Sly said as he shook out a purple shawl. It was far too small for Kahled, it was no less detailed and lovely than the rest of his wardrobe. "I started this after he took off. I figured he needed a minute to mope over his negative self-image, so I kept myself busy."

Sly decided not to take Kahled's discouraging reaction personally. He didn't know what the vampire looked like before Nosferatu's Curse manifested, and he didn't know how long it'd been since Kahled could look at himself without revulsion. Sly was still getting over his first terrified impression, and it had been more than a month.

"You..." Walters hesitated. "Made a fort?"

"Yep."

Sly rose onto his tiptoes and hung the shawl over the entrance with a flourish. He stepped back with a satisfied sigh, hands on his hips as he admired the random collage of fabrics hanging over the bed. It wasn't the prettiest thing, objectively speaking, but it made Sly smile.

Walters, however, was frowning as she inspected the construct. "What on Earth—"

"If you can't say something nice," Sly chirped, "don't say anything."

She tilted her head sideways, squinting. "You put a hole in a centuries-old Afghan to hang it from a light post?"

Sly grinned. "Technically, Kahled made the hole. I just widened it a little. Neat, huh?"

Her expression suggested she disagreed. With a look like feces were dangling beneath her nose, she shook her head and made for the exit.

"He could use a little interior design!" he called after her.

Whatever Sly lacked in talent, he liked to think he made up for with passion. The vampire would most likely cringe when he saw what happened to his precious clothing, but Sly hadn't touched anything wearable or brand new and, most importantly, he didn't get rid of anything. He hoped Kahled found it amusing.

Laughter, Sly knew, was good medicine, and a decent apology for unwelcomed advances.

He crawled onto the bed and lay in its center so he could take in the full effect. The purple shawl was thin, and the day lighting filtered through it with a warm glow. A few of the other fabrics had a similar near transparency at the right angle, but the shawl's makeshift entrance at the foot of the bed was the most eye-catching.

With a pleased hum, Sly sat up and began rearranging pillows. He fluffed each one and attempted an artful mountain against the wall that smothered the damaged headboard. He smoothed out the blanket and was considering a nap when the vampire finally returned.

A low, rolling growl announced him.

Sly stilled, then tossed the cushion in his hands and scurried to the subtle divide in the hangings with his customary lack of grace. He poked his head out between the shimmering shawl and a sheet partially shredded into tinsel.

Kahled stood inches away, jaw tense and hackles raised as he stared.

"What in the great cosmos did you do to my room?"

Grinning, Sly smacked the cloth draping past his shoulder. "I made a fort."

Kahled's body slowly uncoiled as his alarm faded. "Is that what this is?"

Sly rolled his eyes. "Everybody's a critic."

"... Why?" Kahled peered at a hole high on the wall like he'd never noticed it before. "Are those my pants?"

Sly followed his bemused gaze. The lounge pants in question were part of the chain that linked the hole to a bedpost.

"Looks like it."

Kahled gaped at his knotted trousers hanging overhead.

Sly's face was growing too warm, so he slipped back behind the shawl. The meager privacy did nothing to calm the heat creeping up his neck, and his heartbeat was speeding up with the dawning possibility that he'd made a stupid mistake.

The hangings beside him rolled and waved in a flurry. Sly scooted back just in time to avoid Kahled's knee as the vampire fumbled his way through the flimsy curtain. None of Sly's hard work was damaged.

Kahled flicked strands of mangled sheet off his shoulder, watching with a soft frown as the pieces fluttered to stillness. He turned to Sly with an expectant raise of his eyebrows. With him kneeling at the end of the bed, there was no space left for Sly to breathe.

"I might have miscalculated," Sly commented as he wiggled back into the pillow mountain. "This isn't a big enough fort for you. I see that now."

Kahled's focus slipped off Sly, wandering about the space. Sly watched him study the arrangement with a strange fluttering in his gut, but the vampire's face gave nothing away.

"You did this?" Kahled asked with a softness Sly didn't recognize. He tilted his face toward the ceiling, and his head moved with his eyes as he inspected the patchwork canopy.

Something unnamable sent jitters of anticipation sparking through Sly. He plucked a pillow into his lap and fidgeted with the stitching.

Sly scoffed down at the pillow. "Who else around here has the nerve to mess with your shit?"

"You made me a nest."

Sly glanced around at all the plush randomness. The devastated bedframe wasn't visible inside the fort. There were no claw marks in sight. Everything was colorful and textured, a multitude of exquisite materials overlaying each other and reflecting comfort and warmth. It made the bed seem small, but not claustrophobic.

"Yeah," Sly breathed, "I guess I did. Do you like it?"

Kahled's stunned gaze made another circuit around the mismatched hangings before settling on Sly. "Yes. I think I do."

The giggle that escaped Sly then made him cringe. "Yeah?"

"Yes. It's unique." Kahled brushed the back of his most humanoid fingers over an Afghan with golden embellishments. "Unorthodox, but interesting. Creative, even."

"That's what I was going for!" Sly crowed, toes wiggling in the bedding. "I mean, yeah, it's a little clumsy and a bit of an eyesore, but it's homey."

"*Homey*?" Kahled mocked, a familiar condescension in his smirk.

Sly kicked him. Just a little, hardly more than his toes

pressing into Kahled's thigh. He couldn't help but notice it was a very firm thigh.

"It might not be up to your royal standards, but it's homey to me," Sly insisted, jabbing his toes harder into the vampire's leg.

Kahled's hand ensnared his ankle. His eyes were bright as he caught Sly's eye.

He spoke with an intense, lilting voice. "Thank you, Sylvester."

"You're welcome." Sly looked away, his spine stiff and every inch of him focused on the warm, gnarled hand against him. "About what I said earlier—"

Kahled cut him off, "I never asked Kamari to find me a donor."

Startled, Sly glanced up to see the vampire watching him with the same attentiveness he'd aimed at the fort moments ago. He studied Sly with more than his eyes, his whole body shifting as he took in every feature, from the copper highlights in Sly's hair to the stubborn calluses marking his toes.

"I certainly never asked him for a Companion," Kahled continued, his voice soft but strong. "It's been years since my own kind could stomach the sight of me. I couldn't fathom the possibility of a human who would welcome my touch, least of all one who survived to adulthood without splicing."

"You don't have to explain anything to me, Maestro." Sly offered a weak smile. "I'm just the hired help."

Kahled uttered a quiet growl that wavered between irritation and amusement. He released Sly's ankle and sat back on his haunches. "No one else on Kamari's payroll can look me in the eye without flinching. Even Emmeline's uncomfortable around me, though she tries to hide it."

Sly snickered. "Pretty sure that's nothing against you. She seems uptight in general."

Kahled's mouth softened into a slight smile. "Perhaps. It doesn't help that I remind her of my mother."

"Probably not," Sly admitted as he hugged his chosen pillow to his chest. "Tahliah, right? Tell me about her?"

Kahled did. In the cozy confines of a ridiculous little fort, the vampire spoke, and the human listened. Somewhere along the way, stilted words flowed into smooth conversation, and awkward chuckles gave way to full-bodied laughter. Time passed, and neither of them had the inclination to go to Gorbon for the evening's bloodletting, so they stayed put.

No one mentioned the hours passing by. Neither of them suggested Sly should stay the night, doing nothing more than talking and sleeping on opposite sides of the bed. It happened anyway.

WHEN SLY WOKE UP FOR THE FOURTH DAY STRAIGHT IN Kahled's bed, he wasn't safely enveloped in a blanket on the far side of the mattress. He was tucked in nice and snug along Kahled's side, his cheek smooshed against a scaled shoulder and his leg stretched across Kahled's middle. The sleeping vampire had his nose buried in Sly's hair and a hand loosely closed on Sly's lower leg.

The realization of where and just how comfortable he was hit Sly like a jolt of lightning. He scrambled out of bed before Kahled woke and raced back to his designated guest room.

He didn't go back to sleep. He called Blythe.

"I need a distraction," he said the moment her image appeared.

She frowned. "What's wrong?"

"Nothing. Everything. I don't want to talk about it." His eyes narrowed as he surveyed her projection. Her hair was a tangled mess around her shoulders, her makeup not up to its usual flawlessness. "What's wrong with you?"

She rolled her eyes but did so with a smile. "You're not the only one having a bad day. Phink finally let me back on the stage last night. It didn't go great."

Sly's stomach clenched with alarm. "What happened? Those purist dirtbags aren't giving you problems, are they?"

"Don't worry about it, Sly. Instead, how about you do me a solid and call Le Vau?"

Sly recoiled, grimacing. "Why would I call Le Vau?"

"To get the bloodsucker off my ass," Blythe said. "He keeps asking me to apologize to you on his behalf, and it's getting weird. What happened between you two? I'm starting to feel bad for him."

It took him a long moment to track down the memory. "Don't waste your time. He was being a creepy ass, as usual. Tell me about Centrism."

"There's nothing to tell!" Her eyes darted around, like she was preoccupied with something Sly couldn't see. "Phink put me backstage when you left, and we spun it like I just started splicing and got a bad batch. It was time to put myself out there again, and not everybody liked the new look. That's it."

Sly hummed in doubt. It was hard to tell through the poor quality of Blythe's transmission, but he thought there were bags under her eyes.

She sighed. "Have you talked to your dad yet?"

He winced, pulling back from his comms. "You're supposed to be distracting me from my worries, not compounding them."

Truthfully, Sly could have tried harder to reconnect with his old man. He tried a few times since Gorbon gave him the new unit, but John Spurgeon was stubborn as ever and refused to answer. Thanks to Blythe, he knew his old man was alive and settled back into the house, but that was it.

They never went so long without talking before.

"Call your dad," Blythe insisted. "I told him he better respond this time if he wants my help replacing the front door airlocks."

Sly groaned. "Again? At least tell me he bought the replacements brand new this time."

"Just call him. And let Phink know you're alive too. He acts like my reassurances aren't worth crap."

She disconnected, and Sly's feed went dark.

He tried to follow her direction and touch base with everyone else back home. He wasted an hour warning Phink away from targeting the Vauqeulin Harem for a needless rescue attempt. He ate up another twenty minutes letting Phink complain about HEPP's administrative leadership and how all of Sly's Nocturni regulars were acting like cheap, jilted asshats.

He didn't bother asking Phink for Le Vau's contact info. One moody vampire at a time was all Sly could handle.

The reminders of home worked like a charm, and Sly felt settled in his skin again. He fluffed out the pillows on his bed, nodding at their softness, and he started looking forward to burying his face in them that night till he fell asleep.

With that reasonable, safe plan in mind, Sly made for the kitchen and some much needed breakfast.

❧

Mae found him with a muffin stuffed in his mouth. Next thing he knew, Sly was following her toward the medical bay with a napkin of morning sausages wrapped in pastries and a mug of steaming liquid that smelled like honeyed pine and all things green.

She was half a step ahead him the whole way, but she kept shooting furtive glances back at him every few strides. Sly was too busy eating to ask her why.

She didn't leave him wondering long. Mae waited for him to set his edibles on the sprawling desk in Gorbon's office, then she descended on him with big pleading kitten eyes.

"Doctor Gorbon sent me to the Master's suite to find you," she said, "but you weren't there. Did Master Kahled kick you out?"

Sly blinked at her, sausage caught between his teeth.

Her lower lip wobbled. "You left. Didn't you?"

"Um…" Sly cast about for Gorbon as he tried to swallow.

Mae stepped back, her spine rigid as she clasped her hands in front of her. "Of course, you're not pursuing a Companionship. I almost forgot."

Sly choked back the food trapped in his throat as she ducked her head and turned away. "It's a temporary deal."

"I know," she rushed to say, shooting him a tight-lipped smile.

Sly opened his mouth again, unsure what to say. He was spared by the arrival of Gorbon and Walters.

"Good morning, Mr. Spurgeon," Walters greeted him with a full smile, causing Sly to look around for the cause of such an uncommon expression. "I trust you slept well?"

Sly gave her a careful once-over with his hesitant answer, "Yes?"

"Excellent." She breezed past him on her way to one of Gorbon's monitors.

"Thank you for bringing him, Mae." Gorbon clapped the young woman on the shoulder as he passed her on his way to

Sly. "How are you, Sly? We haven't spoken much this past week."

For no apparent reason, Sly flushed. "Take it up with Walters. She's the one who told Kahled I needed a babysitter."

"I did no such thing," Walters interjected without raising her eyes from the screen.

Gorbon chuckled and picked up Sly's mug to force it into his hand. "You'll want to drink that while it's still warm."

"Right," Sly accepted the mug. "What is it again?"

"Tea," Mae chirped. "Didn't I explain that while I was preparing it?"

Sly opened his mouth to apologize for his earlier inattention, but Gorbon steamrolled over him. "It's dirt water. Tastes horrible, but it's invaluable in combating iron deficiency and fatigue."

Sly sniffed at the earthy liquid with interest. "It's medicinal, then?"

Gorbon nodded. "Special order from Ethos. Which is ironic, considering Europe was once renowned for its tea consumption. This particular breed of leaf is only cultivated by the Harems, though, as a dietary supplement for human donors."

"It's not absolutely necessary," Walters added, abandoning the monitor to join them. "But if you're going to continue letting Kahled feed directly from your vein without supervision, you'll want to capitalize on every tool at your disposal."

The heat drained from Sly's face. "Wait. It's been convenient, but it's not like we're planning for that to be the preferred bloodletting method going forward."

Three pairs of eyes snapped to him. Silence reigned.

Sly's shoulders sagged. "What?"

Gorbon frowned at him, stroking his beard in thought. "Convenient, you say?"

Walters braced her fists on her hips and raised her chin in his direction. "Mr. Spurgeon, you've spent the better part of a week holed up with Kahled in his room."

Sly shrugged. "So? He's lonely, I'm bored. It doesn't take a genius to work that one out." He sipped the tea and nearly scorched his tongue. "Shit!"

"Just to clarify," Gorbon said, "you're *not* sleeping with him then?"

Sly stopped fanning his tongue to gape at the doctor. "No! Why would you ask that?"

Nearby, Mae snickered.

Walters crossed her arms, lips pursed as she studied Sly. "Mr. Spurgeon, do we need to have a conversation about your intentions toward my charge?"

Sly turned his incredulity on her. "What?"

Gorbon sighed. "Let's not get ahead of ourselves, everyone. Sly, finish your tea, then I want to go over some blood work with you. Emmeline?"

She lifted a brow at the doctor in response. Sly did a doubletake, he was so used to seeing that expectant expression on Kahled.

"Remember what we said about reasonable expectations," Gorbon said with a pointed look.

Walters glanced at Sly, then Gorbon, and stomped off with a haughty "humph."

Once the tea was cool enough to drink, Sly downed it without dwelling on the grainy taste, and Mae was quick to snatch it from his hand and exit the suite.

Sly joined Gorbon at his desk before a large monitor. There were enough charts and numbers on display to make him dizzy, but none of it held any meaning for Sly.

"Now that you're better acquainted with Kahled..." Gorbon shot him a wary look as he clicked through digital folders. "I want you to see this. You need some context."

He opened a graphic file and slid from the seat, pausing to gesture for Sly to take his place.

Despite the tea's warmth lingering in his mouth, Sly's tongue felt like a dry lump trapped between his teeth as he took the offered seat.

The image filling the monitor made him frown. It wasn't captured on Earth, that much was obvious by the cerulean skies and gentle clouds in the background, beyond the jagged spikes of a shattered glass wall. There was dark, ultramodern furniture and polished floors, but the décor wasn't worth noticing under all the blood and gore.

Sly didn't look at it for long. He turned to Gorbon, sick to his stomach as he asked, "What am I looking at?"

Gorbon's somber gaze remained on the screen. "This is the Vauqeulin Harem's primary house on Ethos, taken roughly sixteen months ago, right after Kahled eviscerated two of his kin."

Sly's heart dropped as he glanced back at the screen. "Kahled did this?"

There were no bodies in the picture. Only blood. Only pieces.

"He killed an Elder."

Sly flinched away from the desk. The Nocturni weren't simply long-lived, they were the closest thing the universe had to indestructible. Their deaths were rare. Monumental even.

Gorbon was watching him carefully as his continued talking. "He nearly killed a cousin who was part of his security detail and left her scarred. Have you ever seen one of the Nocturni so badly injured, they couldn't fully repair the damage?"

Gorbon didn't wait for a reply. One hand settled on Sly's shoulder while the other reached over for the keypad to move onto another photograph.

"This was the final straw that forced Kamari to send him here."

There were countless pictures. Details of the decimated room with its shattered wall, and similarly designed spaces beyond it that sported familiar claw marks and trails of deformed footprints in nauseating shades of crimson. Gorbon didn't pause long on any of them, only enough to ensure Sly understood the extent of the destruction.

"I can't tell you how many times we avoided a similar incident here by filling him with enough tranquilizers to kill a grown human twice over."

"Stop." Sly shrugged off the doctor's hand and leaped from the chair. "What's the point of this? If I shouldn't be alone with him, maybe you should have mentioned that before now."

"If you were open to having this conversation six weeks ago, I would have." Gorbon grabbed him by the arm. "But now? With your blood in him? Sly, we haven't used a single sedative since the day you came to us. You've been a miracle."

Sly jerked out of Gorbon's pleading grasp with such violence they both stumbled.

The doctor didn't reach for him again. Eyes wet and trained on Sly, Gorbon leaned toward the computer desk. A few taps of his fingers, and the horrific pictures were replaced by a line chart. Gorbon indicated it with an insistent swipe of his hand.

"You're curing him, Sly."

But Sly was shaking his head side-to-side before the doctor finished speaking. "No."

"It's slow, but consistent. With enough time—"

"I'm glad he's improving," Sly said in a rush, backstepping with every word. "Seriously, I am. But all I'm doing is holding him over for a few months. That's it."

"You could do so much more, Mr. Spurgeon."

He backed up straight into Madam Walters. Her wizened hand was gentle and soft on his arm, but it made him jump a foot in the air.

"Fuck's sake, wear a bell or something!" he yelled as he wheeled around to evade her.

She stood still and tall, tracking him with her gaze like a practiced predator. With the fierceness in her tight expression, Sly was convinced she spliced with something lethal, like a bird of prey. She hunted him with all the determination Kahled lacked.

"You promised," she reminded him. "You told the Harem's scion that you would consider a true Companionship while you were here."

Sly flung out his hands and glared back and forth between the two of them liked a cornered animal. "What do you think I've been doing? I'm here, aren't I? I'm even spending time with him now, and guess what, I haven't seen anything worth giving up my life as I know it!"

"Is this not enough for you?" Walters stole his breath with the cold amazement in her tone. "We want for nothing here. We have comfort and security most of our species would envy. And this—" She waved toward the monitor with uncharacteristic passion. "This is the opportunity to save a life. To make history. What greater purpose or selfish desire could you possibly have?"

Sly didn't know why his chest felt so tight, why his eyes

stung, or why he kept shaking his head over, and over, and over, like an idiot. He only knew how to answer because it was the only answer available.

"My family needs me," he said. "They need me to get them off this rock before it self-implodes and, coincidently..." He lifted his chin and spat. "*That* is the only thing in this fucked up universe I desire."

He whipped the wetness from his eyes as he stomped past her.

THAT SHOULD HAVE BEEN THE END OF IT. IT WASN'T.

As he promised himself, he returned to his guestroom for the rest of the day and buried himself in pillows till after dinner. He didn't sleep, he just hid away and felt sorry for himself. He was bundled up in silken sheets and breathing top quality air as he sniffled into pillows lined in literal golden thread, and he felt sorry for himself.

He hated it. He had the gut-wrenching thought that he might hate himself.

He called his dad. No answer.

He started to call Blythe, but he hesitated. He found Phink's contact in his comms instead.

"Sly?"

Sly wasn't transmitting his image, but Phink was. At the sight of his fuzzy face and furrowed brow, Sly's tear ducts started up again.

"Hey, Phinkly," Sly croaked then cleared his throat. "If I ask you something, will you answer me honestly?"

Phink's face scrunched with confusion and more than a tinge of worry. "I'm always honest, Sly. What's wrong?"

He had to force the words out through a constricted throat, and it hurt. "Am I selfish?"

Phink's eyes and mouth went wide, and Sly wondered why he was still showing him his face when it wasn't reciprocated. After a moment of stunned silence, Phink closed his mouth into a pouty frown. "Sylvester Spurgeon, what in sun's blazes is going through your head?"

Sniffling, Sly wiped under his eyes again. "Just answer the question, Phink."

Phink's projection blurred as he shook himself, an angry twitch he'd had longer than Sly had been alive. "No, Sly. You're the least selfish person I know, and if anyone says differently, you send them my way, okay?"

Sly gave a weak nod before remembering Phink couldn't see him. "Thanks, Phink. I'll be home soon."

Phink's expression did not ease with the reassurance. If anything, the words made him wince as if he were masking pain.

CHAPTER 11

*S*ly underestimated the Nocturnus. Kahled wasn't stupid, and when Sly and his blood failed to appear before him that evening, he knew something was wrong. Sly expected an annoyed ping via comms or perhaps Walters to come knocking on his door. He didn't expect Kahled himself to walk into his guest room around noon without warning.

The vampire looked around as if he'd never seen the place. He frowned at the decent-sized wardrobe as if offended and perched himself on the corner of Sly's bed. The furnishing was a fraction the size of what lay in Kahled's room, and the wooden foot board supports groaned and sank under his weight.

"Are you trying to break another bed?" Sly asked in a deadpan tone.

Kahled was still glaring at his closet as his hand found Sly's foot, gripping it tight through the bedding. "I need to feed, and that means you need to eat."

Sly squirmed to roll over with a dismissive huff, but Kahled's grip tightened on his foot and willed him still.

"When I ran the Harem," Kahled began in soft, rumbling

tones, "I had to accept that my peoples' happiness was not within my control, but I was at least able to ensure their needs were met. I try to do the same here with this household."

Sly sat up to level an unimpressed stare at the vampire. "I'm not one of your people though."

Kahled met his gaze with a raised brow. The grip on Sly's foot tightened. "You may be in my brother's employ, but so long as you're here, you're my responsibility."

Sly frowned. "No, I'm not. This isn't a real Companionship—"

"No," Kahled agreed with a nod, "but we're supposed to be treating it like one. Which means this..." He gestured between them. "...Needs to be a mutually beneficial arrangement. You've given me more peace than I have known in years, Sylvester. The least I can do is see you properly fed and clothed."

As if on reflex, the vampire's attention strayed toward Sly's wardrobe.

"I have enough clothes," Sly assured him, smirking despite himself.

Kahled's lips pursed around his fangs as he uttered a quiet growl. "That's debatable."

Sly used both palms to shove Kahled off his bed, to no avail. "All right, get out and take your overindulgent ideas with you."

"I will once you promise to take care of yourself."

Sly rolled his eyes. "I'll eat when I feel like it. Relax, Maestro. I'm not starving."

The vampire huffed as he stood. "Feed yourself," he commanded. "Call your family more often. Don't miss another bloodletting appointment with Gorbon and, for moon's grace, stop letting me put my mouth on you if it's too great a burden."

Sly gave him a lazy salute. "Yes, sir."

Kahled headed out with another huff but with a distinct note of amusement in the sound.

Upright in bed, Sly twisted his fingers in the sheets and frowned at the warping fabric. He heard the door click open and said, "It's not a burden, you know."

Kahled stilled in the doorway. Sly didn't need to lift his head to know those pale eyes were watching him.

"It's fucked up, but if things at home were different..." Sly trailed off with a sad little laugh. "If Earth wasn't such a mood killer, I could see myself wanting this."

Kahled's considerable weight shifted beyond Sly's view. "By this, you mean...?"

Sly shrugged and smoothed the sheet over his legs. "All of it, I guess. The fancy accommodations, the contract." He started lifting his eyes, but nerves got the better of him. "You."

Kahled said nothing for a long time. Sly was ready to throw himself back into bed and smother himself with the blanket by the time he said anything.

"I've never been interested in Companionship or any permanent relationship. My Harem was always commitment enough for me." Kahled stepped out the doorway, then paused.

Sly finally looked up to catch pale eyes trained on him with a pearlescent shine that was too beautiful for Earthly standards.

Without thinking, Sly murmured, "But you don't have the Harem anymore."

Sly flinched the moment the words escaped his mouth, but Kahled didn't. He considered Sly a moment and bobbed his head in a soft acknowledgment of the truth. "If I were ever fit for Companionship, it would have been with someone like you, Sly."

Then, he closed the door and walked away.

KAHLED'S PARTING WORDS RAN CIRCLES AROUND SLY'S HEAD for two days straight. He got out of bed and took care to eat three full meals each day, earned himself two fresh needle marks from bloodletting, and wasted time roaming the manor and sending Blythe random messages. Through it all, Kahled's voice and the glowing pallor of his eyes lingered in the back of his mind like a persistent but soft-spoken ghost.

No one suggested Sly visit the Master's rooms. Kahled himself had effectively disappeared, and Walters and her staff gave him the cold shoulder, speaking to him in curt, monosyllabic messages. Gorbon still conversed readily with him in the evenings, but he kept it professional and mild; he strayed from that approach only to assure Sly that the household wanted to respect his boundaries and give him "space to process," though he never clarified what he meant by that.

Sly tried contacting his father again, but there were no answers there either.

A few nights after Kahled visited his room, Sly stood in the hall between Gorbon's rooms and the elevator, his feet waiting for him to decide which way to go. He was tempted to stay put and start ripping his hair out instead.

The med bay's door slid open to reveal Felix, hands in his pockets and glasses slipping down his nose as he frowned at the floor. He glanced at Sly before grimacing.

"You're late. Doc just sent me to find you."

Sly shrugged. "He knows I have a comms now."

Felix scoffed and stepped aside with a halfhearted wave for Sly to enter. "Most evolved societies consider it rude to use an electronic summons in the span of a single building. I shouldn't be surprised you don't know that."

Sly stayed put and folded his arms. "Last I checked, you're not much more evolved than me. When's the last time you spliced, anyway?"

Felix's cheeks reddened as he made a sharp gesture for Sly to get moving. "That's none of your business."

Sly leaned in without budging his feet, peering at the other man. "Is that why you hate me so much? Because my unrefined American blood makes me a more ideal Companion?"

Felix took a threatening step forward. "Shut your mouth."

Sly gaped at him. "Seriously? *That's* your problem?"

Felix jabbed a finger into Sly's chest, his expression thunderous. "I don't give a shite about your blood, Spurgeon," he spat. "You're no purer than I am. The only difference between us is that you have a golden opportunity laid at your feet, but you're so stupid or heartless that you're wasting it!"

Sly flushed, and a gross shiver ran down his back despite the heat on his face and neck. "Fuck you. You don't know a thing about me."

If he had to keep looking at Felix's flustered face, he was going to punch something, so Sly turned away and went straight for the elevator. It wasn't until the doors opened into the coolness of Kahled's foyer that he realized there was no escape to be had.

"Fuck," Sly hissed under his breath, grabbing fistfuls of his hair.

This was not the time or place to fall apart though. No matter what type of person Felix imagined him to be, Sly wasn't about to put a dying Nocturnus in the awkward position of comforting a perfectly healthy human.

Kahled would have heard the elevator opening to admit him. After taking a bracing breath, Sly made his way toward Kahled's room and knocked.

"Come in."

Sly's breath hitched when he caught sight of the intact fort. It was glowing from the inside, a soft-blue sheen behind the multitude of fabrics. After a moment's hesitation, a hand sporting a single claw peeked through the hangings and pulled them aside.

"You kept it up?" Sly asked as he came closer.

"I like it," Kahled said while he held the entrance open. "Besides, I couldn't think of any better uses for all the parts."

Sly knelt on the edge of the mattress, barely inside the nest's border. It was enough to see the dim evening lamp in the center of the bedding, loose papers and pens scattered around it. The topmost page showcased a rough sketch of a large modern building with lots of windows.

"Is that Ethos?"

Kahled nodded, watching Sly as he picked up the drawing. "It's where Kamari lives."

"It was your home, then?"

He didn't get an answer. Sly looked up from the picture to see Kahled staring at the fabric ceiling with such wistfulness, it made Sly's chest ache.

Objectively, Sly knew Kahled must have been handsome before the curse warped his fangs and painted bruises around his eyes. It was still there in the symmetry of his features, the sharpness of his jawline, and the thick flow of his hair. Then there were his eyes. His eyes glittered like iced silver in the lamp light, and not even the worst of the scales could detract from the sight.

"When you said we were supposed to treat this like a real Companionship..." Sly paused to clear a dry throat. "Did you mean it? I mean, do you want us to be like that?"

Kahled quirked his head to the side as he studied him. "I will give you an honest answer if you do the same."

Sly sat up straighter. "All right."

"I've never been to one of HEPP's Houses," Kahled said with a precarious calm, "but I can imagine what it must have been like for you. You make your living by displaying your humanity to every vampire and highly spliced human who can afford your time."

Sly blushed. "You make it sound so dirty."

"No," Kahled shook his head. "You provide for a viable audience, Sly. My point is that you have substantial practice ignoring inhuman paws chasing after you."

Kahled raised his left hand between them, his fingers splayed so that the light glinted off the talons and armored platelets of his middle and ring fingers. The scales crept over his knuckles and created a random trail over the back of his hand and wrist. The patches grew firmer and larger the further they went up his arm.

Face grave, Kahled met his eye over his brandished extremity. "Can you honestly tell me you want this touching you?"

Sly considered his hand without shying away. "Well, we'd have to be extra careful where fingering is concerned, but sure."

Kahled cut him off with a sharp growl, but his voice was unnervingly calm. "This isn't a joke, Sly."

"Why are you asking me for honesty if you're not going to believe me anyway?"

The vampire's jaw tightened, and he lowered his arm.

Sly caught the deformed hand before it could land in

Kahled's lap. "Just for a minute, could you stop comparing yourself to whatever perfect Nocturni leader you used to be? Because this—" He gripped Kahled's hand in both of his and shook it. "This is all I know you as."

Kahled stared at him, eyes wide and bright, his face unreadable. He didn't pull away, and he didn't interrupt, he just let Sly talk.

"I already said I wanted you to kiss me," Sly didn't shout, but his vehemence carried the same weight regardless. "What more reassurance do you need?"

"You should be terrified of me," Kahled whispered even as he leaned forward.

Sly laughed, and it was quiet and fragile, the amusement faint. "Weeks ago, maybe, but right now? Seriously, Maestro. I've folded your underwear. You don't scare me."

With his double grip on Kahled's hand firm, Sly tugged him closer and sucked in an inaudible gasp when the vampire followed the gentle pressure.

"I want to believe you," Kahled murmured, his breath a warm puff on Sly's cheek.

Sly wasn't stupid or heartless. He knew where this was going, and he was powerless to stop it. He doubted why he bothered trying in the first place.

Sly licked his lips, eyes locked with liquid-silver orbs. "Can we just exist for a bit? Leave history behind us? Your Curse, my family, all of it—can we pretend it doesn't exist for a little while?"

"Yes," Kahled said, and the word slid from his mouth to Sly's with the slightest brush of their lips.

Sly didn't let go of the vampire's hand. He held the palm tight in his and used the other hand to comb his fingers through the ebony waves tucked behind Kahled's pointed ear while he rose up on his knees. Once Kahled didn't have to hunch over to meet him, Sly initiated a proper kiss.

It was like no other kiss in Sly's experience.

They took it slow. They were gentle and cautious in their movements, first from a mutual wariness of the fangs and then from the unexpected eroticism of such gentle exploration. There was little pressure and no rush as they nuzzled closer. They shared breaths as their lips caressed one another.

Sly enjoyed the rasp of Kahled's facial hair and marveled at its difference from the substantial tresses flowing through his fingers. The vampire's lips were so smooth and plush, Sly doubted they'd ever been chapped in his life. Before long, Sly's curiosity ran away with him, and his tongue slipped out for a light swipe across Kahled's lower lip.

It was the final push that sent them over the edge of Kahled's inhibitions. And the bed.

Sly gasped as he fell backward from the force of Kahled's lunge. His stomach lurched as he fell out of the nest and into cool air. Everything spun around him, and Sly grunted as he landed, not on his back with his skull crashing into stone, but onto his side, with a broad palm protecting his head.

And there was Kahled, facing him, on the ground, one of his legs still stretched over the bed after an inelegant tumble.

Sly snickered.

He shut up a second later when he was flat on his back on the floor with Kahled crouched over him on all fours. His eyes were so bright, they seemed to burn white for a moment.

"I won't hurt you," Kahled vowed, panting. "Can I…? I want to just…"

His eyes darted over Sly's body, and Kahled bit at the inside of his lip like he couldn't think straight.

Sly wrapped his arms around the vampire's neck and said, "Go for it, Maestro. I'll tell if you if I need to stop."

With a distracted nod, Kahled bent down and kissed him again.

Sly gasped.

It wasn't soft and sweet this time. It was tremulous, still slow, but hungry and deep. Kahled's tongue invaded his mouth, and while his fangs effectively kept him from eating Sly alive, he compensated by being thorough, very thorough. Kahled licked into him and a low, pleased growl vibrated through Sly's mouth and traveled to the back of his tongue.

When Sly's surprise abated enough for him to respond, Kahled rewarded him with a groan and shifted above him. Sly got the briefest thrill of a hard body rubbing over his before Kahled threw him for a loop, almost literally.

"Stars above," Sly laughed as he bounced back onto the bed.

He had time to blink once before Kahled was on him again. The vampire crawled into the fort and straddled his hips, and Sly's breath caught when he saw the bulge of Kahled's arousal. His hands found Kahled's hips without conscious thought, and then they were grinding, and Sly couldn't think at all.

He hadn't been with anyone in a long time. Probably not as long as it'd been for Kahled, but long enough that he was primed for explosion much too soon. The slightest movement felt like fireworks shooting up his spine, and Kahled's weight was perfectly positioned, and—

"I'm going to come if you keep doing that," Sly warned as he dug his fingers into the topmost curve of Kahled's ass.

Kahled made a low, guttural purr, and then he was gone. Strong hands grabbed Sly's hips and flipped him over onto his hands and knees. There was a hint of a claw point over his hipbone, then his pants and underwear were sliding down his legs with a speed and seamlessness Sly never managed on his own.

With a breathless laugh, Sly reaffirmed. "I definitely have a manhandling kink."

"Convenient," Kahled commented as he rubbed a palm over Sly's naked rump.

Without further warning, Sly's knees were pushed apart, and a hot wet tongue dragged over his balls. Sly yelped. He would have faceplanted in the bedding if Kahled's careful grip wasn't keeping him in place. As it turned out, Kahled needed both hands to hold him still while he put that talented tongue to use. Sly found it impossible to stop himself from pushing back into the pressure of Kahled's face against his backside, to test the grip on his hips and chase after the pleasure Kahled was offering him.

A corner of his mind knew he was tempting fate. The fingers on his hips were already bruising, and there were fangs way too close to his junk. Such thoughts were banished from his mind long before they could take root, though.

It was wet and messy and exhilarating. There was woefully little suction thanks to Kahled's oral impairments, but there was heat and pressure and slick, and Kahled had all the enthusiasm of a starved animal. The random flicks of tongue over his cockhead sent jolts of electricity rocketing through Sly, only to be outdone by the laving at his balls or the frantic slurping strokes over his asshole.

It lasted long enough that Sly started shaking. He reached down to give himself a helpful tug, but Kahled slapped his hand away.

He was yanked back with such force, his face crashed into the mattress. There was an indecent sound of a slobbering mouth, then Kahled was licking him again from balls to hole, and a wet open palm was rubbing over his cock with a matching rhythm.

Sly screamed into the mattress as he came.

He lay panting in a puddle of his own fluids when Kahled crawled over him with a reverberating hum. Kahled's hand planted in the bedding beside Sly's face, one talon shredding through layers of padding. A blanket of naked skin spread over Sly's back.

"Please," Kahled whimpered as his cock slid between the globes of Sly's ass. "Can I? Let me… I just…"

Loose-limbed and struggling to calm his heart and breathing, Sly wrapped his fingers around Kahled's wrist and squeezed.

That was all the reassurance the vampire needed. Sly was too spent to anticipate being breached, but it was a nonissue; Kahled didn't attempt penetration. He rutted against Sly, his cock huge and hot as the length dragged between Sly's cheeks, every thrust eased by copious precum and their combined sweat.

Sly's groin was still tingling in the afterglow, and the minor friction with the sheets was almost too much, but he canted his hips back with a groan and was relieved from that side effect of Kahled's movements.

"Sly," Kahled slurred around his fangs as he chased his release. "Sly, please. Can I— Can I—"

Sly wasn't sure what he was asking until he felt Kahled's free hand on his back and a claw tapped his skin.

"Please," Kahled begged.

Sly reacted on instinct. It was the most natural thing in the world to shift his cheek over the bed and place a chaste kiss on the closest part of Kahled he could reach. A scaled knuckle pressed to his lips.

Kahled gasped, and his thrusts stuttered.

"Take what you need," Sly told him.

A sharp pain streaked over his shoulder blade. Sly gasped, and before the sound finished exiting his throat, it shifted to a noise of pleasure as Kahled's mouth sealed over the wound.

It didn't take long for Kahled to reach completion after that. His hand curled into a fist in front of Sly's nose, and the blanket ripped with a loud tearing, but Sly didn't let go of his wrist. Even as Kahled's thrusts grew harder and his rhythm faltered, Sly held him. It was easy. Almost comfortable. He hardly had to do a thing. Just lay there, lax and present, and hold on. His grip on the vampire wasn't solid enough to be noticed.

With his heartbeat starting to calm, Sly tried giving Kahled's wrist a firm squeeze. He was so close, and saw no harm in it, so he placed another kiss on the same uneven spot. He was tired, and it wasn't as deliberate, but it felt important.

Hours later, after a well-deserved nap, Sly discovered he was a sticky, crusty mess, and his pants were nowhere to be seen. Every muscle was loose, and his head felt like it was floating.

Sitting up, he noticed how dark it was in the nest. The lamp was out, overturned among the pillows and a few crumpled papers. Sly turned to locate the drawing of Ethos, and he found Kahled passed out beside him.

Sly stilled, staring.

There was something different about the vampire while he rested. The perpetual furrow of his brow was lifted, the stress on his face eased. His fangs were prominent as ever, but his mouth and chin were relaxed, softened in a way Sly had never noticed. With his eyes closed, Sly wasn't distracted from the straight line of his nose or the smoothness of his skin. There were no scales on his face, only the short bristles of a new beard.

He was beautiful, deformities be damned.

Sly didn't fight the impulse to trace the curve of a sharp cheekbone with one finger. His touch slowed when he felt Kahled's flesh shift over the bulk of a fang. Cautiously, he stroked over the vampire's upper lip and noted the strange dips and curves.

As he pulled his hand back into his lap, Sly realized Kahled was still clothed, though his lounge pants rested dangerously low on his hips. There were telling stains on the matching top, and Sly imagined how Kahled might react to find his precious clothing soiled.

The thought made him chuckle as he lay back down.

TIME MEANT NOTHING IN THE COZY CONFINES OF THE NEST. By unspoken accord, that single night's reprieve from the real world stretched on, and Sly rarely left Kahled's rooms. Food was delivered to the door, and Sly discovered the master bathroom was more expansive and indulgent than the one in the guest wing. They spent hours talking and hours more in silent, cuddly contemplation. They lived in a cocoon of comfort where nothing and no one else mattered.

Sly left his shiny new comms on the floor beyond the bed and didn't bother picking it up when it came alive with alerts.

Kahled's comms was mysteriously absent. He allowed Gorbon to intrude on them occasionally for health checks, but, otherwise, the vampire greeted each knock on his door with a snarl. He ignored Walters's every attempt at conversation in favor of nuzzling into Sly's throat or the sensitive softness of his belly.

It was indulgent and rude of them, but they didn't care.

For the first time in far too long, there was pleasure. Sly

never had a lover so attentive, so preoccupied with driving him to new heights that he disregarded his own pleasure for hours. The constant stress dragging on Sly's shoulders lifted further away with every shuddering moan and captivating kiss. Sly never realized how selfish sex had been before, but then Kahled taught him how the giving could be at least as satisfying as the taking.

More than once, Kahled responded to his touch with great, relieved sobs. His claws were always safely stowed in fistfuls of mattress, but he leaned in to Sly's slightest caress like a touch-starved animal.

It wasn't all physical either.

The nasty pit in Sly's stomach was gone. Its absence would have been alarming if he could be bothered to investigate, but he didn't. Instead, Sly let himself be distracted from his Earthly worries. He floated away on a fantasy built by a deep, strong voice and words cultivated by a life beyond his wildest imaginings.

"You're beautiful like this," Kahled whispered in his ear one morning as Sly stretched awake.

Sly peeked at him over his shoulder, frowning. "Bedhead and drool does it for you, huh?"

Kahled pressed close, and his facial hair tickled Sly into a lazy smile.

"Normally, you bounce around like a ball of frantic energy and boisterous affectation," Kahled purred against his cheek. "You're rarely so restful. Even in your sleep, you move constantly."

Sly snickered. "Oops."

Kahled nuzzled him with a playful growl. Sly's heartbeat sped up as a thick arm curled around his waist.

"You're impossibly tempting so early in the day," Kahled

murmured as he licked his neck. "So quiet and soft, all that biddable, untainted human flesh."

Kahled rolled back, making Sly gasp as he was dragged along. A little graceless shifting and awkward chuckles later, he lay on his belly atop the vampire. One arm pinned him in place while the other hand drew teasing trails over his ass and thigh. Sly could feel the tip of a claw, faint and cautious against his bare skin and the hot steel of Kahled's cock under his belly.

"You would tempt the most self-controlled vampires I know," Kahled continued musing as his eyes roamed the curves of Sly's throat and shoulders. "You're small and lively like the perfect prey. And you're uncommonly fair. Your skin begs to be marked up by the right fangs."

Sly flushed and bit his lip. "That should not be as hot as it sounded."

Kahled lunged up for a darting lick across his jaw. While Sly giggled, he shrugged and said, "I have as much beast in my genes as I do human. Arguably more."

"Excuse you." Sly poked him in the chest. "I guarantee there's nothing but fresh humanity being added to that mix lately. Give me a little credit."

Kahled rolled his eyes. "Then maybe it's my humanity that makes me think you should be hunted down and ravished."

Grinning, Sly rewarded the smooth talk with a love bite to the vampire's collarbone.

Kahled tilted his chin out of the way with a pleased hum. As Sly's lips journeyed across his chest, he breathed, "You're perfect."

Sly's chest constricted around his heart, and his breath caught. After days in bed together, he was used to Kahled's poetic tendencies and his fetish for bestowing compliments, but there was a new softness to his voice. It sounded like emotion too thick to name, like something dangerously close to awe.

It was humbling. It stunned Sly into stillness.

The arm around him tightened the slightest bit, and a bearded chin rubbed against his forehead.

"What I wouldn't give," Kahled whispered against his hair, "to see you illuminated by raw starlight."

Sly distracted him from further romantic notions with his mouth. In the afterglow, Kahled curled around him like a mythical dragon around a precious horde, and Sly hid a smile in the pillows with tears in his eyes.

THERE WERE MANY MOMENTS LIKE THAT IN THE FOLLOWING days. Those days blended into weeks without Sly's notice.

Kahled would say something or look at him in such a way that made it difficult to breathe. Sly facilitated between weightless enjoyment and nauseating confliction.

"I dream about you," Kahled whispered one night.

Sly lay nearby, his naked body swaddled in silks as he dozed, but he opened a blurry eye at the sound of Kahled's voice.

The vampire wasn't looking at him. Pale-gray eyes were glued to the sketchbook in his lap, a pen caught between the humanoid fingers of his right hand as he drew. His focus was so absolute, Sly began to wonder if he'd spoken at all.

But Kahled continued, softly addressing the page, "I dream about drinking your blood with perfectly formed fangs. I remember what it's like to bite a willing partner in the heat of the moment, the right fit between my lips, the complete absence of fear that I might harm them beyond repair."

Sly was too sleepy to comment, but the wistfulness in Kahled's tone deserved a response. With lazy movements, he pried an arm from the bedding and reached out to set his palm on Kahled's knee.

The gentle scratch of the pen tip on the page hushed, but Kahled didn't react otherwise. He resumed sketching.

"In dreams, it's almost too easy to blend the fantasy of you into memories. I used to whisk pretty boys like you off Ethos every once in a while. For decades, it was the only peace I allowed myself." His soft words broke on a weak laugh. "I avoided the Elders and my duties so I could lose myself among the stars and a warm body. I thought it was preserving my sanity."

Sly's fingers clutched at a scaled knee, but Kahled's legs were folded to support the sketchbook and the skin was stretched too tight over the joint for his grip to find purchase. Even so, Kahled's unoccupied hand found his and acknowledged his comforting gesture with a fond pat.

The drag of the pen resumed in the background, and Sly closed his eyes. It was a surprisingly soothing sound as he burrowed deeper into the bedding, but not as nice as the thrum of Kahled's deep voice.

"I would have taken you above the clouds, shown you the galaxy from the private viewing deck of a luxury spacecraft. It would have been just us and the cosmos." He sighed, and the sound made Sly's heart throb. "I would have worshipped you till you begged for my bite, and ruined you for any human lover."

The pen's motioned slowed as a heaviness collected in the air of the fort. Sly's sluggish thoughts searched for something to say, but the still moment only stretched on and on. Eventually, Kahled set down his artwork and eased down on the bed along Sly's side.

Kahled whispered, "It's intolerably selfish of me, but I know I can't be your first. I hope no other vampire's fangs ever break your skin."

Sly frowned as he drifted off to sleep. His dreams that night were a warzone, his father's hatred pitched against the fragile suggestion of Kahled's affection.

CHAPTER 12

Kahled kept him entertained for an uncommonly long stretch, but Sly grew bored before too long. While Kahled slept, he explored the rest of the Master's suite and learned the various rooms were massive and underutilized. The only space worth noticing was the spare room where Kahled's sketchbooks had been dumped.

Sly settled himself on the barren stone floor and pulled the first of a few storage containers into his lap. It was open when he found it, with a few untouched booklets resting at the top of the contents. One was encased in hard leather, another had supple covers of pale green, and yet another had deep engravings etched into its front. Each unused sketchbook felt heavy and rich in his palms.

He set them aside and uncovered a treasure trove.

There were bound collections interspersed with loose sheets. Black and white figures and pages and pages bursting with colors and mediums Sly couldn't name. There was a range of images from unintelligible lines to in-depth portraits and detailed landscapes. A few times, he noted an acclaimed monument or thought he recognized Kamari's likeness. There was an entire sketchbook dedicated to brown ink drawings of ancient symbols and calligraphy from a rich culture that had abandoned Earth centuries before. He spent a long while admiring the beautiful writing without comprehension, then he set it aside.

The next handful of papers were loose and far less polished. A brief flip through them, and Sly was grinning from ear to ear.

"What are you doing in here?" Kahled rumbled from the doorway. Sly looked up from the drawings to see him leaning in the doorway with a pouty scowl on his face.

Sly held up a loose page with a flourish and peered around it at Kahled. "I think this is my favorite one so far."

Kahled snorted.

It was a simple sketch, the black lines old and faded in the rough likeness of a couple bodies intimately entwined. It was imperfect, far from the detailed images brimming the container, but it was compelling. Wild. Sexy.

"Can I have it?" Sly asked. "If you're just leaving all this to rot, I might as well have it framed."

"It's trash."

"It's awesome," Sly countered. "You're a very good artist."

He glanced up in time to see Kahled shrug. "I'm all right."

"Bullshit." Sly held his newest gift, displayed taut and smooth between his hands for Kahled's optimal viewing. "I'm going to have it framed. You have no idea how satisfying it would be to hang your work on my dad's living room wall."

Sly snickered, but his heart sank. He knew he would

never show it to John Spurgeon. It wouldn't be worth the risk if the old man ever learned the creator was a vampire.

When Kahled didn't comment, Sly shot him a curious look and asked, "Does your Harem know you're a pornographic portrait hobbyist?"

Kahled glared at him. "You're not as amusing as you think you are."

"Excuse you." Sly fanned himself with the drawing. "I'm fucking hilarious. I managed to make Walters chuckle once."

"Now that I don't believe." Kahled scoffed as he pushed off the doorframe. "She has better taste."

Sly tapped a finger over the pulse in his throat. "And I was beginning to think you liked my better taste."

Kahled's eyes gleamed so bright in the hallway light, for a split second, Sly thought they were glowing. It was so startling, he almost missed the way the vampire's nostrils flared and the muscle in his jaw twitched.

"You're trouble," Kahled grumbled under his breath as he turned toward the bedroom.

"Hey, Kahled?"

The vampire tossed his head back with a put-upon sigh. "Yes, Sly?"

Sly glanced around at all the scattered works and bit his lip as nonsensical heat crept up the back of his neck. "Why is all this stashed away back here? It just seems more convenient if you had them closer to you, maybe in your room."

"Why?"

The snap to that single word chilled Sly to his core. When he lifted his attention from the paper mess, Kahled's eyes were still gray, but shadowed.

"You all right, Maestro?"

Kahled shook his head, blinking rapidly, and his eyes

lightened again. He sighed and rubbed mutated knuckles over his brow. "Don't call me that, Sly. I'm decent with a pen, nothing more."

Sly studied him as he climbed to his feet, and the provocative sketch felt fragile between his fingers. "I disagree."

"Then you're wrong."

Sly stared from the bins of sketchbooks to the vampire responsible for them back to the piece in his hand.

Kahled took a stiff step into the room and crossed his arms, huffing. "Get that sad look off your face, Sylvester. If you like it so much, take it, but don't make it a big deal."

Sly perked up with a sassy lift of his brows. "Really?"

Sly's breath caught. Kahled was blushing. It was faint beneath the even bronze of his skin, but it was there in gentle pink splotches high on his cheeks. It deepened to a rosy red under Sly's attention.

Kahled scoffed as he spun on his heel to limp out of the room. "For the love of Luna, Earthling, you wouldn't recognize real artistry if it paraded right under your nose."

Sly chased after him.

"*Maestro*," he laughed, bouncing along in the vampire's disproportioned footsteps. "You spout fucking poetry when you say anything longer than a sentence, and you draw ancient symbols absentmindedly like it's as easy as breathing. Easier, I bet, considering the air quality in these parts."

Kahled growled. "No."

"You've got a romantic streak a mile wide," Sly interrupted, jabbing his finger into Kahled's back with each word: "You. Are. Such. A. Fucking. Artist."

"And you're a nuisance. Why are you still here? Don't you have some sorry Earthly port to get back to?" He glared at him over his shoulder, but there was no substance to it. "Why am I still wasting what's left of my time with you?"

"Because you have nothing better to do." Sly smiled as he retorted. Then, he fluttered his eyelashes. "And because you like the way I suck your— Ah!"

As Kahled flung him over his shoulder and carried him off, Sly cackled. The vampire was good and distracted from the chaotic splay of books and pages in the spare room and, for a time, so was Sly.

DAYS LATER, GORBON DROPPED IN ON THEM TO DRAG Kahled down to the medical bay for a thorough check. Sly was careful not to look to closely at the creases of tension carved into the doctor's forehead as he hurried Kahled off for privacy.

The ball of dread in Sly's gut gave a nasty pulse, so Sly went looking for a distraction. He took a quick inventory of the storage containers in the spare room before he tiptoed down to the basement.

Sparks flew, and not in the good, proverbial way. Sparks flew in the literal, fire-hazard way.

"Shit!"

Sly leaped back from the intercom's control panel with a spectacular display of wild limbs and squeals.

Tilla's golden face gaped at him from where his comms was perched on a nearby shelf. "Was that supposed to happen?"

"Nope." Sly shook his hand till he could ignore the small electrical sting on his finger. "But don't worry, it's not the first time old tech has spat in my face. The Guard's system was downright violent in comparison. It took me months to get it working the first time Dad asked me to have a look."

Tilla frowned as they watched him give the panel door a fond pat. The sheet of dented metal swung closed under the attention only to bounce back, but the tangled wires within the cabinet didn't zap him again. He was nearly done fixing the functional damage Kahled had done weeks ago, and the dented door wouldn't bother him if it hadn't revealed the internal chaos of dusty, unlabeled wires.

Sly held the door shut with his foot and braced his hands on his hips as he asked Tilla, "Could you add some wire insulation to my order while you're at it?"

"About that..." Tilla hesitated as they studied Sly from head to toe with narrowed eyes. "I've offered to discount off-world goods for you before, but you've always said no. What's changed?"

Sy shrugged and poked at the stubbornly unstuck door with his toe. "Not much. I just have a little extra income right now."

Tilla snorted. "I don't need to visit Centrism to know the mess you're tangled up in, Sly. Your name's been all over the American Port, on the tongues of all her interplanetary traders since the moment you signed that contract."

Sly waved them off. "Yeah, Blythe already told me."

"Is it true?" Tilla's frown was so severe, it might have qualified as a pout on someone less imposing. "The Vauqeulin Harem forced you into Companionship?"

Sly tensed, the blood draining from his face. "Don't believe everything you hear, Tilla. Fuck. Is that the nonsense my dad's buying into?"

As a rule, he and Blythe avoided talking about John whenever possible. She made sure the two men knew the other was alive and well, but she hadn't offered to push messages on either Spurgeon's behalf in weeks. For his part, Sly stopped asking her to. He also stopped trying to contact John directly, though he couldn't say when it became a conscious decision.

"I don't know, Sly." Tilla bit at their lips, their visage shrinking as they leaned away from their comms. "I touch down for work, but I haven't stepped outside the port's galactic market since I learned you were gone. I could ask around though?"

Sly yanked at his hair with a frustrated hum.

Tilla wasn't a friend. They were a client, or at least, they used to be. Sly wasn't sure what this conversation meant for their relationship, but it was their first interaction beyond Centrism's walls. Sly had to beg their comms code from Phink this morning to make this conversation happen. Technically, Sly supposed this made *him* their client now, but it had the uncomfortable feel of a personal investment there could be no turning back from.

Sly sighed. "Don't bother yourself, Tilla. You're already helping me out plenty if you can get me the stuff I asked for."

"The insulation and..." Tilla shot him a prodding look. "The paints?"

He nodded. "Yep. That's the stuff."

They did not look convinced. "As in pigments?"

"Yes." Sly nodded with a bit more force. "Paint. Like the stuff you make pretty crap out of!"

"You're confused, Sly. Crap is never pretty."

"Are you being serious right now?"

Tilla's face was stoic as they assured him, "No excrement is attractive. Not on your world or any other."

"Sunfire strike me now." Sly groaned. "Whatever. Paint, Tilla. That's all I want. And brushes. Whatever a person would need to make something with the stuff."

Kahled's storage containers were full to the brim with drawing journals and utensils, but even Sly's untrained eye knew what was missing. There were sharp, clean cases of charcoal sticks and pens in various sizes, shades of dark inks, and even an unopened case of real, wood-encased graphite that should have been displayed in a museum.

But there was no color.

It didn't sit right with Sly.

"Maybe ask the other traders," Sly suggested without meeting Tilla's eye. "I don't know enough about art to know what he'll need, just get me something usable. With a lot of color. That's important. And make sure it's decent quality, okay?"

Tilla's expression hardened.

"If you can't find anything in America's Port, don't stress about it," Sly added. "Just keep me in mind if you come across anything between now and the next time you're Earth-bound."

Tilla's stony expression didn't shift, but they hunched their shoulders in dissatisfaction. "I only came to Centrism for you. I see no reason to go out of my way to deliver a gift to the vampire who poached you from us."

"Temporarily," Sly stressed.

"You're a terrible liar."

"Eh, screw you. Will you try to find me some paint or not?"

"If it's convenient."

"If this was my comms, I'd throw you across the room! Right out a window to fry!"

"Very impractical of you."

"Just find me some artsy stuff," Sly whined. "Pretty please?"

Tilla's posture shifted, easing enough to make Sly feel

like cheering. "We will see. Is this vampire of yours footing the bill, then?"

Sly shrugged as he examined a box of spare parts on the shelf bellow Tilla's projection. "It's sort of a surprise."

Tilla made an unhappy hum.

Sly prodded at the box, jostling it with a satisfying clank. "He's not so bad for an obscenely rich vamp. I figure he'll need something to occupy him when it's time for me to leave, and—" For some unknowable reason, he had to pause to catch his breath. "And I want to give him something. To remember me by."

The gasp that escaped Tilla was almost inaudible. "You like him, don't you?"

Sly gave a jerky nod as he pushed the unsuspecting box of parts away as if it offended him.

"He's not so bad," he repeated, flushing. "It's a good thing I'm out of here in only a few short months. He's a total sap, and he's shit at hiding it; if I gave him the time, he'd probably try something ridiculous and start trying to *woo* me."

He broke into a laugh, but it fell flat. Judging from the pinched look on Tilla's face, the attempt at levity wasn't convincing. The gross pit in his gut only reinforced it with a pang.

Tilla sighed, and Sly winced at the disappointment lacing the tiny sound. "I'll find you some paint, Sly," they said, so soft and gentle as if they were saying goodbye and expecting to never hear from him again.

Sly's voice broke as he said, "thanks," then he hurried to disconnect the call.

∾

HE FIDDLED SOME MORE WITH THE INTERCOM CONTROL PANEL before he made a slow, but direct trek toward Kahled's rooms. When he got there, he found the vampire pacing the length of his bedroom in long, limping strides. The talon growing from the big toe of his right foot punctuated each step with a crisp click on the stone floor.

Kahled stilled and faced him when the door closed behind Sly with a snap.

The vampire tensed and ducked his head as he scrutinized him. His face was blank, his voice cool as he asked, "Where were you?"

Sly threw out his hands in a careless shrug. "Around."

Kahled's face remained neutral as he resumed pacing. "I thought you left."

Arms going lax at his sides, Sly gave a short, sardonic chuckle. "And gone where? Not sure if you know this, but I don't know-how to pilot any of the vehicles in your hangar, and I'm not actually stupid enough to try walking my mortal butt back to America."

Kahled didn't respond. He shot him a single glance as his pace slowed, but otherwise he kept glaring toward his busy feet.

Sly gave an aimless hum as he moved toward the bed. "So, what now?" he prompted as he pulled apart the shredded sheets obscuring the foot board so he didn't topple the fort when he sat down.

Kahled didn't seem to hear him.

Sitting down with the hangings tossed over his shoulder, Sly raised his voice and tried again. "If you want me to leave, you can just say so."

Kahled huffed a reluctant laugh. "I don't want you to leave."

That hurt. It shouldn't have, but it did.

Kahled kept pacing, and Sly closed his eyes instead of watching him. He wished the Earth would hurry it up and split apart already; the least it could do was implode conveniently enough to get him out of this situation. His insides twisted themselves into knots as he struggled to find something to say.

He was spared.

"I thought you might have come to your senses," Kahled said as one foot came down with a pronounced thump. "You don't need to entertain me because you're bored or you pity me—"

Sly blanched. "I don't!"

Kahled spoke over him, his lopsided gait uninterrupted. "There are less than three months left on your contract, and I will gladly abuse that time if you let me, Sly."

Sly stood up but faltered on his way toward the vampire. "I'm not— What? What are you saying?"

Kahled finally stopped stomping back and forth and turned to face him, his jaw and brow set with determination. "Doctor Gorbon informed me—"

Sly's heart lurched as he reached for the vampire. "Are you okay? Is the Curse getting worse?"

Kahled shook his head as he held up a hand to wave him off. "This isn't about me."

"Actually, it is!"

"You cannot let me take advantage of you!" Kahled snapped.

Sly blinked. "Huh?"

Kahled made a long, rolling growl as he pressed a fist to his brow in thought. When he lowered his hand and looked at Sly, his eyes caught the light and flashed white.

"Kamari coerced you into this," Kahled said, his tone hard and insistent. "But no contract can give me blanket permission to use you however and whenever I like. And Gorbon—"

He cut himself off with a sneer, and Sly thought he saw a shadow flit across his sclera. The vampire shuddered, his whole body bristling as he collected himself.

Kahled chose his words with greater care. "The doctor suggested that your behavior and prolonged stay in my bed was surprising. Perhaps a bit alarming, considering your determination to leave at the end of the contract..."

As Kahled trailed off without meeting his eye, Sly's jaw dropped. "What the fuck, Maestro?"

Kahled's lower claws screeched on stone as he shifted his weight. "If Kamari, Emmeline— If anyone pressured you to give me anything more than blood—"

"Stars above, Kahled!" Sly guffawed. "You're not taking advantage of me. My blood's bought and paid for, sure, but I wouldn't be sleeping with you unless I genuinely wanted to. How is this in any way unclear?"

But Kahled wasn't looking at Sly in all his righteous indignation. Those sad gray eyes were trained on the monstrous digits of his left hand, perhaps staring past it to the further mutated foot, where the largest claw was still aligned with the latest scratched carved into the floor.

Sly scoffed. "Fuck Gorbon and whatever he's insinuating."

It was so easy, so very, very simple, for Sly to forget his own misgivings in that moment. Blythe and John, Centrism and the port, none of them mattered when Kahled was right there within arm's reach and yet lightyears away at the same time.

Sly crossed the room faster than he knew his legs could move. He wrapped his puny human fingers around Kahled's hand and held on tight till the vampire looked at him.

"I can't stay with you," Sly affirmed, up-front as always. He hugged the hand to his chest and offered a cheeky smile as he added, "But I'm perfectly capable of enjoying myself while I'm still here."

Silently, Kahled slipped free of Sly's grasp so he could cup the human's face in his palm.

Sly leaned into it with an undetectable sigh of relief.

Kahled's thumb brushed over his cheek. He watched him with soft eyes beneath a furrowed brow.

"I can have this," Kahled whispered, as if confiding to himself. "Scales, claws, and all, but I can still have you. For a short while."

Sly set his hands on Kahled's hips, kissing the vampire's wrist. "Yeah, Maestro. For a little while."

"It's enough," Kahled assured him before bending to kiss Sly's forehead. "It's more than enough."

Sly wasn't entirely sure what Kahled meant by that, but he didn't question it further as their mouths met in a cautious kiss. They crawled into bed, and the future was a distant worry that had no place in their little nest.

WITHOUT SLY'S NOTICING, THE BED AND ITS FABRIC hangings somehow morphed into a mere backdrop to the sanctuary of Kahled's arms. Sly spent the next few days ignoring his comms and making sure Kahled knew his deformities weren't the deal breaker he thought they were. When Kahled was ready to let him out of bed for longer than five minutes again, he had an impressive array of passion-induced bruises.

One evening, while Kahled fed from a cut on his arm, Sly

prodded a red and purple spot on his inner thigh. He hissed as it sent a dull ache creeping toward his groin.

"You like leaving marks, I noticed," Sly teased.

Kahled lifted his head and licked a smear of blood from his lip as he tugged Sly closer by the waist. "I've never been inclined before, but then, I've never had the opportunity to play with skin like yours."

The word "play" swam circles in Sly's head, distracting him from his self-led physical exam.

"What do you mean?"

Kahled's tongue lapped at the cut on his arm, unperturbed as he answered between licks. "You're pale."

Sly rolled his eyes. "No shit."

"Most humans have more pigment in their skin," Kahled commented as he began nuzzling up Sly's arm, leaving the latest cut to scab over.

"I'm aware," Sly assured him. "Blythe says I'm the whitest boy she knows, and considering I know everyone she does, I'm inclined to believe it."

Kahled uttered a thoughtful hum as he mouthed at Sly's shoulder. "History books claim it was evolution's futile response to the sun's growing intensity. The only people I know as pale as you are Nocturni."

Sly held up his hand and considered it. "Yeah? I think Walters and Felix are close to my color."

Kahled lifted his head, frowning. "Who?"

"Felix?" Sly snickered at the clueless look on Kahled's face. "You know, the posh blond bastard who's always glaring at me over Gorbon's shoulder?"

Kahled quirked his head in thought. "I thought his name was Philip."

Sly barked an inconsiderate laugh as he imagined Felix's reaction to that statement. Sly hadn't spoken to the other man since their little spat in the hallway, and he didn't regret it.

It seemed Kahled had even less to do with the grouchy staff member. With a dismissive shrug, the vampire returned to kissing Sly's collarbone.

"He's a shade or two darker. Now, you," Kahled purred as he nuzzled the hollow of Sly's throat, "are less peach-toned and more, hmm… alabaster."

Sly rolled his eyes as he blushed. "There you go again, waxing poetic with your fancy words."

Kahled licked over his pulse with a low, promising growl. "You're as fair as fresh snow."

Sly snorted forcefully enough to make Kahled pull away with a sneer. "You're just picking on me now, and it's ridiculous."

Kahled settled beside him on his side, his upper body balanced on one elbow as he admired Sly. "How would you know? Witnessed many snowfalls, have you, Earthling?"

Sly shook his head in answer as he burst with mocking laughter. The humor caught in his throat as he felt finger pads and the fine-tipped point of claws whispering up his inner thigh. It made him shiver in the best way. Breathless, Sly inched his knees further apart.

There was nothing humorous in Kahled's manner or expression as he continued petting the human's vulnerable areas with barely-there strokes.

"You're not as light as some of The Nine Bloodlines, but you're better." A possessive edge infused Kahled's voice as he glided his fingers over a fading bruise near his hip. "You show marks so brilliantly, and they linger for days, slow to heal and slower to fade, so unlike the Nocturni. Like a real human."

Sly trembled. "That's me. Real human."

He held his breath, waiting on Kahled's words. Sly could sing, but he had no gift for creating lyrics; Kahled's way of speaking felt like the exact opposite. He wove sentences into music without melody or recognizable tune, and it was beautiful.

Sly felt beautiful under the intensity of Kahled's regard. Silver eyes and gentle fingers roamed his skin like it was composed of the most fragile gold leaf. The words accompanying that avid attention did not disappoint.

"All manner of reds and purples are already blossoming," Kahled murmured as his featherlight touch traced down to a love bite on Sly's inner leg, just above the knee. "I can still see the indentation from the blunt edge of my teeth."

Sly closed his eyes and went limp against the pillows. Kahled pressed on the mark in a faint mimic of the delightful pressure his mouth had used hours earlier to create it in the first place. Sly moaned.

"You're like a living canvas. Every time I touch you, I…"

His deep, soothing voice faded away, and the promising caresses stuttered to a halt. Sly opened his eyes, and the vampire was staring at his splayed body with a stricken expression.

Before his brain could catch up with him, Sly raised a hand to comb through Kahled's hair in steady, glacial passes. "What're you thinking about, Maestro?"

Tentative, Kahled raised his gaze to Sly's face. "I was never a violent person before Nosferatu's Curse."

Twirling an ebony lock between his fingers, Sly smiled. "I'm not surprised."

Kahled leaned into his hand, and the motion was so catlike, it summoned Blythe to Sly's mind. His heart panged.

"Tell me," Sly murmured, scooting closer. "Every time you touch me, you… what?"

Kahled closed his eyes and hid his face in Sly's open palm. "You're so pale," Kahled spoke, soft and aching as if the statement suddenly hurt. "I get distracted by the blue of your veins. Then I remember the red of your blood, so deep like rubies against your skin…"

The thinnest line of wetness seeped from Kahled's clenched eyelids into Sly's palm.

"I never want to hurt you," Kahled said after a moment's recovery. "I'm glad you'll be gone before I have the chance."

"Don't talk like that."

Sly rolled into him so he could pepper kisses along Kahled's jaw and throat. Kahled accepted the affection stoically for a moment before he wrapped an arm around Sly's waist and hugged him tight.

"Hush," Sly whispered, though Kahled hadn't uttered a sound. "We don't need to think about that right now."

But it was too late to avoid the chilling reminder that had snuck into their nest. They didn't speak of it, but it burdened the air around them, as if the patchwork hangings wilted right in front of Sly's eyes. Kahled slumped against him, the tear tracts dried on his cheek, and Sly held him close while he sang them to sleep.

CHAPTER 13

*T*hree more weeks passed, and the small fortune's worth of Lunar clothing in Sly's guestroom closet somehow made its way into Kahled's rooms. He brought his toiletries up himself after he realized Kahled's bed was so much more inviting than his own, but the clothes were another matter. He still hadn't touched most of them, including the dress Kahled had discarded on him a while back.

In fact, Sly had no distinct memories of carting any of his clothes through the elevator, but Walters assured him that her staff was not responsible. Considering Gorbon and herself were the only humans Sly ever saw in Kahled's rooms, he believed her.

The only explanation was that Kahled was the one responsible.

That idea brought on a series of startling realizations for Sly.

Somehow, well over half his contract had eclipsed without much fuss. Sly couldn't remember the last time he traded more than a few passing words with Mae, Felix, or any of the manor staff for that matter. He thought about Blythe and Phink, his life at Centrism, and those thoughts floated like a warm, gentle breeze to the forefront of his mind; he wasn't sure when he stopped missing them with the visceral ache of homesickness.

He didn't think about his dad, nor their mutual noncommunication.

Instead, Sly threw his focus toward the greatest distraction currently available on Earth: Kahled Vauqeulin.

There was all the sex he could want and soulful talks late into most nights. There were decadent breakfasts in bed and indulgent bubble baths where water droplets scattered rainbows over Kahled's scales in fascinating patterns. There was laughter and a fair amount of sobbing, and the easy flow of lullabies and sentimental pop songs whenever Sly could be convinced to sing them; Kahled convinced him often.

When Walters or Gorbon managed to bully Kahled into the medical suite for hours of testing and monitoring, Sly jumped onto slightly adjacent distractions.

"He's a twice-damned romantic," Sly complained to his comms one such afternoon.

Blythe's disembodied voice sounded from his wrist, "And that's a problem... how?"

He was back in the basement's communications center, buffing out the final replacement parts while Kahled was busy conferencing with Doctor Gorbon and Kamari Vauqeulin. It was a decent task for keeping him preoccupied. His antsy hands were kept busy at least, but it wasn't enough for Sly to ignore how frequently Kahled was beginning to send him away whenever Gorbon was around.

"It's a problem," Sly snarked back at Blythe, "because my life is a cosmic joke and the first time I meet a guy potentially worth more than a long-term booty call, he has to have a terminal illness!"

He took out his frustration by kicking the dented door to the internal wiring. It snapped back at him with a sharp sting to his shin.

"Fuck!" Sly hissed, rubbing at the spot.

"You all right there?" Blythe asked.

"Fine," he grumbled as he shook the pain from his leg.

They weren't using the video features of his upgraded comms. He turned the feed off shortly after connecting with her so he could focus enough to relabel the intercom's controls. Days ago, Mae found him a laser engraving gun, and he was halfway through assigning each relay on the control panel to the appropriate room in the manor.

Without visual cues, Blythe still tried to test his concentration.

She drawled, "You really like this vampire, huh?"

"No," Sly snipped, grabbing up the label gun. "He's a jerk."

"Then he must be your type."

"I don't have a type." Sly shot a perplexed look toward the comms, forgetting she couldn't see him. "I can count the number of lovers I've had on one hand, and I don't see any commonalities. And that's assuming we want to count that holiday party where Phink—"

"That didn't count," Blythe snapped.

Sly winced as he recalibrated the gun for a new label. "Sure about that?"

"Sylvester," she whined. "You swore there was no penetration of anyone's orifices!"

"There wasn't!"

"Then it doesn't count!"

"Whatever." Sly waved his hand, the sharp line of the

comm's metal blurring with the motion. It didn't affect Blythe, but it satisfied him all the same. "My point still stands. I don't have a type."

As he positioned the laser marker over the appropriate spot on the panel, Blythe snickered at him.

"You might not be picky about your bedpartner's looks, but look at the people you bother to cultivate any sort of relationship with."

"I'm perpetually single," he deadpanned over the quiet sizzle of the laser. "It's a side effect of being one of the few human Earthlings in a generation and not having a fetish for wrinkles and sagging skin."

"Not all relationships are romantic, smart ass. Otherwise, you and I would have shacked up years ago."

"Well," Sly paused thoughtfully. "You *are* my life partner."

"Ditto, you little miscreant. But I'm not ever fucking you."

He gave a loud, mournful sigh, "You do lack the proper equipment to get the job done right."

"Excuse you!" she wailed with dramatic affront. "I have *all* the equipment."

Sly groaned, but she cackled over him.

"But seriously, Sly." Her humor began to cool. "How's that vampire treating you?"

"Good."

"Sylvester," she huffed. "I know he's feeding you like a pig to slaughter, and if you mention that Jacuzzi one more time, I'll scratch your eyes out. I'm not talking about that." She repeated her question with pointed emphasis, "How is he *treating* you?"

Sly frowned, the hand holding the labeler dropping to his side. "Is this your way of asking me about my sex life?"

She made a sound far from complimentary. "Yes."

He laughed and lifted the gun to switch up the input.

"Sylvester," she demanded. "I haven't been laid in weeks! Let me live vicariously through you!"

"You'll be disappointed." Sly grinned as he zapped another label into place. "By your penetration-dependent definition, we're not having sex."

"Bullshit," she spat, sounding scandalized and doubtful. "Not even oral?"

Sly snickered, relieved she couldn't see the flush on his cheeks. "Okay, fine. We have sex!"

"Seriously? With those fangs?"

"He's very gentle and considerate," Sly said, his defensiveness spurring her into a bout of giggles.

"But no butt stuff?"

Sly shrugged, "It hasn't been a priority."

He wasn't about to tell her of Kahled's squeamishness anytime Sly mentioned fingering. The vampire couldn't look at his lethally mutated hands with any thoughts for pleasure, and Sly's willingness to do all the prep work himself only seem to hamper Kahled's mood.

It was a minor disappointment, as far as Sly was concerned. He hadn't needed to rely on his own hand in weeks.

Blythe sighed. "Remember the good old days, when I had all the Nocturni lovers at my disposal, and you were still too prudish to let a vamp anywhere near you? Where did we go wrong?"

Sly laughed, shaking his head. "Why the dry spell, Blythe? Do your droves of admirers think your time backstage has tarnished you more than those spots?"

He expected her to scoff, maybe share a chuckle before she corrected him for besmirching her reputation. She didn't.

Sly's insides churned with warning bells. "Blythe?"

It took her too long to answer, and her voice was uncharacteristically soft when she did. "I wasn't ready to be back on stage. Phink's letting me stay behind the bar for a while longer."

Sly set the label maker on the control table's surface so he could bring up the comm's video projection. Blythe wasn't expecting him to turn it back on, and her device was positioned in such a way that he only saw a portion of her profile. She wasn't wearing makeup, and the bags under her eyes were new.

"What's going on with you?"

She glanced toward her comms with a halfhearted smile, but she didn't reposition herself within the frame so he could have a better look at her. "Don't worry about me. You have your hands full enough with your vampire."

Sly frowned. "He's not my vampire, and you're deflecting."

She rolled her eyes, but her smile lifted to a more believable expression. "I'm glad you're enjoying yourself, Sly. You seem happy there."

His eyes narrowed on her, his frown deepening. "Yeah. It's not a bad gig."

She righted her comms so he could see her head-on, and he knew it wasn't the lack of concealer that made her look so tired. "I have to get back to work soon, but I wanted to tell you something."

Sly braced for bad news. Either she was sick or John was, or HEPP was replacing Phink at Centrism. Maybe anything and everything was going to shit in his absence.

He wasn't ready when she gave him a wistful little smile and said: "Phink and I were talking. We think you should reconsider this whole Companionship thing."

Sly interrupted with a testy, "That's the whole point of this temporary contract—"

"Sly."

He shut up when she sighed his name. It was sad and hopeful, and it reminded him of the way she used to talk about dancing on the moon someday. They were kids back then, back when she still bought into his daydreams of making it off this rock for brighter horizons.

Throat tight, Sly wondered what Blythe would make of Kahled's stories about starlight and a galaxy bursting with colors and possibilities.

"You've always been a caretaker," Blythe said, a strange waver in her voice. "If it wasn't your mom, it was me or John or—"

"I thought we weren't talking about him?"

"I'm not. I'm talking about you." She folded her arms in front of her and rested her chin on it, her smile small and patient. "It's like you said, Sly. Companionship isn't a bad gig. I think you're suited to it."

"It's a job, Blythe." It was his voice, his words, but it felt brittle leaving his tongue. He shook his head and pressed on, regardless. "And one with a literal dead end, by the way. Thanks for the reminder."

Her lips trembled, but she kept smiling, even as her eyes watered. "You're the only man I know who would get involved with the one Nocturnus in the universe he could outlive."

They didn't stay on comms for much longer.

Afterward, Sly was in no mood to finish the labeling endeavor. He stared at the control display, at the motley array of repurposed metals he managed to scrounge into a functional machine hub. It was worlds nicer than the equipment waiting for him back home with the Guards, sleeker and shinier in comparison.

It was an eyesore compared to the beauty it had been before Kahled wrecked it.

Sly closed his eyes on that thought and was bombarded with recent memories. Kahled and his brilliant silver-gray eyes swallowed up by shadows that inspired dread in the pit of Sly's stomach. His disfigured feet and the scales that mottled his tawny skin. Sly wondered how long his puny mortal blood could keep it in check.

If Sly decided to stay, would he even recognize Kahled by the end?

HIS MORBID THOUGHTS PERSISTED THROUGH THE AFTERNOON till he gave up on the labeling project and returned to Kahled's rooms. The moment the elevator doors opened to admit him into the foyer, he could hear raised voices.

"I never asked for this!" Kamari Vauqeulin's voice rang shrill and hoarse from the bedroom.

Sly's footsteps froze at the sound of a barking growl. It was short and sharp, Kahled's voice cracking the air like a whip. It was deliberate, but far from human. When Kahled spoke, Sly almost didn't recognize him. The tone was brisk and commanding in a way Sly never witnessed. There was real, rational anger behind it, and a wealth of emotion too tumultuous to untangle.

"And I didn't ask for a premature death sentence, but here we are."

Sly could hear the snap of the vampire's gruesome fangs and the thud of his careless footsteps from down the hall.

"We both inherited raw deals from our mother. Do you

really want to get into a pissing contest over who has it worse?"

Whatever Kamari Vauqeulin said in response, it was too quiet to overhear from the foyer. Sly glanced back at the elevator as the doors slid closed and considered finding somewhere else to while away another hour. Before he could decide what to do, another noise erupted in the bedroom and shocked him still.

It was the brief, piercing yowl of a mournful beast. The terrible sound echoed off the walls as it was followed by the snap and crackle of metal and electronics being torn to pieces.

"Damn it, Mari," Kahled hissed.

Heart racing, Sly stepped away from the elevator and inched down the hall. "Kahled?"

He was still several steps away when the door swung open, it's edge groaning in complaint under Kahled's white-knuckled grip and one embedded claw. His eyes were gray, but they were dark as they sought out Sly's face.

"Do you have any siblings?" Kahled asked in a strained voice, tilting his head in that inhuman way he sometimes exhibited.

Sly shook his head with a halfhearted smile. "Pretty sure I was all the kid the Spurgeon household could handle."

The shade of Kahled's irises seemed to lighten, but he didn't look any happier. "You're fortunate," he said without inflection, before releasing the door and slipping away into the bedroom.

Sly followed after him and stopped dead in the doorway.

The shattered remains of a gold-plated comms lay on the floor. There was blood speckle on various pieces.

"What happened?" Sly gasped, eyeing Kahled for injury. "Are you hurt?"

"I'm a vampire, Sly," Kahled reminded him with a snarky edge to his tone. "It's already healed."

Kahled waved a hand in an indifferent gesture, and Sly crossed the room to grab hold and inspect it. There was a thin pink line bisecting Kahled's palm; depending on the depth of the wound, it was the equivalent of days or weeks of human healing.

Cradling Kahled's hand, Sly frowned up at the vampire. "Was this an episode? Should I go get Gorbon?"

Kahled stared at his recently injured hand, lax in Sly's hold, and shook his head. "This wasn't the Curse's doing," he said with a weary sigh, "Just my own. And my brother's."

"What happened?" Sly repeated as he led Kahled over to sit on the bed. "I heard shouting, but I wasn't trying to listen in."

They sat side by side, and Kahled sagged, his burly shoulder falling into Sly like a warm weight being unloaded. He stared out at nothing, his face drawn and exhausted.

"You don't have to tell me if you'd rather not," Sly suggested, rubbing the vampire's knee.

Kahled heaved another sigh, and Sly swayed as the larger body relaxed that much more against him.

"I was born to serve my Harem's needs." The vampire didn't refocus his absent gaze or glance toward Sly as he spoke. "Nocturni don't generally rush to breed, we're so long-lived, but our mother... sometimes I wonder if she knew her time would be so short. She raised me to succeed her, and when it happened a century sooner than it should have, I thought myself lucky for those decades of grooming. I thought I was ready."

He trailed off with a single note of mirthless laughter, and the resulting silence was too stiff for Sly to tolerate long.

"Were you ready?"

"No." Kahled shook his head, slow, sad, and distant. "I was too young. Too inexperienced and nervous to prove myself. I would have ruined us if the Elders hadn't guided my every move. But we were fine. I was good at listening to those who knew better. Kamari always had to learn things the hard way for himself."

Sly curled his fingers against Kahled's thigh and dragged his nails up and down his leg in an encouraging scratch. He tried to imbibe his tone with some humor as he asked, "Is he fucking up all your hard work, then?"

His words fell flat, and Kahled's distant effect was unchanged. "He's not ready for this. I wasn't ready, but at least they tried to prepare me for it. How were we supposed to anticipate a once-in-a-millennium disease would strike at us twice in a row?"

"You couldn't have," Sly assured, winding his arm around Kahled's waist. "No one could have. It's shitty dumb luck."

"I tried to help him," Kahled continued in that deadened tone. "I turned the Harem over publicly, and I tried to ease him into the position, but apparently, I just kept doing the job for him until the Elders ran out of excuses to keep me on Ethos."

Only then did Kahled turn to look at him, and Sly's heart ached at the dry, defeated look in his eyes.

"They should have exiled me years ago, if not the moment I was diagnosed, then once I lost control of my splicing abilities and the deformities became obvious."

"But they didn't," Sly countered, squeezing him. "They didn't give up on you that easily. They needed you." He hesitated before adding, "It sounds like maybe Kamari still needs you."

Kahled didn't seem to hear him. "When I took up our mother's position as the Harem's Heir, it demanded all the time and energy I could spare. I never wanted that for Mari."

They lapsed into silence again, and Sly's throat closed as if he were suffocating on Kahled's weak misery. His recent conversation with Blythe lurked in the shallows of his thoughts, and Sly felt light-headed with the rising need to rediscover who his lover was, who he used to be. He needed the despairing atmosphere to ease; he wanted Kahled's dry, dark humor and his lilting phrases to smooth away the heartbreaking heaviness.

Sly rested his cheek on Kahled's shoulder and asked, "What was it like growing up on Ethos? With Kamari."

Kahled sneaked his arm underneath Sly's, crossing them so he could set his palm on the human's knee in reciprocal comfort. They were pressed so close, Sly felt the vampire's body heave a tough breath, but he didn't speak.

Sly nuzzled him and offered, "When I was little, about six, my mom took me to this event HEPP was hosting in the port's convention center. They had all these people and stuff from Luna and a couple more distant planetary colonies. We couldn't afford any of it, but I remember standing in front of this stand of moon-grown produce and gawking at all the colors and the shapes of raw, whole fruits. We spent a long time there, just inhaling the sweet citrus and talking about what we thought it tasted like. Mom said someday, when we had the money and she could talk Dad around to it, we would visit Luna and see about eating berries or apples straight off the vine."

Kahled's shoulder shook with the briefest chuckle. "Apples grow on trees, not vines."

"Same difference to me." Sly shrugged without lifting his head. "It's all curated in greenhouses free and clear from this planet anyway."

"Fair enough."

As the quiet began to settle around them again, Sly clear his throat and continued. "There was a photographer with his own booth there, too, and we talked to him for a while. He traveled the galaxy for HEPP, helping their campaign to get more humans off the planet before it combusts. I've still never seen stars or clear blue bodies of water in real life, but back then, I swore his pictures were the most amazing thing I'd ever seen outside of a theater."

There was a small but distinct smile in Kahled's voice as he commented, "This artist made quite the impression on you, did he?"

Sly shrugged. "I've never really thought of photos as art, but sure. You could say he predisposed baby me to consider rich, stargazing artists in a favorable light."

They shared a quiet laugh, and Sly felt Kahled's chin rub over the top of his head, the bristles of his beard scratching Sly's scalp through his hair.

"Mom said it was sad how he didn't have a place he called home," Sly murmured, "but I thought his life sounded like an adventure."

He meant to finish the story there, on a wistful high note. As Kahled sat in the circle of his embrace Sly could feel the heartsick weariness seep from his muscles into a reluctant looseness. Something in the release of tension inspired him to keep talking.

"I didn't understand why she smiled so sadly then, but I get it now." The words weren't planned, but they flowed from him with an easy breath that tasted like truth. "I've wanted nothing more than to get off this rock since she died. Sometimes, I think if we'd lived someplace like Ethos or Luna, maybe she'd still be alive."

Kahled kissed his head and whispered, "Ethos would be lucky to have you."

"Tell me about it?"

There was a beat of stillness, a return of tension, and Sly thought Kahled wouldn't pick up the bead he'd dropped for him.

"We have two suns on Ethos," Kahled began. "Twice the solar power of Earth, but we could go outside wearing nothing but our skin, if we wanted. Even the humans."

Sly released the breath he'd been holding. As Kahled's deep voice washed over him, he closed his eyes and snuggled into the vampire's side.

"There's nothing quite like the feel of sunlight on your face, warming you as fresh air tickles your skin to cool it. You would have to be careful, though. Even with Ethos's atmosphere intact, the sun would burn you before too long."

Sly shuddered. Once, when they were walking home from school, Blythe took off a glove on a dare. For a moment, they'd watched in awe as the sunlight glinted off her glossed nails, but then Blythe screamed as the blisters began to bloom. She'd been wrapped in bandages for weeks.

The sight was horrific, and it did nothing to prepare him for the trauma of seeing his mother burn to a crisp months later. By the time port authorities came to clean up after her, there was nothing but ash and charred bone.

"I'm not sure I'd risk it," Sly mused aloud. "If I ever make it off-world, it'll take me forever to gather the nerve to step outside without cover."

"I hope you do it someday," Kahled said. "I hope you get to swim in an ocean that won't boil you alive and visit preserves where you're allowed to feel the grass between your toes."

Sly kissed Kahled's shoulder with a watery smile. "Think

I'll ever get to pet a cat? The closest I've ever been to one is a couple furry clients at Centrism."

Kahled responded with another kiss to his brow. "I hope you do."

They cuddled quietly for a long, shaky moment. Sly wasn't sure when their grip on one another tightened into something desperate and soul-aching, nor which of them tipped the scale from soothing embrace to something stronger. It didn't matter, it just was.

"I wish you could show me your home," Sly murmured against Kahled's jaw.

The vampire gave a stiff nod and corrected him. "It's my brother's home now. I have nothing left to show you but this."

Kahled pulled back enough to make eye contact, luminous silver orbs staring into Sly with a universe's worth of sorrowful wishes. Then, he kissed him.

CHAPTER 14

S ly woke days later to Walters barging into the room and yanking the hangings from the side of the bed.

Kahled growled. His arm around Sly's middle threatened to crack a rib as he burrowed into the pillows. Sly slapped at the vampire to loosen his grip, but it had no discernable effect.

Walters glowered down at him with one hand on her hip while the other held the hangings aside.

"Mr. Spurgeon. Why there is a merchant trading vessel requesting to dock in my hangar without Harem security's preapproval?"

Sly's brain hustled up to speed as he blinked up at her. "Huh?"

Beside him, Kahled shifted till he could perch his chin on the crown of Sly's head. "What's happening?" He yawned.

She bristled. "There is a heavily spliced person loitering outside our gates demanding they be allowed to park in our hangar bay for a delivery. There's been no advance notice, and I have no confirmation from Master Vauqeulin or Harem security that they should be here."

"Send them away, then," Kahled grumbled, shoving his face into Sly's nape.

Walters clicked her tongue with pronounced disapproval. "They claim to have packages for one Sylvester Spurgeon."

Sly surged out of bed and Kahled's hold with an exuberant cry. "Tilla!"

Twenty minutes and one rushed explanation and many apologies later, Sly bounded down the grand staircase in the estate's entrance hall like an excitable pet. Walters and Kahled trailed behind him, the former with a haughty click each time her heels touched the floor, and the latter with a grouchy grimace as he clutched a black and gold receiving robe tight over his sleepwear.

Tilla waited between the stairs and the double doors leading to the garage. They stood head-and shoulders above the few manor staff who were hanging about, their golden hair roped into a thick braid that had grown all the way to their waist. The leathery jumpsuit plastered to their muscular build was thick and durable, suitable for versatile space travel in a way Tilla's provocative casual wear never suggested when they visited Centrism. The high-tech gun holstered to their thigh was new, too.

Sly stumbled on the bottom stair, staring at Tilla. He was all at once overwhelmed by the comforting sight of their features and stunned by the professional badass persona standing in front of him.

Tilla's eyes were browner than he remembered as they smiled at him. "Sylvester."

Thoughtless, Sly raced the final few feet between them and threw himself at the familiar figure. Tilla caught him with ease, and it was only after they set him back on his feet with a fond sigh that he remembered hugging was a personal boundary they never crossed before. He blushed up at them, opening his mouth to apologize.

A low, suspicious growl echoed throughout the stone hall.

The room and its occupants froze.

Tilla's brow rose as they stared over Sly's head toward the stairs, and Sly turned in time to see the darkness melt from Kahled's eyes in a rush. The growl cut off, and Kahled shook himself.

Walters stood at the vampire's side, her face pinched with concern as her hand hovered over his arm. She didn't touch him, as always, but as Sly watched her chin tremble and her eyes soften, he wondered if Kahled was wrong about everyone's perceived disgust and disdain for his mutations. In that moment, Walters looked like she wanted nothing more than to hold the vampire, but she held herself in check for fear of rejection.

Kahled took no notice of Walters, though. His eyes, blessedly gray, were trained on Tilla.

"You're Sly's friend?"

Tilla nodded, their gaze darting between Kahled and Sly twice before settling on the vampire. "And you are Sly's vampire?"

Kahled's brown cheeks pinkened as he said, "I am."

They both looked to Sly then, and for no good reason, Sly felt his body warm by several degrees.

Sly shuffled his feet and gave Tilla a forced grin. "Does this mean you got the stuff?"

"What stuff?" Kahled demanded.

"I'll have my men unload it, if you like," Tilla said, still casting scrupulous glances between himself and the vampire.

Sly's eyes widened. "*Unload*? Shit, how much did you get?"

Tilla shrugged and turned toward the hangar to oversee

the delivery. As they did so, they caught Sly's eye with a baffling wink.

Behind Tilla's back, Kahled strode over to grip Sly's wrist. "What stuff?" he insisted, brows furrowed. "If you needed something, you should have told me. The Harem is supposed to provide for you as part of the contract."

"This isn't part of the contract, though."

While Kahled pouted, Sly left his wrist in the vampire's hold and led him into the hangar. They found Tilla stationed at the foot of a ramp connected to a two-story craft composed of sleek metal beneath layers of coppery dust and streaks from wind and solar burns. Under Tilla's stern direction, a couple men in similar attire were carting crates down the ramp and offloading them near the entrance hall's doors.

There were multiple cases of varying sizes. One of them was longer than Sly was tall, but it was thin and lightweight; it nearly toppled over when Sly poked at it.

"Tilla?" Sly worried aloud. "You're sure my budget covered all this?"

Tilla continued scrutinizing their workers, unperturbed. "You asked for quality materials, and the search was easier than expected. Our American suppliers had a surplus collecting dust in their warehouse. They were happy to be rid of it."

"Materials for what?" Kahled grumbled at Sly's side.

As the final box was dropped among the others, the ramp reeled into the ship with a mechanical hiss.

Tilla eyed Kahled. "It's for you. I would warn you not to waste my effort and Sly's money, but I made out on this deal. Turns out, Earthlings don't have much time for such extravagant hobbies, and there's more where this came from. We'll sell the rest on Luna and turn a handsome profit."

Kahled's hand tightened on Sly's wrist as he bent to

grumble in his ear, "Just what have you brought me, you little menace?"

Sly rolled his eyes. "You have such a unique way of saying 'thank you, Sly. I really appreciate you thinking about me and potentially squandering your hard-earned cash on a gift for my bored, overgrown ass.' Seriously."

Kahled growled at him, but it was less angry and more… nervous.

Sly met his eyes, scant inches between them, and finished with a minimum of sass and a lot of inopportune sincerity, "You're very creative. I can't wait to see what you do with it."

Kahled reared back on his uneven heels, staring as if he didn't know what to make of Sly.

Sly swatted at Kahled's arm till he let go of him then motioned him toward the delivery. "Go. You're welcome."

Movements stiff and eyes narrowed in suspicion, Kahled slouched off toward the crates. He kept shooting searching glances back at Sly, even as he stretched a claw out to part the packaging of the topmost parcel. He stopped once he got a look inside, his eyes fixated inside the box as he blinked down at it.

Sly gnawed on his lip as he watched the stillness of Kahled's face.

After a long moment, the vampire reached inside and pulled out a black bundle wrapped in fine twine. Sly didn't have a clue what it was, but Kahled plucked at the knot and unwrapped it with practiced hands.

"What is it?" Walters asked, peering at the item with cautious curiosity.

Kahled unrolled the black material and swallowed hard before answering, "Brushes. Paint brushes."

Sly opened his mouth to make a sarcastic remark, but he

stopped himself. He watched, silent and wary, as Kahled slipped a single brush from the wrapping with a softness to his face that was unfamiliar. There was nothing so evident as a smile, and Sly wondered if he'd made a mistake.

The brush's pale stem looked fragile in the vampire's grasp. Kahled balanced it between humanoid digits, and he brought the half-inch of silver that joined the hairs to the wood to rest on the scaled pad of his mutated finger. He was gentle, the twirl of the tool a lazy and graceful sweep that was unencumbered by the claw or swollen knuckle.

Kahled didn't look up from the brush in his hand as he croaked, "Thank you, Sylvester."

Sly huffed a quiet laugh as he remembered to breathe. "Good. That's good."

Kahled returned the brush to its packaging and cradled the set against his torso as he reached again for the box. There was the slightest tremor to his hand as he rifled through the remaining contents, and Sly was overcome with the urge to give the vampire some privacy.

Clearing his throat, Sly turned to thank Tilla.

He wasn't expecting Tilla's full attention to be trained on him. While everyone else, from Walters and her curious staff to Tilla's men watched Kahled explore his gift, Tilla watched Sly. Their golden-brown stare was heavy, direct in a way it never had the chance to be when watching him on Centrism's stage.

Sly twitched under that stare. "What?"

Tilla shook their head, slow and deliberate. "You're an interesting Earthling, Sylvester Spurgeon."

"Thanks?"

Tilla's schooled expression didn't clarify whether or not they were complimenting or insulting him. They tilted their head toward the manor doors, arms still crossed. "Usually, I don't make special deliveries for individuals. A real Companion would probably offer me a drink for my trouble, at the very least."

Sly glanced back at Kahled and Walters, their heads bent close together over another box. The vampire still held the brushes in a tender grip, but he indicated items with the other as he spoke freely to the old woman. Walters nodded along, her hands clasped before her hips as she hung on his every word.

Sly patted Tilla on the arm as he sidestepped toward the door. "Come on, I'll show you my favorite room in the place."

SLY HADN'T TOUCHED THE BILLIARDS ROOM BAR SINCE HIS first week in residence, and he nearly embarrassed himself when he couldn't find the appropriate glasses for whatever liquor Tilla picked up.

Mae showed up with impeccable timing and offered to mix them each a cocktail.

"I can bring you or your men something from the kitchen, if you like," Mae suggested after pouring Tilla's drink. She stood in front of the door, the consummate serving girl in her pressed skirt and gentle attentions.

The bulk of Tilla's focus remained on Sly, but they spared Mae a glance. "Thank you, but I'm fine. The guys would probably appreciate it, though."

"Of course." Mae gave a deep nod and shot Sly a warm smile. "If you or your guest need anything, find my name in your comms, all right?"

"Thanks," Sly muttered as she strode from the room.

He made for his favorite seat in the center of the sectional couch, and Tilla followed him. He sank his ass into the leather upholstery with a superficial sigh of relief, but inside, his guts lurched. How long had it been since he last sat there? Not since he invited himself into Kahled's bed, that was for sure.

Tilla sat a full two couch cushions away from him. They settled onto the furniture with ease, relaxing with one leg crossed over the other. It struck Sly as odd that Tilla would seem so comfortable in the room while he had to fight not to bounce his leg with mounting nerves.

"Four months I've been here," Sly said with a short laugh, "and Mae's never once offered to make me a drink. Is it because you're prettier than me?"

He eyed Tilla as he sipped his drink; it was fruity and light, the alcohol a thrilling zing to an otherwise mellow flavor. Considering he wasn't looking to get drunk and Tilla presumably had a ship to pilot, it was a perfect refreshment.

Tilla didn't answer. They drank, watching him over the glass's rim with an unwavering expectancy.

Sly abandoned his drink on the coffee table. "What's with that look?"

Tilla shrugged one shoulder as they sipped. Lowering the glass, they stated, "You didn't tell me you were in love with this vampire."

Sly recoiled. "Woah. That's a thought. Where did you get that idea?"

Tilla frowned. "Are the rumors true? Is he dying?"

Sly spluttered and wound up on his feet without any conscious decision to leave the couch. "How about you answer my question first so we can have a friendly chat instead of a gossip-based interrogation?"

Tilla spun their glass loosely between their palms as their

frown softened. "You told Phink and Blythe this was a job, Sly."

"It is."

"Centrism was a job," Tilla said, mild and simple as if reciting a textbook. "Myself and every other soul who sat in your parlors were a job. You've never looked at any of us the way you look at that Nocturnus."

Sly laughed and threw up his hands. He glared around the room, but there was nothing around to inspire him with the right retort.

"Nocturni don't condone the splicing he's done," Tilla commented in that level tone. "It doesn't take a genius to see there's something wrong with him."

Sly sighed and yanked at the hair sprouting over his forehead. "I'm helping him with that. That's why I'm here."

Tilla stopped spinning their glass. They sat up straight, staring at him with crushing gravity.

Sly's shoulders sagged. "I'm helping him," he repeated.

Tilla's mouth tightened into a hard line, wholly unsurprised and saddened. "You're asking to get hurt, Sly."

His mouth went dry and every inhale was starting to hurt, so Sly didn't argue. Instead, he swallowed around the jagged rock materializing in his throat and nodded.

There wasn't much more to be said. He knew it. Tilla knew it. Sometime later, Mae returned to notify them the delivery crew was fed and ready to go, and as she escorted Tilla out of the room, she shot Sly a pained little half-smile that told him she knew it, too.

Alone in the billiards room, Sly felt the manor walls closing in. He sat on the couch and wondered if Kahled was still in the hangar bay picking through art supplies like a starving man before a buffet.

~

ANY DOUBTS SLY MIGHT HAVE HAD ABOUT HIS GIFT'S reception disappeared that evening when Walters led a parade of staff through the elevator to Kahled's spare room.

Kahled didn't scold her or argue. Not at all. He carried his new brushes to his bedroom in a mild daze, occasionally sending unreadable looks in Sly's direction.

Sly wasn't sure what Kahled would say once they were alone, and he couldn't bring himself to follow the vampire into the cozy nest. Instead, Sly stopped in the doorway and scurried down the hall after Walters.

Despite her initial displeasure at Tilla's arrival, the Head of House leaped on the opportunity the creative materials presented. Sly slipped through the doorway into the spare room and gaped at the flurry of activity inside. Several staff members were busy rearranging Kahled's storage bins to accommodate the new arrivals, and more than one box was being emptied to reveal pallets of paint, slabs of various textured surfaces, and countless items Sly didn't recognize. Walters stood stock still in the middle of the hubbub, towering over an open container of charcoal and ink sketches.

While her people bustled about them, Sly peered over her shoulder. She held one of Kahled's journals between her palms, open to a two-page spread of hypnotic black and gray swirls.

"I had no idea," she murmured to Sly when he joined her. "He never told me he had such talent."

"I don't think he considers it a talent, just a hobby," Sly offered, his words lame next to the evidence in her hands. "But yeah, he's really good."

"You knew."

The look she gave him then made him flush. It wasn't

quite a smile, but there was a lift to her thin mouth as tears glazed her eyes. It was more than gratefulness; if he didn't know any better, he might have called it maternal pride.

"He told you," she said in a soft voice he never heard from her before. "I've known him most my life, but he never shared this part of himself with me. He only showed you."

Sly shrugged, looking everywhere but her face. "It wasn't like that. I stole a sketchbook from under his nose because I was peeved at him."

He turned away and watched as Felix slipped by with another man, the large, lightweight box balanced between them. He could feel Walters's gaze burning into the side of his face, but he kept his attention on Felix with the hope she would move on. She didn't, and Sly watched Felix peel away the brown packaging as if he were witnessing something historic. The parcel in question turned out to be three enormous canvases stretched across sturdy frames.

Felix leaned all three pieces against the far wall with a bemused look on his face. "Master Kahled asked for this?" he asked, patting the taut face of the topmost canvas. "What for?"

Sly crossed his arms as he glowered at the blond. "Whatever he wants."

Felix raised a brow at him then at the canvases. He looked like he was going to say something cutting, but he didn't get a chance.

"Felix," Walters said, crisp and polite as ever, "would you mind taking a quick inventory to see if we have a spare desk or anything suitable for a workstation? I'd like to make this a functional studio." Then, wonder of wonders, she turned to Sly and asked, "Do you think Kahled would like that?"

Sly glanced around like he expected someone else to answer her.

"Mr. Spurgeon?"

"Sure." Sly faced her again with a jerky nod. "I think he would."

Maybe Tilla was right. Maybe, just maybe, he wasn't helping Kahled as much as he was setting himself up for heartbreak.

CHAPTER 15

*L*ate the next morning, Sly woke up alone.

Heart pounding and mouth dry, he slipped down the hall and knocked on the closed door to the newly instated studio. There was no answer. He set his comms on his wrist and powered it on before he remembered that Kahled's personal device got destroyed last week.

He wandered down to the kitchen to find Mae and Gorbon lingering over the remains of the breakfast spread. They turned to him with bright, eager smiles on their faces.

"Good morning," Mae chirped.

"Did you sleep well?" Gorbon asked, handing him a steaming mug of tea.

Sly accepted the beverage with a wary glance around the room. "Have you seen Kahled? We didn't get a chance to talk last night."

Silence greeted him, and when he stopped eyeing dark corners for suspiciously absent vampires, he found Mae and Gorbon grinning at each other.

Sly blushed. "We didn't talk because we were sleeping," he clarified.

Mae's grin widened with a near-silent giggle.

Gorbon was more composed as he gestured toward the food. "Eat, Sly. Kahled's undergoing a few tests for me today, but once he's done, I'm sure he'd love to speak with you."

Sly narrowed his eyes on the doctor. "He's been in the medical suite a lot this week."

"Has he?" Gorbon shot over his shoulder as he began prepping a second mug for tea.

Cupping his hands around his drink, Sly leaned his forearms on the island counter and scrutinized the doctor. "Is there anything I should know about?"

Gorbon stirred cream into his tea as he frowned at him. "Like what?"

"Oh, I don't know. Maybe my blood's becoming less effective?"

Mae giggled. Sly shot her a dark, searching look, and she blushed. "You're plenty effective, Sly. Promise."

She set a plate of fruit-stuffed crepes and sausage in front of him then skipped out of the room without further comment. Sly blinked after her.

"Did I miss something? Why's she so perky?"

Gorbon chuckled. "Mae's parents worked here since before her birth. She's lived her entire life beholden to the Vauqeulin Harem. For the top-tier accommodations and fortified shelter from Earth's elements. For the food in her belly and the quality of the air in her lungs. She and her family could have immigrated to Luna years ago at the Harem's expense, but instead… they stayed here."

Sly picked at his crepes as his stomach curdled. "Why? I can't imagine having that chance and wasting it."

"Because Nosferatu's Curse has plagued the Vauqeulins for as long as Nocturni have existed." The doctor joined him at the kitchen island, still stirring his tea with that small smile on his round face. "People like Mae volunteer to live here, maintaining this ancient estate and preparing for the possibility that the Harem they owe so much might need the extra support."

Gorbon sighed and abandoned his mug to the side. "Sly, Mae doesn't know Kahled like you do. He hasn't given her that opportunity, but he's been the Harem's leader for all but the last few years of her life. She grew up knowing his name and seeing his influence on every aspect of her existence. Did you know, Kahled personally approved and funded her medical training, years before he could have known he would benefit from it?"

Sly shook his head, the food in front of him growing cold.

"Some Nocturni may consider themselves better than us mere humans," Gorbon continued in earnest, "but most of the original bloodlines understand and value the smallest people connected to their Harem, including humans. Without us, they wouldn't exist. Mae is only one example; she could go anywhere, do anything with the resources and skill the Harem would provide her, but she stays."

Sly found his mind whirling with hazy imaginings. It might have been a byproduct of the unbridled excitement in Gorbon's voice or maybe it was the memory of Kahled's stunned face as he held those brushes. Either way, for one heart-stopping moment, he let himself enjoy the fantasy of what his life might look like if he took the easy path Kamari Vauqeulin laid before him.

Even when Kahled died on him, he could be free of Earth and its inherent threats. Sly's eventual escape from the planet was bound to be explicitly stated in bold on any Companion Contract the Harem was likely to offer him.

"Do you understand, Sly?"

Musings interrupted, Sly jerked to attention to find Gorbon leaning over the counter toward him.

"That's who Kahled is, what he means to Mae and the others," Gorbon said with a quiet, tremulous laugh. "And yesterday, they finally got to know him, if only for a moment. Mae and Emmeline, all of them, they've been tending to the walking corpse of their personal hero, and yesterday, you brought him back to life with a bit of paint."

For the life of him, Sly couldn't think of a way to respond to that.

SLY FLITTED BETWEEN KAHLED'S SUITE AND THE BILLIARDS room the rest of the morning. He told himself he was anxious to know what Kahled thought about his surprise and Walters's consecutive studio construction, but that didn't explain the sick edge to his impatience. Every time he passed by the medical bay without catching sight of the vampire, Sly's mood darkened further.

Eventually, Felix caught him in the hall and told him off for lurking. Sly managed to refrain from slapping the superiority off the blond's face and decided to stop carving a path between the elevator and the billiards room for a while.

He retreated to the basement. By late afternoon, the intercom was fully labeled and functioning again.

Dinner time was fast approaching, and there was no word from Kahled. What the hell kind of tests was Gorbon running?

Walters found him in the control center as the manor's lights dimmed for the evening. He was seated in the lone stool, his feet propped up on the console and the laser gun in his hand; she caught him in the middle of engraving nonsense into the dented circuitry access door for fun.

"I thought I might find you here."

Sly sprang from his seat, nearly dropping the engraver. "Shit! Make a little noise next time."

As his heart calmed down, he tossed the tool onto a shelf. If he was lucky, Walters wouldn't notice the messily lasered door that now read: *Operable comms courtesy of Sylvester Spurgeon, mismatched hardware courtesy of the Evil Overlord*. Her eyes skimmed over the fresh engraving with several slow blinks, but she didn't comment.

When she addressed him, her tone held nothing but professional politeness, "Kahled sent me to find you."

"Cool," he nodded as he moved to slide past her. "You know, if he got a replacement comms, he could have just summoned me—"

She held her arm out, blocking his path.

"...Himself." He met her shrewd stare and finished with a huffy, "What now?"

She smiled, and it was hawkish like she'd caught him in a trap. "He's in the ballroom. Do you know where that is?"

Sly puffed out an irritated sigh. "Of course he is. Since when did this place have a ballroom?"

Her smile sharpened as she spun on her heel and indicated he should follow. "Right this way, Mr. Spurgeon."

THE VAUQEULIN HAREM'S EARTHLY ESTATE ONCE HOUSED hundreds of Nocturni and a full staff besides. The couple dozen human servants Sly grew accustomed to in his time there were the skeleton crew responsible for maintaining the property. According to Walters, it was unrealistic, bordering on absurd, to expect so few people to keep a full estate of such size running smoothly at all times, so they oscillated between differing wings every decade or so.

Only the medical bay and the Master's suite were permanently accessible. Even the kitchens alternated. Sly learned there were three of them in total as Walters led him through a recently unlocked door and down a disused hall.

"I feel like an idiot," Sly muttered as he swiped at a giant picture frame that spanned half the hallway. It was covered by a white, dusty tarp. "All this time, I never thought twice about how big this place was. Little did I know, there were six or seven attached houses just a day's hike away."

She acknowledged his commentary with a resigned sigh, but otherwise ignored him. "The ballroom normally wouldn't be aired out for years yet, but after yesterday, it seemed Kahled was inspired to muck about with my established schedule."

Sly snickered at her obvious derision, but he managed to stifle it.

Walters said, "Here," as she paused before a set of doors twice as tall and embellished as the entryway to the dining hall. One of them was ajar, its handle was the size of Sly's forearm and freshly polished, and there was just enough space for a large man to squeeze through. Sly was relieved he wasn't expected to pull the enormous door open on his own.

There was nothing but darkness inside the room.

Sly glanced from the door to Walters. Twice. "You want me to go in there?"

She nodded and waved him on, her expression expectant.

Sly's eyes darted to the black gap between the doors and back to her again. "Are you sure?"

Her shoulders dropped as she sighed.

From the void came an impatient growl. "Get in here, Earthling."

Walters sighed again, heavier. She strode back down the hall without another word, shaking her head.

Sly leaned on the open door and peered into a whole lot of nothing. "You know, Maestro, the only humans who can see in the dark are heavily spliced, and from an outside perspective, you're coming across as super creepy right now."

He strained to catch sight of Kahled but had no luck.

There was a low, rumbling purr of a large animal, and Sly thought he recognized the awkward thumps and clicks of Kahled's gait, but it was too quiet. Then, it was too fast.

There was no other warning, no visual cue or spoken words. One moment, he was searching blindly for Kahled, the next, a clawed hand snagged the front of his shirt and yanked him inside.

Sly yelped.

The door thudded closed. There was nothing but pitch black, and before his body could decide between fight or flight, his feet left the ground. Sly took a breath to scream, but then the pressure at his back and under his knees registered.

His would-be scream slipped out as a confused "ugh."

In the dark, Kahled scoffed into his ear. Then, there was a sense of motion, and Sly's brain caught up.

"Are you carrying me?"

"Shut up before you ruin it."

"Ruin *what*?"

Sly jerked in Kahled's arms, and he grabbed for the vampire's shoulders on reflex. "Don't you dare drop me."

Kahled laughed at him. The sound was deep and warm,

and it melted away the afternoon's anxiety like it was nothing but a figment of Sly's imagination.

Then, there was softness and smooth fabric all around him as Kahled set him down. He wasn't positive, but it felt a lot like he was sitting in the middle of their bed. In a ballroom. In complete, cavernous darkness.

"I am so confused," Sly stage whispered. "Am I supposed to be excited or terrified?"

"Hush."

"Are you going to murder me? 'Cause this seems a tad unnecessary—"

"Sylvester," Kahled purred.

"Yes, Maestro?"

"Shut up and watch."

Sly wanted to respond with an appropriate quip about the lack of visibility, but Kahled shifted in the dark, and an electronic whir sounded nearby. He was struck speechless.

The dark vanished in a burst of brilliant color.

Sly's eyes adjusted in a few blinks, and his breath caught. His heart stuttered. Time went still.

"Stars," Sly whispered in awe, staring up toward the ceiling. "These are stars?"

"Yes."

And they were. They could be nothing else. He was watching the stars. In full color and large-scale imaging, projected onto darkened walls and shrouded ceilings. A serene nebula played out across the darkness in so many shades of blues and greens and silver, sparkling lights. A galaxy's worth of interstellar beauty spun in lazy waves around them, dotted by distant planets and pearly streams of star dust.

Sly had seen videos and photographs, of course. He lived in an Earthly port, not under the rock. He'd even seen a handheld planetarium once, from a crowd of gawking Earthlings. The memory did not compare to this.

Sly stared up at the heavens and trembled.

"It's just a recording," Kahled murmured.

Sly could feel the vampire's presence, solid and warm beside him, but it didn't draw his gaze. His eyes stung as he stared, fixated on all that otherworldly color.

"It's just clouds here." Sly swallowed a terrible croak in his voice before it could embarrass him. "Sunfire storms. The sky, it's always been deadly." His voice broke anyway. "It's not... this."

This was beautiful. Inspiring. Endless possibility. He didn't have Kahled's way with words, but he wanted to say something profound. He couldn't think beyond how the sight made his insides hurt with want.

He couldn't imagine greater. It was so *much*, even in a planetarium made from black drop cloths and a home projector. It was a glimpse into a world so far beyond his dreams.

Kahled cleared his throat, so soft and quiet, like he didn't want to intrude. "Do you like it?"

"Oh, Kahled." Sly sighed, tears wetting his lashes. "I love it. This is incredible."

Breathless, Sly pried his eyes from the overarching show to look at the vampire, but Kahled wasn't looking at him. His face was lifted toward the ceiling, the look on his face heartbroken and sweet.

"Holy shit," Sly breathed.

The Nocturnus was gorgeous. The artificial starlight showered him in a soft glow that made his eyes and scales gleam with an eerie, cold beauty. The familiar lines furrowing his brow and the corners of his mouth melted away in wonder. He seemed younger. Healthier.

It was surreal, like Sly was stepping back in time and sneaking a peek at a Kahled he'd never known.

"I should have thought of this before now," Kahled brought a hand to his mouth and stroked his beard, attention locked on the overhead display. "I've been so bitter, caught up in missing all I had that I ignored what remains within my reach. This isn't real, but it makes me miss the wider cosmos a little less."

The vampire lowered his focus to acknowledge Sly's staring, and Sly nearly swore aloud when the starlight reflected off those gray irises like white lasers.

"Under different circumstances," Kahled continued in devastatingly soft and alluring tones, "I would have moved entire civilizations to show you this for real. I would have flown you off this miserable little rock and never looked back."

Sly's throat convulsed around a sudden blockage. He turned his attention heavenward, but he couldn't make sense of the swirling hues and fluctuating lights as heat crept up the back of his neck. He tried and failed to ignore the gravity in Kahled's voice.

"It's beautiful," Sly said, shaken.

Kahled purred, "Yes."

"I always wanted to see the stars. For real. It's kind of the ultimate Earthling goal," Sly blabbed. "The Port Science Museum used to do this thing every month. They had this blow-up hut, kind of like this, but cheap. The holograms were old and the projector probably even older, and everything was dulled with age, but Mom used to—we used to love it. Shit. Now, there's no going back. You've ruined me for any mediocre, under-funded stargazing gimmicks forever."

He cut himself off with a laugh. It was forced and raw, nothing like the lightweight chortle he was aiming for.

Kahled laughed with him anyway, small and quiet, but genuine.

"Glad to see my goofy charm still works." Sly flopped backward onto the mattress. He laced his fingers together behind his head like a boney pillow and swallowed the last of his tears. "Damn, I'm good. "

"No, Sly," Kahled said as he lay down next to him. "You're extraordinary."

Sly couldn't breathe. Stars winked down at him as Kahled settled like a smoldering bolder along his side. Dangerous fingers skimmed over his belly, and Sly's lungs refused to cooperate.

"Extraordinary," Kahled repeated, plush lips brushing Sly's ear.

"Not really." Sly kept still, stiller than he could ever remember being, and he trained his gaze on the bright flare of a distant planet. "I'm just some Earthling—"

"You might be all I have left."

Sly winced. "Don't say that."

"My Harem, led by my nearest and dearest family, left me here to die," Kahled said with a scoff. "Emmeline and Gorbon speak a lot of encouragement and promises that lead nowhere, and the rest of the humans cower when I enter a room."

Sly shook his head without daring to look at Kahled. "That's not true. You're projecting—"

A heavy, scaly palm clapped over his mouth.

"No one," Kahled stressed, an intense growl in his voice. "I don't say this lightly, Sly, but not *one* living soul has shown me the same care and consideration that you have lately."

Sly pushed Kahled's hand away and sat up in a hurry.

"You're welcome for the art supplies, but this is little much, even for you."

"And there he goes," Kahled sighed, "destroying a perfectly lovely moment with that abysmal tact."

Sly reared up, spluttering nonsense. He silenced himself when Kahled reached up to cup his chin and tug his face close.

"Let me say thank you, Sly."

Sly blinked twice, wide-eyed and terrified. "You're welcome."

Kahled's hand shifted against the delicate skin under his chin, and a thumb brushed his bottom lip. Kahled warned him, "I'm going to kiss you now."

Sly shivered and leaned into the vampire's touch. "Okay. But I'm not sure that's a good idea."

Kahled paused, not quite ready to follow through on his threat. "Isn't it?"

"Only if you mean it." Sly demanded through a constricted airway. "I'm not playing at Companionship anymore. Okay?"

Kahled inched closer. "Me neither."

"And don't you dare fuck me out of misplaced gratitude or some shit!"

"No," Kahled growled. "I'll fuck you because I want to."

Kahled kissed him.

Sly gasped into it. His mouth opened, startled, but pliant and warm and absolutely, unabashedly eager. Thick arms wrapped around his waist before Sly could process the taste of him on his tongue, before he could marvel at the familiarity mixed with a new rawness that didn't have a name. Sly locked his hands around Kahled's neck and gave back as good as he got.

Kneeling on the bed, Kahled yanked him forward with a

growl, bringing them flush together. The vampire didn't have to tackle him the way he did, considering Sly was already in his arms. Even so, they tumbled across the mattress, and Sly lost track of whose limbs were whose as they rolled over each other.

Something was different. *They* were different. Sly grabbed at the rich fabric of Kahled's shirt, and neither of them cared when it wrinkled and tore. In return, Kahled shredded the clothes from Sly's back with a rare disregard for his claws, and red welts streaked Sly's back with a thrilling burn. Kahled's blunt teeth latched onto the ridge of Sly's collarbone to suck his skin between his fangs, as if the vampire could draw blood without any punctures. He used his front teeth and minded his fangs, but he left many, many marks.

Through it all, Sly's body thrummed with an incessant, bubbling energy. He couldn't lie still if he tried, and he saw no good reason to bother. He scratched at Kahled's skin, admiring the red lines of his nails even as they healed right before his eyes. He pulled at Kahled's ebony hair, even though the vampire never seemed to notice, because it felt silken and glorious wrapped around his fingers.

"Stars and moons," Kahled moaned as he slid between Sly's legs.

Sly clung to the vampire's shoulders as he smiled up at him from his back. "You really want me?"

"You know I do."

Their movements became lost in the undulating starlight, and Sly stopped trying to make sense of anything. He wasn't sure when Kahled's pants disappeared or where the lube bottle came from. He didn't care. Before long, Sly had three of his own fingers knuckle-deep inside his ass, with no distinct understanding of how he'd gotten to that point.

All he knew was the heat and heft of Kahled's body against his. The deep rumble of his lover's moans in his ear. The perfect, thrillingly tight grip of the hands on his hips.

When Sly's hand guided Kahled inside him for the first time, they both whimpered. It stung in the best way, and Kahled didn't give him much chance to wilt before he began moving, rolling his hips and grinding into him like a dream come to life. Sly didn't last long with Kahled's abs rubbing over him with every thrust, but the orgasm was too intense and all-encompassing for him to care.

Kahled's thrusts stuttered as Sly went limp under him. The vampire buried his face in Sly's neck and whined.

"It's okay," Sly panted as he kissed Kahled's temple and rubbed his back. "Go on. I've got you."

Kahled took him at his word, his lower body regaining a fluid rhythm. Sly held on as the continued friction sent jolts of exaggerated pleasure up his spine. He had the wayward thought that the pleasure was sharp enough to become painful if it went on long enough. That was a concern for another time, though.

Kahled pushed his upper body off Sly, tossing his head back with a roar, and it was over. He panted, poised over Sly and haloed in cool tones that glinted off his scales as if he were shedding starlight from his very pores.

"Beautiful," Sly murmured, splaying his hand over Kahled's heaving pec. It was solid, thick muscle, warm and alive to his touch.

"Yes," Kahled said, but he was looking up at the false universe. "It is."

Sly didn't try to correct him. He stroked over Kahled's chest, from a dark nipple to clavicle and back. He did it again and again, petting at the same rate his heart was beating till it slowed to normalcy. That was when he noticed the newest patch of scales emerging on the other side of Kahled's chest. Right over his heart. Sly's whole body went cold at the sight, but he recovered before Kahled could notice the pause in his caress.

Kahled didn't seem to notice. He relaxed into Sly's touch as their bodies separated, settling back on his heels between Sly's thighs.

"I'm sorry," Kahled murmured.

"For what?"

The vampire caught his wrist, interrupting Sly's caresses so he could raise it to his face and kiss into Sly's palm. He didn't quite meet Sly's eye as he admitted: "I think I'm falling in love with you."

CHAPTER 16

*S*ly never responded to Kahled's declaration. They lapsed into silent, introspective cuddles, showered in fake starlight and suspended in heartbreaking confusion. Then again, maybe it was only Sly who felt limp and lazy with soul-heavy want.

Kahled fell asleep curled around him, clutching him gently with the faintest scratch of a claw on his arm, the roughness of scales settling over Sly's belly. His hot, even breaths wafted against Sly's cheek like a calming breeze, the sort of natural phenomena Sly never had the chance to experience on his decaying world. Not for the first time, the vampire reminded him of a covetous dragon, enthralled and protective of his greatest treasure even in sleep.

But Sly couldn't rest. He didn't have the mind or strength to wriggle his way out of Kahled's hold. His body was sore in the best way, and his heart kept launching into a chaotic dance every time he replayed Kahled's words in his mind.

I think I'm falling in love with you.

His mind churned in pointless circles around those simple words. Endless. Exhilarating. Painful.

The ballroom was quiet. Nearby, the hologram projector whirred softly like an eerie lullaby, and the galaxy swirled overhead with a hypnotic calm. The misplaced mattress and plush blankets were an indulgent addition to the homemade solarium that invited all manner of ease and relaxation. At the core of it all, Kahled lay warm and cozy against him.

But Sly couldn't sleep.

He stayed put in Kahled's arms, his lover's tender words ringing in his head. In the quite stillness, such thoughts compounded and tumbled into a cluster of other memories, other voices and other sentiments.

Bloodsuckers, John spat from the darkest corners of his mind.

Blythe's voice echoed with: *you're the only man I know who would get involved with the one Nocturnus in the universe he could outlive.*

And his father intruded with a brusque reminder: *those parasites cheated!*

Then, there was Tilla. *You didn't tell me you were in love with this vampire.*

Eventually, when the insistent thoughts felt like a noose crunching down on his throat, Sly shivered out of Kahled's arms. He sat hugging his knees at the edge of the bed.

That was when he noticed the woven basket set on the floor beside the projector. It didn't have a lid, but from his vantage point, he could see the corner of folded cloth napkins and the protruding neck of a gleaming amber bottle. It wasn't the sort of thing Sly expected to see outside the borders of a hologram or a screen. It took a moment for his eyes to accept it was real.

Sly chuckled at the romance, the corniness. His voice broke right before his eyes started watering.

"You found the rest of my surprise, I see."

Sly glanced over his shoulder to see Kahled watching him, naked and relaxed where Sly left him. He was hugging a bundle of blanket in Sly's stead.

Sly nodded toward the basket. "You know the whole wine-and-dine-thing is supposed to happen before jumping into bed together, right? It's like a rule. Courting 101."

"Oh?" Kahled sat up and slid to the edge of the mattress, bringing himself to Sly's side. "We're courting now, are we?"

Sly's chest constricted. He shrugged. "Maybe?"

Kahled frowned at him.

Sly tilted his head back and set his sight on the false cosmos. "I don't know what we're doing, actually."

Kahled made a noncommittal noise and shifted forward. Sly sensed him leaning toward the projector, and the glorious overhead display dimmed to nothing, encasing them in darkness. For a long moment, nothing happened. Then, there was a click, and the machine hummed, the sound rolling into greater volume.

Then it went quiet.

"Wow," Sly commented dully as his eyes dried. "Very impressive, Maestro."

"Shut up," Kahled growled, but there was a softness, a humor in the sound that made Sly ache.

Then, there was light. Two of them. They were close together, near the device. For a wild second, Sly thought it was a new recording of two singular, distant stars, but then he blinked.

Sly gasped.

It wasn't a projection. It wasn't a trick of the light.

It was Kahled. In the pitch black of the dance hall, with his unaltered human vision, Sly was staring straight at him. At his eyes. They glowed.

"Kahled?" Sly grabbed at the vampire's arm, riveted. "Your eyes..."

"Ignore it," he ordered, refocusing on the projector.

"But—"

"Just another symptom of the Curse. It's not a big deal. Ignore it."

But that was impossible. Kahled blinked, and the dark closed in for a split-second reprieve from the brightness of those twin orbs. It wasn't the cool sheen of reflected light in Kahled's normal gray irises, they were white-hot as if backlit by strong blue flames. It was bright enough for Sly to make out the details of Kahled's facial hair.

Sly stared. He couldn't help himself.

Before he could utter another word, Kahled smacked the unhelpful projector with a resounding crack. It wasn't the newest technology, and Sly suspected it was rescued from the dusty shelves of the basement's communication center.

"...Kahled?"

He smacked it again, harder. Sly jumped, as if the blow were aimed at him, and the projector whirred to life obediently.

The blank canvas of dark walls was drenched in liveliness. Colored light and roiling, wave-like movements surrounded them. It was nothing like the serene cool-toned spacescape from earlier. There was too much color, too much drastic, glorious activity. It was startling, hypnotic, and excruciatingly vivid as the old device gave them a modern clip of celestial activity.

It was impressive. Far enough above their heads, the hologram conveyed enough detail to distract him from whatever was happening with Kahled's eyes.

Sly made a soft, strangled noise as the sight stole the air

from the room as effectively as a vacuum. He fell backward, lying flat beneath the renewed sky with his eyes wide open.

A burst of brilliant purple and pink light scattered overhead. The fuchsia explosion battled the cooler hues swarming from the opposite direction. The effect sent colors and shadows cascading like magic over their naked bodies.

Kahled cleared his throat. "Do you like it?"

"It's incredible, Kahled." Sly sighed. "Is this really what it looks like? Away from Earth?"

"Yes. It's the Carina Nebula," Kahled explained as he stretched out beside him. "Roughly two centuries past, I believe. Kamari forwarded me the recording from our Harem's archives. I thought you might appreciate it."

Sly didn't blink as he watched sparkling green clouds bubble across the ceiling, too fast and chaotic to predict or deny. "This is... Oh, Kahled. It's beautiful."

He winced at the sound of his own voice. There was a strange quality to it that echoed in his head, something raw that made his throat constrict and his heart hurt. He couldn't decipher it, if it was good or bad, but it was a lot. Terrifying. Amazing. Inevitable.

Kahled rolled onto his side, his nose nuzzling into Sly's cheek.

"You're watching high-energy currents colliding over and over," he explained in a hush, "and collapsing gas columns. You're watching stars being born."

Sly's bones felt heavy, anchoring him with a monstrous weight. It felt as if his ribs were threatening to crush his chest, like he'd never catch his breath again.

"It's an area of extreme stellar activity." Lips against Sly's skin, Kahled whispered, "Perpetual motion."

"It's incredible."

"Yes. And intense."

Kahled slipped a hand over Sly's belly, taking his opposite hip in a solid grip. He licked over the pulse point in his throat, and Sly trembled.

"Turbulent, chaotic, dangerous..." Kahled added, each word accompanied by a chaste kiss. "But glorious."

Sly swallowed thickly.

Squeezing his hip, Kahled placed a final, slow, and weighty kiss on his temple. Somberly, he admitted, "It reminds me of you. Or I suppose… you remind me of it."

Sly uttered a stilted laugh and finally tore his gaze from the fake stars. His eyes ached, stinging with reemerging tears. He blinked rapidly to clear his vision.

Colors coiled and raced over so much brown skin. Light beams glinted off so many scales, and those eyes—those luminous, ethereal eyes—were still shining in competition with the stars.

Mouth dry, Sly said, "I love it..."

"But?" Kahled prompted, his thumb stroking over Sly's hip in careful sweeps.

Sly chewed his bottom lip. "I want to see it for real, Kahled."

"Of course you do."

Sly shook his head. "No. No, you don't get it. I've never seen true starlight, Kahled."

"I know—"

"No, you don't." He didn't say it meanly, but with the hard edge of absolute, miserable conviction. "I've spent my entire life hiding from a sky that could kill me in a second on its nicest day. I'm giving the literal blood in my veins to someday look out a window and see a horizon that wasn't on fire."

Sly's words came faster and quieter, panicked. He couldn't watch the sympathetic frown crease Kahled's face further, and he couldn't stand the sight of all the vibrancy playing out overhead. He squeezed his eyes shut and pressed his palms over them for good measure.

"I watched my mother walk outside and turn to ash instead of facing another minute barely surviving here. This place—this planet—it's a death trap."

He felt Kahled deflate against his side, then his warmth disappeared as the vampire pulled back.

Sly hated himself as he whispered, "I can't stay here, Kahled."

"I understand, Sly," Kahled assured him, voice calm and level. "I came here to die, after all."

Wincing, Sly pulled his hands from his face. "Kahled—"

"It's not your fault," Kahled continued smoothly as he sat up. "And I'm not your responsibility. It is, however, our joint misfortune to be here together."

The insidious *for now* at the end of that statement went unsaid.

Sighing, Kahled hefted the basket onto the mattress and set the bottle and two glasses on the dance floor; he upended the rest of the contents on the bed. All manner of choice morsels tumbled onto the space between them, collected in thick glass containers and clear wrapping. The air filled with the thick scent of clean citrus and rich sugars.

Sly watched, silent with wetness lingering on his lashes.

"I wouldn't wish this fate on my worst enemy," Kahled commented as he picked through the foodstuffs scattered between them.

"You deserve better," Sly agreed. "We all do."

"I've had better, Sly." Kahled nodded distractedly, but there was no self-pity in his voice as he plucked something small and dark from the selection. He considered it with a bland expression as he continued, "I didn't appreciate it as much as I should have. Now I'm land-locked, and I'll never go stargazing again."

Kahled looked at him as he rolled the item between his fingers. The colored lights of the hologram twirled around them and highlighted the lines of his face, from those dark brows over shining eyes to the chiseled curve of his cheekbone and straight shoot of his nose. There were no creases or wrinkles from a scowl or despondent unhappiness. He looked calm and settled in his skin.

"Maybe—" Sly paused and bit his lip. "Gorbon thinks I could cure you. Maybe I could keep donating from a distance, or—"

"The Harem's wealthy, but not that wealthy," Kahled interrupted, the corner of his mouth lifted awkwardly over a fang in an involuntary smirk. "We didn't get that way by gambling on uncertain expenses."

Sly flushed with anger. "What about all the investments you've made in people like Mae? Kamari's an idiot if he thinks you're not worth at least that much chance."

Kahled's smirk widened, and Sly thought his amusement was genuine. "No. He's not. Impulsive, but not an idiot. Between the two of you, you might have browbeaten the Elders into reconsidering my exile. Unfortunately, you're a year or two too late to be my hero, Sly."

Sly scoffed at that, his mouth wide with a retort on the tip of his tongue.

Kahled stopped him with an upheld hand. He offered the dark little sphere by waving it under Sly's nose. Sly recognized the rich, nutty cream scent in an instant, even though it had been years.

His jaw unhinged. "Is that chocolate?"

Kahled grinned, and the pride on his face made his fangs seem smaller. "It is."

Sly leaned away from the delectable, eyes narrowing on the vampire. "What are you up to? You've already seduced your way into my pants. Why all the unnecessary charm and bribery?"

Kahled rolled his eyes, lowering his hand. "So suspicious."

"I'm a realist." Sly snatched the chocolate from Kahled's hand, earning a laugh. He took another hit of the decadent smell as he eyed the vampire. "You really think you're falling in love with me?"

Kahled met his stare and held it fast. There was no snark in his voice when he said, "Obviously."

Sly lowered the stolen sweet to his lap, feeling it begin to soften from the heat of his palm. "I like that idea," he said with matching sincerity. "But I still want to go home to my family and leave this place—leave you—behind me."

Kahled's smirk cooled to a resigned smile. "I know."

"I'm an asshole."

"Yes, but I like that about you."

Sly's laugh broke into a sob.

A scaled hand cupped his chin, forcing him to raise his face for the gentlest kiss on the tip of his nose.

"It's okay to be selfish," Kahled murmured, his thumb stroking Sly's jaw. "I don't have the power to make all your dreams come true, but I want more than this for you. I want you to experience the universe without constraint."

"I wish I could take you with me!"

Kahled held him as he cried. The chocolate melted, forgotten.

THE NEXT MORNING, SLY LAY NAKED AND ALONE, WRAPPED IN

an expensive blanket that felt like sin personified, but he felt cold and uneasy. There was no thick arm locked around his waist, no impressive wall of muscle and warmth plastered to his back. It should have been too early for Kahled to be out of bed.

The vampire should be snuggling with him, not rushing to see Gorbon without so much as a goodbye peck to Sly's cheek.

He made his way to the closet and was pulling on loose-fitting pants with a snug waist when he noticed the bruising on his hip. The marks were dark, blues and purples and blacks, and the perfect size to mimic the pads of Kahled's fingers. There was a thin red scratch beside the largest one.

Sly recalled the dull pain from Kahled's grip when he fucked him under the projected spacescape, and his stomach gave a nasty churn. The bruises looked worse than he thought they should.

He finished dressing right as the lights began to brighten with the dawn. When he stepped out of the lift into the main house, the halls were still and sleepy but illuminated for the day.

His footsteps slowed as he neared Gorbon's suite and all its medical necessities. He lingered outside the entrance, fidgeting with the hem of his shirt, pulling at his hair. The wide sliding door had never seemed so clinically imposing before.

Walters appeared at the opposite end of the hall. They saw each other at once, but neither of them said anything as she strode toward him. She studied him with shrewd, cunning eyes the whole while, before coming to a standstill in front of him. She folded her hands in front of her skirt; despite her age, she was every bit the composed, genteel woman Sly once spied in Kahled's sketchbook.

"Did you enjoy the stargazing?"

Sly nodded. "Yeah. It was… a lot."

Her smile was slight and sad.

Sly passed away from her and the med bay door. "I can't stay here." He turned on his heel and shook his head harshly as he journeyed back the way he'd come. "I can't. I won't."

Walters didn't react.

He kept moving. "I'd hate myself if I did. I'd end up resenting him. I won't do that to either of us."

He glanced at the old woman, and she was as serene as he'd ever seen her. In that moment, the lift to her chin seemed less pompous and uptight and more considerate.

"Stop it," Sly snipped without any bite. "Stop standing there staring at me like that. It makes me feel like you're about to swoop down on me and sink your talons in."

She chuckled.

Sly wasn't ready to be on the receiving end of her compassionate sorrow, and it jolted him out of his frantic pacing.

"I was his mother's Companion. Did you know that?"

"Kahled told me."

Her smile waned, weighed down by grief and a lifetime of memories, but it didn't disappear, not entirely. "I never understood why Tahliah settled for me instead of trying for a cure. I spliced as regularly as anyone else in my youth, and by the time I met her…" She sighed, and her eyes fluttered as if the lids were too heavy. "Like his mother, Kahled was born preoccupied with the Harem's concerns. It's what they were raised for, their purpose and their right. Like her, he is meant to be here to care for himself rather than others, and instead, he's been coasting."

There was a cinch in her armor of professionalism. She turned away, the loose skin on her throat rolling with a heavy swallow. It made Sly feel weak, almost light-headed; in the months he'd known her, Sly never saw her falter.

"Kahled didn't come here to get better," Walters murmured, her voice quivering. "I wish he had, but he didn't. He came here to die, alone and far from home. Just like my Tahliah."

Sly took a halting step toward her, twitchy fingers outstretched as if to give her a hug. He stopped himself.

"You loved her," he said lamely.

"Yes."

"You knew she was dying, but you stayed with her anyway." He shifted his weight and followed her vacant stare off toward nothing. "Was it worth it?"

She hesitated to speak. The quiet delay sent his stomach twisting into nasty, sick spirals.

"I wonder if she knew," Walters commented in an even tone, as if discussing the décor. "Tahliah asked me to look after this estate when she was gone and to help any of her kin who might need it. At times, I think she chose me for his sake, so this place and its people might be ready for him."

Sly brushed his knuckles against her arm. "But was it worth it?"

She didn't answer him. Not exactly.

"Even if my blood was as pure then as yours is now, there was nothing I could do to save her. She was ready for it to end long before I came along." She met his eye with a sympathetic smile.

Sly stepped away, shaking his head. "Never mind. Forget I asked."

He couldn't look at her, not even as she took his hand to cradle in her own.

"Take it from someone who knows," she murmured,

"you've already brought him more peace than he hoped to find on this world."

He didn't look at her, but he could hear the warbling tearfulness in her voice. If he looked at her, they would both start crying, and he didn't know if he would ever stop.

"Whatever you do next," she said with renewed strength, "you can do it with a clear conscience and the knowledge that you brought meaning back into his life, even if it was at the end."

Sly's appetite was nowhere to be found, and Walters hadn't incentivized him toward company, so he forwent breakfast. He ignored the path toward the kitchen and dining hall and retreated to the billiards room. He opened the door and immediately regretted that decision.

Felix sat in a corner of the expansive couch, legs tucked under him and a tablet screen bright and alive on his lap.

Sly groaned and spun around to leave.

"It's a community space," Felix drawled after him. "I have just as much a right to use this room as you do."

Sly laughed mirthlessly. "No shit? That's why I'm leaving instead of kicking you out."

From behind, he heard a haughty scoff. "As if you could make me do anything or go anywhere."

The rage that spiked up Sly's spine was a force of nature, strong and immediate and undeniable. He did an about-face and stomped toward the couch. The only reason he didn't swing at the snotty blond was because the damn furniture got in his way.

One hand white-knuckle tight on the backrest's padding, Sly reached over for the nearest couch cushion and threw it. The fluffy square smacked into Felix's face with a satisfying thud that sent the bastard's eyeglasses flying over the armrest and clattering across the floor.

Felix gasped as he lurched to his feet, a hand over his nose.

"I don't know what your issue is, and quite frankly, I don't care!" Sly spat. "You want to fight? Fine. Bring it!"

"You're mental!" Felix gaped at him as he scrambled around the far side of the couch to retrieve his glasses.

"Fuck you!"

Sly lunged for him, and it was downright hysterical how Felix flailed out of range. It didn't seem to matter that the better half of the room stretched between them.

Neither of them was laughing.

Sly's vision blurred, his breath strained, and his eyes stung as he shouted and gesticulated, "I should kick your ass for all the bullshit you've been throwing at me and your holier-than-thou attitude! I should be tearing this place apart for dragging me away from my life! My home! I should hate all of you and walk away without ever looking back, and you have no right to keep trying to make me feel like shit for it!"

"Then leave!" Felix snapped the moment Sly paused to catch his breath. "You keep saying you don't want this, but you're still bloody here!"

"I have a fucking contract!"

"But you don't want it, do you?"

Then, Felix was in his face, his hands balled in the front of Sly's shirt. Sly grabbed at the guy's wrist on reflex, but he didn't know what else to do as Felix shook him like a ragdoll.

"You keep spitting on the idea of Companionship, but that doesn't keep you out of the Master's bed, now does it?"

"Fuck you," Sly hissed, trying unsuccessfully to pry the hands off his person. "It's not my fault Kahled doesn't want you!"

Felix let go, and they stumbled away from each other.

"You're an idiot." The blond stared at him with a stunned

shake of his head. "An absolute idiot. You think I'm jealous that you're with the Master?"

Sly blinked, spluttering. "Aren't you?"

Felix laughed nastily. "I barely know him!"

"Then what the hell, man?" Sly threw his hands up. "Why are you always so mean?"

For a moment, Felix hid his face in his hands and uttered an insultingly amazed chortle. Then, he glared at Sly as if he were being difficult on purpose. "Do you have any idea what I would give to be in your position?"

Sly blanched. "What?"

"Companionship," Felix stressed, as if struggling to explain a complex issue to a thick child. "It's a golden ticket off this miserable little rock..."

"Oh, I'm aware."

"And into a life of easy leisure and endless opportunity!" Felix hissed over him. "You realize if you signed the bloody contract, you would spend the next four or five years in the lap of Earthly luxury, and after the Master's gone, the Harem would set you up for the rest of your life? You could go anywhere, do anything, ask for any bloody thing, and Master Vauqeulin would hand it to you on a silver platter!"

Sly huffed, astounded more than amused. "Is that what Kahled is in your head? No *personal hero* for you, just a convenient cash grab?"

"What on Earth are you on about?"

Sly's whole body burned with revived anger. "Do you even care that he's dying?"

"This conversation's going nowhere." Felix made a sharp, dismissive gesture and turned to snag his tablet from the couch. He made to strut past him, glasses back on and tablet in hand.

Sly grabbed him by the forearm. "I asked you a question."

Felix yanked his arm free, glowering. "Why, Spurgeon? Because it'd be so convenient if I were this callous, shallow person you could feel good about yelling at? Well, go ahead, then. Yell away! Maybe it'll make you feel better for self-sabotaging your way back to a dead-end port."

Then, he walked away, head up and a furious flush on his high cheekbones. Fuming, Sly let him.

CHAPTER 17

Felix's sharp-tongued words and Walters's unwanted sentiments were still wearing on his nerves by dinner time. Sly hadn't eaten anything all day, but instead of joining the staff in the dining hall, he snagged a tray of food from the kitchen and carted it off toward their room.

Kahled's room. Not Sly's. Not *theirs*. Kahled's.

He didn't make it to the elevator.

Gorbon's door glided open as he passed, and Mae swayed, blinking up at him in surprise.

"Thank you," she chirped, relieving him of the food tray. She tilted her head toward the med bay. "Come on."

Sly's gaze darted down the hall toward the elevator before refocusing on Mae as she walked off with his dinner. Sighing to himself, Sly hopped through the doorway to Gorbon's suite and fell into step beside her.

"I'm surprised you didn't show up earlier," Mae commented, shooting him a grin.

Sly hunched his shoulders. "No one told me to."

She laughed, and it was light and easy. Maybe he was

imagining the tightness around her eyes as he followed her into the main exam space.

Gorbon was seated at his desk, intent and frowning at a monitor. He didn't seem to notice Sly's arrival.

There was no sign of Kahled. The opulent, manacled hospital bed was missing from view, the curtain pulled clear across that corner of the suite.

"Kahled's been here all day?" Sly asked.

Mae set the tray on the exam table. "Not quite. I think he went upstairs for a nap around midday. Didn't you see him?"

"I was watching a show in the billiards room," Sly murmured as he approached Gorbon.

Over the doctor's shoulder, he could see various graphs, charts, and lengthy paragraphs of text too fine to read at a distance.

Mae was unveiling the food, chattering as if nothing worth mentioning was going on. "I'm surprised he didn't call for you. He must have really needed that nap." She giggled. "He's quite fond of you, you know. He's been sketching your face all afternoon. Who knew he was so good with a pen?"

"You're very chatty today," Sly commented as he leaned one elbow on the desk beside Gorbon.

"The Master's been in a good mood. I guess it's contagious."

Sly nudged Gorbon. "Why are you frowning?"

Gorbon continued glowering at the screen as he leaned back in his chair, arms crossed. "I'm trying to make sense of the nonsensical."

Sly scowled at the screen, but the better view revealed nothing. "Is this about all those tests you've been running on Kahled lately?"

Gorbon gave a noncommittal hum, his attention trained on the monitor.

Then, Kahled's voice sounded from behind him. "Sly?"

Sly turned around to find Kahled standing just behind the exam table. His shirt front was open, and while his abs might have been distracting at any other moment, they couldn't hold Sly's notice once he spotted the fresh bandage taped over Kahled's hip. It was large, wrapping around his side beneath the hanging shirt, and the other end nearly reached his navel.

"What happened?" Sly demanded as he pushed off the desk to hurry toward him.

The vampire did nothing to stop him as Sly patted his fingertips over the white gauze. There was no reaction at the contact, no sign of pain or worry.

"What are you doing in here?" Kahled asked.

Sly bristled. "I could ask you the same thing!"

Nearby, Mae pouted from Sly to Kahled. "You didn't show him?"

Kahled growled. His eyes darted in her direction for only a moment before returning to Sly.

Mae flushed and pattered off to Gorbon's desk as Sly poked at Kahled's chest. "Show me what?"

Kahled sighed, but he didn't pull away as he raised one hand to peel back the medical dressing.

Sly gasped.

Kahled was covered in scales where there had been bronzed human skin just the night before. They were not the same scattered bits of reptilian platelets that Sly had grown accustomed to. Even beyond the reach of any direct light, they gleamed like glass. Smooth. Hard. Like actual armor. They didn't rest on the skin. They didn't try to blend into the human body. They protruded. Heart pounding in his throat, Sly went to touch the mutation. Before his fingers made contact, he could feel the heat emanating from them, a noticeable degree hotter than the rest of Kahled's body. He didn't need to touch to know the markings would feel hot and solid as metal under the sun's glare. He pulled his hand back.

Kahled's breath hitched, his body tensing. Sly glanced up to see a flash of hurt cross his face before it was schooled into calmness.

Throat tight, Sly rushed forward to blanket the largest patch of new scaling with his palm. It was hot, not enough to burn, but it would be uncomfortable if he kept contact for long. Sly refused to pull away too soon for a second time.

Kahled held back the unsealed edge of his bandage and let him.

"It's hot," Sly observed in a stony tone.

Kahled's abdominals crunched tighter under his palm, beneath the glassy heat of the scales.

"I needed a sample for a biopsy," Gorbon explained. "They're tougher than the previous formations of that phenotype, and we had some difficulties extracting—"

"We tried shaving some of it off," Kahled interjected with a dull, resigned voice. "It didn't work."

Sly glanced back at Gorbon, and the doctor shrugged, leaning out of his chair. "All we got was friction." He cleared his throat as he glanced at Kahled, then added, "And a few sparks."

Sly lifted his palm to peek at the scales again. "Is that why they're so even? They're sanded down?"

"No." Kahled growled as Gorbon choked.

Sly's hand was knocked away as Kahled reapplied the bandage with jerky, impatient movements. "They're unchanged from when I woke up. Nothing he did worked."

Gorbon grunted, rubbing at his beard. It seemed grayer than Sly thought it had been the other day, but maybe he was projecting.

"So… no biopsy?" Sly prodded.

Gorbon's confirmation wasn't verbal, just an awkward blend of nodding and shrugging. In the past five months, Sly couldn't recall him communicating so inefficiently.

Sly huffed, and before his brain could catch up with his hand, he grabbed for the reattached gauze and yanked it clear off Kahled's body.

Mae screeched Sly's name, scolding him. He didn't care though. It was meaningless background noise.

He could see the rest of the area the bandage had covered now. The pristine scales weren't a uniform coat but scattered dots that crept over a hip and rounded the torso. Each scale, regardless of size, was thick and glossy, growing outward from the skin like tumors.

There was one area of exception.

"What did you do?" Sly whined.

A deep groove of raw, ugly red was etched among the gem-like scales. The skin surrounding it was pink and inflamed, and Sly knew the ragged edges to the wound would match the width of Kahled's claws.

Kahled took the bandage from him with a wretched gentleness. "I was angry," he said as he settled the white over all that red, "Gorbon needed a sample, and nothing was working. The—my claws did."

As Sly watched, a corner of medical tape rolled back from the new scales. The vampire sighed and pulled the gauze tighter across his body before putting it back down. Like it was a minor inconvenience. Because the tape wouldn't adhere to the mutated flesh any more than a scalpel would scratch it. That was why the bandage was so large, Sly realized with nauseating dizziness.

"Does it hurt?"

Kahled shook his head, but Sly only saw it in his periphery; he couldn't tear his eyes from the covered wound.

"This happened overnight?" Sly pressed, his voice wavering.

"While I slept."

"The growth became visible while you slept," Gorbon corrected before giving a weary groan as he rose from the chair. "I've been tracking the mutations on a cellular level for weeks now, and it's been speeding up. It's not entirely surprising to see another anatomical change emerge, but..." He ended on a frustrated sigh.

"Wait. Stop." Sly wiped under his eyes with one hand and pulled at the hair tickling his forehead with the other. He couldn't stop staring at the obvious bandage. "I thought my blood was halting the mutations?"

"It was," Gorbon said, "more effectively than we hoped, too. But then… I don't know what changed, but the disease is reasserting itself. He's mutating again. Differently than before, but still involuntary."

Kahled took Sly's shoulder in a warm grip, fingers flexing in a minute massage that did nothing to ease Sly's tension. Sly forced down the urge to pull away from the touch, eyes locked on where a glassy, worrisome growth was creeping across his lover's lower abdomen. It didn't matter that the sight was hidden away like a shameful secret; he could still see it all too vividly. Sly wouldn't retreat though, instead, he reinforced the contact by gripping Kahled's wrist.

"It's only affecting my body," Kahled murmured in a deep, careful purr. "My mind is as clear as ever. I have you to thank for that."

"I don't understand," Sly whispered to no one. His free hand clutched over his middle as his insides contracted and threatened to burst in a mess of emotion.

Kahled set a finger under his chin and lifted his face till he met clear, gorgeously gray eyes.

"You're not curing me, Sly. And that's okay. I never expected this to work, but it's been a wonderful reprieve."

"You can't say that to me." Sly shoved Kahled's hands away from his face, glaring at him with accusation. "You don't get to tell me you're in love with me one day and then throw in the towel the next!"

"That's not what this is."

"What if I gave you more blood?" Sly argued. "We could do feedings twice a day for the last few weeks while… while I'm still… I'm here. I'm still here!"

"It's all right, Sly," Kahled whispered as he enveloped him in his arms, the damned gauze crinkling between them.

He was wrong, but Sly didn't have the energy or the words to explain how. It was simpler—not easier, never easy —to drop his weight into Kahled's waiting hands and let his sobs wash over them both.

SLY SLEPT UNEASILY THAT NIGHT, AND WHEN KAHLED warned him over breakfast in bed that he would be spending the day with Gorbon again, Sly hugged him and waved him out the door without a word. He stayed in bed till an indecent hour.

Eventually, he couldn't stand the quiet emptiness of Kahled's cozy little nest. On a whim, he slipped into the first set of Lunar garments he could find in the closet that would fit, padded barefoot down to the elevator and through the halls, and ultimately planted himself on the billiards room couch. He was numbing his mind with trash reality shows when Blythe joined him via comms.

"What are you doing, Sylvester?" Blythe murmured during a lull in the holographic drama.

Sly's muscles tightened to the point of pain as he shut off his visual transmission.

"Sly? Where'd you go?"

"You're supposed to be helping me verbally eviscerate *The Real Companions of Luna*," Sly reminded her, "If you're going to turn all soulful on me right now, I'm not going to give you the benefit of seeing every tiny thought and emotion run across my face."

He folded his arms, the comms on his wrist squished between his arm and torso. It wasn't comfortable, but it was better than glaring at the cold metal every time Blythe's voice pitched with too much concern for him to ignore.

"Sly. Hun." Her sigh came, muffled from beneath his arm, with none of her reliable sass. "We need to talk about this. What are you doing?"

Despite the fact she couldn't see him, Sly's hand flailed toward the entertainment display. "I would think that's obvious!"

"I'm not talking about the damn show, Sly."

Sly muttered another terse "obviously" under his breath.

"I like it when you talk about him," Blythe said softly. "Your vampire."

"He's not my vampire," Sly snipped. "He's not my anything."

"You're full of shit."

Despite the commonness of those words from her tongue, her absent attitude grated on his nerves. He sat up straighter, stiffer, and shifted his weight from hip to hip on repeat.

"You can't go five minutes without bringing him up," Blythe continued. "I know you like him; I can hear it in your voice."

"Maybe you're the one who's full of shit," Sly suggested.

She gave a quiet, distracted chuckle. "Maybe. But I don't think I'm wrong here."

He snorted as he punched the controller to shut down the show. The hologram disintegrated, and he flopped back into the cushions with a scowl. With his full attention and bad mood trained on the comms, he noticed various noises from Blythe's end. Her apartment was usually quiet, but he could pick up the distant backdrop of *The Real Companions of Luna* from her end.

There was also an irritatingly familiar whir of old plumbing and filtration systems.

"You know, when you first told me what you were doing, I was scared I'd never see you again," Blythe continued, wistful and soft. "Then, you called and told me about this house and this guy, and I was so convinced you would abandon me, and I was going to have to deal with my problems on my own now."

"Don't be stupid," Sly said without feeling, rubbing at his stomach as if it would do anything to ease the cold lump of disquiet festering there.

The noise of celebrity personalities bickering in the background became muted. Blythe's voice came through clearer. More direct.

"I'm fine, Sly. You know that, right? We'll always have each other, but you don't have to come running every time I hit a bump in the road. You can do something just for you. It doesn't have to benefit anyone else."

Sly scoffed, and he didn't need her to tell him that it sounded lackluster and reflexive. "Yeah."

"If you wanted to stay, I wouldn't blame you."

"Do you know why I'm here, Blythe?" Sly jumped up, ripping the comms from his wrist because his hands needed something to do, and the damn thing was starting to feel like a shackle. "Don't paint me out to be some sort of martyr. Yeah, I miss you and Phink and my dad, but my life doesn't revolve around you! I came here, and I'm leaving in a few weeks for *me!*"

"Okay."

"You know how badly I want to get off this fucking rock!" He was shouting at her, at the universe, at everything. "I need more than this! I deserve more!"

"You're right, Sly. I—"

"Do you seriously think I would give up my dreams for a guy?"

In the stunned silence that followed, Sly's heart was ready to burst out of his chest. He stared at the device in his hand, his knuckles white around it. He felt hot and sick and so very, very tired.

"Okay," Blythe eventually whispered. "Just know that we're okay. Me, everyone at Centrism. Even John."

At the mention of his dad's name, the incessant buzz of Blythe's surroundings stuttered in a telling way. Sly knew the sound of pistons and airlocks in disrepair.

Sly frowned. "Are you at my dad's place?"

"Yeah." Blythe heaved a reluctant sigh. "I come over every now and then. Checking in on him, you know?"

"Yeah?" The skin on the back of his neck prickled. Sly plopped back onto the couch and braced his elbows on his knees to curl over the comms. "And he hasn't thrown you out since seeing your new beauty marks? I'm surprised."

Blythe couldn't hold his eye as she said, "It's been months, Sly. They're hardly new. And John…"

Sly held his breath. "Yes?"

She took a while to answer, and Sly began gnawing on his lip, frowning as the wait dragged on.

"He's trying," she said, words coming slow and

measured. "It's not easy for him to accept us living our lives so differently from what he envisioned for us. There's been some not-so-passive-aggressive comments. But he's trying. He misses you."

Sly laughed meanly. "Is that why he hasn't talked to me in months?"

"Just give him time."

"Listen to you, getting all wise and mature."

She didn't deserve the harsh edge to his sarcasm. Her answering chuckle seemed forced. It made his heart hurt.

"Hey," he murmured as he tugged at his hair. "I miss you, you know?"

"I know, but you love that vampire more."

Sly slumped against luxuriant leather of the Harem's furniture. It was so plush and opulent, it practically swallowed him. He was tempted to sleep there for a bit. The thing was more comfortable than anything waiting for him at home. He leaned his head back and closed his eyes.

His mind was ready with a vivid memory of a rich dance hall masquerading as a galactic lightshow. Deep, needful whimpers in his ear. A warm weight on his chest that held him together with easy strength.

"Yeah, I do," Sly admitted. "But I love you too. Sometimes, it's just not enough."

For the life of him, he wished he knew what he was talking about.

"You know what your problem is, Spurgeon?"

Sly froze, and it had nothing to do with the fact he was elbow-deep in the industrial-sized refrigerator in the main kitchen. He leaned back to peer around the fridge door.

Felix was leaning against the island counter, hands balled into fists and a peeved, pinched look on his face.

"You," Felix stressed, "are precisely the type of Earthling that gives humans a bad name in greater galactic circles."

Sly closed the fridge door and put a couple extra inches between himself and the blond. "Didn't know I had that much influence, but okay."

"A Companion's more than a vampire's house pet or trophy donor."

Sly glared at him. "I never said they weren't."

Felix huffed like he thought Sly was intentionally missing his point and stormed off. He came close to knocking Mae and another female servant over on his way out. The two women leaped apart with stricken looks on their faces. They shared a worried glance before the second woman rushed after Felix.

Mae offered Sly a strained smile as she joined him on the other side of the kitchen.

"Don't let him get to you," Mae murmured as she reached for the tea kettle. "He's just jealous."

"Not according to him," Sly grumbled, glaring in the direction Felix had stomped off in. "Why isn't he Kahled's Companion if he cares so much?"

Mae's practiced fingers paused as they prepped a mug. Her shoulders hunched.

Sly turned to her with his hands on his hips, foot tapping. "He implied he's as pure as I am. What gives?"

"He's from Luna," Mae said, shooting him a meaningful side-eye he couldn't interpret. "But he's not from the Vauqeulin Harem."

Sly frowned and threw up his hands. "Then how'd he end up working for them?"

"He followed Gorbon here." She turned away, her cheeks

flushing pink as she hesitated to add, "You know, as his patient. I think."

Sly deflated, flummoxed. "What?"

She shrugged, the pink on her face deepening with discomfort. "He got here shortly after Gorbon did. After Master Kahled was diagnosed, but years before the Elders sent him here. Gorbon was ready and waiting for Kahled, I thought Felix was, too, but they never tried for Companionship."

Sly tried to wrap his mind around that, tried to make it make sense with every uneasy interaction he'd had with Felix so far. He drew a blank.

Mae side-eyed him as he thought. Rolling back her shoulders, she sighed and retrieved a second mug and filled it with tea, water, and honey. She slid it over to him as she sipped her own beverage.

He fiddled with the handle. "You're sure he's here as a patient?"

Her head bobbed in a noncommitted answer. She set down her tea. "I don't know the details. I think he has a blood disorder. Postmodern anemia, I think."

Sly's insides shriveled. "Well, shit."

Mae nodded, shooting that nervously encouraging smile at him again. "You're on the cusp of living his dream, in a lot of ways."

Sly replayed every disdain-ridden conversation he'd had with the blond. He wasn't blind to his own contributions to the antagonism.

"Shit. I might owe him an apology."

CHAPTER 18

*T*he following week passed in a dreamlike blur. It didn't feel real.

There was the reassuring heat and press of a solid arm locked around his waist and the impressive body attached to it. There was sweet freshness set in his mouth by the spearpoint of a claw, clear, floral water to bathe in, and powerful, misshapen hands to brush droplets from his skin. There was the grainy texture of charcoal smeared on his cheek when he interrupted Kahled's drawing, and the poignant scent of acrylic paint whenever he followed the vampire into the studio.

A numbness washed over him. It was gray and endless, highlighted by gorgeous moments filled with the crystalline shine in Kahled's eyes. It didn't feel real, but Sly thought it might be preferable to reality.

"I HAVEN'T CHANGED MY MIND," SLY SAID WHEN WALTERS

caught him between the med bay and the elevator. "Nothing you say is going to make this better."

Walters remained unperturbed. "He's in love with you."

Sly turned his back to her as he dropped his face into his hands. "I know."

"I suspect he's not alone in it."

Sly's eyes stung. He'd shed more tears in recent days than he had in years. He was getting sick of it.

As the elevator doors began to close between them, he couldn't meet her eye. He said, "It doesn't change anything."

SWEETS WERE A RARE LUXURY IN THE PORT, AND FRESH FRUIT even more so. Sly would go to his grave still dreaming of chocolate covered strawberries. Kahled fed them to him by hand. It should have been corny. It wasn't.

"I'll make Kamari gift you a box every year for the rest of your life," Kahled threatened as he kissed fruit juice from his lips. "Once a year. To commemorate my death. You'll never forget me that way."

"You're an idiot," Sly mumbled into the next kiss. "I could never forget you."

GORBON JABBED AT A PURPLE AND BLUE SPLOTCH ON SLY'S inner thigh, and Sly wailed as he slapped the doctor away.

"You should put a stop to that," Gorbon advised as he opened a supply cabinet and fished out a jar.

Sly frowned at the old man. "Stop what? Letting Kahled use me as a chew toy? Because I'm kind of contractually obligated here."

"Your obligations begin and end with bloodletting. And only for three more weeks, as you keep reminding everyone."

Sly folded his arms tight over his chest. "Your point?"

"I have every confidence in your intelligence, Sly," Gorbon said as he opened the jar and held it out to him. "Surely, you realize how much more difficult you're making this?"

Sly didn't say anything as he scooped out a dollop of medicated cream to rub into the latest evidence of Kahled's amorous attentions.

"Kahled has become attached." Gorbon pulled his chair over to the exam table so he could sit before Sly, hands folded in his lap as he peered up at him. "So have you, for that matter."

Sly scrubbed the medication into his leg till his foot started twitching from the reverberations of dull pain.

"I'm not talking about mere sentimentality, Sly. You and Kahled share a rare chemistry. You've been invaluable in his treatment—"

"Stop," Sly said through gritted teeth. "I know. You're grateful. He's at peace. His mind's stable. Yay. Great job! But guess what? He's still dying. My blood's not the miracle cure you were hoping for after all."

"True." Gorbon nodded once, his frown thoughtful. "But the quality of the life he has left is significantly better than what he was facing before you."

"I can't stay."

"You could."

"I can't." Sly shook his head in a fit that made his vision blur. "I want to, but I can't. What about my family?"

"Forgive me..." Gorbon placed his palms on each of Sly's knees and squeezed. "But what makes your family worth more than your own happiness?"

A long, terrible moment passed as Sly struggled for an answer.

"You will not die on this planet," Gorbon said, slow and confident. "Kahled won't let you. He may not be able to follow you off-world, but he would do anything to secure your future if you let him."

Sly's heart stuttered out an awkward, wishful tempo, and his chest ached. Unable to find words for whatever nastiness was growing from that dark pit in his gut, Sly settled for shaking his head.

Gorbon only gripped him tighter, but it didn't hurt. It was grounding. Real. Impressing.

"You could be together," Gorbon implored. "With you, he could have years left. Maybe you can't stop the physical mutations, but his mind, his soul, his heart—he's still here."

"And when he isn't?"

"The Harem can take care of you," Gorbon promised, shaking Sly's knees in tiny jostles. "All you need is the legal precedent in place."

THEY HUDDLED IN THE NEST. SLY SAT CROSS-LEGGED, INCHES from where Kahled mirrored him. Sly's comms unit lay on the blanket between them, its metal harsh against all the comforting fabrics. Sly stared at it with a deep furrow to his brow. He might have stayed that way for an eternity if Kahled didn't help him out of it.

Silent and indisputable, Kahled picked up the comms and looped it around Sly's wrist. There was no scratch of talon, no hesitance or fumbling of his mangled digits. He was graceful, handling Sly and the device with the same care he used to wield a paintbrush.

Sly would know. In the week or so since Tilla's visit, he spent countless hours watching Kahled at work.

The vampire went so far as to turn on the comms for him. Then, Kahled sat back and gave an expectant nod. There was a challenging arch to his brow as he waited for Sly to act.

Under the steady awareness of those perfect gray eyes, Sly tried.

John Spurgeon did not answer his call. Again.

THE NEBULA RECORDING WASN'T HALF AS FANTASTICAL WHEN superimposed over the mismatched hangings around Kahled's bed. It was still pretty, if a little too chaotic. Between the nebulous array of colors and activity and the stationary textiles with all their patterns and textures, it almost hurt Sly's brain to study it too closely. As sweat and lovemaking cooled on their skin, and the energy in the nest calmed to make room for intrusive thoughts, Sly was grateful for the distraction. It was lively. Vibrant and beautiful. It apparently reminded Kahled of him, but Sly couldn't afford to look too closely at the sentiments buried in that information.

Sly watched a star spark to life over a backdrop of checkered purples and reds, careful not to think too much. Kahled didn't let him coast like that for long.

"Kamari could set up a trust fund," Kahled said without moving his stare from the cloth ceiling. "We could figure out a clever excuse to give you the money you need to get him off-planet."

Sly replied, prompt and toneless, "Dad's a stubborn jerk, but he's not stupid."

Kahled didn't try to reassure him otherwise. They lay on their backs, side by side, faces aimed at the pretend sky; they didn't need to move much for Kahled to take his hand and intertwine their fingers. Sly was impressed at the vampire's dexterity; there was no hint of claw glancing off his skin.

The silence returned, but Kahled's words had already damaged Sly's deliberate mindlessness.

He sighed, fingers lax in Kahled's grip. "I don't even know if he wants me to come home."

Kahled gave his hand a squeeze.

"Even if he does," Sly's voice quivered, "I'm in for a rough time convincing him to leave with me."

Kahled said nothing as he rolled onto his side to face him. Hands still joined, Kahled kissed his brow and nuzzled close. He was solid and warm and comfortable along the full length of his body, from shoulder to knee. At that angle, Sly couldn't feel the unforgiving outline of the protruding scales on Kahled's torso.

"I'll never convince him to do it using Nocturni resources."

Silence reigned. There was no comfort in it. It became unbearable after a few stiff moments.

When Kahled spoke, his lips moved against Sly's temple, and fangs combed his hair back. "What if you went without him?"

Sly opened his mouth to answer then snapped it closed. Once more. Three times.

"You can help him fix up the house. Update the weather seals. Kamari could even get you an air filtration system from Luna that could outlast him."

Sly closed his eyes, head shaking as if he could ward off the idea. He didn't raise a hand to block his ears though.

He heard the heavy grief and wistful hope in Kahled's voice when he said, "You could leave him behind to the life he wants and still take care of him."

Sly wasn't sure who he was speaking of. It felt like a punch to the gut.

"DON'T FREAK OUT," BLYTHE'S VOICE ANNOUNCED FROM HIS wrist the following morning.

Sly stalled out in the hall, a stone's throw from the elevator that would take him back to Kahled and the cozy confines of their nest. The steaming tea in his hand sloshed, but it stayed in the mug despite his abrupt halt.

Blythe's harried tone was almost as alarming as her words.

Sly raised his comms and activated the visual feed. Blythe's face appeared in front of him, and she was a gorgeous sight of glowing, spotted skin, precise eyeliner, and artful curls. Try as he might, he couldn't detect any shadows or creases under her makeup. The ball of dread growing in his belly stopped ballooning so fast. Her grimace kept it from deflating.

"What's wrong?"

She winced and attempted to mold the grimace into an embarrassed grin. "Nothing's wrong exactly. Things are just… unusual."

"Blythe."

"I'm moving!" she announced with forced cheer. "Into a house! Yay me!"

He squinted at her. "Whose house?"

She flushed.

"New girlfriend?" Sly pressed. When she shied away from her comms, he changed tactic. "New boyfriend, then?"

She glowered at him.

"Whose house?" he demanded with all the authority their shared history afforded.

She bared her teeth in a would-be grin. It looked painful. "Your dad's?"

Sly didn't know how to respond to that. He wasn't convinced he heard her correctly.

"I told you, I've been checking in—"

"You are not screwing my father."

Her jaw dropped with indignation. "Sylvester! Ew! No!"

"Good," Sly pronounced as the balloon of dread burst with a rush of relief. "Now, what the fuck, Blythe? You're rooming with my dad?"

Her giggle was uneasy. "I needed a change of scenery. And lower rent. Working the bar doesn't match up to stage tips."

"Blythe!" he barked. "What happened to all your savings? Stars above, retirement in Europe can wait a couple more years if it means keeping your roof over your head."

Blythe groaned. "This is why John told me not to tell you. We knew you'd overreact."

Sly spluttered and dropped his mug. Ceramic shattered on the stone floor, and scalding liquid splashed over his toes. Sly leaped back with a yelp, and the lid on his volume was thrown far and wide.

"I thought you weren't talking to him about me anymore?" he shouted. "So, he gets to tell you to keep shit from me while I can't even mention his name without needing to change the subject?"

Blythe grimaced. "That's as much your fault as it is mine."

"Oh, fuck off." And he ended the transmission.

Behind him, he heard the easy hum and glide of the

medical suite entrance opening. After a few halting footsteps, he heard Gorbon speak.

"Sly? Is everything all right?"

Instead of answering, Sly tossed his head back and screamed through clenched teeth.

KAHLED WAS A MIRACLE WORKER. THEY MADE LOVE LIKE IT was going out of style. They talked about nothing and everything, from the painfully important to the slightest asinine thought that crossed their minds. It was everything Sly needed to let his anxiety and guilt float away like so much meteor dust. Despite Sly's moodiness and everything hanging over them, the vampire managed to ease them into conversation and indulgent, mindless touching at regular intervals.

There was no telling which of them needed it more.

There were moments of glorious, heartfelt laughter. Stifled snickers as Kahled's beard tickled Sly's neck. Soft, lazy chuckles as Sly regaled the vampire with stories of his childhood in the port and notable nights at Centrism. Whenever one of them uttered an unexpectedly sassy comment or a surprisingly light anecdote, they fed into each other's mirth till it burst from them in unrestrained roars.

Kahled sat up in bed after a particularly boisterous bout, and Sly's relief vanished. There were new scales, more of that enhanced growth appearing along the curve of Kahled's shoulder blade. It was no more than seven or eight platelets, but they rose from the skin and gleamed like shards of metal embedded in his flesh.

In an instant, the pause they had set on the world broke apart, and reality reasserted itself.

Kahled felt him staring and turned to quirk a brow at him. "I can hear you thinking."

"Yeah?" Sly scooted closer and leaned on Kahled's arm so he couldn't see the emerging mutation. "What am I thinking then, Maestro?"

"Too much."

A thick arm curled around Sly's waist. It tightened, warm and perfect and inescapable without being painful. Sly rubbed his cheek against the sculpted curve of Kahled's shoulder and raised a hand to trace the cords of muscle spanning the vampire's ribs.

He was strong, intimidatingly so, and while Sly suspected he'd been smaller before the disease conquered his body, he found it impossible to imagine Kahled as anything less. Even if he'd been wholly human, Kahled was bound to be head and shoulders taller than himself.

In a seamless haul, Kahled lifted him into his lap. He lipped at Sly's ear and ordered, "Stop thinking."

Kahled could have hurt him beyond recovery at any point in recent months. Sly was always aware of it, but in that moment, he realized how complete the disparity was. Kahled wouldn't need claws or fangs to destroy him. He probably never needed them to assert himself.

He simply chose not to.

"What's wrong?" Kahled asked, bumping their noses together with so much intent and affection.

"Nothing." Sly chuckled quietly. "Everything."

It was a shitty situation they were in. Kahled was no more at fault than he was, and he was going to let Sly run free from it without him.

Sly said, "I love you."

And Kahled said, "I love you, too."

The vampire pulled back enough to frame Sly's face in

his hands. A lone talon pricked at Sly's head through his hair, but it wasn't important.

Sly was no Moon Diva. His skin was rough and creased from stress and a lifetime of poor quality water and air. His hair was plain and boring up till the moment Walters and her tailored products got weeks to work their magic, and even then, it only brightened the coppery reds like a cruel mimicry of Earth's skyline.

But in Kahled's hands? Under his crystal clear eyes? Sly almost felt beautiful. He felt worthwhile.

They made love because the moment demanded nothing more or less.

Kahled growled, "Mine," against his cheek as he came, and it was so perfect, Sly's eyes watered.

Sly was overwhelmed. Kahled *took* and he *owned*, and Sly let him with an ease that was terrifying. For once, just once, he allowed himself to imagine never wanting anything else. Then, he was plummeting head-first off a ledge he never expected to reach in the first place.

The relief—for the love of the cosmos—the relief was devastating.

There was no mass of responsibility weighing him down. All the worries and grief, the dreams and people, the Earth and the sky—it all fell to the wayside. He floated away.

For the first time in his life, Sly felt free.

THAT FREEDOM DIDN'T EXTEND BEYOND KAHLED'S PRESENCE. He had two weeks left. Less. One week and six days. Maybe a handful of hours. Sly told himself he would be home soon, but it made him feel hollowed out and weepy. It felt like a lie.

Then, Phink reached out to him.

His soon-to-be-reinstated boss grunted through the comms, "When are you going to be back?"

And Sly didn't know what to say, what to do. His mouth worked without uttering a sound.

"I can't put Blythe back on stage, not to mention as my headlining act." Phink huffed and puffed, his projection bristling like the spitting image of an agitated animal. "The Nocturni are getting antsy with both of you out of the spotlight. Yesterday, Le Vau threatened to sue HEPP on your behalf for wrongful indenture or some nonsense like that. Can you believe it?"

Sly responded with a lackluster hum.

"Stars above, Sly," Phink bellowed. "Of all the times for you to learn how to hold your tongue, you pick now?"

Sly shook himself and tried to rally his thoughts. He really did try. "I don't know, Phink. I'll be back soon. Le Vau and the others can be patient for a few more weeks."

Phink wasn't pacified. "The House's profits are dropping. I never marketed you as pure, but you drew in big money. Without the Lunar Harem's trickling through the door for a glimpse of your skinny ass, I'm not meeting HEPP's quotas. And with Blythe's shit going on, I'm starting to worry they might ask me to resign."

It was like the world was spinning into overdrive, gravity crushing down on him with unrelenting force from all sides. Sly slumped under it all and didn't have the gumption to straighten up again. He sighed, and it didn't begin to express how exhausted and heavy-hearted he felt.

Phink didn't seem to notice. His fur-lined eyes darted around his un-projected office in a constant loop as he ranted. "Tilla has touched down three or four times since you left, but they haven't stepped outside the trade warehouses once. I hate to say it, Sly, but I need you here. We don't have to promote it or anything, but it wouldn't hurt to leak a minor suggestion that you went to work for a Harem because you're pure—"

"Phink," Sly interrupted at that point. "My blood status has gotten me into enough shit lately. Don't you think?"

Face falling, Phink raised a hand in acquiescence. "You're right. I shouldn't have suggested it."

"Probably not."

"Yeah." Phink's laugh was disturbingly unfamiliar, hoarse and resigned. "It's long past time I start listening to you. You're a rude little shit when you want to be, but you've always been smart."

"Aw!" Sly crowed, hand over his heart in affectation. "Phinkster! You say the nicest things."

But Phink wasn't listening. His gaze was distant, and there was nothing teasing in his tone as he grumbled over Sly's snickers. "I should have paid closer attention when you warned me about the Humans First crowd. Blythe, too, for that matter."

Sly's humor evaporated faster than a puddle under the sun's glare. "Did something happen?"

With a distracted shake of his head, Phink said, "Not really. Posturing, for the most part. They tried staging a boycott, but it turns out that purity extremists don't have the numbers for that to be effective. Since then, we've chased a few vandals off. Had to call the Guard a couple times, but it's just for show."

Sly's shoulders began to unwind. They shouldn't have.

"I mean, it's not really Centrism they have an issue with, anyway," Phink continued. "I just wish I could do more for Blythe when she's not here, especially after what happened."

Sly perked up. "What?"

Phink frowned, shifting about as he focused on Sly. "Blythe didn't tell you?"

"Tell me what?"

"A couple Humans First jerks..." Phink's lip curled with distaste. "They showed up at her apartment a while back. Scared the shit out of her."

The lump of awfulness festering in Sly's gut iced over.

BLYTHE DIDN'T ANSWER ANY OF HIS ATTEMPTS TO CONTACT her. Neither did John, but that was nothing new. Sly might have worried himself into literal sickness if it weren't for Kahled.

They were in the studio. Kahled sat at a carved wooden table that Walters had repurposed for his desk, a sketchbook splayed out under his hands. Sly didn't know what he was working on.

The human was too busy stomping in circles round and round the room as he fretted.

"I knew she was hiding something!" Sly carried on without pause. "I've been so wrapped up in you that I didn't press, but I should have!"

"Maybe she thought it wasn't worth worrying you over?" Kahled suggested, still intent on his drawing. "She might have been spooked when she told Phink, but she calmed down enough to realize that was all it was. She's clearly unharmed, and you've more than suggested she had a tendency toward dramatics."

"She moved in with my father," Sly said, deadpan. "A trained Guard."

"That doesn't necessarily mean anything."

Sly scoffed at that. "And it's such a convenient

coincidence she's dodging my calls now that Phink tattled on her?"

Kahled raised his head to shoot Sly an unimpressed look over his shoulder. "You're not the center of her universe, Sly."

Sly flushed. "I know that!"

Kahled chuckled. He set down his pen and rose from his chair so he could lift it. It was a solid piece, sturdy enough to hold his bulk, but the vampire maneuvered the thing as if it weighed nothing and set it back down facing Sly. When he retook his seat, he set one deformed ankle over the opposite knee, hands resting on his thighs. His undivided attention was trained on Sly.

Sly swayed, struck dumb.

In that moment, Kahled didn't look like he was dying, he didn't look like someone Sly had any right to touch. He looked like a king. It was in the proud ease of his posture, the cool yet sympathetic composure in his voice. The hot temper and sharp sarcasm Sly usually expected from him were nowhere in sight, replaced with determination and a practiced calm. It wasn't quite like he'd donned an authoritative mask but more like he'd slipped into a well-worn coat.

Not for the first time, Sly wondered about the Nocturnus Kahled had once been.

Sly deflated. Every cutting word and raving sentiment poised on his tongue dried up. He felt childish under that knowing gaze.

If Kahled noticed the change in his demeanor, he didn't show it. He waited, still and patient, till it was obvious Sly wasn't about to open his mouth and keep going.

"Walk me through this," Kahled said, and while it didn't have the hard ring of an order, it was an irrefutable direction all the same. "Let's say Blythe told you the moment she was confident her unwanted visitors were gone. What purpose would that have served?"

Sly started bouncing his leg as he thought that scenario through. "I could have helped her. Maybe."

"How?"

"We'll never know." Sly threw up his hands and let them fall back to his sides with a resounding smack. "But if the past's anything to go on, I could have done something."

Kahled's eyebrow lifted. It was difficult to tell around the fangs, but he seemed to be fending off a smirk.

Sly squirmed and added, "Probably."

"I see. Then, you have experience mediating with aggrieved Humans Firsts activists, do you?"

Sly thought back to all those poker nights John had taken him to as a kid. He'd spent most of them goofing off at the bar or trying to teach himself how to count cards to no success. The moment he was old enough to be invited to the table, Sly decided to let John go on his own from then on.

"Not exactly," Sly admitted, frowning.

"Smart," Kahled commented, "but unhelpful where your friend's situation is concerned."

Sly snorted. "She should have just listened to me in the first place."

"Sometimes, we need to make mistakes." Kahled shrugged one shoulder. "It's how we learn."

"You are being infuriatingly calm about this," Sly scowled, hands tight on his hips. "Come on, Evil Overlord, Mr. Renowned Harem Leader. Isn't it the tiniest bit concerning to you that someone close to me might be targeted by these people?"

"Not especially," Kahled said as he rubbed at the dark scruff on his chin. The beard was getting long, thicker than anything modern humans could grow without splicing, and

Sly wondered if Kahled would let him help shave again. He now knew shaving lather was a poor substitute for lubricant, but there was a thrilling intimacy to holding a razor to a lover's skin without harm.

The thought was distracting.

So, naturally, Sly doubled down. "What if they kidnap her and hold her hostage?"

Kahled paused, a baffled frown crunching his features. "Why would they do that?"

Sly made a rough gesture at him. "To get to you! Through me! If Humans First folks know where she lives, they probably know she's friends with me and that I'm shacking up with a vampire. They'd jump at a chance to use someone who personally offended them against a Harem. They're probably plotting away in some dive bar to use her to force me to do something terrible like—" Sly canvased the room for inspiration, and he spotted a wrapped canvas on the desk with "*For Mari*" scrawled across it. "Like make me set up Kamari for an ambush!"

Kahled responded with a confounded sneer. "But Kamari never goes to the ports."

"How do you think he found me?"

Kahled rolled his eyes without dropping his royal demeanor. "They missed their chance, then."

Sly huffed. "You say that, but when we start getting packages with Blythe's toes in them, I expect an apology for your lack of faith."

Kahled shook his head as the smirk he'd been denying bloomed across his face.

"Oh!" Sly strode toward Kahled to jab a finger into his chest. "And I'll need your complete and unrelenting assistance in bringing her home safe."

"Of course, Earthling." Then, Kahled hooked a human

finger in the front of Sly's waistband and tugged. "Now, stop pouting, and get over here. I have something more pressing for you to worry about."

BLYTHE GOT IN CONTACT WITH HIM BEFORE THE SUN ROSE THE next morning.

"You don't have to worry about me," she said, but Sly was critical of the weary drag in her voice.

"Turn on your video," he demanded. "Let me see your face."

She sighed. "It's getting late, Sly. I'm in my pajamas. No makeup."

"So? I've seen you naked."

She groaned. "Just don't freak out, okay?"

Sly's gut burned with heightened alarm. "You're not helping your case. Show me."

Blythe took her time. When her likeness glowed into being over his wrist, Sly uttered a sharp cry before clapping a hand over his mouth. It wasn't the blueish bags under her eyes or the unkempt state of her hair that startled him, though that was concerning, too. The skin on her cheek was mottled with the sick greens and yellows of a healing bruise.

"Why didn't you tell me?" Sly whimpered.

Blythe shrugged, her lips pursed and gaze downcast in embarrassment. "There was nothing you could do from the other side of the planet. I figured it was time I learned to fight my battles on my own."

CHAPTER 19

*D*ays later, a sharp, feral snarl rang in Sly's ear in the dead of night. He jolted upright in bed, but there was only darkness within the nest's fabric hangings. Darkness and the persistent, rolling voice of a beast.

"Kahled?"

Sly's heart pounded. Blind, he got to his knees and reached for the vampire. He could feel where the bed dipped toward a mountain of body heat, and he found Kahled's shoulder in the next moment.

His voice trembled when he whispered, "Maestro?"

Kahled vibrated under his touch with gurgling growls. Sly eased his palm over the curve of a familiar shoulder to rub at his bicep, and every internal alarm he had shrieked anew as he discovered thick, armored platelets.

"Shit. Kahled?"

Fingers featherlight and slow with nerves, Sly explored what could only be another patch of mutated skin. It was large. Shaking, Sly used both hands to circle Kahled's arm, and there was an inch's worth of hide along the outer side of

265

his bicep. The impenetrable sleekness of the new scales was uninterrupted from joint to joint. Kahled's elbow felt rough and wrong, the scales smaller than ever, like embedded pebbles.

"Are you awake?" Breathing hard, Sly shook the vampire.

The bestial noise was cut off. The resulting silence was nauseating, and Sly imagined he could hear his own heart sprinting through it.

Sly never heard a yawn, never felt the terribly developed arm under his palm tense for movement. He never sensed Kahled waking fully. One second, he was sitting in absolute darkness with a wary hand on an unknown disfigurement, and the next, he was flying back from a whirlwind of heavy motions and haphazard flashes of light.

Kahled gasped upright, coiling into a crouch on the far side of the mattress.

Sly could see him now. It was impossible not to. Kahled's eyes were glowing again, wide and panicked and illuminating the nest in a cool silvery sheen. It might have been beautiful if it weren't so concerning.

"Hey!" Sly whispered in a hurried hiss as he raised his hands in deference to whatever episode had hold of his lover. "Kahled? Calm down, okay? What happened?"

Kahled wasn't blinking. Sly wasn't sure if he was breathing as he turned his head every which way, searching for threat or risk like a cornered animal. He was quiet, still, and poised precisely like a predator in wait.

Sly's gaze wavered, and he noticed the scales.

"No," Sly whined. He dropped his hands as he fell back into the pillows.

The scales were exactly like the ones blooming over Kahled's hip from the previous week. Glassy smooth and indomitably strong, they blanketed Kahled's upper arm and, worse, the patch on his torso had spread far beyond its previous scope, streaking over his ribs and slowing to a trickle over the side of his chest. The patterned growths diminished in size as they neared his navel, down to the pinprick spots of scaling Sly thought he'd felt on the elbow.

As alien as he looked, as horrid as the implications were, none of it was as heartbreaking as the frightened anticipation on Kahled's face.

Sly got back on his knees and held his arms open. "Hey, Maestro. Look at me. Please, Kahled."

He did, and his eyes were too large and bright to meet head-on. Sly winced.

"Sly?" Kahled asked in the voice of a scared child.

"Right here," Sly murmured, going to him with his heart clogging his airway.

Shuffling on his knees, he didn't have to go far before Kahled met him partway. Neither of them expected his massive form to move with such fluid speed.

Then, there was pain, sharp and brief as it streaked along Sly's jaw.

"Oh!" Kahled cried, jerking away.

Staring back at Kahled, Sly lifted a hand to his own face and felt a thin line of blood welling to the surface. It took a long while before he realized what had happened.

Kahled whined, "I cut you!"

That wasn't right. Kahled was always so vigilant about his claws. In their months together, sleeping side by side, Kahled had never cut him, not once, without the intent of bloodletting.

Sly gave the wound a tender pat. Blood smeared, but it was minimal, already scabbing. Sly ignored it as he reached for his lover again.

Kahled shied away, shaking his head.

"It was an accident," Sly reassured, chasing after him. "I'm fine."

"I cut you."

Sly refused to acknowledge the aching resignation in Kahled's voice. The vampire's face smoothed into blankness as Sly took each of Kahled's hands in his.

Sly gasped in fresh hurt as a fine point jabbed into his palm. Uncomprehending, he looked down to see the new claw on Kahled's pointer finger part from Sly's hand. It was small, the same size as the nail had been when they fell asleep wrapped up together, but the surface was thick and hardened like metal, growing into a short, wicked point. It wasn't like the talons on his three monstrous digits, but it was well on the way there.

As Sly stared, Kahled slipped out of his hold.

"No." Sly latched onto the vampire's wrists. He refocused on Kahled's face, but there was no visible reaction to glean anything from. "It's okay. It's purely physical. We'll work around it—"

"I should send you home early."

"No." Sly crawled over and wrapped his arms around Kahled's shoulders. "Don't you dare shortchange me. I'm still here. I'm still with you."

Kahled's voice was dull as he countered, "It's not safe for you."

"Fuck that. You've always had claws. I don't care."

He clung to the vampire, thrumming with a nervous energy that had no outlet.

Kahled didn't hold him back. He didn't push him away either, but Sly could feel the distance growing nonetheless.

"What can I do for you?" Sly begged, his nose against the fine point of the Nocturnus's ear. "Let me help. Just tell me how, and I'll do it."

He felt Kahled's throat shift as he swallowed. "I don't want to hurt you."

"Then let me hold you. Let me help." Sly tightened his arms till his muscles screamed. "Can I sing for you?"

It took forever for Kahled to nod, once and weak, but it was enough. It had to be enough.

Sly hopped onto Kahled's thighs and wrapped his legs around him, clinging as he sang "Starlight Daydreams" into Kahled's ear. He managed three versus before his voice broke and finally—*finally*—Kahled hugged him back.

KAHLED DRAGGED HIM DOWN TO THE MEDICAL SUITE SO Gorbon could superglue the scratch shut and assure them it wouldn't scar. Sly found the liquid bandage more irksome than the red line under it would have been on its own, but Kahled wouldn't stop fretting till it was professionally cleaned, examined, and bandaged.

After that, Sly was banished from the room so the doctor could do his real job and tend to the vampire. It was still dark when Sly was being looked over, and Kahled was holed up with Gorbon before the dawn lights turned on for the day. Sly wanted to be in the room with them, but Kahled didn't look like he could handle that. He didn't want Sly watching whatever medical bullshit Gorbon had to do to him.

Around breakfast time, Walters found Sly sitting on the floor across from the medical wing's entrance, his back against the wall.

"Come along, Mr. Spurgeon. We have something to discuss."

He expected her to lead him back to Kahled's rooms or perhaps down to the kitchen for a rare meal removed from the rest of the household. Instead, he followed her with uncharacteristic silence right up to the billiards room doors.

"Here?" He stared as she flung one of the doors open. "Really?"

Shoulders back and back stiff, Sly followed her inside. When he pounced on his preferred spot in the center of the sofa, he found himself curled into a squished ball of useless agitation. He watched Walters with blatant distrust as she connected her comms unit to the large holographic display.

Kamari Vauqeulin beamed to life in actual size and detailed rendering.

Sly blinked and uncurled to raise his head in surprise.

He almost didn't recognize the Nocturnus. The fine fur that once lined Vauqeulin's face was gone, leaving him perfectly smooth and pretty in comparison with his high cheekbones and aquiline nose so exposed. The only hair that remained on his face was a tasteful goatee and a sculpted version of Kahled's thick brows. His eyes were still golden, his ears large and pointed with canine affectation, but the gold was receding to brown, and the ears were less furred and smaller than he remembered them. His hair was tamed into a severe braid. His attire was subdued from the unique purple outfit Sly remembered last seeing him in. The new suit was black and refined, with a pale green blouse tucked under the blazer.

He was the picture of a powerful leader of an elite Harem, a true scion of the original bloodlines. His projected visage looked like a staged advertisement.

"Nice getup," Sly said, eyeing the vampire from head to toe. He breathed a little easier when he noticed the glittering stiletto heels on Vauqeulin's feet. "How's Ethos treating you?"

The Nocturnus's mouth twitched with a sneer, but he fought it. "We're not here to talk about me."

Sly rolled his shoulders back and sighed. "Kahled?"

"Of course."

Walters settled on the couch beside Sly, ankles crossed and hands folded in her lap. "It's time to negotiate, Mr. Spurgeon."

Sly glared between them, exuding suspicion. "Negotiate what?"

They answered in unison, "A Companion Contract."

Sly groaned.

"Kahled adores you," Walters cut straight to the chase. "Surely, you know that?"

"Yeah. He loves me." Sly's throat closed, and he couldn't meet their eyes.

"And that means nothing to you?" Vauqeulin asked with measured calm.

"It means everything!" Sly snapped, leaning forward with his fists clenched over his knees. "But it changes nothing. I have people waiting for me in the port."

"You mean your father?" Walters prompted without shame. "The man you haven't spoken to the entire time you've been here?"

Sly glared at her. "My family disputes are none of your business."

"Enough."

Sly's head jerked around, convinced he'd see Kahled in the doorway. But it wasn't Kahled who spoke; it was his brother, Master Vauqeulin. Kamari.

The Harem Heir had his hands raised in placation, but his expression was full of warning. Both humans heeded the unspoken command to be quiet, but Sly noticed he didn't have his brother's presence, his effortless authority; Sly doubted the virtual attendance was a big factor. Kamari gave off the impression of a child imitating their role model.

"Sly," Kamari said, grave and shaken, "I want to give you a formal offer for Companionship."

Sly was shaking his head before the statement was finished. "Kahled won't agree to it."

"He doesn't have to." Kamari shifted, his unease obvious despite the confidence in his words. "Strictly speaking. I'm in control of all the Harem's resources, and if you and I make an agreement—"

Sly cut him off with a cold laugh. "I don't care how rich or entitled you are, that's not how consent works."

Kamari sighed, and it was irritated and sad, and it made Sly want to throw a couch pillow through the hologram.

Walters gifted the Nocturnus a moment to compose himself. "Kahled should not be your responsibility..." she said, setting the pads of her fingers against Sly's shoulder. "But the fact remains, you've made a significant impact. And that's not limited to a biological level, but mentally and emotionally as well."

Sly snipped, "Not sure if you noticed all the time he's spending with the doc lately or all the shiny new phenotypes taking over his body, but it looks like I've barely delayed the inevitable."

"You're right," Kamari huffed. "The disease is adapting too fast for you to stop it, and in ways we've never seen. For all we know, you might be exacerbating the physical mutations."

Sly interrupted, "You're not blaming that on me."

"But think of his mind, Sly!" Kamari shouted over him, wolfen eyes pleading. "His soul? His heart? All the best parts that make him who he is, they're still intact, thanks to you. Are you really going to condemn him to a short, miserable existence when you have such power to drastically increase the quality of whatever life he has left?"

Sly's insides felt rotten. The evil lump in his gut had only grown stronger and more noxious in recent days, and Kamari's speech doused it with fuel.

"He loves you," Walters repeated.

Sly squeezed his eyes shut. "I know!"

"And I know you feel something for him."

"Look!" Sly cut her off with a rough flap of his arm, wheeling between her and Kamari's projection. "Yes. I love him too. There aren't words for how badly I wish this would work, but it won't! He doesn't want me to stay here any more than I want to be!"

That was the point that broke him. In a rush, tears flooded his eyes, and the avalanche of emotions he'd been holding at bay since Tilla's visit came crashing down. Standing untethered in the billiards room, Sly hid his face in his hands and cried.

Kamari and Walters let him. They didn't intrude. He had no clue if that was good or bad.

Sylvester Spurgeon was not the most creative of men, and it was frightening how easy it was to imagine the future they were offering him. He could see himself calling up Blythe and telling her to come visit sometime because he was never coming back and maybe, just maybe, he deserved to be happy for a change. Sure, he would miss his dad and Phink and all the folks at Centrism, but Kahled's dry humor, his teasing, and his misshapen smile seemed like a fair trade. It wouldn't last, but while it did, it would be wonderful: hours making love under artificial skies and eating culinary treats from the luxury of a designer mattress dressed in Lunar silks. He would be free to lose himself in this tiny corner of the world, this sliver of the universe where Kahled existed and made him weightless with laughter.

And when Kahled was gone, he would catch a one-way ticket off this hellscape and never look back. Alone.

Panting through his sobs, Sly moaned out his final argument, "Even if he were healthy, he'd outlive me half a dozen times over, and he'd have to get over it eventually, anyway." His voice croaked, the words strangling, "At least this way, things aren't drawn out. We don't have to watch the end coming straight at us."

"So, you get to run away?" Kamari's voice was cold, and Sly was glad he hadn't lifted his face from his hands. He didn't want to see whatever expression Kamari was regarding him with. "You get to leave him first, rather than hold his hand so he can die on you?"

"Yes!" Sly ripped his hands over his face and into his hair, nearly scalping himself with his nails. "Since those are my only shit options, then yes!"

He met Kamari's stare, and the mournful anger on that lovely face felt like a punch to the gut.

Then, Walters was beside him, her thin, wizened hands firm on his arms. "I understand," she said, full of heartache and determination. "You didn't ask for any of this, and it's not fair. The kind of chemistry you and Kahled have is rare, even for Companionships."

He glared at her with stinging eyes and a wet, messy face. "Why are you making this so hard?"

She wasn't crying, but her throat flexed with empathy that threatened to be debilitating. "I won't lie to you. Watching someone you love die is the most difficult thing you could ever do. But it's worth it. I would do it all again in a heartbeat."

She held his gaze, held his weight upright in her hands, and Sly had never understood another person so well. He felt weak and small, insignificant and aimless, and she reflected it all back onto him with years of experienced conviction. She was with him, not only in the moment, but in spirit.

John wasn't there. Blythe wasn't either.

Sly waivered.

And Kamari fucking Vauqeulin saw it.

"We'll take care of you," the vampire murmured.

Despite the unfathomable distance between Earth and Ethos, Sly thought he could feel him at his shoulder. A damnable whisper in his ear. Promises too good to be true.

"Stay with him, ease him through this last struggle, and I swear, the galaxy will be laid at your feet. You could live out your life on any planet of your choice at the Harem's expense. You won't have to lift a finger if you don't want to."

Sly felt sick. He swayed on his feet, and he knew, beyond doubt, that he was going to hurl all over Walters's pristine, pleated skirt.

"Your father will want for nothing," Kamari soldiered on. "I'll talk with my contacts at HEPP, and they'll make sure he's taken care of. He never has to know the Harem was involved."

Sly squeezed his eyes closed again, clenching harder than ever. Instead of relieving darkness, all he saw was Kahled, moping in a miasma of despair, reduced to the mess he was the first time Sly entered their bedroom.

Their bedroom. That wrecked bedframe and it's whimsical, slapdash canopy. The nest he made for Kahled with his own two hands, the one he pictured on reflex when he thought of home.

He opened his eyes again. He met their expectant stares. His throat closed, and dark spots popped into view as his knees threatened to give out. He heard himself speak, but it echoed in his head, distant, as if someone else were speaking.

"How long?" he croaked. "How long do you think I could have with him? If I stayed?"

Ultimately, the answer was longer than expected, but not long enough.

SLY MET KAHLED IN THE FOYER. THE ELEVATOR DOOR SLID back, and Sly was greeted by the sight of his lover leaning on a cold empty stone wall waiting for him. His fine clothes hid the most damning of the deformities like they usually did, but the gauze mitten on his left hand gave Sly pause.

"What did you do this time?" Sly demanded. "Pry off a fingernail for Gorbon? I'm pretty sure that's considered torture, and that's probably illegal on most worlds."

"It's just a necessary precaution." Kahled glanced down at his wrapped hand, his face stoic. "I didn't want to cut you again."

Sly scoffed. "You won't."

"I might."

"Not on purpose."

"That's not good enough—"

"You're good enough."

Kahled's mouth snapped closed. He gave Sly an unamused glower.

Sly stepped closer with a shrug, willing himself into a nice, casual pose as he joined Kahled against the wall. "You're good enough for me. Exactly as you are." Sly wove his arm through Kahled's, hugging his much thicker limb.

"Scales and all."

Kahled scoffed. "You're impossible."

It was a curious way to say *I love you*, but Sly understood it. In response, he rested his cheek on Kahled's chest, and the vampire bent to kiss the top of his head. It was so soft, it tickled, and the fangs didn't even register against his scalp.

"Will you hate me when I leave?" Sly asked. A chill stole over him as he tacked on an unhelpful qualifier, "Next week."

"I doubt it," Kahled nuzzled him, beard tangling in Sly's hair.

Sly slumped, forcing the vampire to take his full weight, but there was no complaint. Sly sighed. "I might hate myself for leaving."

"You shouldn't."

"I shouldn't be investing myself in love affairs with terminal people either."

Kahled chuckled, and it was deep, rumbling, and heartfelt. There was a tinge of melancholy to it, but it was no less genuine.

"I want to leave," Sly said with faked calm, "but I don't want to leave you."

"I know." Kahled pried his arm from Sly's grasp so he could sling it around the human's shoulders. Pressed close and cozy, he steered them down the hall. "That's a worry for next week. Not right now."

SLY SLEPT HARD. THEY CUDDLED AND TALKED WELL INTO THE night, and after they each soaked a pillow or two with tears and their stomachs ached from laughter, they fell asleep. It was the good, deep sleep of catharsis.

Dreams carried him away, far, far away from reality.

He dreamed of Kahled and starlight and an infinity of easy affection where there were no such things as judgmental parents or crippling expectations. He imagined Kahled as he always knew him, big and fearsome, but so gentle with that monstrous weight on his bones. He lost himself in a fantasy where claws raked his skin without cutting, where Sly himself was impervious to their harm.

Then, the dreams shifted.

He was languishing in a familiar bed with a familiar body along his back. There was all the detail and comfort of a memory, shrouded in sleep's haze.

There was no accounting for the sinister air twisting around him like a tangible trap.

Kahled was no different in Sly's subconscious than he was in real life. His soft snores gurgled in Sly's ear with a touch of animality, and he kept his touch featherlight, claws teasing and harmless as they trailed down Sly's belly. Sly recognized the hungry purr against his neck as a heavy hand slipped between his legs with utmost care and zero pain.

Sly ignored his arousal to grab Kahled's wrist and say, "Something's wrong."

"It's all right," Dream-Kahled promised, nuzzling and licking him, "I'm here. I'll protect you."

In real life, Sly would have laughed and teased him for such a comment. In the dream, Sly willed himself to believe him.

He let the fantasy unfold like it always did. There was pleasure and heat and low, greedy growls that made him grin. It was slow and heavy, and every movement made him shudder in the best way.

The wrongness persisted.

"Something's wrong," Sly repeated, panting against Kahled's shoulder.

He reached for Kahled's hand, and there must have been a lapse in the dreamscape's timeline because the musculature in Kahled's arm didn't flow quite the way he expected it to. When he reached the knuckles of Kahled's right hand, he expected to find the ring finger with its lone talon and warped knuckles, but all he found was simple, mortal skin.

"Did I cure you?" Sly asked as noxious hope raced up his spine.

Kahled answered him with a guttural moan. It was more beast than man.

Sly's arousal waned under a flood of unease. He tried to kiss his way around Kahled's shoulder to inspect his hand, but the dream didn't cooperate, because he wasn't laying on his back after all. He was on his front. Kahled was still on top of him, hard and ready and so sweetly cautious, but that caution was moot since his claws were gone.

"Wait!" Sly hissed, trying to lift himself from the mattress despite Kahled's weight. "Are you cured?" Kahled showed no signed of hearing him as he rubbed himself on Sly's ass and lower back.

"Kahled? I need to know if I cured you!"

A gruff whisper brushed the back of his neck. "Mine."

And a large, fully humanoid hand shoved under Sly's body, going for his sex. The grip was dry, but firm and good. It felt like being touched by a stranger.

"Mine," Kahled repeated, and it echoed in Sly's head like a spell had been cast.

Hot fluid sprayed onto Sly's lower back.

Sly came fully awake, gasping as he jerked his face up from the pillow. He didn't move far on account of the full weight of a naked vampire pinning him facedown on the bed.

Kahled groaned above him as he finished. He pawed at

Sly's shoulders and hip, and Sly cried out in relief when he registered the thin rasp of a few claws.

"Thank the stars," Sly whispered into the pillow, then he lifted his head to tell Kahled, "I'm not mad, but we have to have a talk about somnophilia— Woah!"

Sly caught a flash of brightness out of the corner of his eye before he was plunged face-first back into the bedding with Kahled splayed out on top of him. Then, there was slobber everywhere, the wetness getting into the hair on the back of Sly's neck as the vampire covered his neck and shoulder with messy kisses and slurping licks.

The wild noises leaving Kahled beckoned the wrongness from Sly's dream.

"Maestro?"

When Kahled continued to mouth at him, his significant weight crushing Sly like never before, Sly suspected Kahled wasn't fully conscious.

The thought was paralyzing. Sly's entire body tensed, and the last of his arousal was doused.

Kahled took notice. He paused for all of a second before nuzzling into Sly's neck with a concerned whimper. He didn't speak. Not as any sentient being would.

"You awake, Maestro?"

The only answer he got was a rolling purr of pleasure and relief, then Kahled resumed licking him. Grooming him. Like an animal.

"You better be asleep," Sly huffed under his breath.

He tried to reposition his arm so he could force Kahled conscious with a pointed jab. It wouldn't hurt the vampire, but Sly hoped it would jolt him out of whatever episode had a grip on him. With an irritated grunt, Sly jerked his elbow backward into Kahled's gut.

Pain lanced through his arm, rippling along his nerves from his elbow. Sly shouted.

Kahled growled, and his weight became suffocating on top of him. An unforgiving hand snatched Sly's forearm and trapped the offending limb against the mattress.

There were no claws cutting his skin. There wasn't a hint of a point anywhere on his arm.

The raw dream in Sly's mind transfigured into a nightmare, and Sly craned his neck to look. His heart stopped.

Kahled's arm was covered in glassy armor, the scales stretching from his shoulder to each fingertip. The claws were still there, but they were smaller and uniform across all five digits. In the cold glow of Kahled's mutated eyes, his hand almost looked metallic, like a shackle keeping Sly in place.

Sly recoiled, turning his head so he could gulp back a panicked breath. He shouldn't have.

Sharp, deep pain struck beneath his exposed ear. Hot— burning hot blood—began leaking onto the sheets, and Sly wondered if he wasn't still caught in the dream-turned-nightmare.

It was only when he heard Kahled scream for help that he realized how badly he'd been bitten.

Black spots popped in and out of his vision. The world spun. He didn't hurt, he didn't even feel scared anymore, but sort of floaty and cool.

"Sylvester?"

Kahled's face appeared in front of him, sleek scales gleaming on his neck and devastation etched into his handsome face. There was something else, something different about Kahled's appearance, but Sly was having trouble concentrating.

"No," Kahled whimpered. "No. No. No. Sly? Please. No."

Sly's ears stopped working right at that point. He had the

vague notion that there was something he needed to do, but everything was muffled. His ears, his thoughts, the world. Space and time turned funny and distorted, and he thought he was moving fast, air swishing past his naked body, but he couldn't be sure.

He couldn't be sure.

He couldn't be...

CHAPTER 20

*A*n obnoxious beeping sent pulses of ache echoing through his head and forced him back to consciousness. It was beyond jarring. Wasn't he having some weirdly intense sex just a minute ago? Sly frowned. He stretched and went to scratch an itch on the side of his neck, but his fingers found a thick bandage instead of skin.

Shit.

"Kahled!" Sly gasped as he sat up.

The medical suite spun, making him nauseous as he dropped back into the bed. Sly's heart thumped a spastic rhythm behind his sternum, rushing too little blood through his veins. He gagged.

Nope. He was puking.

"Easy does it," someone—Mae?—murmured as they rubbed his back. "Doctor? He's awake!"

There was a hushed conversation nearby, maybe in response to Mae's alert, but Sly didn't catch any of it. He was too busy heaving, bile and snot and hot, bulbous tears dripping from his face.

Kahled bit him. He really bit him.

Sly tried to calm down, tried to slow his heart so it wouldn't keep pumping whatever blood he had left faster than he could probably afford. During the struggle, he caught sight of Felix.

It wasn't Mae rubbing soothing circles on his back. The blond sat by his hip, letting Sly lean over him so he could spew into the pink plastic bin Felix held in his other hand. He was silent, with a disgusted grimace on his face that didn't mesh with the soothing motions against Sly's back.

"Is Kahled okay?" Sly had to clear his dry throat, and it caused the bandage to shift. There was no pain. Only fear and worry. "Something was wrong—"

"Don't worry about the Master," Felix said, and the subdued timbre of his voice felt like a slap across Sly's face. "Worry about yourself for a change. You could have died."

"Like you care." Sly slumped away from him and dropped his panting, useless self into a mountain of pillows.

Deep-blue pillows. In the medical bay.

Sly jolted upright and turned to investigate his surroundings. The black blossoms of dizziness made an immediate reappearance.

"Stars and moons, Earthling!" Felix shoved him back down. "Do you want to pass out again?"

Sly ignored him. He spotted the manacles on the headboard. He recognized the white curtain drawn around the bed. This was Kahled's spot, reserved in the medical wing just for him.

"I shouldn't be here," Sly whispered, more to himself than to Felix. "Something's wrong with Kahled. He wasn't himself. This bed is his, not—"

"Don't worry about Kahled," Gorbon interrupted as he slipped through the curtain. The tablet device in his hand was beeping in a constant, even rhythm that kept the doctor's eyes darting between Sly and the screen. "He's fine. You're the one who nearly bled out."

Giving the vertical thing another try, Sly leveraged himself into a reclined position against the headboard. "Don't be dramatic. Bleeding's what I'm here for."

"This isn't a joke, Sly."

Gorbon pulled up a stool, and the look on his face as he settled across from Sly was graver than his words. He set his beeping tablet on one leg so he could take one of Sly's hands in both of his, and Sly knew he was going to hate whatever came out of the man's mouth next.

"The Curse got the better of him," Gorbon said, voice worryingly cool and level. "Whatever episode led him to tearing your throat out ended just a moment too late. You needed a transfusion."

Sly's brain wasn't firing at full speed yet. He shook his head and tried to figure out why those words set off so many internal alarms. Gordon cleared it up for him in the next breath.

"You were lucky, Sly. Very lucky. You remember the extra vials I filled every time we siphoned off your blood for Kahled's daily dose?"

Sly nodded, but it was weak and reluctant.

"I was trying to cultivate a supply we could use after you left. With proper rationing, I thought I could use it to help him last another year, but…" Gorbon's grave eyes welled, shiny and disappointed. "I gave you everything I had. We nearly had to supplement with spliced blood."

Sly jerked back, ripping his hand from Gorbon with a harsh gasp. "Am I spliced? My blood? Is it—" He swallowed, the ugly word caught in his throat. "...tainted?"

He would be useless to Kahled if that were true. That thought raced through his head three times before he dared to consider how his dad might react. Sly's voided stomach threatened to rebel again.

"You're all right." Gorbon stood, hands rubbing Sly's arms as if trying to warm him up. "I had enough of your blood in storage to keep you alive, but you'll be weak for a bit."

"Mae's already gone to get you some tea," Felix interjected from where he sat, legs crossed at the foot of the bed.

Sly was tempted to kick him off. With more venom than warranted, Sly spat, "What are you still doing here?"

Felix's answering smile was sharp and fake. "Helping."

"That's debatable," Gorbon muttered. "Clean out that bucket, then go check in with Madam Walters. She may need help with Kahled."

As Felix slinked out through the curtain, Sly clutched at Gorbon. "How is Kahled? What happened?"

The doctor sighed, and his rounded face seemed to sag under his beard. He retook his seat, but he kept a bracing grip on Sly's arm.

"He didn't mean to do it," Sly insisted. "I was half-asleep when the episode began, and I think he was too—"

Gorbon held up a palm to hush him. He waited for Sly's panting breath to calm down before speaking.

"Kahled's been reacting to your blood on a microbiological level since day one, Sly. I made the mistake of letting my optimism get in the way of the science, and I mistook continued mutation for cellular repair."

"What is that supposed to mean?" Sly wailed.

"It means I was wrong." Gorbon met his eye without faltering. He looked older than ever. "And I'm sorry for it. Your blood has done nothing but alter the path of his mutations."

Sly's insides shriveled. Breathless, he asked, "I wasn't helping him at all?"

"Oh! That's not true, Sly. You might not have stopped the disease, but you've made him happy! You gave him peace! Do you have any idea how much that means to him?"

Sly shook his head hard enough to make himself dizzy. He tried to swing his legs down from the bed and push past Gorbon, saying, "I need to talk to Kahled."

Gorbon urged him back into the bed. "You need to rest and rehydrate."

"Where is he?" Sly swatted Gorbon's constraining hands away. "I need to talk to him."

"You can't!" Gorbon snapped.

Sly's heart stuttered in his chest. "But why?"

The doctor pushed out a rough exhale and slouched on his stool. "He's confined to his rooms for now. We're monitoring him for any further changes, and once we're confident he's done manifesting any reactions to your blood, he'll be free to roam the manor again."

Sly spluttered, "How long is that going to take?"

Gorbon frowned. "It doesn't matter."

"Like hell it doesn't matter." Sly fumed. "He needs to know I don't blame him."

"Sly." Gorbon rested his palm on Sly's knee, his eyes beseeching. "Neither I nor Kahled are prepared to risk him biting you right now."

"That won't happen!"

"It already has."

Sly's jaw snapped shut. There was nothing he could say to refute the fact.

"It's going to take a couple weeks with significant supplements before you can bleed for any vampire," Gorbon continued with uncommon firmness, "and your contract ends in four days, anyway."

Sly gasped, turning away as if Gorbon had slapped him. Four days? He was supposed to have a week left with Kahled.

"Kahled and Emmeline talked it over with Master Vauqeulin. We're sending you home early."

Silent tears streaked down his cheeks, but Sly was too stunned to do anything about them.

"HEPP's sending a shuttle. It should be here tonight."

Sly's voice shook as he asked, "If I hadn't woken up just now, were you going to cart me off without explanation?"

Gorbon took his time answering. When Sly turned an accusing glare on him, he shook himself and chose his words with care. "HEPP knows what happened. They would have given you details as soon as you asked."

Sly's spine gave out. He flopped back into the majestic medical cot, but he found no comfort in it.

"You weren't going to wait to let me say goodbye?"

Gorbon closed his eyes, covering his mouth with a closed fist.

"None of you?" Sly pressed.

"It wasn't my decision. It was Kahled's."

Sly's breath hitched. "And now he's in lockdown? So I don't get to say goodbye anyway?"

Gorbon didn't raise his eyes from the floor as he said. "He doesn't want to see you."

"Oh, fuck him!"

"He woke up yesterday to find himself covered in your blood and your body going cold in his bed." Gorbon sounded sympathetic, but there was a hard edge to his voice. "He may not be human, Sly, but even the Nocturni have their limits. He would never get over it if he killed you."

Sly heard him, his ears caught the words, and they were

definitely English. He couldn't process it though. They made zero sense.

He wanted to rage. He wanted to lash out and smack the fucking tablet away till it shattered on the floor and stopped that incessant beeping. He wanted to throttle Gorbon and go scream at Kahled's door until the self-sacrificing asshole let him in. He wanted so much.

He did *not* want things to end like this.

SLY WOULD GO TO HIS GRAVE WITHOUT ADMITTING HOW HARD it was to get himself to the ensuite bathroom, barely eight feet from the bed. Mae was kind enough not to comment when she had to support him for the walk back. Then, Walters brought him steak and leafy salad that tasted like dirt underneath its fixings. The act of chewing so soon after the trek to the toilet exhausted him.

He told himself it was all to do with blood loss. It was mostly true.

"Mr. Spurgeon?"

Sly jolted upright. He'd barely begun to doze, but he felt groggy, and it still took too long for him to focus on the man in front of him. Once his eyes got with the program, he groaned.

"Seriously? They sent *you* to fetch me?"

HEPP's bug-eyed, stick-thin representative stood at his bedside, the curtain drawn back in his hand. The faded patches on his suit were laughably shabby with the Harem's immaculate, high-tech suite as a backdrop. Sly remembered him on sight, but he had trouble remembering his name. Michaels?

"Well..." The man shifted past the curtain as he

straightened his suit jacket. "I am the agent assigned to your father's case. Which has become your case, of course."

Sly tried to make it make sense but drew a blank. "What case?"

The man—Miles?—frowned. "Your Assessment Contract?"

Sly kept staring, waiting for clarification with blatant confusion.

The guy kept frowning, like he expected Sly to know what he was talking about. When the quiet started to feel awkward in record time, he cleared his throat and added, "Mr. Phink filed the agreement you made with Kamari Vauqeulin in association with the Harem's offer to clear John's debt. Normally, the two incidents would be treated as unrelated, but, well, given the circumstances..."

The man trailed off, his cheeks pinking as if he were embarrassed to speak further. His astounding unhelpfulness managed to jog Sly's memory.

"Myers?"

The agent straightened up, meeting Sly's eye with relief. "Yes, Mr. Spurgeon?"

Impatient, Sly prompted, "My circumstances?"

The sass did the trick, and Myers blurted out, "It was the surest way to guarantee your safe return."

In a rush, Sly remembered how concerned he'd been the last time he'd been home. He replayed Phink's greedy hope in the face of his own dread at the prospect of Companionship. With wide eyes, he reconsidered the reluctance and pessimism he started out with. He'd been so convinced the Harem would entrap him somehow, that the parasitic villains of John's nightmares would steal him away, and he'd have to fight to make it home.

The memories came readily, not even six months behind him. It felt like a lifetime ago.

Dazed, Sly asked, "What if I wanted another contract?"

Myers perked up. "Of course! After listening to Phink, I didn't dare hope you would be interested, but we're always looking for Companions. HEPP has long recognized that humanity's future depends on successful emigration from Earth, and the Harems are by far the most stable option. How Companionship remains so unpopular is really quite a mystery—"

"Great." Sly had to stop himself from snapping his fingers under Myers's nose. "How soon can you get me something to sign?"

Myers blinked those bulbous orbs like he wasn't sure he'd heard right. "How soon? Well, um… Mr. Spurgeon, you won't be eligible until you've fully recovered—"

"Bullshit," Sly snapped, and Myers backed away as he began gesticulating. "I can recover right here perfectly fine, probably better than I could in the port. Let's just sign the contract with a date two weeks from now!"

Myers paled, bug-eyes going disturbingly wide. "Oh, my stars. No, that won't happen."

Sly tossed his hands as he yelled, "What kind of organization wastes money on pointless personnel transport just for the sake of a technicality?"

Myers's chest puffed out, his face reddening as he sputtered, "No, Mr. Spurgeon! You misunderstand. What you are suggesting is not only illegal and counterproductive to HEPP's mission to safeguard human welfare, it isn't even possible!"

"Why not?"

As he watched Myers's face fall, Sly's worry soared higher.

"Companionship requires two interested parties, Mr. Spurgeon," he explained, grave and gentle.

"Yeah," Sly snipped. "Me and Kahled. That was always Kamari's endgame anyway!"

"Yes, but the Harem terminated your contract with its intended scion..." Myers hesitated, glancing around in pronounced unease. "And Master Vauqeulin is, we might say, *unwilling* to sign you up with anyone else."

"I don't want anyone else!" Sly fumed, fisting the blanket over his lap.

Myers was in full retreat as he patted the curtain to find its partition. "And Kahled Vauqeulin can't be reasoned with, so... you know."

"No!" Sly shouted after him. "I don't know!"

"He won't take you back, Mr. Spurgeon."

Sly went cold and still. He felt more lifeless than he'd been while bathing from his own artery.

"I'm sorry, Mr. Spurgeon," Myers chirped as he fussed his way through the privacy barrier. "I really am. These things don't usually go like this."

The curtain swished back into place. Sly could make out Myers's shadow as he inched toward the exit.

"Anyhow," Myers murmured, "I just came to let you know I'm here. The Harem's being kind enough to restock my transport, and then we'll be leaving."

Myers was gone before Sly realized he was crying.

WITHIN THE HOUR, SLY WAS IN A HOOVER CHAIR, WATCHING Walters stuff Sly's fancy new wardrobe into a crate. They were in the foyer to Kahled's suite. At least, Walters was. Sly was stuck with the front end of his chair sticking out of the elevator; there was no room for it in the foyer while all of Sly's belongings cluttered the space.

"It shouldn't have happened," Walters grumbled.

She didn't look at him as she worked. She was folding clothes Sly didn't recognize, her movements brusque and pointed. Her voice and manner were irate, more uncomposed than he previously knew she was capable of being.

Sly remained in the elevator, waiting for her to scream or cry.

"He shouldn't have been capable of biting you," the woman ranted, "considering his physical deformities and the progression of the disease, we were confident it wasn't a risk."

When she stopped speaking to catch her breath, Sly offered an unconvincing reassurance, "It's fine."

"It is not!" Walters scoffed, shaking out a shirt with a vicious snap. "We knew he was assuming new traits—unpredictable traits, even—but did we bother routinely measuring his fangs? No!"

"It's not your fault," Sly said without feeling.

"How did we miss it?" She stilled, the finest of clothes wrinkling in her shaking hands. "His fangs were shrinking, and we didn't notice until the moment he could fit them around your throat."

Sly stiffened. "Don't blame him either. He wasn't in control."

She gave a short, choked laugh. "I know. How reckless of us to assume his mental decay had ceased when nothing else had."

Sly's stomach twisted along with her miserable chuckles. He didn't know if he believed it when he said, "He went months without an episode. It was a reasonable assumption."

Walters didn't argue with him. Her prim and proper

293

posture broke, her upper back curving with an uncharacteristic slump, as she turned in a slow circle to survey the discarded items.

"None of this is mine," Sly commented.

She sighed and resumed folding the item in her hands. "It is now. A gift from the Harem."

He watched her work in uneasy silence for a long while. Sly couldn't remember touching half the clothing items he saw her stow in the shipping bin, and there were a few boxes filled with stars-only-know-what that Walters struggled to lift on her own.

Walters saw his uneasy expression when she finished loading them. "It's not all from Kahled. Most of it is, but there are some goods from storage. If you're smart, you'll sell it off and use the funds to make your way to Luna." She patted her skirts and turned away from him as she huffed, "Or wherever strikes your fancy."

Sly felt sick with impotent anger. An unfair amount of it leaked into his voice when he said, "This isn't how I wanted it to go."

She sighed, still not looking at him. "It makes no difference in the end, Mr. Spurgeon. We all did our best, and it wasn't enough. Not for you. And not for him."

Sniffling, Sly wiped at his eyes. "That's not fair."

"No. Reality rarely is." She faced him then, hands folded in front of her and a watery smile on her face. "I wish you all the best, Mr. Spurgeon. Truly."

Sly nodded, his throat too tight and his gut too volatile to attempt words. He saw her farewell for what it was, a condolence for his loss.

Kahled knew he was there. He could probably hear Sly's heart breaking from down the hall. He never showed himself. He never said goodbye.

It was infuriating. Unacceptable. Sly never let Kahled ignore him before, he couldn't let it slide now.

Utilizing the touchpad on the chair's armrest, Sly backed up into the elevator and left Walters to her business. He had blushed and complained when Mae first brought him the chair, but he could barely make it down the hall on his feet without risk of passing out; the thing was especially helpful at getting him down to basement level in record time.

There were lots of metallic shrieks and crashing as Sly hoovered his way into the communication center. It was crammed like never before, and Sly didn't care as his chair shoved shelves out of the way and knocked over the lone seat Sly passed so many hours in over the recent months. He had to pull up parallel to the console in order to reach the controls, but he managed to do it without making himself nauseous, so he counted that as a win.

He needed the win, small and meaningless as it was.

He activated the intercom with shaky fingers and brought the microphone into his lap. He was linked to Kahled's rooms and Kahled's rooms only. It wasn't private enough, not close enough, but it was at least something.

"You are a colossal douchebag, Kahled Vauqeulin."

His anger tempered the sorrow in a way that made his voice seem strong. He hoped it lasted; he would hate to get weepy on his last intercom transmission.

"I don't care that I'm rocking a shiny new scar thanks to you. I'm not mad you bit me. Hell, I'm not even bothered by the fact you humped me in my sleep like an animal. I was kind of into it in the moment. But this shit? Throwing my unconscious body into Gorbon's tender care and washing your hands of me? Fuck you, Kahled. Were you hoping HEPP would cart me off before I woke up so you wouldn't have to deal with me?"

Sly paused, panting. He needed a moment to calm down, to figure out what he needed to say. He needed to think. There was a problem though because the anger spurning him onward was starting to flag. He was weak and hurt and not much else, but he managed to hit the mic's transmit button one more time.

"News flash, asshole. I love you. I know this was right around the corner, but... not like this. Come on, Maestro." His voice broke with a sob. "Don't end it like this. I want to see you. Hug you. Please? At least let me say goodbye."

The mic fell from limp fingers. Sly didn't care. He set his elbows on the hoover chair's armrests and shoved his fists over his eyes to stem the waterworks.

The control panel beeped, and Kahled's voice whispered from the speaker. "I'm sorry. Goodbye, Sly."

CHAPTER 21

S ly stepped off the shuttle in a daze. The grime and bustle of the American Port's transport station was like a dream: awkwardly familiar but indistinct. Unimportant. There was none of the relief or pride he once expected to feel when his feet found home ground again.

The world snapped into focus with a vengeance when a timid hand gave his shoulder an awkward pat.

"Well," Myers muttered, "the Harem requested we get you home safe, so… where would you like to go? Your official address is still listed as your father's place, but I could just as easily escort you to HEPP. We could examine your options."

"Myers?"

"Yes, Mr. Spurgeon?"

"Fuck off."

With the agent flustered in his wake, Sly turned into the crowd of travelers in a daze. He was home, but none of it felt real. It was as if the Vauqeulin Harem's estate and all its splendor had traded places with the rest of the world, somehow cementing itself as reality while relegating everything else to an unimportance.

Myers chased after him. "Where are you off to, then?"

Sly tried to pull himself together enough for intelligent conversation. "Anywhere that's not with you."

But Myers kept up with him, an irritating shadow at his heel. "I know the timing isn't ideal, but it's never too soon to think about your future."

Sly quickened his step.

"I can personally guarantee HEPP would love to work with you again. Your status is a rare investment opportunity, and I can only imagine—"

Sly stopped. Myers walked into him. Other pedestrians were jostled, but Sly paid none them any notice as he spun to glare at the humanoid bug.

"I'm confused. Am I a 'human interest' story to you or a cash grab?"

Myers balked. "Oh! That's not what I—"

"Which is it? Answer the question."

Myers continued trying to defend himself against the accusation in Sly's tone, but Sly was having none of it. Sly kept talking over him, demanding over and over and over again that Myers answer the simple question. Passerby started giving them a wide berth. Several people stared.

Sly jabbed his finger into the agent's chest and shouted, "Give me a fucking answer!"

Foot traffic paused as Myers gaped at him. Before the man could compose himself, the onlookers got moving again.

Myers's Adam's apple bobbed as he swallowed and reapproached. "Maybe you're both, Mr. Spurgeon."

Sly fumed, but he didn't keep shouting. "That's not an answer."

He made to keep walking, fully intending to lose Myers in

the crowd. Instead, his arm was caught in a thin but insistent grasp.

"Yes!" Myers hissed in his ear. "You have a goldmine swimming through your veins. Just because we might profit from it doesn't mean it's not the best thing for you to do. You're smart, Mr. Spurgeon; you know how quickly the wrong people would jump at the chance to take the choice away from you. At least with HEPP, you can negotiate a fair deal."

Sly tilted his head to stage whisper back, "The only deal I want is with Kahled."

"It won't be long before people start suspecting you're pure." Myers let him go with a sigh. "I suggest you get off-planet before word gets out you're back. Phink and the Guard won't be able to shield you for long."

"Thanks for the advice."

As he walked away, Myers's fading voice made one last appeal. "It's not your fault that vampire's a doomed martyr. Don't squander the chance he's giving you!"

"Fuck off!" Sly shouted, and the crowd leaped out of his way to support his exit.

He walked away from Myers with next to nothing on him. The crates of superfluous gifts Walters had boxed up for him were being unloaded into one of the station's storage facilities until Sly could figure out what to do with it. He had the shiny new comms on his wrist, a certified and fulfilled copy of his contract, and a significant severance check in his pocket. That was it.

Belatedly, he noticed he didn't have an adequate coat to step outside the station. He hadn't needed one in months. No coat, no masks, no protective outer gear of any kind; none of it was necessary on the estate. Earth-bound as it was, Sly was never at risk for atmospheric exposure while on Harem property.

That was never true at any other point in his life.

It was a world-shattering epiphany at precisely the wrong moment. He was already stranded in a busy public space, between jobs and still weak from blood loss. The profound appreciation for all the security he'd left behind with his pulverized heart couldn't have come at a worse time.

Sly sat his ass on the cold grimy floor of the station.

He was lost. He knew exactly where he was, where his people were, and how to contact them, but he was lost all the same. Hours passed, but Sly couldn't make himself care.

"Sly?"

The familiar voice reached out to him like a beacon through fog. It was surreal to look up from his knees and find his boss standing there, fur on end and teddy-bear eyes wide and amazed.

Sly pried himself off the floor and plastered a grin on his face. It had only been six months since he last put on a front for the stage, but the cheery act felt stiff and uncomfortable as if it had been a lifetime.

"Hey, Phinkly. What brings you here?"

The fuzzy guy didn't take his outstretched hand in greeting. He stared at him in a mixture of awe and concern.

Sly dropped his hand. "Thanks for the warm welcome, Phinkerton. You shouldn't have—"

"Myers sent me."

Sly's shoulders dropped.

"It's really you?" Phink peered at him, his fuzzy brow crunching low. "You're back?"

Sly snorted an unconvincing laugh. "Try not to sound so disappointed. Weren't you recently begging me to come home and fix all your problems?"

Phink's hair stood on end, and for one wild moment, Sly thought he might witness the boss cry. "Master Vauqeulin told me what happened. Sly. Kid. You were supposed to *want* to come back to us."

Sly felt small as he avoided Phink's direct gaze. "Can we do this later? I'm tired."

"You're not tired. You're exsanguinated." Phink's expression only darkened as he drew nearer. "We didn't expect to see you again. Not really. Blythe kept telling me how deep into it you were getting with that vamp."

Sly reacted. His insides gave a vicious churn, and while he wasn't sure exactly what his face did, it made Phink's go blank and carefully impersonal. Professional.

It was all wrong. Phink didn't bother with professionalism where his staff was concerned. Phink called him Earthling and tutted at him like they were dysfunctional siblings, and it was perfectly comfortable without encouraging any sort of personal bullshit. It was one of the main reasons Sly worked for him for so long.

"So, about Blythe..." Sly cleared his throat and surged ahead with the change of subject. "Is she seriously shacked up with my old man? What? What's that look for?"

Phink shuffled backward, wincing. "So… what exactly did she tell you about her place? About your dad?"

Sly's brain screeched to a halt. The universe shuddered to an abrupt stop. The slow, maudlin thoughts that plagued the background of Sly's mind all day halted. The fantasy of crystalline gray eyes, the scent memory of chocolate and visions of make-believe nebulas, even the stinging resignation that he was home, all of it was shoved aside. Recalibrated.

It was like waking up from a wickedly good dream with a totally shit ending. Sly took a breath as the mantle of familiar expectations resettled on his shoulders, and he felt like himself again.

"What happened?" Sly demanded.

Phink toed at a broken tile on the station floor with absolute focus.

Sly propped his hands on his hips and scowled. "Phink!"

Phink sighed, shoulders slumping. "Fine. You were right. Let me just admit that up-front and get it out of the way so you can spare me the—"

"Phink. Get to the point."

"All right! So, marketing Blythe as pure-blooded wasn't the safest move—"

"What," Sly bit out coldly, "happened?"

"It's not that big a deal anymore. It happened weeks ago!" Phink held up his hands as if to ward him off. "I thought she told you. She ought to have told you—"

"Spit it out."

"One of her Humans First guys set her building on fire."

Sly blanched.

Before he could react further, Phink rushed on. "No one got hurt! She wasn't even there when it happened. She was having dinner with your pops. Guess even out in the middle of nowhere, you were still watching out for her ass."

His throat was too tight. It hurt to force words out. "And my dad? What was she supposed to tell me about him?"

Phink shrugged. Again. "I don't know the particulars, but... some sort of health scare, I think. Minor? Pretty sure. It was a couple weeks earlier. It's been months, now, Sly."

Sly brought a fist to his mouth like it would keep his gorge from rising.

"I think the Guard had to cut him loose. She's been helping him cover expenses, and after the fire... well. It just made sense for her to move in and consolidate their resources."

For a split second, Sly thought the world was finally crumbling to pieces beneath his feet, just as it had been threatening for centuries. Everything went shaky, his legs unsure and his vision blurring. There was no way of telling if the ground was truly unstable or if the storm was trapped inside him for a change.

"Ah, shit, Sly. Don't cry—it's not that bad."

It was that bad. He was gone for six months too long, wasting time in a fairytale while his family limped on without him.

"They managed well enough. Blythe probably didn't see any point in worrying you."

He was going to hurl.

"She had to take some time off when he got out of the hospital, but things turned out okay."

Sly squatted down right where he was, face in his hands.

"...Sly?"

"I need a minute."

"Okay. Yeah. Take your time..."

This close to solid ground, he didn't feel quite so untethered. His insides still spasmed at random, and he barely managed to stifle a gag, but he worked through it. He pressed his palms into his eyes and dragged air into his lungs. It was a mockery of the breathing technique Walters tried to talk him through on his first day in the manor.

It made him think of Kahled and the practiced way he could just breathe to let the tension leach from his massive shoulders.

His heart gave a wrenching pang, and he dissolved into silent, wrenching sobs.

Sly wasn't sure what he expected when he paused outside his childhood home. The sinking in his stomach suggested he should prepare for abject squalor, but the exhaustion dragging on his bones made everything seem unremarkable.

The door looked the same. Dingy. Weather-beaten. Filthy and dinged as it ever was, no more or less. The sealed pistons were as janky and threadbare as he left them. The cute welcome mat he expected outside of Blythe's place was missing, but not surprising since John Spurgeon was never one for inviting sentiments or throwing money at anything he couldn't find at a liquor store.

There was no accounting for the sense of wrongness pressing down on Sly from all sides. If it weren't for the uncommon clarity to his skin and the layers of quality dieting on his bones, he probably looked much the same as the day he'd left. Months of clean water and well-balanced meals were nothing a few weeks back home wouldn't downgrade to a mere memory.

Nothing had changed and everything had. Same town, same wretched skyline, and same dreary, decaying buildings. Same him. Except not.

The outer gear Phink brought him felt disgustingly heavy as he lifted his arm to knock. His body was stronger than ever, and he wasn't dumb enough to think the damn coat was the sole reason he was struggling.

The outer door unlocked. Sly stepped inside. In the long minutes it took for the atmospheric seal to reestablish and signal the inner door was safe to open, he tried to get comfortable with the eerie familiarity. The entry way was dusty and poorly lit, a weak, ugly yellow callback to his childhood.

It was worlds different from the warm glow that had represented daytime at the Vauqeulin Estate.

Sly couldn't muster the energy to regret the way things languished between him and his dad. Trying to think it over only made him long for soothing mood lighting against a makeshift canopy and a strong body to cradle him through unchecked hours.

The inner doorway to the apartment popped open, and Sly snapped back to reality.

Blythe stood there in all her glory. Miles of deep-brown skin and athletic curves beneath sweatpants and a skimpy top. Beautiful and strong as ever. There was a quality to her face that didn't seem quite right, but Sly supposed it had to do with the ample splay of jaguar spots crossing her temples and the full span of her shoulders. The faint discolorations had darkened into true markings, vivid golds and stark blacks. Irrefutable splicing side effects, but she pulled it off well.

She looked good, even with the defensive set of her jaw.

"Who are you, and what do you want?" Blythe demanded, her hand tight on the door.

Words seemed too difficult, so Sly reached up to remove his mask in silence.

At first, she didn't react. He stood with one of Centrism's extra masks in his hands and watched her stony stare melt away as she recognized him. Her slitted eyes widened, just a smidge.

"The fuck are you doing here?" She glared, propping the door with her hip so she could cross her arms.

Sly fidgeted with the mask. "Last I checked, I sort of live here?"

Her shoulders rolled back like she was considering

clocking back for a blow. He could tell by the jut of her jaw that she was peeved, probably because he surprised her.

"Oh, really?"

Or not. There was too much weight behind her stare, too much knowledge.

Sly faltered. As her face softened, he said without inflection, "He terminated the contract early. Just a few days, but… yeah."

That was all he needed to say. Her lips pursed in a wavering pout, and she dropped her arms open. "Come here, you pitiful thing. Tell me all about it."

He wanted to. He meant to. The moment he felt her arms around his shoulders, his brain went on hiatus. He collapsed into her familiar embrace, shaking apart and not fighting it in the slightest. He didn't remember making it into the house or choosing to use her hair as a snot rag; neither of them made a snide comment about her letting him. He didn't care that his dad wasn't around. It was loud and messy and it hurt, from the croaking in his throat all the way down to the wicked festering lump that had finally burst in his stomach.

It was like the day his mother died. Blythe was there, too. While John was at work, she held him back from chasing his mom into the harsh light of midday. When he finally calmed down and caught his breath, they were huddled together on the threadbare couch, and the springs creaked under the shifting of their combined weight. He peeled her damp curls from where his sobs plastered it to his cheek.

He laughed weakly as he removed himself from her lap, "That's what's up with me. How about you?"

She didn't answer. She just kept looking at him with gut-wrenching sympathy.

Snorting back the last of his meltdown, Sly glanced

around the house without taking anything in. He didn't look at her. He couldn't. "Where's my pops at?"

Blythe slung an arm around him and drew him back in. She set her chin on his shoulder with a heavy sigh. "He's at the doctor's for a follow-up. He should be back soon."

Sly didn't have the energy to press for details. Not yet. He huffed and slumped against her.

Her sigh was startling, exhausted and mature in new and heartbreaking ways. "He got let go from the Guard and went off on a drinking binge. Landed in the hospital."

"Alcohol poisoning?" Sly was impressed with his cool tone. No hysteria here.

She gave him a squeeze. "Not exactly."

"Liver failure?"

"Nope."

"Drunken brawl then?"

Blythe said nothing.

Even his wince was weary. "How bad was he beat?"

"It wasn't like that..."

"Just tell me."

His voice was dry and scarily resigned. Detached. It sounded like he was half-asleep, listless and wholly uninvested. Maybe too invested.

"I don't know the details," she answered, words stilted with reluctance. "I'm not even sure the booze had anything to do with it. He got bit. Jumped by a loner vamp."

It was like being doused in ice water from behind. The weary fog evaporated, and Sly jerked upright as adrenaline raced through him. His grip on the back of the couch turned his knuckles white as he leaned back to stare at her.

"A Nocturnus attacked him? Are you sure? Absolutely, undeniably sure?"

She nodded. "Positive."

"How did that even happen?" Sly bounced from the force of his gesticulations. "Even if he was still working for the Guard, he has no business in vamp territory!"

"Oh, it didn't happen downtown," she assured him with a disbelieving huff. "Right around the corner from Mickey's, actually."

His eyeballs tried to jump from his head. "Bullshit. Bloodletting isn't allowed in public spaces! Dad would have never offered, and that makes it assault—"

"No shit."

Unable to stop himself, Sly jumped to his feet, stomping like a child throwing a tantrum. "Vampires don't just do that to people!"

Blythe shrugged as she leaned back on the couch, arms crossed as she scooted into the far corner. "Vamps don't usually go for people who can't pass a sobriety test at a glance either, but that's what happened."

"What! But that... that's not..." He floundered. "The Nocturni don't... they don't just... they don't do that!"

Except when they did. How often did John and his coworkers complain about the climbing rate of unsolicited vampire bites? Sly's childhood was rife with constant warnings.

For the life of him, he never imagined coming back to such a clusterfuck of a situation. His heart raced, and a sickening cloud of dread pervaded the room. It made no damn sense. He flopped back down onto the couch and braced both feet on the floor, elbows on his knees and fistfuls of hair in his hands.

"I don't understand," he said slowly.

"What's up with you?" He could feel her concerned and baffled stare boring into the side of his head. "Yeah, it's shitty, but it happened weeks ago. He's mostly recovered. You don't have to worry about this."

"No, no, it's not... You don't get it."

He didn't get it either. The sensations rocking through his body, the upset in his head, the heaviness of the air in his lungs, there was a disgusting, nostalgic quality to it. It reminded him of those disquieting seconds in the medical bay, tucked into a cushy bed and waiting for Gorbon to announce he was being banished from the estate. It was like being back at HEPP, sitting through the fallout of John's disastrous gambling all over again. It was how he'd felt when his mother set the treat of a freshly cooked meal on his plate and kissed his hair before she walked outside without her gear.

It wasn't the end of the world, but it sure as hell felt like it.

He was struggling to breathe again and, at the same time, smash together the puzzle pieces that were poking random holes in his head as they jostled around. It rendered his focus into complete shit.

He was understandably distracted when the front doors opened then shut.

"Sly?"

His dad's voice hit like gas on a fire. Sly whirled around to stare at the man by the door.

"Dad?"

But it wasn't his father, it was a mess of an old, failing man. The protective gear he'd worn most of Sly's life hung off him as if a parachute had dropped out of the sky above him. The hollows of his cheeks were dark, darker even than the purple-gray bags under his eyes. From across the room, Sly could tell the fingers gripping his mask were skeletal, far too thin beneath his gloves. His dry lips were peeling. His forehead seemed oddly huge and misshapen where his hairline had receded. Less hair, but much grayer. In six months, he'd aged a decade.

John looked closer to death than Kahled ever had.

Sly could only stare—at John, Blythe, the house—he stared between the two most important people in his life, but couldn't find the words to express himself. He was speechless. Shaken. Wounded like he hadn't been when Kahled bit into his jugular.

Blythe hugged herself under his heavy attention and glared at the floor.

When Sly next turned to him, he caught John's hopeful expression go stony. "So," he said, "you're back."

John had never spoken to him with such indifference before. Sly watched him shrug the protective layers off and hang them on coat hooks, disrobing like it was any other day. He didn't glance at Sly as he hung his mask and shucked his boots.

Sly swallowed the rock lodged in his throat. "Did you even try contacting me once?"

"I could ask you the same thing."

"I did call!" Sly blubbered. "Damn near every week!"

John didn't react as he crossed over to the kitchenette and opened the icebox. "Blythe? Did you move my beer again?"

Sly laughed, high and cold, and John flinched.

"Were you going to tell me you were attacked by a vampire and hospitalized?"

John stiffened. "Bloodsucker took a lucky shot at me." He sneered, but he didn't face Sly as he yanked a bottle of water from the fridge and slammed the door.

Sly scoffed, tugging at his hair till his scalp screamed. "Do you even care that you're not the only one? I almost needed a transfusion with spliced blood, Dad. What would you have done then?"

John raised the bottle, and a thin bandage peeked out from his sleeve, wrapping one wrist. "You should've been prepared for that the moment you signed up to be some parasite's chew toy."

"Are you fucking kidding me, Dad?"

Blythe reached for his flailing arm. "Sly!"

He evaded her. Rounding the couch, he pointed at John's bandage furiously. "It's been weeks since you were bit? Really? What'd he do, gnaw you down to the bone and leave you for dead on the street?"

Finally, at long last, his father looked at him. He raised his chin to glare down his nose, even though Sly was taller. His glare darted down to the bandage covering Sly's throat for only a moment. "By now, I figured you'd be intimately familiar with what a bloodsucker's fangs could do."

Sly's mouth snapped shut without his permission.

"Or is that why you're back?" John asked, cool and mean. "Finally learned your lesson the hard way, huh?"

"John!" Blythe barked.

Her scolding tone was buried by Sly's reaction. "What the fuck's that supposed to mean?"

John squared his shoulders and propped a hand on his hip, the water bottle in the other gripped with white knuckles. His arm pushed back the tarp masquerading as a shirt so it revealed the belt barely holding his pants up on the last hole. The posture was so reminiscent of the able-bodied Guardsman he'd once been, it made Sly sick.

John Spurgeon never seemed so small.

"Things must have gone badly," he said calmly. "That's the only reason you'd come back after choosing a vamp over me."

Sly laughed in amazement. "You think that's what happened? That I chose Kahled over you?"

"Oh!" John held up his hands in mocking affront. "It's Kahled now, is it?"

"John!"

"Shut up, Blythe."

Sly shoved a finger under the old man's nose and yelled, "Fuck you!"

"Why so upset, Sly?" A hint of something sympathetic and fatherly flickered across John's face. "Please, don't tell me you let that soft heart of yours get attached to a bloodsucker."

Sly's fists clenched at his sides. "Fuck you," he repeated.

The old man's jaw clenched and his face went crimson. "You're the one who chose to debase yourself and all of humanity by chasing after a damn parasite. Bad enough you abandoned me and Blythe—"

"Are you delusional?"

"—without a backward glance—"

"I did this for you!"

"Bullshit!" John spat. "For years, I tolerated your obsession for the inhuman variety because I love you, but the truth is, you never wanted a damn thing to do with humanity or our way of life! I've had months to think it over, Sly, and the only thing that surprises me is that it took you this long to find an excuse to take off for some grand existence you can't imagine finding on Earth!"

Sly shook his head. "I literally cannot count the number of things wrong with what you just said!"

"Cut the shit, kiddo. You've been looking for a chance like this since your mother died!"

"No." Sly shook his head again, harder. "No. The only

thing I have done is tie myself in knots trying to save what's left of us!"

"We don't need saving!"

"Look around!" Sly gestured wildly toward the reinforced windows caked with dirt in their ill-fitted frames. "There are entire worlds out there with clear skies and breathable air, and there's no good reason we shouldn't have that!"

"There's plenty of good reasons, Sly. You just don't want to acknowledge them."

"You! You—" Sly sputtered. "You're a closed-minded old fool!"

John rolled his eyes. "Don't go taking it out on me because reality didn't match up to your fantasy."

"Okay." Blythe stepped between them, holding Sly back with a hand on his chest. "That's enough. Sly, just let it—"

"No, he's right."

He didn't push her away, didn't budge an inch, but her hand fell away just the same. His cool tone must have startled her after all the yelling. It certainly made his dad stall out.

"Yeah, you're right," Sly repeated, loud and proud. "It was nothing like I imagined."

John muttered a token, "Sorry to hear that, kid."

"It was better!"

John sighed, and Blythe winced as she got out of the way.

"That's the truth." Sly slapped his thighs, and the sound echoed with finality. His words came faster, louder with every volatile second. "I took a job to cover your ass, and I expected to come back a week from now to waste another decade or more trying to recover our money and my motivation to get your dead weight off this rock before it implodes!"

John fumed right back at him. "Don't talk to me like that in my own damn home!"

"That's what I expected. That's all," Sly continued, gaining traction in leaps and bounds. "Not to make it onto a ship before you were dead, but to just keep pretending we were headed that way! If it wasn't for your outright refusal to face the facts and leave, it would have been more drinking binges or maybe another dangerous gamble. Either way, you were never going to let it happen, you've just been—I don't know—pacified? Willfully ignorant? Fucking comfortable enough with the status quo to continue letting me throw away years and opportunities of pursuing anything better for myself!"

John raised a hand with a nasty snarl. "I have never told you what you could or could not do. Don't you dare blame me for your shitty decisions!"

"Every moment, every action, every fucking plan for my future!" Sly yelled, his eyes wet. "It's always revolved around you, whether you wanted to own it or not. And, even now, you're too damn stubborn to see how it's been killing me!"

"I wanted what's best for you!" John screamed back. "You're my son, dammit! My boy, and a fucking human being with a born right to the ground beneath your feet!"

"I. Don't. Want. It." Sly yanked at his hair, heedless of the tears streaming down his face. "I want more than to live an unremarkable life and die a useless death on a planet that won't keep turning much longer after I'm gone!"

"You don't know that!"

"I want stars!" Sly clutched a hand over his chest as he gasped out the words, trying to stop his heart from bursting out of him. "There's an entire galaxy only a ship's ride away, and I deserve to see it at some point!"

"Sly!" Blythe pleaded, reaching for his hand. "Hun, come on."

He smacked her hand away. It left his own stinging.

"The only person in my entire life who has done everything possible and made sacrifices to support me is Kahled Vauqeulin," Sly declared, spitting vindication. "A Nocturnus!"

"Then what are you doing here, Sly?" John asked, his face cold with indifference. "Because I'm having a hard time understanding why you'd invite yourself back into my simple Earthly life when you're so in love with some bloodsucker."

"Good fucking question!"

"You know what?" John threw his water bottle into the kitchen sink, and it burst with a resound crack. "I'm done with your shit, Sylvester."

"Good!" Sly crowed. "Because I'm done carrying yours!"

John jabbed a finger at the front door. "Get out of my house!"

"Gladly." Sly huffed, snatching up his outer gear.

"Wait!" Blythe snagged his arm on his way toward the door, her expression stricken as her eyes darted between the two men on a loop. "Why don't we all take a minute and calm down? Can't we try to talk this out?"

John glared at her. "This doesn't concern you, girl."

Sly whirled on him, and Blythe's restraining grip was the only thing keeping him from throwing a punch. "Don't talk to her like that!"

"You don't get to tell me shit!" John sneered, the vein in his neck popping as his cheeks purpled with rage. "I should have stopped you from hanging out with splicing addicts when you were a kid, but your mother talked me out of it! If she could see us now, she'd be sick!"

Sly was stunned silent. As Blythe brought her hands to her mouth with a sharp gasp, Sly began shaking his head.

"She was sick," Sly said with disconcerting calm. "You were too stubborn to see it, and I was too young, but she died because of the fucked up vision you have of humanity's birthright."

John stumbled back a step, staring at Sly like he didn't recognize him. "You don't know what you're talking about."

"You killed her," Sly said, voice shaking and eyes stinging. "You and this planet."

"Fuck you," John whispered.

"I'm not going to let you do the same to me."

Trembling with useless rage, Sly snatched his mask off the couch and stomped toward the exit.

The venom in John's voice was weak with disbelief as he sputtered, "You walk out that door boy, don't you dare think about coming back!"

Without another word, Sly donned his gear and walked out.

CHAPTER 22

*W*ith no other tenable options, Sly ended up at Centrism. Fortunately, Phink had a softer spot in his heart for his Earthling staff than he generally admitted.

"This isn't a charity," Phink grumbled from the doorway of his office after letting Sly take over the space.

"Thanks, boss," Sly murmured from his temporary bed.

Phink stepped aside, and Blythe squeezed into the doorway. She still wore her outdoor layers and had a stuffed bag slung over her shoulder. In her other hand, she was dragging a fold-out mattress, much like the one Sly sat on.

Phink waved her in with an unenthused grunt. "Go on. You'll have to set your bed up in the corner between my desk and the filing cabinets along the far wall since Sly's claimed the prime real estate where my guest chairs were."

With a somber nod, Blythe moved to do as he said. Sly watched her through blurry tears, his chest and throat tight as he trembled. She would have to crawl off the foot of her mattress to get to her feet, and it was inevitable that they would trip over each other.

Phink folded his arms and glared down the hall in a

decent imitation of a grumpy stuffed toy. It should have been laughable, but it wasn't.

"I know a guy who might have an apartment vacant," he offered. "I'll give him a call."

Their boss closed the door on his way out. There was a beat of silence as the privacy settled, then Sly loosed an upbeat whistle and drummed his fingers on the desk. "You didn't have to follow me."

Blythe sighed.

"I'm clearly the one he has the bigger problem with."

"Shut up." She sat on the edge of his makeshift bed with a groan and glared at him, arms straight and hands braced behind her. "He only let me in the door because I didn't give him a choice. It wasn't going to last much longer anyway, now that he's back on his feet."

Sly's fingers stilled as he stared at her wetly, "I love you."

"I am quite lovable." A smirk graced her lips before her arms gave out. She fell back against Phink's desk and continued magnanimously, "Besides. I'd rather be homeless with you than living slightly more comfortably with that old fart."

Sly choked on a laugh as he wiped his eyes. "Sure."

"I wish you never came back."

He wanted to be offended, to scowl and turn the conversation into a joke. He didn't have it in him. He slumped, the proverbial stick up his ass snapped clean through.

"We were all right." Blythe tucked her hands beneath her head, but the casual position did nothing to hide her rigidity. "I know it doesn't look that way to you, but we were adjusting. Without you, I had to wizen up, and I think John was just starting to recognize reality for what it is."

"Wow. You sure know how to cheer a guy up—"

"You were happier with that Nocturnus than you've been in years," Blythe said over him. "Hell, Sly, the way you laughed when you talked about him—I haven't heard that since we were kids."

"Yeah," Sly admitted sadly, "I wish I never came back too."

∾

THREE DAYS LATER, CAMPING OUT IN PHINK'S OFFICE WAS getting old fast.

"Move your shit, I need a file," was their boss's new catchphrase.

Things only got worse once the situation became public knowledge.

"I'm officially swearing off dick," was a sentiment commonly overheard in Blythe's vicinity, along with, "If another man offers to be my Sugar Daddy, I'm going to castrate him."

Centrism's clientele had likewise adopted certain sayings. Barely an hour went by without some iteration of: "Sly? Is that really you?" or "We didn't expect to see you again!" The combination of disbelief and confusion on everyone's face when they recognized him behind the bar was sickening.

Sly stayed quiet. Phink wasn't pushing him to get back on the stage just yet, the big softie.

"Sly? You're really back?"

The words were unsurprising, but the tone was something else. Instead of pity, it rang with something suspiciously hopeful.

Sly whipped around, smacking himself in the face with a dish rag.

Standing on the other side of the bar was Quin Le Vau.

319

His hands, fancy gloves and all, were splayed on the counter, and his handsome face gaped at Sly as if he were a ghost.

Sly took an awkward step forward and stowed a tumbler below the counter. "Uh... Hi, Le Vau. Yeah. I'm back."

Luxuriously thick leather warmed his skin as Le Vau cupped his jaw. Sly shouldn't allow the touch to linger, but he did.

"It's really you," Le Vau whispered, his hand trembling. "I thought I lost you..."

Sighing, Sly patted Le Vau's wrist away from his face. "You never had me to lose anyway."

Some of the overwhelming emotion receded from the vampire's face. He drew back his hand. "Of course. My apologies—"

Sly opened his mouth to brush him off.

"—for my behavior last time we spoke, specifically."

Sly's mouth snapped closed. He stared at Le Vau and his guarded expression, perturbed.

Le Vau nodded to himself. "I realized how out of line I was, and there hasn't been a moment since where I haven't regretted driving you to such extreme lengths."

"Holy shit," Sly gasped. "You're serious?"

In the years he'd worked there, diligently evading Le Vau's flirtations, he'd never seen the vamp so subdued. So genuine. Certainly never so contrite. His attitude was unrecognizable.

First Phink was being nice, then Blythe was growing up and holding her shit together, and now Quin fucking Le Vau had a conscience. Maybe his absence had done everyone more good than harm.

"I wouldn't joke about this, Sly," Le Vau continued despite Sly's attention wandering into the territory of ground-shaking epiphanies. "I know we've never been close, but there are reasons I began frequenting Centrism after you came along. I made a rash decision when I chose to break ties with my Harem, and watching you on that stage was one of the few comforts that let me live with that choice. You have no idea what isolation does to a Nocturnus—"

"I do," Sly cut in. Thoughtlessly, he slid his hand across the bar to squeeze Le Vau's fingers. The leather was uncommonly thick and creaked under the pressure of his grip. "We're not that different, you know. Your kind are every bit as socially dependent as humans are. You're lonely."

Le Vau froze, staring at their joined hands. "Yes." He slowly turned his hand over to return the comforting grip. "I suppose I am."

Sly nearly choked on the convoluted emotions welling up inside him. "I've spent some time lately appreciating how important personal connection is. For all of us."

He gave Le Vau's hand another squeeze before tugging free. In his wake, gloved fingers gripped at the air almost forlornly.

"You're being awfully sweet and not-creepy," Sly replied with forced cheer. "And it's nice to see someone glad I came back, so… apology accepted."

A hint of familiar flirtation colored Le Vau's smile. "Good. I suppose Vauqeulin's loss is my gain, then."

Sly laughed, but it sounded fake. "I don't know about that."

That fang-filled smile softened. "You fell for him, huh?"

Sly refocused on polishing glasses and shrugged. "Something like that."

cot the moment he entered the office that evening after his shift. "Let's run away together."

Sly paused with his hand on the doorknob. "To where?"

"Anywhere! Anywhere but here. Between my savings and the crap the Harem gave you, we can afford two tickets off-world to wherever we want!"

Sly stared at her from his own tiny cot, his face blank and his body exhausted. "Why?"

"Why what?" she scoffed. "Because we can. Because there's no reason not to. Because it's what you've always wanted! Pick a fucking reason, Sly. I don't care. Let's just go. There's nothing keeping us here now. Let's just do it."

Sly swallowed repeatedly before he could manage intelligible words. "I don't want to leave—" he cut off with a croak and cleared his throat before trying again, "I didn't want to leave him."

Blythe's face crumbled. She popped off her cot and bounded over to his so she could wrap him in her arms. "I'm sorry things ended badly with your vampire, Sly."

He sniffled, but didn't cry. He'd done enough of that.

"You're not the only one who's had shit hit the fan lately. Let's get out of here and do something with ourselves."

The defeat in her voice was foreign. It made her seem like a world-weary woman rather than the smart-assed brat he left behind months ago.

"Please," Blythe begged hopelessly. "I'm ready, Sly. I've spent half a year trying to catch up, but I can't be you. I can't pull your weight the way you did for me. I wish I could, but I can't."

The truth of it was etched into every new line in her face. She was no less gorgeous, but the signs of hard-won wisdom were there, lightly carved into her brow.

Sly bit his lips and whined. "What happened while I was gone, Blythe?"

She shook her head with a tight smile. "Nothing you didn't see coming. I knew I had a few Humans First sympathizers among my regulars, but one was actually in it. He bitched about me to his friends, and they decided I was worth making an example of."

Sly dropped his face in his hands. "Fuck, Blythe. They really lit up your apartment?"

She withdrew her arms to rub the goosebumps from her legs. "They, uh… it was complicated. There were letters. A few threatening packages. That sort of thing. I reported it, but the Guards kept saying they had to prioritize petty squabbles between humans and Nocturni. Human-on-human harassment is just an inconvenience, apparently."

"Stars above," Sly whispered, gripping her knee in solidarity.

"Then, the fire happened, and I knew. I need to leave."

"Okay."

"I think you need to come with me."

"Yeah. Probably."

Neither of them sounded happy about it.

Sly couldn't stand the oppressive sorrow cloying the room. After an intensely uncomfortable stretch of time, he shrugged out of Blythe's hug and clambered toward the door.

"Sly, wait—"

He closed the door and ran from the pleading sympathy in her voice.

THE SUPER SHITTY PART ABOUT BEING BETWEEN HOMES WAS the distinct lack of privacy. At least, that was what it felt like in the minutes it took to snatch his borrowed protective gear from the office and escape before Blythe could lock him into a well-meaning-but-intolerable hug. He couldn't handle her touch just then. Any comforting touch might shatter him.

Naturally, he was just fumbling with the straps of his mask and cussing himself over it when none other than Quin Le Vau caught him in Centrism's airlocked foyer.

"Sly?"

"Fuck!" Sly shouted, whipping the mask around and nearly smacking the vampire across the face with it.

Le Vau deftly avoided the collision with a raised brow.

"Can you get through a single fucking night without creeping on me?" Sly snarled before his brain could catch up with his mouth.

He braced for Le Vau to bare his fangs at him or threaten to shove him out the door without his mask. Even without the prestige of a Harem at his back, Le Vau was leagues higher up the social (and animal) food chains than Sly. He should have met Sly's antagonism like a reasonably predictable loner vamp and dished it back out in soul-crushing force.

Instead, Le Vau offered a contrite grin and said, "I suppose I could try."

Sly gaped at him. Then, he burst out laughing. The sound busted out of him, unprecedented and uncontrolled. It doubled him over and had him gasping. It was possible he was crying, but he was going to ignore that for as long as the vampire did.

He shouldn't have run off on Blythe. He was too raw, too desperate for something he couldn't have. A forced heart-to-heart with his best friend was at least a better option than losing his shit in front of a veritable stranger.

"Are you all right?"

"Okay." Sly nodded as he dried his face with his coat

sleeve. "Who are you, and what did you do with Quin Le Vau?"

The grimace he got in response was almost ugly around those huge fangs. Which was an absurd thought in light of the recent months Sly spent panting after a guy with a bigger set. That thought sent Sly into renewed shouts of tearful laughter.

To his credit, Le Vau waited him out. He shifted his weight and glanced about in blatant dismay, but he waited.

When Sly managed to calm down, he noticed they were alone in the foyer.

"Oh wow," Sly panted, staring about as his reluctant humor morphed into an uneasy chuckle.

"Wow?" Le Vau prompted as he shuffled closer. He wasn't all that threatening with his hands shoved deep in his pockets like a naughty child caught in a practical joke.

Sly slumped in defeat and admitted, "I'm a walking dick joke. It's not the size that matters, boys, it's how you use it. Well, fuck me..."

Le Vau hummed and took another measured step closer. His smile was small and charming, and around those uncommonly fearsome fangs, Sly's heart only saw Kahled.

Sly shuddered and shook himself to banish the thought. Pining after Kahled was pointless—maybe dangerous—if Myers hadn't been exaggerating to lure him into another contract. Blythe was right, he needed to move on with his life.

"While that is a tempting invitation, Sly," Le Vau said with none of his familiar teasing, "for now, I'd rather make up for my transgressions by offering a sympathetic ear and a stiff drink."

Sly frowned dubiously at the vampire.

Le Vau held up his hands and stepped toward the exit. "No strings. No expectations."

"I repeat..." Sly's eyes narrowed. "Who are you?"

Le Vau's face fell. "You really think so little of me, don't you?"

"Honestly?" And because Sly didn't have the energy to be anything but blunt, he went right ahead and said, "I can't remember the last time I thought of you at all."

Le Vau winced, his lip lifting awkwardly from his fangs. Sly always thought he was handsome, despite the unpopular splicing choice; visually, Le Vau was fit, a consummate Nocturnus specimen, but that was before Sly had anything significant to compare to. Next to the likes of Kamari Vauqeulin and his delicate eyeteeth, Le Vau's fangs were an insult to modern trends.

In comparison to Kahled, well... There was no comparing Quin Le Vau to Kahled.

Le Vau had no scales, no deformed hands and feet. The only thing he had in common with Sly's new standards for attractive Nocturnus features was uncommonly large fangs. Sly paused to considered whether that alone would be grounds for a Nocturni to be exiled from their Harem. Then, he promptly felt like a fool.

"I never asked how you ended up so far from your Harem," Sly mused, eyeing him. "And you never said why you chose to leave."

Because Le Vau, Sly reminded himself, was nothing like Kahled. He chose to become a loner, immigrating to the American Port decades before Sly ever stepped onto Centrism's stage. He wasn't cast out by his family due to no fault of his own. Sleazy comments and inappropriate overtures aside, Le Vau had never forced him into bloodletting, even by association. In the years they had known each other, this Nocturnus had never bitten Sly. He never put Sly in a hospital bed, only to turn around after the first mishap without so much as a fond farewell.

If the past six months had taught him nothing else, he at least knew better than to judge any vampire too quickly.

With such bittersweet thoughts in mind, Sly asked, "Do you want to tell me about it?"

The vampire gaped at him in surprise. It was so uncouth, so strange on Le Vau's genetically tailored face, that it made Sly laugh. A real, genuine, startled laugh.

Le Vau recovered with a faint pink on his cheeks. "I'd love to!"

Throat tight, Sly raised his mask to his face and nodded toward the exit. "Come on, then. I know a place that does a decent cocktail even at this hour of the morning."

CHAPTER 23

*S*ly hadn't been inside Mickey's bar in years, not since he stopped shadowing John to poker night in his early teens. It was a long and narrow hole-in-the-wall sort of place, just a few blocks away from Centrism, and Sly and Le Vau made it inside well before it closed at dawn. Mickey's was a little dingy and slightly disreputable, but it had the widest variety of human- and Nocturni-appropriate menu items for several blocks.

The owner was a clever asshole, happy to cater to clashing crowds for the right profit. If Sly remembered right, they were slipping through the door toward the tail end of the Nocturni's happy hour. If Mickey's was as greedy and strict as they used to be, all the humanity purists would have gone home hours ago.

The layered doors sealed behind them, and Sly flung his mask off.

Le Vau was more reserved as he slipped off his mask and hood. His nose wrinkled as he eyed the stained grout of the tiled floor, and Sly realized the place might be grossly below the vampire's expectations.

"So," Sly sang the word as he set down Phink's spare mask on the nearest booth table. "I realize this probably isn't up to your usual standards, but I promise, the drinks are just as good as anything we serve at the House."

Le Vau bumped their shoulders together with a teasing smirk on his way toward a seat at the booth. "Don't worry about it, Sly. It's not like I'm one of the Vauqeulins."

As the vampire chuckled, Sly flushed and scratched at the back of his neck.

"Word got around then, I see," Sly begrudged as he sat across from Le Vau.

"About you moonlighting as the Vauqeulin heir's personal blood bag?" Le Vau snickered at whatever look appeared on Sly's face, and there was a glimmer of his old creepiness in it.

Sly was almost relieved by the hint of familiarity. Probably, he was just grasping for something normal to tether himself to in his new reality.

"Yes, Sly. Word got around," Le Vau continued, his amusement fading fast. "So, it's true, then? I told myself I wouldn't believe any of the rumors unless you confirmed it."

"I can appreciate that." Sly sighed and raised a hand to flag down the bartender. "I guess it's true. A little more complicated than servicing the Harem's Heir, but true enough."

As Sly shrugged off his coat, Le Vau leaned back and stretched his arm over the back of the booth's bench with his outer gear still on. It was jarring to see him so cool and relaxed in a setting that wasn't Centrism. Then again, it wasn't like Sly had a wealth of experience socializing with the guy outside working hours.

The bartender, an old, gruff, pot-bellied man, swung by for their drink order. The moment he stepped away, Le Vau's foot nudged Sly's ankle under the table.

"How did they treat you?" Le Vau asked with no further prompting. "I hear that Harem's leading family are a bunch of pompous posers. More bark than bite, so to speak."

Sly flopped back into his seat with a chorus of creaking upholstery. "You're familiar with the Vauqeulins? Why am I not surprised?"

"You shouldn't be. They're one of The Nine." Le Vau's smirk widened, and he winked as he added, "And it's a small universe."

Sly snorted.

They lapsed into a tense quiet.

It lasted till Le Vau nodded toward the digital menu glowing a cheerful neon green behind the bar. "I noticed they don't post the percentage or donor species of the blood in their cocktails. How much would you bet that they water it down?"

Sly snorted again, but with greater enthusiasm. "I'm not about to bet against anyone who can afford real leather gloves."

Le Vau surveyed his hand with a thoughtful expression. "You recognized it was real? I'm impressed."

"Don't be. I had a lot of time to get overly familiar with a couch."

Silence fell between them for the second time in as many minutes. If it happened again before their drinks arrived, Sly was going to write the outing off as a failed experiment and make a polite excuse to leave.

That wasn't quite the turn their evening ended up taking.

Le Vau huffed under his breath and repositioned himself so he could lean on the table. "Can I tell you a secret?"

Sly already knew he was desperate for distraction, but it was still embarrassing how fast he chirped back with an eager, "Sure!"

"Do public schools still teach you about the original splicing formula that birthed the Nocturni?"

Sly frowned, taken aback. "Yeah. But I haven't had to refresh my memory since I was… I don't know. Nine years old? What're you getting at?"

Le Vau's fangs forced his grin unfortunately wide. "So, one of the key ingredients way back then was bat DNA. Today's vamps don't like to admit it, but it's an integral part of our makeup, so even though bats have been extinct for a couple centuries, most of us still have a little something from that species. And what do you know, my flying vermin ancestors are the dirty little secret behind the sharpest ears in the world."

At Sly's uncomprehending stare, Le Vau tapped his ear. Like most Nocturni, his narrowed into pointed peaks at the top, though not as obvious as Kamari's or Kahled's.

With a start, Sly remembered how sensitive Kahled's ears were, how they twitched at the grating sound of Sly's fork the first time they met.

"Do all Nocturni have superhuman hearing, then?" he asked.

Le Vau shrugged, his grin never fading. "Most, probably. Want to know what the bartender's saying about us?"

Sly guffawed. "You can hear him?"

"Talking shit under his breath." Le Vau nodded. "He's definitely watering down my drink."

Sly made a consolatory noise in the back of his throat. "Guess you'll have to satisfy that vampire bloodlust some other way."

"Are you offering a vein?"

The proposition was polite compared to Le Vau's usual come-ons. The hopeful glance he cast toward Sly's bandaged throat and the way he licked at one overlarge fang were familiarly crass.

Sly jerked back from the conspiratorial little huddle with a stiff chuckle. "Nope. No way. Actually, just in case you're getting any ideas, I couldn't right now even if I wanted to." Sly shielded the injury with one hand as he hastened to say, "The last time someone bit into me, it didn't go so well."

"Why?" A deep frown erased the lascivious hope on Le Vau's face. "Are you all right?"

Sly shrugged, hyperaware of the healing skin pulling on his neck beneath the gauze.

The vampire made a soft hum and rose from his seat. "I'm rethinking that drink. Something tells me you could use alcohol far less than you could use a shoulder to cry on."

Sly shook his head fiercely, eyes comically wide. "Oh, no. Nope, I'm fine—"

"Sly."

A heavy hand came down on his shoulder, opposite the injury. It sent an unpleasant shiver down Sly's spine.

Sly met the vampire's eye, and his breath caught. He'd never been so close to Le Vau before. From no distance at all, the small flecks of blue in Le Vau's hazel irises were beautiful.

"Why don't you come to my place?"

Sly recoiled. "Seriously?"

Le Vau grimaced, and Sly thought he felt the fingers on his shoulder pinch briefly through the combined layers of his shirt and Le Vau's glove.

The vampire backpaddled with a charming chuckle, "I simply meant that you could use the privacy to air your thoughts, and my place is, admittedly, a lot more comfortable—"

"Ah," Sly interrupted, squeezing past him and out of the booth. "There's the Quin Le Vau I remember."

"Let me make up for the way I treated you before," Le Vau pleaded. His sincerity gave Sly pause, and he couldn't help but notice the blue in Le Vau's eyes that much more.

"There's always an agenda with you." Sly affirmed, not unkindly. "Even when it's well-meaning and honest. I don't have the energy for those games tonight. You can't feed off me right now. Stars above, but do you even know why you want to so bad?"

"I thought it was obvious." Le Vau's cocky smirk made another reappearance as he gave Sly's shoulder an encouraging squeeze. "You're beautiful, clever, and wildly entertaining, Sly. What more could a warm-blooded male want?"

Sighing, Sly took them both by surprise by stepping forward and placing a palm on the vampire's chest. "You're a Nocturnus and *I*, goofy little Sylvester Spurgeon, am quite possibly the only human you've ever met with completely pure human blood."

Le Vau's eyes widened. The blue in them was never more obvious, and the shade was just pale enough to make Sly's heart hurt at the reminder of a completely different vampire.

"You're not interested in me, Quin," Sly said with a solid pat over the vamp's heart. "Not really. Your hindbrain is just fixated on my pheromones."

"I don't understand... You're—you've never spliced?" Le Vau sounded breathless. "Not ever?"

Sly shook his head as his arm dropped back to his side. "It doesn't matter right now, anyway."

"The hell it doesn't." Le Vau gaped at him in astonishment.

No, it wasn't mere surprise. The vampire's face went

slack and his eyes glazed over; Le Vau had the look of someone who's entire worldview was shattering before his eyes. The foreign emotion colored his face made Sly's skin prickle with goosebumps.

"For the love of the cosmos," Le Vau whispered. "It makes so much sense now..."

There was no mistaking the clenching of the vampire's hand on his shoulder this time around.

Sly winced and tried to tug free. "Ease up, Le Vau. That kind of hurts."

The vampire yanked his hand away as if burned. "I'm sorry."

"It's okay..." Sly frowned and rubbed at the sore spot till he was confident it wasn't bruised.

"I would never hurt you, Sly. You have to know that, right?"

"What?"

A gloved hand cupped his jaw with startling tenderness. "I always knew you were special, Sly. But this... You're precious. You don't even know."

Sly blushed. "Actually, I kind of do. Which is why I'm going to ask you not to go shouting about it from the rooftops, okay?"

"Please," Le Vau stepped into his personal space, close enough for Sly to feel Le Vau's coat buttons brush his shirt "Won't you let me have a taste?"

Sly stiffened.

"Just one taste, Sly. Please—"

"No. I don't think that's a good idea..."

But the vampire was nodding, heedless. "One taste. That's all I'm asking for, Sly—"

"No, Le Vau!" Sly repeated firmly as he pushed the vampire away with both hands.

Le Vau stumbled back, his crowded mouth open in shock. "Sly, please! You don't know how much I need you."

Sly gasped. "What the fuck?"

It was as if the final pieces to an intricate puzzle were popping into place by magic. As Sly stared at Le Vau, all the little things that used to bother him about the loner started to make sense. He scrutinized those enormous fangs with the benefit of experience. He reconsidered the unprecedented blue in Le Vau's eyes and cast a wary glance at the ever-present gloves. Sly wondered how long it'd been since the last time he saw the vampire's hands bare, safe from exposure inside Centrism's walls.

"You're a Vauqeulin descendant," Sly whispered, "aren't you?"

Le Vau's shoulders lifted, tense like a cornered animal. It was too easy for Sly's racing mind to project Kahled in his place, bristling with anger.

Sly took a deliberate step back. "Why did you leave your Harem, Le Vau?"

"You don't know what you're suggesting, Sly," the vamp warned.

"Yes, I do," Sly said, as soft and non-antagonizing as he'd ever tried to be in his life. He did rather well, despite all the sudden sprinting of his pulse. "How long have you known you were Cursed, Quin? Have you sought treatment?"

Le Vau growled. "Stop."

"We can get you help."

"Yes." Le Vau stalked forward. "You can help me, can't you? All this time, I've had a cure prancing around right under my nose."

"No, it's not that simple."

"It is."

"No!" Sly ripped the bandage from his neck with

fumbling fingers, breathing fast as he revealed the raw stitches. "See? This is what happened the last time the Curse got the better of a vampire. Vauqeulin hoped I could cure his brother, but it didn't work."

Le Vau froze in his tracks. He stared at the scar with a focus as sharp as his teeth.

"Kahled cared for me at least as much as you think you do, and he still nearly bled me out," Sly explained in a rushed whisper. "If you bite me now, you'll kill me. Or worse, I'll need a transfusion with spliced blood." He gave a strangled, humorless chortle. "Tainted blood, Le Vau. Either way, I'll become useless to you if you bite me now."

The fangs were too large for Le Vau to close his mouth properly, but he swallowed around them anyway. "He fed from you directly?"

Sly nodded frantically. "For months. I wasn't there just to be his Companion—"

Le Vau cut him off with a growl loud enough to demand the barkeeper's attention.

"Everything all right, gentlemen?" the man called from behind the counter.

Le Vau snarled in response without tearing his gaze from Sly's vulnerable throat.

"Hey!" the bartender hollered. "I don't tolerate racial disputes in my bar! Keep it up and I'll call the Guard!"

The blue was starting to glow in Le Vau's eyes. Just a little. Just enough. Sly only caught it because he was looking for it.

"Call the Guard," Sly said with forced calm.

A vicious shiver rattled through Le Vau. He stomped closer.

Scars notwithstanding, if Kahled was coming at him like that, Sly would have dropped to his knees, ready to go in an instant. The idea of letting Le Vau get that close had Sly quaking in his boots.

He never should have come back to the port.

A short, spinechilling laugh burst out of him.

"You think this is funny, Sly?" Le Vau bit out, the dark growl in his voice unmistakable.

Sly clapped a hand over his mouth with a whimper, shaking his head as the bartender scurried off.

"You taunt me with everything I could possibly want..." Le Vau snarled. "And then you laugh as you tell me another Nocturnus stole you from right under my nose!"

But the irony was choking Sly. Kahled had sent him away for his own safety, only to put him in the least safe position of his miserable Earthling life. No, no, no, the irony wasn't choking, but it was, quite possibly, going to get him killed.

"Please—" Sly gasped through a cloying mix of tears and laughter. "Le Vau, I'm not—I'm not laughing at you. I just... You have no idea what I would give to not be in this scenario right now— Ah!"

He jumped, nearly straight out of his skin, as Le Vau crossed the scant space and forced him back into the booth. Sly's shoulders hit the table with a dull thud that was more terrifying than painful. He flinched when Le Vau's fist planted itself inches deep in the plaster beside his head.

The blue was glowing white-hot now. Anyone could see the danger.

Sly tried to clear away his useless tears with a few rapid blinks. Le Vau stopped him from using his hand by pinning his wrist to the table.

"He bled you," Le Vau rumbled, hot breath ghosting Sly's face. "And he fucked you. Didn't he?"

Le Vau shook him, and the next thing he knew, Sly's head bounced off the table and started ringing with pain. Someone shouted. Someone snarled. Something broke. Searing agony exploded up his left arm and Sly's stomach heaved. All the while, Sly watched the ceiling swirl, and black spots popped in and out of sight.

Then, Le Vau was crouched over him, hot rage and hotter calculation distorting his features.

"I should have known what you are."

Spittle dotted his face as the vampire snarled.

"As if Vauqeulin stealing you away wasn't clear enough, I should have figured it out after I realized your father's blood was so much heartier than any I've ever tasted."

Sly's breath froze in his lungs.

"But no!" Le Vau sneered as his hand closed on Sly's throat. "I was so stupidly possessed with the idea of you coming home to take care of him, I never slowed down enough to put it together. That's what I get for thinking with my dick, I suppose."

Sly slapped at the steel grip locked on his neck, blocking his air supply. Darkness crept in and threatened to smother the terrified realization of what Le Vau had done.

"He'll pay! That fuck of a vamp is going to pay!"

The pressure lifted. Sly had enough time to gasp in a lungful before the chance was gone, and his mouth was blocked by hard lips and harder fangs in a bruising kiss. It was mercifully brief.

"I'll be back for you."

CHAPTER 24

*W*hen adequate air was making its way to his lungs and his head mostly stopped ringing, Sly discovered Phink's mask was crushed to bits on the floor. The sleek comms unit the Harem had gifted him was cracked and useless, pinched into his bruising skin.

The barkeeper insisted on calling Emergency Services, but Sly didn't have time for a hospital trip just for a minor concussion and bruised wrist. It was a good thing Centrism was only a few blocks away, and Blythe was quick. Sly wasn't all that coherent when he summoned her via the barkeeper's comms, but the shaken old man was.

"Mickey's," he barked at her after yanking his wrist from Sly. "Get this kid out of my bar before I have the authorities take care of him."

Minutes later, Blythe plowed through the door. She got one look at Sly and fumbled for the latch on her mask as she cried out, "What the hell happened to your hand? Is it broken?"

Sly glanced down at his injured wrist and winced. The

decimated comms was surrounded by a disturbing patchwork of bruising and swollen veins creeping over the back of his palm. He tugged a glove over the injury.

"It's nothing. I need help. I think Le Vau's about to do something stupid."

The second glove didn't go on so smoothly. He grimaced as he tried to get the tendons in his crushed wrist to move his fingers the right way. It hurt, but he could move them. It wasn't broken. Probably.

"What happened?" Blythe demanded as she took over.

She slipped the glove on his good hand without fuss, then reached for the other with a wince of reluctance that didn't stop her. Sly hissed in pain as she rolled the glove back to expose the mangled metal and began plucking at the cracks with nimble fingers.

"Le Vau," he said, voice numb as he watched her slip a nail between his skin and metal. With a weak snap, the comms released and the rush of blood tingling into his fingers made Sly gasp. "Shit! Ow. Yeah. So, Le Vau's Cursed, too."

Blythe dropped the ruined comms as she startled back, staring at him with her jaw dropped.

"I figured it out." He raised his injured hand and waved weakly. "And he learned a few details about me and Kahled that didn't sit too well with him."

"Wait." Blythe winced like her head hurt. "Quin Le Vau? He has the same disease as your vampire?"

"Did you bring me a mask? I need to get back to Centrism. HEPP needs to alert Kamari Vauqeulin."

Like a true friend, Blythe let her questions go in favor of helping him into her extra mask. It was small on him and stepping outside made the exposed skin by his ears itch, but it got the job done. Sly pinched his hood tight beneath his chin and manage to survive the outdoors for the mad dash back to Centrism without breaking out in a rash.

Once they were back inside, Sly ripped the tight gear off, and not a moment too soon.

"Sly! There you are! We were just looking for you!"

Phink was waiting for him in the House's foyer, just inside the sealed doors. He wasn't alone.

"Tilla?"

"Sylvester!" Golden arms looped around his neck, and he was smothered in muscular cleavage. "When Vauqeulin told me what happened, I almost didn't believe it!"

"Sly. Sly. Sly!" Phink pawed at his shoulder. "Is this a joke? Can I borrow it? I could put it in the public lounge for a month, and I bet it'll buy you some more time before I need you back on stage!"

Tilla held him at arm's length to talk over Phink. "He paid me twice my usual fee, and I thought he was crazy, but then I saw it, Sly. Then, Vauqeulin gave me his message."

Blythe shouted, "What the fuck are you talking about?"

Sly tried to collect his bearings and parse out the meaning of their jumbled words, but the world was spinning out of control too fast for him to keep up.

"The painting!" crowed Phink.

At the same time, Tilla frowned and Blythe demanded, "Didn't you see it on your way out of here?"

"We thought that was why Blythe went running to find you." Phink stared from Sly to Blythe and back with slow, owlish blinks. "She didn't tell you?"

Blythe sputtered, "Tell him *what*?"

Phink and Tilla shared looks of stunned confusion before they turned toward Sly with disheartening expressions

"Master Kamari Vauqeulin," Tilla said with a gentle frown. "He summoned me from his Earthly estate two days ago. I was still haggling a deal in Europe's Port, so it was no big deal to double back, certainly not at that price—"

"Tilla?" Sly interrupted, his insides chilled with anxiety. "I have some time-sensitive shit to get to. What are you doing here?"

Tilla shot Phink an infuriatingly hefty look, then they spoke to Sly, "Master Vauqeulin gives you his thanks, and he promises that he will try to talk sense into his brother."

Sly's heart lurched into his throat. He choked on it audibly.

"If Kahled cannot be swayed within a week or two..." Tilla continued, biting their inner lip and not meeting Sly's eye. "Master Vauqeulin will come to personally escort you and yours off-world."

Sly clamped his eyes shut against the implication.

"He said, if it comes to that, he suspects it will be a condition of Kahled's last request."

"No." Sly held up a hand to stop them from saying more. "No. The Curse isn't so advanced that they'll put him down like a rabid animal. He has more than two fucking weeks left in him!"

"Sly," Blythe murmured, reaching for him.

Sly waved her off with a vicious jerk of his arm. "I don't have time for this! I need a properly fitted mask and a way to contact the Harem! Either help or get out of my way!"

Tilla sighed. "Vauqeulin left his personal contact information with the package he asked me to deliver."

"Where?"

"My office," Phink offered.

Sly took off. Like some sort of troop of self-appointed Guards, Blythe, Phink and Tilla followed him all the way to Phink's office.

Phink hustled ahead of him to reach the door first, shooting Tilla an unreadable look. The door opened.

Sly froze.

"Holy shit," Blythe breathed.

"Gorgeous, isn't it?" Tilla asked.

"It's..." Sly swallowed, but he couldn't think of anything to say.

It was red. The canvas leaning against the foyer wall was nearly waist-height and primarily crimson toned. While the browns and yellows and all manner of peachy hues were evident and well-applied, they only seemed to emphasize his least favorite color. It was so red. So very, very red.

But it was unlike any red Sly knew. Red was fire, the color of smog and a decaying planet. It was death. It wasn't alive. It wasn't bursting with energy and majestically beautiful.

Then again, neither was he, last he checked.

The human male portrayed in the painting was him, but not. Smooth-faced and pouty lipped, flushed and expressive with shining eyes. The hair wasn't auburn-brown and unremarkable, it was highlighted with ruby and oranges that made the dried paint seem to dance like active flames. Shimmering honey tones highlighted the eyes, and the warmth stroked into the skin promised comfort and sensuality. He was breathtaking.

Sly swayed. "That's...?"

"You," Blythe affirmed as she steadied him. "Kahled painted it, didn't he?"

Sly gave a wobbling nod. He didn't trust himself to open his mouth.

"He did you justice," Phink commented. "A little heavy on the sexiness, but, otherwise, it sure looks like you."

Nothing more needed to be said, not that Sly would have

noticed either way. He was too busy weeping like the forlorn lover he absolutely was.

Blythe wrapped him in her arms. "Oh, Sly!"

"Oh, no! Don't—it's all right!" Phink blustered.

"Shut up, Phink! Let him cry. You cry as much as you want, Hun."

Sympathetic hands petted his shoulders, back, and the crown of his head. He couldn't tell who was offering the comfort. He didn't care. He buried his face in his hands and sobbed.

"Okay. Let's give him some privacy," Phink huffed.

He was jostled and dragged on unsteady feet. He bobbed along blindly through a cacophony of concerned voices and unhelpful murmurs. Only once he felt the cot under his ass and heard the snap of the office door muffle everything else did he find the strength to lift his head.

Blythe sat beside him, her hand rubbing his back. Tilla was perched on the corner of the desk, face stony-still and posture soft, like a golden statue of a merciful and powerful god.

Sly tugged his shirtsleeve from the wrist of his coat and tried soaking up the wetness on his cheeks. He tried to smile, to give them some belief that their presence was helping, but neither of them looked reassured.

"What now?" he whimpered up at them. "I love Kahled, and I think I just sent a deranged vampire in the middle of a psychotic break after him."

Sly didn't know what to do. There was no plan, no motivation, just a dark, empty hole in his gut. It was like Le Vau had reached in and ripped out the lump of dire worry and upset festering inside him all these months. Somehow, while he'd been trying his damnedest not to notice, that gross tangle of negativity had sucked up all the care and hope he had in him. Now, it was all gone.

He was numb. Untethered. Lost in more than one sense of the word.

Good thing he wasn't as alone as he felt.

While Sly languished on his cot like a limp noodle, Blythe yanked Phink into the office and caught him up to speed.

She ended with a terse, "What do we do about this?"

Phink stared at her, shaking his head. "No. No, I can't get involved in whatever Harem drama—"

"Phink. It's *Sly*."

She said his name with all the gravity of a top-security code word, but Sly couldn't make himself care. Her demand and Phink's silent acquiescence were worth taunting them over on any other day. But it wasn't just any other day.

The last time he felt so hollowed out with regret, there was still an ashen patch on the lawn where his mother had fallen. Nothing mattered. Everything that did was gone, and no amount of logic would convince him it wasn't his fault.

"I can shoot the Harem Heir a message," Phink said in slow, stilted words. "But with Sly no longer under contract, it could be days before he bothers looking at a message from a HEPP employee, especially one from the entertainment side of things. I just don't have that much sway, Blythe."

Blythe said, "What about contacting the estate directly?"

"We don't need to," said Tilla. "Harems normally contact me through stringent business avenues, even for private deliveries, but this Harem's leader came to me personally as Sly's friend."

Blythe's excitement stirred something small and fiery in Sly's chest as she cheered. "You have a direct line to Kamari Vauqeulin?"

No one spoke, and Sly looked up to find three of the most heavily spliced people he knew huddled in front of the desk. Tilla remained half-seated, their head and shoulders towering above the others, and a warm glow of projected figures hovered over their wrist. Phink and Blythe wore identical expressions, brows furrowed and lips bitten, as they focused on the display.

His dad wasn't there. He wasn't included in the little troupe readying themselves to dive into a mess of Nocturni legacy for no better reason than to defend Sylvester Spurgeon's soft heart.

Sly's throat closed tight, his chest throbbing painfully.

A hard voice sounded from Tilla's wrist where golds of spliced skin and rich metal blended against each other, "Who in the great cosmos is this?"

Kamari's voice washed over Sly like a sunstorm through so many protective layers. Sly gasped and jumped to his feet.

"Kamari Vauqeulin?" Tilla leaned over their wrist. "I'm the merchant you chartered to deliver the painting to Sly Spurgeon."

Kamari's voice softened, but he did not turn on his video feed to show himself to them. "The delivery was successful, then?"

Tilla, Blythe, and Phink glanced at Sly with stiff faces.

Blythe muttered, "You could say that."

The hard edge returned to the vampire's tone. "Who was that?"

Phink cleared his throat, making a rude gesture to silence the woman. "Master Vauqeulin, this is Phink, the manager of HEPP's House, Centrism. Tilla was kind enough to lend myself and select employees their comms so we could issue you a warning."

Kamari made a sound, soft and gruff. Sly couldn't tell if he was laughing or growling at them.

Phink soldiered on in his most polished business voice, "It seems your Earthly estate is being targeted by a known loner Nocturnus—"

"Is this a threat?" Kamari interrupted, voice heavy with incredulity. It was the first time Sly had heard him sound so stereotypically… rich? Pompous?

"We're trying to *warn* you!" Blythe snapped, grabbing Tilla's wrist in her impatience.

The vampire responded with mocking patience, "You do realize, we are one of the wealthiest and most capable Harems in existence? I'm a direct descendant of The Nine—"

"We know!" Sly interrupted, squishing himself in between Phink and Tilla.

"Sly, is that you?"

"Quin Le Vau is one of yours!" Sly yelled at the comms, "He's Cursed too, Kamari! I saw it!"

"He nearly broke Sly's wrist!" Blythe said, matching his volume.

"And he attacked my dad!"

Everyone froze, staring at him with wide eyes.

Sly met each of his friends' gazes. "Didn't I mention that?"

"No!" Blythe and Phink chimed with matching scowls.

Their attention was diverted as Tilla's comms lit up with an incoming visual. Kamari's face materialized in the air. His intricate braid was too long for the comms to capture, and his ears were completely divested of fur, but he looked otherwise the same as he'd been portrayed in the estate's billiards room. His expression was serious, but schooled smooth as he focused on Sly.

"I'm sorry about your father, Sly. Truly. But I have no

responsibility for or power over vampires who choose to break ties with the Harem."

"He's Cursed, Kamari," Sly stressed.

"That's not possible. Nosferatu's Curse is rare—"

"Yeah. I know. Gorbon told me ages ago. Tahliah should have been the once-in-a-millennium occurrence, but she wasn't. Kahled mentioned how worried the Elders were when he got it too, less than a century later, and they were right to worry. He's not the only one! Le Vau's Cursed too!"

"It's not possible," Kamari hissed.

There was a pinch to the corners of his eyes and a shrug to his mouth that made him look young. For a moment, Sly was struck dumb as he saw the Harem Heir as the untrained child Kahled probably saw. That in mind, Sly made an aborted gesture to reach for him.

Hand falling to his side, Sly sighed. "I know this doesn't make your life easier, Kamari, and the implications for your bloodline are absolute shit at best, but you have to believe me. Le Vau seemed fine one second—better than normal, actually—and the next, he did this."

Sly raised his injured hand and pulled back his sleeve. Kamari's jaw tightened right before he covered his mouth with an open palm.

"Stars above, Sly," Phink hissed, reaching for his arm. "You need a hospital."

"It's just bruised," Sly muttered, eyes locked on Kamari. "Le Vau may not be connected to the Harem, but he has resources. I bet he's already on his way toward you."

Kamari blanched. "You're sure? You really think he's after Kahled, on his way here?"

Phink stiffened.

Sly nodded. "That's what he said—Woah!"

Tilla grunted as Phink tried to swipe the comms from

their wrist. When that didn't work, he brought the whole arm close to his face to convey his urgency. "You're there? At the estate? Master Vauqeulin, you need to leave!"

Kamari blinked. "I beg your pardon? I'm not about to abandon my brother—"

"Then take him with you?" Blythe suggested, her tone unimpressed.

Everyone ignored her as Phink shook Tilla's wrist and shouted, "You are the third leader your people have known in a given century! What do you think will happen to the Harem if you die?"

Kamari's likeness shrank as he reeled back from his comms.

Blythe looked from Sly to Tilla and back, alarmed. "That's not a thing. Right? Le Vau's beef is with Kahled, not his brother or the Harem. Right?"

At Sly's continued wide-eyed silence, she turned on Phink.

"Right?" she snapped.

Phink closed his eyes and pinched the bridge of his nose. "Fuck, guys. He's Cursed! Le Vau's been on Earth longer than I've been alive, and there's no way of telling how advanced his condition is. For all we know, his plan amounts to nothing but causing as much havoc as possible."

Paler than ever, Sly neared the comms again. "Kamari?"

He could sympathize with the stricken tremble in Kamari's voice. "Yes, Sly?"

"Kahled told me he killed someone. Other Nocturni. That's why you exile the Cursed ones from Ethos, right? Because they're dangerous, even to your kind?"

Kamari shook his head and switched off his video. Once his face was out of their sight, he croaked. "I have a personal security detail waiting for me in the hangar bay. I might… I will have them patrol the area while Walters and I evacuate the manor."

Mouth dry, Sly asked, "And Kahled?"

Kamari was slow to answer. "They won't allow him on my craft, Sly. It's a luxury star farer, it doesn't have adequate space to put him…"

"You're not leaving him there?" Sly hissed, aghast. "What about Walters? Gorbon? They have shuttles—"

"You know him as well as I do, Sly." The sadness weighing Kamari's every word stole the breath from Sly's lungs. "Do you really think he'll be willing to trap a handful of humans in close quarters with him for any length of time? Especially now when his episodes are so unpredictable?"

Sly didn't answer. There was no answer, at least not one that he could stomach.

"I'll come for him," Sly cried. "Tell him I'm on my way back to him."

Kamari sighed, "Okay. I'll try." Then, he was gone.

Blythe glowered at Tilla's wrist. "What an asshole."

Tilla drew their arm close to fold over their chest, discerning gaze trained on Sly. "I tried to warn you, Earthling. But you just had to go fall in love with a dying vampire, didn't you."

It wasn't a question, and Sly made no attempt to deny it. "You have no reason to help me, Tilla. You've already done so much more than I could repay you for. But will you? Will you help me get back to him?"

Tilla's shoulders heaved with a silent sigh. Their expression told him nothing as they said, "All right."

"All right!" Blythe repeated, voice fierce as if to compensate for Tilla's bland response. "Let's go save Sly's vampire prince!"

Sly shook his head at her. "He's not a prince."

"And you're no knight in shining armor, so I guess you're well-matched."

"We should go." Tilla passed between them toward the door. "Le Vau may not know the way, but he's a couple hours ahead of us. We'll have to be very lucky if we hope to beat him there."

CHAPTER 25

One of Sly's earliest and fondest memories was of a rustic orange sky and billowing brownish clouds seen through the spot-marked window of public transit. At the time, he found it pretty, so much burnt amber stretching into forever and so very, safely far away. It had all the beauty of the Unknown, the Untouchable, and his ignorance made it blissful. In that memory, he was safe and comfortable in his mother's lap, cocooned by the double layers of his protective gear and hers.

He didn't mind the cumbersome garments. He didn't mind the mask either when his mother was right there, tickling his imagination with suggestions that they were space explorers aboard a daringly rigged craft that was about to launch them through those gruesome clouds. She bounced her leg and hugged him tight, and he giggled as she described the vehicle's awkward roll as a harrowing build up to flight.

The transport turned a corner, and they passed through the clouds together. For real. Ugly puce grays and mottled browns blotted out the view, shrouding every window on the transport till the driver was forced into a full stop until the sunstorm passed. When it finally did, the pretty orange sky was obscured by black smoke and flickering flames that made his mother gasp. They were no longer playing pretend.

Years later, the echo of that childhood disappointment and incomprehension rolled over Sly. It was like he was six years old again, on an unfamiliar craft, staring out a dirty window and watching flames wreak havoc in place of a beaconing horizon.

Phink gripped his shoulder. Blythe held his hand. Tilla piloted their weather-worn merchant ship.

No one spoke.

When Tilla had announced they were less than an hour from the estate, Sly raced Blythe up to the Command Deck. The full front wall of the giant, curved room was a reinforced window at the highest point on the craft; it would give them a full view of the estate unlike anything Kamari's personal shuttle might have allowed for if Sly had been paying attention on his first ride in.

They expected an early view of the estate as they approached. They expected Le Vau might have beaten them there, that he might already be in Kamari Vauqeulin's custody.

They hadn't expected smoke in the distance. It was distinguishable from the fiery smog that perpetually crowded the Earth as it sent up blossoms of ash to further stain the polluted sky. Sly's brain went on hiatus as he waited to see the flames eating away at a place that felt like home.

They crested a hill, and the flames were there.

"We're too late," Sly murmured.

No one contradicted him.

The estate wasn't much to look at from the outside. The building was functional, windowless, and an absolute fortress against the elements. It should have been a solid rectangle, sealed and secured from nature and enemies alike.

There was a crater. The immediate corner of the building was caved in, smoke and flames rising steadily as metal and stone and fabric and stars only knew what else burned into so much dust. Nothing moved besides the fires.

"Fuck me," Sly whispered into his bruised palm.

"Le Vau?" Blythe sounded horrified and breathless, her grip on his good hand ached. "What did he do?"

"He crashed his ship straight into it," Tilla decided. "He must have."

"He's dead then," Phink said. "No one could survive that. Not even the Nocturni."

Sly moaned. It was quiet and warbling, and it inspired Blythe to let go of his hand so she could smack the back of Phink's head.

"Shit! Oh... sorry." Phink patted his shoulder before stepping away.

Tilla glanced over at the three of them without relinquishing the ship's controls. "Stay strong, Sly. A Harem old enough to have an Earthly property is a Harem smart enough to have contingency plans. Chances are, whole sections were locked down and sealed air-tight the moment any part of the interior was exposed."

"And that's assuming the evacuation efforts didn't work out," Blythe added, giving him a rousing shake.

Sly shook his head, biting his lips shut. He didn't know what would come out of him if he opened his mouth, but it wouldn't be good or helpful.

Tilla steered them past the wreckage, and Sly wasn't the only one who fell mute. The only discernable noises were the subtle beeps and taps of consoles and the creak of the fine leather of the pilot's chair as Tilla adjusted their direction. They watched, helpless, as horror seeped through the ship's walls and turned the air rancid by mere proximity.

The crumpled hulk of a crashed craft was worrisomely deep into the house. Le Vau's transport was a long, slender thing, but no further details were discernable. It was blackened and streaked, nothing but jagged metal in some spots and hazy shapes under the flames.

"Stars above," Phink whispered.

They got close enough to see the first bodies.

"Dammit!" Blythe hissed, bouncing on her heels and wringing her hands. "That… that… fucker!"

The crash was responsible for the deaths, yes, but not directly; Sly could tell as much at a glance. If the craft managed to plow into a person or sprayed debris into anyone, it was impossible to tell with all the flesh so devastated by exposure, but the bodies looked too intact for that to be likely.

In an instant, the creeping echo of his memories launched into the forefront of Sly's mind.

The charred remains were familiar, and for a split second, Sly couldn't breathe. He saw his mother falling to her knees as the atmosphere stripped her flesh and shredded her clothes. Then, he realized the clothes were wrong, damaged beyond repair, yes, and familiar, yes, but they were wrong; that black scrap was Lunar-made as it fluttered over an arm sporting blisters that exposed bone.

He thought he recognized a skirt on one of the bodies. Uniform-like. On a small frame. Mae? He hoped he was wrong.

Earth's raw might needed mere minutes to make a body unrecognizable. There was more than one body this time. His mother had been easy to identify. He'd watched her step out the door in her bedclothes and known the entire time as

Blythe fought him into a mask and coat who and what he would find.

This time, though... This time, there were too many bodies. So many bodies.

"No," Sly said as he marched over to Tilla. "No. Not Kahled. Not him. Just... no."

Tilla's hand hesitated on the steering. "Sly—"

"Go around," he said. "Park in the garage like last time. It's on the other side of the building, and so is Kahled's suite. It'll be intact. Perfectly safe."

Tilla met his eye, cool and infuriatingly expressionless.

"It's safe," Sly insisted. "Like you said, they'll have backup barriers. That could be the only area contaminated—"

"Okay," Tilla raised a gentle hand to Sly's cheek, making him freeze.

"Yeah. Okay."

Lowering their hand, Tilla added, "If the garage doesn't seal and the sensors don't read clear, I will not open the doors."

Sly nodded once. "Sure. But they will."

They had to. There was no other option.

They tried contacted Kamari at the first sign of smoke, but there was no answer. If the evacuation was interrupted and access to transportation wasn't secured with breathable air, there was nothing else that could be done. Kamari and his entourage, Walters and her staff, Kahled, they could all be dead.

Some forgotten deity seemed to be looking out for them, because Tilla's trader code worked on the hangar doors, and they closed behind them and sealed up like a dream. The minutes it took Tilla to land and take necessary precautions were agonizing; Sly spent them pacing by the exit with Blythe and Phink bracketing him like watchful shadows.

When the air inside the garage was determined safe, he was out before the gangplank could finish lowering to the floor.

"Sly, wait!"

He ignored Phink's demand for caution and sprinted to the entrance hall doors.

There was no one to greet them. Walters wasn't standing in wait with her neatly pressed skirt and proper welcoming committee of loyal staff members. Sly hit the doorway with clean air frantically filling his lungs and the distant noise of Blythe and Phink hurrying behind him, but there was nothing —no one—else within earshot.

He skidded in the foyer, shouting a relieved laugh as he noted the pristine state of polished floors and intact tapestries and no fire in sight. He stalled out in that giant stone room where he once found Tilla dumping a shitload of art supplies on the unsuspecting household.

Blythe and Phink caught up to him there while he was still staring at the far wall.

The wall was gone. In its place was a seamless slate of shining chrome spanning from floor to ceiling, from the foyer's corner to the foot of the staircase that led to the main house.

Sly took a shaky breath. He didn't dare take it too deep or too easy, but he breathed.

"What is that?" Blythe asked.

Phink jogged up to her side, hands on his hips as he admired the unusual wall. "That," he said, "is the only thing keeping Mother Nature from invading the building. Tilla was right. Emergency backup barrier. They'll be all over the place."

"Then, the rest of the house is safe?"

"Hopefully."

Sly started toward the staircase as he waved at the barrier.

"There's supposed to be a doorway leading to a different wing there."

Blythe cackled mirthlessly. "But of course, they have different wings to their house. Fucking vampires."

Sly was a tad defensive as he led them up the stairs. "We're lucky he didn't hit a more populated area."

"Are we?" Phink grunted as he dragged his extra weight up the stairs behind them. "Le Vau's from their bloodline. He's old. Maybe he knows enough about this place to make a decent guess at where to aim for maximum effect?"

"Thank you, Phink," Sly shouted over his shoulder as he turned into a main hallway. "That is exactly the kind of reassurance I need right now."

"Read the room, Phink," Blythe snipped from her spot at his heel.

Whole stretches of hallway were sealed by sleek blockades. As they got closer to where Sly thought he recognized some of the artwork, his footsteps picked up speed in search of an available door. Any door. He only needed one. So long as they got beyond the hallway, there was a good chance Sly could find his way to the right wing. To Kahled.

Stars above, he hoped the elevator wasn't barricaded.

He found a door. Then, he found the hall leading to the residential spaces. They strode straight past Sly's old guestroom and turned the corner to charge down the major thoroughfare leading to the public spaces. They found themselves at a dead end; the door to the library Sly never took advantage of was visible down the hall, but the billiards room entrance beyond it was blocked. The passageway was cut off by solid, reinforced metal.

Sly slumped. "Shit. No. This needs to be… This area can't be compromised. It can't."

"But this could be good, right?" Blythe grabbed his arm with both hands, her optimism sounding forced. "You said Kahled rarely left his rooms, and there's still a good chunk of real estate between here and the crash. Maybe there's no exposure here, and it's just a precaution to have every barrier possible activated. Right, Sly? I'm right, aren't I, Phink? Tell him."

"Maybe?" Phink wheezed as he tried to recover his breath from chasing after Sly.

Sly nodded, but he couldn't shake the sensation of mounting alarm springing from his gut. "Yeah... He should be... Uh, maybe we could reach his suite from… No. Just... Fuck. The staff. Walters. Where is everybody?"

He spun around, wide-eyed as if he expected a neon sign to miraculously appear to point him in the right direction.

Phink's paw came down on his shoulder. "Calm down, kid."

Sly heard him, but he didn't listen. His ears were busy replaying the soundtrack of his own screams as his mother burned alive.

"Sly?" Tilla's voice reverberated off metal walls. "Blythe?"

And Phink barked, "We're over here!"

It was Mae. The body in the skirt. He knew it. He didn't want to, but he did.

"Breathe, Sly," said Blythe, but she was no calmer than when she stopped him from following his mother outside. "Keep breathing, Hun. Come on."

He couldn't. *He couldn't.*

"Shush, Hun."

His mom was dead. Mae was dead. Walters and Gorbon, maybe. Kahled.

"I never should have left," Sly said through jagged sobs and broken inhales.

He should have signed the Companion Contract the day Kamari and Walters offered it to him behind Kahled's back. Kahled would have been pissed, but at least he'd be alive.

Le Vau could have been left to succumb to his Curse well beyond Sly's awareness, and he and Kahled could have been together. If only. Sly couldn't complete the wishful thought.

There wasn't enough air. There was too much darkness. He couldn't breathe, couldn't think.

He couldn't save them. None of them.

THEY RECONVENED IN THE ENTRANCE HALL. SLY LAY ON THE wide bottom step of the stairs, his head in Blythe's lap. Nearby, people were speaking in harsh, nippy voices, but Sly was having trouble following the conversation. He felt numb. Like he was listening to them through layers of cotton stuffed in his ears. Like he was insubstantial and weightless, even as his head felt too heavy to lift from Blythe's thigh.

"He needs medical attention," Phink demanded. "Europe is the closest port—"

Tilla argued, "If there are survivors here—"

"Big if!"

"—we owe it to Sly to make sure—"

"I am a HEPP employee! *Human*. Existence. Preservation. These two brats are my priority, not some vampire!"

"But Phink," Blythe whined, "all the staff here are human. Wouldn't HEPP want you to help them too?"

"I am not that altruistic, and you know it!"

Sly sat up with a groan, and the bickering stuttered to an end.

After a beat of suspended animation, Blythe nudged him. "So, what's the plan?"

"Why are you asking him?" Phink scowled. "He's the only one who's been checked out this entire discussion."

"Do you have a plan, then?" Blythe snipped back.

"Yeah. It involves getting our asses out of here and reporting this shitstorm to the nearest Guard station."

"No." Sly clambered to his feet, rubbing his forehead like it might jog his thoughts into order. "No, Tilla's right. We can't just leave them like this."

"How?" Phink huffed, fur bristling. "Everything's blocked off. Le Vau broke your comms, so it's not like you can call up your vampire directly. You would have already if you could."

"Oh!" Blythe bounced to her feet, vibrating with inspiration. "Sly! That's it! You can call him!"

Sly frowned down at his wrist, thoughts sluggish. "Without comms?"

He swayed as she hung off his shoulder, grinning. "Think, Sly! Remember how excited you were when you told me about that announcement system? The one you wanted to co-opt for the Guard after you were done pestering your vampire with it?"

Sly's brain flipped through his mental map of the estate, trying to account for all the life-saving inconveniences barring his usual paths. His jaw dropped.

Blythe shook him. "Could it work?"

He took her face in his hands and kissed her. "You are a genius."

She grinned. "I know. About time you rubbed off on me."

"Don't get used to it," he warned as he took off toward the basement.

The trek down to the lower level was unencumbered. As they filed down the cement hallway, their footsteps echoed in a way that made his stomach sink. He never noticed the emptiness in the past, but now the way seemed ominous, as if all the devastation and potential death up above had sunk down to the lowest passages, lying in wait.

For no good reason, Sly braced himself as he gripped the doorknob to access the Communications Control room. Maybe the door wouldn't open. Maybe it would open only to reveal another chrome blockade. Maybe Kahled had destroyed it beyond salvage in a Cursed episode or out of grief or both.

The door opened. Everything was as he left it. The mottled patches, the engraved labels, even the spinning chair. The last person to step foot in there was him.

Phink poked his head over Sly's shoulder in the doorway. "Are we going in or what?"

Sly shook himself, and a moment later, the seat molded to his ass like it was waiting for him the whole time he'd been gone. Sly swallowed the lump in his throat as he powered on the system.

As he did, Tilla stood at his elbow and stared at the console with a doubtful tilt of their golden head. "You know how to operate this?"

"It's practically the same thing the Port Guard uses for in-house announcements..." Sly explained as he reached for the mic. "And I've been micromanaging that shit on my dad's behalf for years."

Blythe snorted as she braced her hands on his shoulders from behind. "No wonder the Guard dropped him like a bad habit after you were gone. You and your free labor were all he had to offer them toward the end."

"It wasn't like that," Sly muttered as he made selections to broadcast to every working speaker on the premises.

"What happened here?" Tilla asked, toeing at the dented door to the internal hardware.

Sly's fingers paused, one hand on the mic and the other poised over the transmit button.

"Kahled," Sly said fondly, "he put his fist through the original dashboard, and that was some of the more superficial damage I didn't bother dolling up."

"...Oh."

"It was perfect before that, though." Sly gave a wistful sigh. "Pristine. Now, it's just decent."

"Decent condition or not..." Phink said, frowning around the room. "This stuff belongs in a museum, not a Harem household."

"Excuse you." Sly tugged the mic closer to his face as he glared at Phink. "This baby was a huge contribution to my sanity for a while. If you don't have something nice to say, don't say it at all."

A final touch of a button, and the hallway speakers crackled to life just outside the door.

"Mayday, mayday," Sly chirped into the mic, but his announcer's affectation was too strained and somber. "This is Sly Spurgeon, speaking to you from the depressing-yet-secure confines of the estate's basement level. If anyone's alive—anyone at all—do us all a favor and hit the little blue call button on the nearest wall unit that looks archaic enough to be part of the announcement system."

He paused, releasing the transmit button while he cleared the choked sobs from his throat before they could be detected in his voice.

"Let me know you're there," he said, tone grave. "Tell me if you're alive. Please."

He set the mic on the console and sat back in the seat, staring at it blindly.

Around him, no one spoke. They held their collective breath. Waiting.

Blythe crouched by his chair, sitting on her heels, head in her hands. Waiting.

Tilla stood like a rock in Sly's periphery, and after a bit, he heard Phink begin pacing in the scant space behind them. Waiting.

The silence settled, stretched on and on, and all the while, Sly's heart raced a little faster with each passing second. He kept waiting.

Phink cleared his throat.

Sly squeezed his eyes shut, ready to deny whatever came out of the other guy's mouth.

One of the console's indicators lit up. The built-in speaker against the back wall hummed awake.

"Sly?" Gorbon's voice warbled from the speaker, weak and shaken, but alive.

Sly snatched up the mic as Blythe lunged to her feet and Phink gripped his shoulder, each of them staring at the little green light that identified an incoming message from the medical bay.

"Sly? Is that really you?"

In the background, Sly caught the distinct shrill of Felix's incensed voice: "He came back? What is wrong with him?"

Sly started crying again, smiling as he spoke into the mic, "I'm here. I have Tilla and a good-sized ship with me. Did Kamari get anyone evacuated?"

The answer was a long time coming. Blythe hung off his

arm and gnawed on a nail while they waited, and Sly wasn't sure which of them was holding up the other.

"We don't know," Gorbon eventually admitted. "We were making preparations to leave, and last I heard, Emmeline and Master Vauqeulin were trying to get Kahled to see reason, but… I don't know." The doctor's voice trembled with tears. "Mae was gathering supplies with some of the others when the bomb hit. Everything shut down. I have Felix and four of the household staff sealed in here with me, but…"

The message cut off mid-sob.

Sly jumped to reply, "It wasn't a bomb, Gorbon. A Cursed loner from the American Port crashed his ship into the building."

The dashboard glowed brighter with a second indicator light. It was labeled: Evil Overlord's Suite.

Sly's chest seized. He released the transmission command and accepted the incoming channel, but it wasn't Kahled who spoke.

"Mr. Spurgeon," Walters admonished, her voice barking from the speaker, "what in the cosmos do you think you're doing here? Master Vauqeulin barely manage to reassure us you were perfectly safe and accounted for in your home port!"

Sly laughed, too high and watery to be considered a sound of relief. Fortunately, he wasn't broadcasting the noise she'd startled out of him. His knees gave out, and he tumbled into Blythe's arms.

As Blythe eased him out of the way, Phink had the presence of mind to commandeer the microphone. "Hello? Hi, I'm Phink, HEPP administrator here—"

Sly and Blythe snorted at that.

"—We're here to offer assistance in any way we can. Woah!"

Sly wrested the mic from Phink and shrieked at it. "Where's Kahled? Is he all right?"

The indicator lights from the med bay and master suite flickered with impatience before Sly accepted the transmission from Walters.

"Get out of here," Walters huffed. "The European Port authorities are already on their way, and the Harem's facilities on Luna have been notified about the threat. Master Vauqeulin's security personnel are combing the manor for intruders as we speak."

"Great," Sly snapped, "but what about Kahled?"

Phink grabbed Sly's wrist to regain control of the mic. "What do you mean they're combing for intruders? You're not suggesting Le Vau survived the crash?"

Sly's fingers went lax around the mic as he traded horrified glances with Blythe.

Walters did not respond. Seconds ticked by with the weight of hours before someone did.

"Mr. Phink, listen to me carefully," Kamari Vauqeulin said, sounding winded. "We need you to get Sly out of here. Immediately."

"Holy shit," Blythe whispered.

Tilla nodded at her. "Le Vau's alive."

"The whole place is locked down," Kamari continued, his speech flowing easier as he recovered his breath, "but if you have a clear path back to the hangar bay, take it. Now."

"Where's Kahled?" Sly demanded.

"Worry about yourself, Sly. Le Vau's loose in the building, and I'm sure he heard your little announcement as clearly as the rest of us did."

Sly stiffened. Everyone in the room did.

"Go home, Sly." Kamari's voice lowered, softened with a plea that made Sly wince. "I'm sorry I didn't take you as seriously as I should have, but I'll pay for that mistake on my own. Please, Sly. For Kahled's sake, go home."

Sly glanced at Phink, but the fuzzy man didn't seem keen on ushering him out of the room. He looked at Blythe, and she stared back, wide-eyed and flushed. Tilla didn't acknowledge him in favor of frowning down at the console. No one moved.

Sly muttered into the mic. "Can I at least talk to him first?"

Kamari's response was hesitant. "I don't think that's a good idea, Sly. He's a bit angry with you at the moment."

Sly's insides curdled into vicious knots. "Is he…? Did he…? I mean... Did I trigger another episode?"

Silence answered him. Sly was ready to press the issue and demand one when a low, distant growl thrummed through the room.

"What the fuck?" Blythe scowled, shifting into a corner, her eyes on the ceiling.

The ball of nastiness in Sly's gut roiled with a frenzied spike. The growl wasn't coming from the speaker.

Sly shut off the system. The electrical buzz cut out, the console lights going dark and the mic useless. The silence was deafening, the stillness oppressive and turning the air sour.

Phink gasped. "Did you hear that?"

"No!" Sly and Blythe snapped.

Then, there was a faint, far-off crunch.

"We should leave," said Tilla, grabbing for the weapon at their hip.

"Agreed," Phink said as he clapped one hand on Sly's wrist and the other on Blythe's and yanking them forward.

Sly was halfway out the door when he pulled himself

together enough to resist. "Wait! What about Gorbon and everyone with him? They don't know what's going on!"

"Not our problem!" Phink huffed, pulling at his wrist.

Sly had to lean back with his full weight to stop the humanoid teddy bear from dragging him into the hall. "They wouldn't be in this situation if it weren't for me! Let me warn them!"

"No!" Phink let go of Blythe so he could focus on Sly with both fuzzy paws. "The bastard survived a crash and who knows how much outdoor exposure, Sly! We are not giving him another chance to kill you!"

"Enough."

Phink let go of Sly as Tilla barged between them. Sly would have flown back into a supply shelf if their golden fingers hadn't snatched him by the collar of his shirt.

"Be quick." Tilla grumbled as they shoved Sly toward the intercom controls. "Then, we're leaving. I don't care if I have to throw you over my shoulder and carry you out. Warn the doctor about Le Vau and let's go."

Sly didn't waste precious time and air arguing.

WHEN THEY MADE IT BACK TO THE GARAGE, TILLA OPENED the door and halked, Blythe along with them.

"Something's wrong," Blythe said, backing into Sly. "Something's very, very wrong."

Tilla raised their nose in the air and took a loud breath. "There's blood."

"Excuse me?" Sly said.

Phink glanced between Tilla's golden mane and Blythe's jaguar spots. "Just how much splicing have both of you been doing?"

"Seriously?" Blythe glared at him, face flushed. "Tilla says they smell blood, and you're concerned about how much we're splicing? You? The poster daddy for splicing?"

"Tilla never said smell." Phink poked her. "But you did."

Sly shouldered past them to press against Tilla's side. "Is it Le Vau?"

Tilla shrugged, their eyes narrowed and scanning the unassuming hangar. "Maybe."

Behind them, Blythe and Phink were still coping via some friendly ribbing. Sly left them to it and crept toward Tilla's ship.

Tilla overtook him within two steps, their gun raised. They rounded a small personal transport, and Sly nearly broke his nose on their back as the bigger human froze in front of him.

Sly peeked around Tilla's side and instantly wished he hadn't.

"What's up?" Blythe muttered, coming up behind them. She gasped.

Phink stepped forward, gagged, and wheeled away with a hand over his mouth.

It was no wonder Tilla and Blythe smelled blood. The six or seven feet between Kamari's small shuttle and Tilla's ship was bathed in the stuff. There were two bodies dressed in black, but neither of their faces were familiar.

Sly didn't try for a closer look, but Tilla did.

"Oh, Tilla, don't touch them!" Blythe whimpered under her breath as she buried her face in Sly's shoulder.

Sly winced away as Tilla crouched near the bodies. "Nocturni," they said. "All three of them."

"Three?" Sly squeaked.

Tilla gestured past the farthest body, but Sly couldn't

make himself follow the direction. "These two have all their limbs. That one belongs to someone else."

Phink retched. Loudly.

"Shh!" Blythe hissed. "Fuck's sake, what if Le Vau's still in here?"

"This doesn't make sense," Sly interjected, grabbing her arm like a lifeline. "We heard him. That growl. It was so far away. Deeper inside the manor. Probably trapped behind at least one or two of the emergency barriers."

"Sly?" Tilla returned to his side, their eyes sad but set. "Maybe it wasn't Le Vau who did this."

Sly bristled. "It was."

"He's not the only Cursed Nocturnus here."

Sly was a sentence away from following Phink's example and upchucking everything inside him. Meals, internal organs, the works. He remembered Kahled's weary description of the last memory he had of home, of the blood on his hands and the body he left on the floor of his childhood home.

"Kahled didn't do this," he croaked.

"Maybe not," Tilla agreed, "but we don't know for sure."

"He's locked up with Walters and Kamari," Sly said, fighting down the sense that he was grasping at smoke with nothing but his bare hands. "It wasn't him."

"It doesn't matter," Phink said. "We need to leave now."

Wordless and grave, Tilla held out an arm to direct them to the ship without trampling the bodies. Blythe was crying big, silent tears as she fell in line behind Phink. Tilla waited for Sly to follow before bringing up the rear, gun in hand.

There were splotches of crimson dotting the ship's outer hull. Tilla didn't seem to notice as they opened the ship and helped Blythe aboard, but Sly did.

They all noticed when a furious howl rent the air.

Sly and Tilla spun around to face the manor entrance, but Phink grabbed Sly's arm in the next moment.

"Time to go, Earthling," Phink said. "That was way too close for comfort."

"I don't understand," Sly murmured. "How did he get through the barriers?"

"Who cares?" Phink snapped. "If he can chew through metal, imagine what he could do to your skinny ass."

Before Phink could drag him into the ship, an electric crackle sounded from nearby. Everyone froze except Tilla, who raised their gun in the general direction.

An unfamiliar male voice hissed through a fractured transmission, "I lost him."

In the tense quiet that followed, Sly caught Tilla's eye. His mind was jumping through conclusions too frantic to put any of them into words.

Another broken creak of a dead man's comms, and the voice demanded, "Is anyone there? I lost track of the intruder, and the Master's not responding. What's going on?"

"Don't," Tilla warned.

Sly ignored them and Phink's aggrieved groan as he rushed from the ship's access point. He didn't dwell on the blood or the lifeless weight of the bodies more than he needed to as he checked their wrists for devices. When he had no luck there, he paused to brace himself before daring to search for the severed limb of the third body.

Thankfully, that was when he noticed a thin line of light jolt across a silver band on the one body's throat. It was a solid circlet of metal resting against the Nocturnus' skin like a tailored collar. Sly had never seen a comms quite like it.

The unknown voice said, "Master Kamari? Armand? Someone answer me, dammit!"

"Sly," Tilla hissed from behind him, "we need to leave."

"Wait," he said as he freed the comms from the corpse. The seamless latch released and unhinged easily enough, but Sly almost dropped it when his fingers slid in a spot of blood. He swiped at it, first to clear the nauseating wetness and then in the desperate hope that it worked the same way a wrist unit would. All he got for his trouble was a warning beep.

Tilla grabbed his arm. "They're private security, Sly, their comms would be on a closed network."

Sly gaped up at his friend. "They don't know Le Vau's taken out three of them. What if this guy's the last one standing?"

What if the stranger on the other end was the only person standing between Le Vau and Kahled? Between Le Vau and Kamari, the last of the Harem's reigning family?

Tilla's grip tightened. "That unit is going to be locked and coded for the use of one specific individual. It's useless to you."

Sly fumbled to get the device around his skinny neck, but it hung loose and awkward as if to reinforce Tilla's point.

"There's nothing you can do, Sly!"

"You're wrong."

The cool calm in his voice startled Tilla into letting him go. Hell, it nearly gave him pause. He was probably in some sort of shock, but Sly wasn't feeling it yet. Rather, it felt like he was slipping into a costume, seconds from going on stage, safe and well back at Centrism. He knew how to let himself go on instinct when those instincts felt so all-consuming and right.

Sly stood tall, whipping his bloody hand on his pantleg as he faced Tilla. "I can use the intercom."

"No."

"Yes! Kamari's guy is in the building, and the system goes to every room. I can tell him about these guys—" Sly threw his hands out toward the scattered bodies. "—then I'll book it straight back here. It'll take ten minutes, tops."

Tilla shook their head the whole time he spoke. "Le Vau may very well be heading there now."

"Maybe, maybe not, but there's no doubt he's Cursed..." Sly winced as he admitted, "and more than a little infatuated with me. He's not that different from Kahled."

"Are you shitting me right now?"

"Sly!" Blythe leaned out of the ship to aim a hushed shriek at him. "If you don't get your cute butt in gear and come here right now—"

"I have a plan," Sly cut in, matching her tone as he looked between Blythe and Tilla. "Listen, all right? I've dealt with this disease before; I'm not talking out of my ass here. Le Vau doesn't have the benefit of my blood. Yeah, he's unstable, and his fixation on me is questionable at best—"

"You're not reassuring me." Tilla scowled.

"Just trust me!" Sly talked over them. "Nosferatu's Curse runs on rage—it's the emotional hair-trigger behind every episode—and as furious as he was learning about Kahled and me, Le Vau never tried to bite me, he barely hurt me."

Blythe hissed, "He fractured your wrist."

"He was disabling my comms!" Sly scoffed, raising his bandaged hand in a wave as if it didn't still throb. "It's not like he tried to kill me."

"That's not an acceptable excuse," Blythe said. "Oh, my fucking stars—Tilla, just toss him over your shoulder! Let's go!"

"I'm not leaving."

Tilla took a step back. "I agreed to bring you here to warn them, not to risk our lives."

"Understandable," Sly agreed, jerking his chin toward the

ship as he sidestepped toward the manor. "But Kahled's part of my life. If there's a chance I can help him, I have to."

"Sylvester Spurgeon!" Blythe seethed at him, Phink's grip on her waist the only thing keeping her from lunging after him. "Don't you dare!"

Sly shot Tilla a hopeful look before jerking his chin toward Blythe. "Do me another favor and make sure she doesn't do anything stupid, okay?"

Tilla's scowl deepened. "Maybe you should set a better example for her."

"Hey!" Sly asserted before giving them his back. "I know what I'm doing!"

When he closed the entrance hall's door behind him, he kept those parting words running across the forefront of his mind on repeat.

CHAPTER 26

There was no sign of monsters when he got back to the basement level. The pervasive dread that mired the hall was unchanged too, so Sly gave into the gut-twisting urge to close the control room's door and lock it from the inside. As if the hunks of metal and wiring could sense his urgency, the system powered up in record time; it made the fine hairs on Sly's arms stand on end.

He stood before the console, microphone gripped in both hands, and let the words fly.

"Hi. Me again. In case anyone's wondering, there are two-point-two Nocturni bodies in the garage, and before you ask, I have no idea where the rest of the third guy is." Sly gulped back more air and hurried on, "I have one of their comms units with me. I can't use it, but I have it in case anyone wants to tell me anything I should know."

He released the transmit button and held his breath, but he didn't have to for long.

"Earthling!" Kahled snapped from the intercom speaker. "What are you still doing here?"

Sly gasped, the sound of Kahled's voice knocking him back on his heels.

"What part of 'get out of here' was too difficult to understand?"

Sly's mouth opened and shut a few times, waiting for his tongue to pick any one of a dozen phrases. He wanted to cry and pour his heart out over the intercom till Kahled knew exactly how much Sly missed him. He wanted to spit obscenities at the whole estate, at Kahled especially, for sending him away like last year's trash. His mind spun with various ways of executing either message, but his physical self seemed unwilling to act on any of them.

Then, a cool, foreign voice spoke from the vicinity of Sly's collarbone, "Sylvester Spurgeon?"

Sly shuddered back into his body. He set the mic on the panel's desktop while the other hand fumbled for his wrist then for his throat before he remembered how useless the comms device was in his hands Groaning at himself, Sly scooped up the mic again and answered the stranger in an open broadcast.

"Yes!" He winced, hoping his new accomplice was as quick-witted as he hoped. "That's, er… me."

Sly's relieved sigh was audible over the immediate message stemming from the borrowed unit.

"I have one Nocturna with me as backup," the stranger said, gruff and grave. "If what you say is true, we're all that's left, and the intruder is successfully circumventing the emergency barricades. Whistle over the intercom if you understand."

Sly whistled.

From distant corridors came a furious howl.

"He's close," the unnamed Nocturnus murmured. "He'll cross us first if he's doubling back toward you."

Chilled tremors raced down Sly's spine. The blood covering the hangar floor was wet, so fresh it was still pooling around the bodies. It took Sly's measly mortal legs minutes to hustle from there to the basement, but that latest howl was so far-off. Too far-off.

What was it Tilla said about Le Vau not being the only Cursed Nocturnus around?

The panel lit up with incoming signals. The med bay. The garage. The Master suite.

While Sly gaped at the console in indecision, the unit on his throat hissed in Kamari's panicked voice: "Kahled's loose!"

Sly's heartbeat went into double-time as he clapped his hands over his neck to muffle the comms. His ears strained, like he expected to hear more howling or anything else to announce the approach of a crazed Nocturnus. All he could discern was the electric buzz of the console and his own thundering pulse.

Under his palm, the stranger hissed an order, "Go now, human. While you still have a chance."

Sly jumped toward the door. He got it unlocked before he thought to stretch back for the mic and issue one last whistle for good measure, then he was out of there. The mic clanged to the floor, and the sound was still echoing when the slaps of his frenzied steps filled his ears.

He was halfway down the hall when a mighty blast shook the walls. Sly skidded to a halt as cement dust trickled from above him.

"What the fuck?"

Sly looked up, but nothing looked amiss. The basement ceiling was the same smooth cement finish as the walls and floor. There were no cracks, no dents from Nocturni fists, or crumbling that might belie structural damage from the crash.

A second impact sounded, and more particles sprinkled down on him. Sly was shaking his head and rubbing at his eyes to clear them of dust when the powerful thudding morphed into a cacophony of shrieking metal and frenzied growls. The basement trembled around him, and the noxious ball perpetually clotting in his gut finally burst as the first cracks appeared overhead.

"Shit," Sly squeaked.

Someone—he didn't know if it was Le Vau or Kahled— but someone yowled from way too near, and the roof was threatening to give out. Sly's reason vanished as the full force of all human evolution sent him scurrying back down the hall.

Run. Run. Run. Hide. Run. Hide. Go. Go. Go. Go.

There was no distinct thought, no semblance of a plan. Instinct took over like never before, and Sly moved as fast as his legs could carry him. He didn't recall racing down to the gym or when he'd decided to pile the padded mats in front of the door. He wasn't sure how he managed to shove one of the weighted exercise machines three feet in that direction either. But he did it. In all the wisdom of his frantic, prey-animal hindbrain, he did it.

He was shaking, hyperventilating as he leaned into the machine. It wasn't budging any further, but if he stopped trying, he was sure his heart would give out.

Something heavy hit the gym doors. The mats wobbled like stacked papers.

"Fuck!" Sly screamed, leaping back from the latest would-be addition to his blockade.

A low, greedy growl vibrated through the doors.

Sly gagged on a sob, fist in front of his mouth. He stared at the hindered doors, his face and body burned as he cried.

Maybe it was Kahled. Maybe it wasn't. At that point, Sly didn't know which would be better.

An ear-piercing roar echoed through the basement level, and a fist-sized dent popped out of the door.

Sly stumbled back, gasping out, "Stars above!" as he fell on his ass.

The animalistic noises quieted at the sound of his voice.

Sly tried to push himself up off the floor, but his arms didn't have the strength. He was splayed in the middle of a wide, open gymnasium, like an actual sitting duck. Unbidden, Sly's harried brain supplied him with a reminder of the first words Kahled likely heard him speak.

I am so dead.

Sly curled over himself with a choked sob. "No," he moaned, then raised his voice in a plea, "Kahled?"

A menacingly pleased rumble answered him.

Sly smacked the tears from his face as he flailed to his knees. "Kahled, is that you? Can you hear—do you know me?"

The slavish sounds and violent pounding eased, as if the creature on the other side of the doors could feel his attention. He didn't go silent, no, but the rolling purr that snuck into the gym was like air rather than noise: slow and insidious, but obvious and unavoidable. Deadly.

Then, Quin Le Vau spoke. "You came after me, Sly?"

Sly's heart dropped. His soul jolted out of his body and, for a second, he wondered if he was going to die from shock after all. Breathing fast and faster still, Sly scrambled further away from the door.

"I can smell you." Le Vau hummed, his tone delighted and creepy as ever. "I hear your heart beating. Mmm. I can practically taste it."

Sly's hand clamped down over his chest, like it would do anything to soften the record-breaking gallop of his heart. His stomach clenched, threating to toss out everything he had, including the stupid loud organ behind his ribcage.

"You could have waited for me at home, Sly." Le Vau's voice was almost unrecognizable, guttural and hungry. There was none of his sleazy charm, no hint of flirtation. "I was always going to come back for you. You know that, right?"

"Fucker!" Sly hissed into his cupped hands.

His body twisted and lurched on its own accord, his attention bouncing all around the room with an influx of adrenaline. There were no other exits, no other doors save for the sauna in the corner.

A piercing streak of claw on stone had Sly jump to cover his ears.

"After I had finished here," Le Vau said from beyond the door, "I was going to come for you. Now that I know the truth, it all makes sense. You. Me. This game between us."

Sly heaved himself up, shouting over Le Vau's vileness, "Don't you dare start that shit!"

Le Vau shut him down with a sharp yowl and a blow to the door that toppled one of the mats. When Sly fell quiet, the beast gave a terrifying moan.

"You talk a lot of nonsense, Sylvester, but your blood speaks for itself. It calls to me. It tells me the truth, how you want me. How you need me."

"Oh, fuck off!" Sly shouted.

Le Vau stopped speaking. He stopped growling. There was no hint of noise, no sign of movement.

A shiver ran down Sly's spine. He reconsidered hiding in the sauna as he kept a wary eye on the beaten door.

Another howl registered from beyond the door. Beyond the hall. It echoed, rageful and determined throughout the basement till Sly's head throbbed with its cadence. It was more than loud, it was penetrative, reverberating off the walls and gym equipment, off the inside of Sly's skull and chest cavity.

It was strong and fierce, and Sly knew the voice.

He didn't get a chance to process, to figure out what was going on. He sat on the floor, alone and exposed, and listened as Kahled's fury faded to nothing. The nothing stretched on and on and on, to the point that Sly's sense of time and reality folded in on itself and trapped him in place.

Le Vau stayed silent. Motionless. Was he still waiting outside the door?

Did Sly dare get up and check?

The quiet wrongness deepened with every thundering beat of his heart. Sly pried himself off the floor in shaky fits and starts, but he managed to get his feet under him without puking all over himself. His gorge rose with a vengeance as he ventured toward the door again; he couldn't force himself to pass the displaced machine he'd left between him and it.

He eyed the fallen mat, the one Le Vau knocked over moments earlier, and a rush of lightheadedness made him sway. There were several others still wedged against the door, but they didn't lie flat; they were warped where the portal behind them bulged inward.

"Le Vau?" Sly whispered.

There was no answer.

He gulped hard, and it felt like swallowing a coarse rock. He rounded the weighted machine and inched forward till his toes touched the edge of the downed mat.

He raised his voice the slightest bit, "Still there, Le Vau?"

No one answered.

Sly counted the seconds that crept by as he waited, not daring to breathe. One. Two. Three. Four.

A distant screeching rent the air, and Sly jumped.

"Le Vau?"

More screeching, like nails dragging on metal. Clanging. A repetitive thudding, distant but growing louder, closer.

The gym doors didn't twitch. The mats stood firm. Sly's body felt cold, down to his very bones.

A crash. Thumps.

Silence.

Sly held his breath.

When the roar came, it resonated. It filled the estate's basement in one booming breath and slammed into Sly like a physical blow. He doubled over, gasping, and the Earth itself seemed to tremble under his feet.

The echo of Kahled's rage was still pulsating in Sly's ears when he recognized the underlying hiss of Le Vau's raised hackles.

Sly reached for the door, calling out, "Kahled?"

But Tilla was right; there was nothing he could do.

He couldn't see what was happening in the hall, and he didn't want to. The noise was horrific enough, like the soundtrack to something leagues beyond his wildest nightmares. There were inhuman snarls and the wet, wrenching thuds of undefinable impact. The shrieks of claws scraping claws, the snap of vicious fangs. Furious, bestial bellows and the sickening squelch of bodies and fluids—

And a single deafening blow into the building. The gym walls trembled hard enough to dislodge dirt and plaster from the high ceiling that extended above the rock wall. Sly smacked at the debris as it landed on his shoulders and in his hair; it mixed with his tears and left muddy lines on his cheek.

He was shaking uncontrollably as he stumbled backward into the rock wall, clear across the room from the door. The back of his shoulders and skull bounced over uneven protrusions as he dropped onto the synthetic padding that blanketed the floor. Sly squashed himself into the corner with his knees drawn to his chest, as snug against the artificial rockface as he could get. His eyes burned, but remained wide and focused on the shoddily barricaded entrance.

There was nothing he could do with his skinny, mortal limbs. There was nothing he could say, no words or songs that could compete with the mayhem happening just beyond his sight. There was nothing around to enable him to call for help. There was nothing. He had nothing.

He could do nothing but listen. And wait.

It went on for years.

Kahled and Le Vau. The violence. They drove each other into walls, closer, then farther, then way too close again. Out of sight but never out of earshot, they clashed over and over and over, cursed with inexhaustive fury and endless bloodlust. They traded blows and wailings, playing off each other in a deadly game no other living creature could stand.

Seconds—or hours—into the fight, Sly's muddled brain couldn't tell them apart.

Sly couldn't think, couldn't breathe. He couldn't exist beyond that moment. He huddled in the corner and evaded every thought about what might come next. He clamped his hands over his ears without drowning out the yowling pain and temper of real-life monsters, and still, he refused to consider what it meant.

There was no way to decipher which horrific vocalizations were Kahled's, so Sly didn't think on it at all.

A vile clamoring forced Sly to lift his face from his knees, hands uncovering his ears as he startled.

Something smashed into the door. The latch broke with a pinging snap as the handle flew off. Sly wasn't sure if he imagined the door flying open for a split second before its momentum slammed it shut again, but afterword, all but one of the substantial mats had toppled. The final mat wavered on its edge, Sly watching with his heart in his throat, before thumping back against the entrance.

Sly's nerves didn't recover. Heedless of the rock wall digging bruises into his back, Sly stood on liquefied knees and watched the door.

Another bang rattled the door from its frame for a fraction of a moment. Sly thought he saw a flash of something big in the slivered view, but it was too quick to be certain. Another thud of impact, and someone uttered a gurgling cry, wet and broken, but angry. A vicious hiss morphed into a taunting sort of yowl.

Sly's heart iced over, brittle and anxious. He couldn't tell which was which, who was wounded, or how badly.

Someone screamed. It wasn't a human scream, but something ferocious and proud. Victorious.

There was no responding growl.

Sly's throat burned. His lungs refused to work right.

The snitch of claws skated across cement, and the noises outside took a disturbing turn. It got quiet, but the vigorous, moist quaffing was too much.

Sly fell forward and his hands hit the floor as he hurled. It was mostly stomach acid, but it was rancid, burning the inside of his nose. His heaving was almost an audio smokescreen over the unseen gore, but it didn't last long enough.

The door blasted open, the final mat flying across the running track.

Sly stayed on his hands and knees, facedown and panting with bile dripping from his lips.

He heard the smack of limp flesh dropping to the ground and the squelching of blood. He couldn't tell who it was. His vision was a mess of tears and deoxygenated black spots, and he didn't have the strength to lift his head. A low confident rumble drifted toward him, and Sly wasn't sure it mattered who the voice belonged to anymore.

He felt the creature draw near. His presence, his body heat. He was so close, Sly could smell the metallic tang of fresh blood on him.

Sly was petrified, caught in the sliver of eternity where he didn't have to face whoever was looming over him.

There were no words uttered as the victor stopped in front of him with a dark, pleased growl. Sly squeezed his eyes shut at the first touch of shadow in his view, before he had a chance to recognized Kahled's deformed toes or Le Vau's polished shoes.

Five perfectly proportioned fingers combed through Sly's hair. Slow. Reverent. Covetous.

Sly shuddered. He shook his head free of those greedy fingers as he recoiled into the rock wall. His eyes popped open.

The sound the left his throat was mangled between a gasp and scream.

Kahled stood before him.

It wasn't the Kahled Sly knew, but it was still Kahled. It had to be, logically, but it was all wrong. What remained of his shirt was torn to ribbons, exposing endless stretches of armored muscle where there should have been warm-brown skin. The impenetrable scales glazed his face in the finest detail, fading artfully into the skin near his eyes and around lips that nearly closed over the functional points of his fangs.

His eyes glowed white. There was no darkness, no touch of gray. No human consciousness.

Kahled's mouth didn't move as he made a demanding purr. He stepped closer, fingers flexing toward Sly with five short, matching claws painted in blood.

Sly flinched.

Kahled paused, growling in blatant warning.

It wasn't just his hands, Sly realized with a sinking feeling in his gut. The gross deformities to his legs and feet were altered. Not gone, exactly, but finished. His humanoid shins and calves were warped into the semblance of an overlarge animal's leg. He had the musculature and general form of a mammalian predator, with his ankles evenly suspended and misaligned from the rest of his legs. Despite that, Kahled's enormous weight was balanced on ten proportionate and reptilian toes, complete with scales. The nails were gone, replaced by thick black talons on each digit. The underlying bone and muscle were as strong and indisputable as his scaled skin.

"Kahled?" Sly whispered, shaking as he raised his head to meet those glowing eyes.

Kahled tilted his head, expression blank as he stared at Sly and seemed to consider the sound of his voice. The motion was so like a beast, but the way it caused ebony hair to fall into Kahled's face was jarringly human.

Sly swallowed his terror and slowly stood up. "Is it still you, Maestro?"

Kahled moved too fast to see. Before Sly could react, a massive hand was on his throat, fingers bruising the far corner of his jaw as he was yanked forward.

Sly gasped and instinctively grabbed at Kahled's arm.

Kahled didn't seem to notice. He didn't snarl, didn't bare his teeth. His facial features never twitched, more refined than ever under the scales and functionally shrunken fangs. He did nothing more than hold Sly's face close to his, breathing.

Sly didn't know what was happening, if he was being attacked or if he was about to be kissed. Kahled's expression told him nothing more than the resting look of an insentient animal could.

After a heart-stopping moment, Sly realized he wasn't being strangled. The palm against his throat was all smooth and supple skin, the grip focused on his jaw rather than his windpipe. Sly's feet were flat on the floor, while Kahled bent over to breathe on his face—no, not breathing *on* him; Kahled was taking long, measured breaths, drawing Sly's scent through his nose, breathing him in.

Sly's voice trembled with hope. "Kahled?"

The air vibrated with Kahled's answering purr.

"It's me," Sly whispered as he brought unsteady hands to Kahled's shoulders. It was like grabbing onto solid stone. "It's Sly. Your Earthling. You know me, right?"

Stars above, but there was blood in Kahled's hair. Thick, congealing splotches of it.

"Talk to me, Maestro."

But Kahled didn't speak. He tilted his chin as he bent closer, breaths deepening as his nose grazed Sly's cheek.

Sly's grip slipped from those beloved alien shoulders, sliding on glassy scales and hot slick blood. Fuck, but there was so much blood, and it was everywhere, on Kahled's chin, crossing his chest, on the rags of his shirt, staining his pants, dripping onto the floor. Everywhere.

It didn't bother Kahled. It didn't stop him from flicking out his tongue to toy with Sly's earlobe.

Sly jerked, gasping, "Kahled! No!"

The vampire growled at him, a wordless demand for silence.

Sly gulped. They were too close for Sly to sneak a glance at Kahled's eyes, but the hot white glow was discernable nonetheless. The intelligence he was used to seeing there was long gone, swallowed up by shocking brightness and blatant hunger.

"So dead," Sly murmured in a disbelieving daze.

He was going to die. The inevitability of it rattled through his consciousness like a gong. Kahled's fangs were smaller now, sharper and more lethal than ever, and they were a breath away from his pulse. From his stitches. Kahled was going to bite him again, and he would be dead. He knew it.

"I love you," Sly said as Kahled licked over the healing mark from their last encounter.

Kahled paused. He pulled back, fingers tight on Sly's jaw and eyes blazing, but he pulled away from Sly's throat. He stared, blank and silent. Expectant.

"I love you," Sly repeated, tears rolling down his cheeks to wash Kahled's scales. "I love you so much, I won't even hate you if you kill me."

Kahled didn't understand him. There was no change, no recognition in his eyes or softening of his features.

"I love you."

Sly wrapped his hands around Kahled's wrist. He didn't pry at the steel hold or try to push it away. He held it, soft and safe between his palms as his thumb rubbed gentle circles on the scales.

Kahled was statuesque. He was so still, Sly couldn't discern his breathing, but he felt the vibration when Kahled made a subvocal purr.

Crying, Sly tried to sing.

The first line of "Starlight Daydreams" fell out of his mouth in a jumbled mess, and Kahled didn't stop him. The second line was still croaked and watery, but clearer. Sly was nearly to the chorus when the vampire finally let him go with a low, curious growl.

Sly held his breath as he watched Kahled's face for any sign of human thought.

Kahled watched him in return. Stoic. Attentive. A curious beast poised for fight or flight at the earliest excuse.

"…Maestro?"

Kahled's lip curled back from his fangs, and he growled. He began pacing.

Sly raised his hands in placation and resumed the song. He kept as still as possible, working his way through the chorus as he tracked Kahled's steps back and forth. The vampire's face smoothed back into impassivity as he trapped Sly in the corner with unnervingly graceful strides.

Despite his constant motion, Kahled's attention remained trained on Sly. He turned his head as he walked, his face aimed at Sly as if they were magnetically attached. Kahled minded him as if hypnotized, with no outward display of emotion. The peculiar glow of his eyes was an uncomfortable spotlight, but Sly was still breathing, still standing under it on his own two feet. He didn't know how or why, only that he was.

Sly was still alive. Kahled was still alive. Maybe, if Sly could keep singing long enough, then maybe, just maybe they could stay that way.

Kahled must have been focused on him with all of his senses, because he didn't react when the sound of hurried feet pounded down the hall.

Sly's heart lurched, but he swallowed it down and kept singing.

He wasn't loud enough to drown out the slowing footsteps as they approached. If Sly could hear them, Kahled's superhuman ears doubtless could too, but the vampire merely continued pacing and watching. People shoved their way past the mangled gym doors with gasps and frantic murmurs, but Kahled never reacted.

Sly didn't dare glance away from Kahled to see who it was. He couldn't shake the soul-rooted certainty that inattention would get him killed. Sly was well into his second recital of the song when he caught sight of Emmeline Walters over Kahled's shoulder.

She was a mess. Her clothing was crumbled, torn, and stained. Her hair was falling from its updo in wayward whisps of gray. She looked skeletal, paler, and thinner than Sly could have imagined, but she stood tall as she raised a clear plastic gun and pointed it at Kahled's back.

Sly sang as she pulled the trigger. Twice.

Kahled froze, tense. His eyes swirled with invading shadows.

Sly sang louder as the gun fired again.

Kahled shuddered, his brow furrowing and mouth folding into an angry sneer.

Sly's voice failed him as Walters fired twice more.

When Kahled's eyes dimmed with relieving grays, the fine scales on his face and neck began to melt away. The lucidity was brief but obvious in the moment before he dropped to his knees and he fell face-first onto the rock wall's landing pad.

Sly sobbed at the sight of all the tranquilizer darts sticking out of his back.

"Sly!" Tilla cried, running toward him.

Strong arms wrapped around him, but the embrace was wrong, from the wrong person.

Distantly, as if through a dense fog, Sly thought he heard the unnamed Nocturnus from Kamari's security team asking if he was harmed. Sly wasn't sure.

He only had eyes for Kahled.

"He wasn't going to kill me," Sly said, speaking from Tilla's arms as he stared at the unconscious vampire. "He was listening to me."

No one acknowledged him.

Tilla hugged him tight. Walters cupped his face in her weary palm before she led him away with the trader's help.

"He was listening to me," Sly repeated.

There were people dressed in tactical gear crouching next to Kahled's body. People Sly didn't know.

"He was listening!" Sly yelled at them over Tilla's shoulder.

Gorbon was there. He shot Sly a wide-eyed stare on his way to join the people crowded around Kahled.

"He was listening to me!" Sly insisted. "He was listening to the song! He wasn't going to hurt me!"

Walters and Tilla dragged him from the gymnasium, kicking and screaming to make them understand. Kahled wasn't ready to die. Sly could still help him. He wasn't lost to Nosferatu's Curse if Sly could still get through to him with a measly little song!

Walters ushered him down the hall with Tilla's reinforcement, and all the while, Sly shrieked, "He was listening to me, dammit!"

But no one else did.

CHAPTER 27

"*F*oolish," Walters admonished a couple hours later. "The lot of you. Complete and utter fools."

They were gathered in the cavernous cargo hold of Tilla's ship. The doors were open, the gangway lowered, and the path to the estate's bloodied garage accessible without the carnage in direct sight. The space itself was made up of harsh metal walls and exposed supports, maybe a few errant shipping crates, but none of it made much of an impression on Sly.

He sat on the floor against the bulkhead, hugging his knees to his chest and staring at nothing. Blythe sat at his side, her arm looped through his and her head on his shoulder; he could feel her trembling, but the awareness was muffled, unimportant next to the sense of loss and frightened numbness obscuring his thoughts.

Tilla was on their feet, positioned in front of Sly and Blythe and glaring at Walters like a self-appointed sentry. "We tried contacting you, but neither the estate nor Master Vauqeulin were responding. Could you have sat idle in that situation with a clean conscience?"

The wrinkled skin by Walters's eyes tightened, but she was otherwise unmoved. Back straight, chin up, and hands folded over her abdomen, she made a decent show of being put together. Sly couldn't help watching the fly-away wisps of her mussed hair, couldn't stop eyeing the singed holes and crumpled lines in her skirt.

"We did not come here for you to scold us like misbehaving children," Tilla said, the aggression in their voice easing a smidge. "We are here to help. If you need it, my ship is available to get your people out of here."

"Kahled," Sly piped up, jerking in Blythe's hold as he looked between Tilla and Walters. "We can take Kahled, right? Kamari said the Harem wouldn't—that they won't have him…"

Tilla's posture softened as they glanced at him. "I don't know, Sly. I have the space but not the means to accommodate his condition."

Sly flinched. Blythe hastened to engulf him in her arms.

Walters bit her lip, eyes on the floor as she said, "Kahled will have to stay here."

Sly flailed in Blythe's stubborn hold as he shouted, "But this place isn't safe! It's barely habitable!"

"The medical wing is still intact," Walters said with a pronounced sigh. "And right now, Kahled is too unpredictable to risk transporting."

"What's that supposed to mean?" Sly squirmed out of Blythe's grasp and stumbled to his feet. Tilla caught him before he could go barreling into Walters face-first. "Sedate him, then! Strap him to that fucking cot and wheel it in here!"

He spun away from Tilla, waving his arms to indicate the spacious ship's hold. His legs were too weak for the dramatics, though, and he crumbled to the floor. His knees throbbed with fresh bruises.

Blythe was on him in an instant. "Stop," she murmured as she flung her arms around his shoulders. "You've done enough, Sly. Let the Harem take care of him."

"Fuck that!" Sly whined. "They'll just kill him and call the job done."

Blythe shook her head, her hair tickling his cheek. "Kamari won't let that happen."

"*We* won't let that happen," Walters corrected. Her thin hand landed on his shoulder, her grip strong. "You must be patient, Sly. No one has ever seen Nosferatu's Curse advance like this before. Between Kahled's symptoms and Le Vau's mere existence, there's ample grounds for concern, yes, but also opportunity."

Sly smacked Blythe's hair out of his face and gaped up at Walters. "What?"

Her hand tightened on his shoulder. "Be patient, Sly."

Before he could question her further, Phink's heavy footsteps came clomping up the gangway.

"Well," he sighed, hands on his hips as he surveyed the group, "HEPP's European branch is swarming the place. They're not too happy with us. Apparently, the presence of three random American employees is nothing but a headache and a shit ton of paperwork, as far as the organization's concerned."

Blythe bristled. "We're hardly *random*."

"Far as HEPP's concerned, we are," Phink countered. "You and I are unaffiliated with the Vauqeulin Harem to begin with and, officially, Sly parted ways with them a week ago."

Sly's breath caught like a jagged rock in his throat, but he managed to say, "This wouldn't have happened if it weren't for me. If I hadn't set Le Vau off—"

"Don't be ridiculous," Walters scowled at no one in

particular. "You are not to blame for the actions of a deranged Nocturnus."

"But—"

"No," she snapped. "You haven't seen his body, Mr. Spurgeon, but I have; he was lucky and irresponsible enough to hide his Curse, but make no mistake, he was well beyond treatment."

Phink cleared his throat, only to shift his weight and avoid everyone's stares. "Le Vau's been around a while. I did some digging, and the Guard's had him registered as an Earth-bound loner for over a century. He was in Europe's Port for a decade before he immigrated to the American Port."

Walters scoffed. "Of course he did. Several of The Nine Bloodlines originated in Europe, the Vauqeulins included. He ran greater risk of having his condition recognized if he stayed in that port."

"Makes sense," Blythe said as she rubbed Sly's arms. "I always wondered why such a rich bastard was hanging around Centrism instead of Europe's Houses. They practically breed Companions over there."

"Hearsay," Phink snipped, glaring at her.

Sly shuddered. "I thought he was just a creep."

"Yeah," Blythe sighed, "but he was also a regular at Centrism long before you or I were born."

Sly yanked at fistfuls of his hair and groaned. "I don't understand. How did he survive under the radar for so long? This can't have been his first episode."

"He had money," Tilla said with a shrug. "And he was dealing with Guards who were ignorant of Nocturni diseases."

"Who knows what got swept under the rug?" Blythe murmured, squeezing Sly tight.

With spectacular bad timing, Sly's foggy brain coughed

up a memory of his father stumbling from a bar stool with his arms around a cruel-faced stranger. *"Fucking vampires,"* John would slur through his grin. *"They'll be the end of the human race if we're not careful. Physical and financial parasites, the lot of them. Hoarding all the wealth isn't enough; they're coming for our blood, too."*

"Sly?" Blythe whimpered. "Oh, Hun, it'll be okay."

"You don't know that." Sly shook his head, pushing away from her. "Stars above, Blythe! What happens when this gets out? When Humans First dirtbags start using Le Vau's name for justifying who knows what?"

He stumbled, chest aching and head buzzing with anxious possibilities.

"That won't happen." Blythe shook visibly, her face ashen as she looked to Phink. "That won't happen, right?"

"Grow up, Blythe!" Sly snarled, his eyes stinging till his sight blurred.

"That's enough, Sly," Tilla said, stepping in front of him so all he could see was their leather-clad chest and golden braid. "Calm yourself. This isn't helping."

"Don't I fucking know it!" Sly screamed as furious tears streaked his face. "All I've done to help—all I *ever* do to help *anyone*—and it means nothing! It does nothing. Kahled's still dying, my dad hates me, and nothing I do is ever enough!"

His foot slid on the floor as he was crushed against Tilla's front. Their arms clamped around him like steel cords, and for one wild, soul-shattering moment, Sly imagined leaping back in time. The slate-gray bulkhead melded into the dark of a stone-walled bedroom, and the person holding him together was the passionate and reliable body of his lover. It was only a second, but it stunned him silent.

"We're here for you, Sly," Phink said. "We've got you."

Sly struggled to breathe under the force of his sobs, but Tilla just held him tighter.

"Isn't there something we can do?" Blythe asked. "We came all this way. Can't you at least let him see Kahled?"

Walters's sigh was so soft and sad that Sly's stunned crying nearly drowned it out. "Let me speak with Gorbon."

～

"YOU'RE MENTAL," FELIX SAID WHEN SLY ENTERED THE medical suite at Walters's side. "Absolutely barking."

"Hi, Felix." Sly gave the guy a halfhearted wave. "Just the person I didn't want to see."

"Likewise," Felix snarked as he spun in his chair to face the computer screen rather than Sly.

"This way, Mr. Spurgeon." Walters tapped his elbow and steered him toward the curtain that sectioned off Kahled's hospital bed. She was stretching out a hand to draw the fabric back for him when Felix gave her pause.

"Any news?" Felix asked, words clipped.

Walters tensed as she glanced over at the blond, but Felix's gaze was locked on the screen. "Master Vauqeulin's people are still assisting HEPP in their search for survivors," she said, her eyes darting between the two young men before she added, "They found Mae's body."

Sly's insides churned nastily. He closed his eyes and took a bracing breath until the urge to hurl passed.

Nearby, Felix sat rigid at the computer desk. His pronounced lack of reaction made Sly's heart break all over again.

"They should have a confirmed headcount of the remaining staff shortly," Walters said before clearing her throat and pulling back a corner of the privacy curtain. "Come, Mr. Spurgeon."

Felix didn't react as Sly slipped by. Neither said a word. Before Felix's mood could settle an extra weighted blanket of pure guilt on Sly's shoulders, the curtain was swinging closed between them.

Kahled was laid up in the cot, his bulk making the princely bed seem small. He was still, peacefully unconscious with the deep-blue bedding pulled up to his throat, but Sly wasn't fooled. The manacles were no longer resting on the headboard's posts, but a segment of the chains that connected them trailed under the blankets like a beacon.

Sly's heart stuttered as he moved closer to examine Kahled's face.

"He looks…" Sly trailed off, breath hitching. "It's like he's almost human."

It was a sick cosmic joke if he'd ever heard one. Kahled was recognizable; the jet-black hair and regal features were just as Sly remembered, the skin the same smooth bronzed sepia. The overwhelming scales weren't gone, but they had retreated into spotty patches on either side of his neck. His fangs were the most startling change; they were negligible in size, no more than two slivers of white between gently parted lips.

"All that?" Sly whispered as he approached the bed. "In barely a week?"

It shouldn't be possible, but Sly's eyes were working fine. He combed Kahled's hair back with his fingers and gasped when it uncovered tiny scales near his hairline.

"He didn't have scales on his face when I left," Sly murmured.

Walters took pity on him and didn't say anything about the full-body coverage the vampire sported earlier in the basement. Had the showdown with Le Vau really happened mere hours ago?

Sly glanced up at Walters, but the need to keep watch of Kahled was insurmountable. Without a clue what Walters looked like or where she stood, he went back to leaning over the vampire, studying his face and counting his eyelashes. "Can he hear us?"

Walters was slow to answer, but when she did, her tone was mild and a bit lost, "I don't know."

Sitting his hip on the edge of the bed, Sly continued petting Kahled's hair. He stroked over the minimalistic scales and marveled at how flat their glassy texture lay against the skin. There were no protrusions, no jarring hardness. The texture was different, yes, but it was subtle, as if these latest scales were part of Kahled's flesh rather than diseased growths.

Sly shook his head as he pulled his hand away. He couldn't afford that kind of wishful thinking. Not now.

"He's still sedated?"

Walters hesitated, shifting in place by the curtain. "We haven't given him anything since I unloaded a full clip into him." After a long moment, she added, "I had to shoot Tahliah once. Toward the end. It took three doses to knock her out."

Sly gnawed on his inner cheek. "How many did you give him this time?"

Walters breathed, "Six."

Sly nodded as his eyes started stinging all over again. "How long till he wakes up?"

"I don't know."

Sly's shoulders sagged.

"Doctor Gorbon's in conference with Master Kamari and the Harem Elders," Walters said as she shuffled back the way they'd come. "I'll send him in to speak with you as soon as he's available. In the meantime," she heaved a breath, and her voice wavered. "Mr. Spurgeon—"

"I'll be right here," Sly promised. He managed to tamp down his bitterness as he added, "I'm not leaving his side till someone drags me away again."

Walters said nothing for a long moment. Sly heard her footsteps and the swish of the curtain falling behind her. Once she was well beyond his sight, she paused. "If he starts to wake, I must ask you to step out where Felix can see you."

Sly stiffened.

"We don't know what state he'll be in," Walters continued. "You don't know what it will do to him if he learns he hurt you again."

Sly stared down at Kahled's restful face, and his whole body felt heavy. "Okay."

Then, she was gone. Felix was still around, but Sly couldn't hear or see him. For all intents and purposes, he and Kahled were alone.

They were left alone for a long time. It was long enough for Sly's insides to start cramping with hunger, long enough for him to accept a grudging five minutes away from Kahled's bedside so he could relieve his bladder. At some point, Sly wedged himself onto the foot of the bed and sat there for a while, cautiously poking at the odd shape of Kahled's lower leg through the blankets.

Kahled's feet were more proportionate to the rest of him now, Sly noticed. His ankle and tarsal bones were still warped into something more appropriate for a legendary dinosaur, but at least they seemed suited to his size. Sly saw for himself how graceful and deadly quiet Kahled could walk with them.

Eventually, Sly wormed his way up the bed. There was no chance of him budging the vampire's body to make room for himself, but Sly managed to nestle against Kahled's side with only his ass hanging off the bed. He wasn't comfortable enough to sleep, not least of all because his stomach kept complaining at him, but he dozed.

That was how Gorbon and Phink found him. They came through the curtain together, and they were such an unexpected twosome that Sly snorted a note of laughter. They made a strangely complementary sight, each of them round and grave-faced. Gorbon's sweater vest was creased and soiled from extended wear and turmoil, while Phink's business professional attire remained as crisp as his fur was frazzled.

"You look ridiculous," Sly informed them as the spark of humor fizzled out, "like a life-sized stuffed toy and his freshly shaved cousin."

Gorbon and Phink considered one another. The former gave a token chuckle as the latter bristled.

"I'm glad to see you again, Sly," Gorbon said as he rounded the bed to stand near Sly.

"Really?" Sly deadpanned as he snuggled Kahled's arm tighter. "I seem to remember you slapping a bandage on my neck and sending me on my way without much fuss."

Gorbon sighed. "None of us handled that well, I'm afraid."

Sly snorted in reply as Phink approached the other side of the bed, peering at Kahled with a curious frown.

"So, this is your vampire?" Phink's lip twitched as he crossed his arms, unimpressed. "He's a lot less scary when he's not covered in Le Vau's guts."

"Or scales," Gorbon added.

"That helps, too."

Sly swung his legs around so he could sit on the edge while keeping a protective hand on Kahled's arm. Despite the obscuring layers of bedding, he could detect the unyielding surface of scales.

He met Gorbon's eye and steeled his nerve. "Is my blood doing this to him?"

Gorbon pushed his glasses up his nose with a gentle shake of his head. "No. It's a contributing factor, at most. The disease itself is mutating." The doctor studied Kahled's face with a flummoxed expression as he continued shaking his head. "I wish I had answers for you and the Harem, but I don't. Not yet, anyway. I need more time to make sense of the data and monitor his state."

"How much time?"

Gorbon shrugged. "It depends. First, I need to determine whether his rational mind can be preserved, whether or when he's done mutating."

"It can," Sly insisted.

Behind him, Phink sighed. "You don't know that."

"Yes, I do," Sly shot over his shoulder before refocusing on the doctor. "He was listening to me before any of you got down there. He didn't hurt me, even fresh from a fight. Some part of him knew me. That means something."

Phink sighed, "I genuinely hope so."

"Don't hope. Believe me."

"I do." Gorbon stroked his beard as he stared from Sly to Kahled and back. "But I can't lie to you. There's no telling how the Harem is going to handle things from here out. Le Vau changes things. Kahled's present condition even more so."

"What's that supposed to mean?"

"It means you shouldn't get your hopes up," Phink interjected. When Sly twisted to stare at him, he shifted in hefty discomfort.

Gorbon set a placating hand on his shoulder. "We don't

know what's happening to him yet, Sly, but even if the answers are encouraging, he's not going to be here much longer—"

"No." Sly slipped to his feet as he whirled away from them in a desperate need for more breathing room. "He's not dying, not yet. I don't care what he did to Le Vau or what the Harem thinks, he's still sentient! They can't euthanize him like a rabid dog!"

Gorbon reached for him again with a cautious hand. "They won't, Sly. Breathe."

"They're not going to kill him," Phink said with a derision that stunned Sly quiet. "They're taking him back to Ethos."

Sly's knees gave out.

"Easy," Gorbon said, catching him and setting his ass on the foot of Kahled's bed.

"Wait. What?" Sly stared between the two older men, back and forth and back and forth, till he started to feel dizzy. The heart tap dancing in his chest stumbled.

Gorbon patted his knee as he leaned on the footboard nearby. "It's complicated, and nothing's certain at this point, mind you—"

"Stars above," Phink grumbled as he shoved Gorbon out of Sly's face. "Pull your head out of your love-sick ass for a minute and think, Sly."

A furry hand pressed on Sly's cheek to turn his face toward Kahled.

"What is he?"

Sly frowned and shoved Phink's insistent paw away. "A sick Nocturnus."

Phink slapped an exasperated hand over his own face. "Does he look sick to you?"

Sly's frown deepened. "No, but he never did."

Phink waved at Kahled's prone form in a frenzy. "Exactly! He's not sick! So, you didn't cure him, that's too bad, but your puny human blood didn't give him a new complexion on its own, Sly."

Sly squirmed across the cot away from Phink. "I don't understand—"

"For the love of the cosmos, Sly." Phink puffed up, the scant skin visible around his eyes and mouth flustered. "He's *evolving*!"

The following silence was deafening, resounding with disbelief.

As the room-wide stupor dragged on, Phink's shoulders dropped. "That sounded a lot more rational in my head."

Gorbon cleared his throat and hip-checked Phink on his way to Sly. "That's a bit more dramatic than I would have said it, but essentially, yes. That's seems the most likely explanation."

Sly gaped at the doctor. "Kahled's evolving?"

Gorbon shrugged. "For lack of a better term. Although, it might be more appropriate to say the *Vauqeulins* are evolving, rather than just him—"

"Woah." Sly held up a hand to stop as an incredulous chuckle burst out of his mouth. "Back up. What?"

Gorbon gave him a patient smile. "Le Vau managed his condition without a Harem's resources for decades, at minimum, and he's the third Nocturni to develop Nosferatu's Curse in the same century. I'll need time and means for a more in-depth autopsy, but between his body and Kahled's, I'd think it's safe to assume something significant is changing in the bloodline itself."

"He's not the only one thinking that." Phink poked his head over Gorbon's shoulder and added, "HEPP's kicking the whole bloodline off the planet."

"I repeat..." said Sly as he bounced to his feet. "What?"

"They're claiming your lover boy is an unprecedented risk to human life," Phink spat, as if quoting someone distasteful, "and they're using Le Vau as substantiating proof."

"Ironic, really," Gorbon said, "since they can't technically prove he was responsible for any particular crimes—"

"Beside the attacks on Sly and his dad."

"Well, yes, but unless they want to claim every human harmed in American interspecies conflicts over the past century were pure-blooded and all their splicing records falsified—"

Sly shouted over them, "Whatever!"

Gorbon and Phink startled back a step, staring at him.

"I don't care about this right now!" Sly flapped his hands at them as he began pacing beside the cot. "What about Kahled? Earth won't house him, but Ethos was the first one to cast him out for an unpredictable disease he still has. Would someone please explain to me how this means anything other than an expedited death sentence for him?"

"Well," Gorbon began, "in as simple terms as I can put it, Kahled is back to being the most valuable member of the Harem. He's the only Cursed Nocturni alive right now, after all."

At Sly's blank stare, Gorbon flushed.

"Surely, you understand?"

Phink snorted as Sly said, "Obviously not."

With a stiff shrug, Gorbon seemed to search for words before repeating, "He's the only one left. As in, he's all they have right *now*, at a point where the Harem is discovering precedent for studying and potentially encouraging survival, rather than..." he trailed off as he indicated their surroundings.

"Exile and premature death," Sly finished, his brain sprinting to catch up as he sagged back onto the cot.

"Yes." Gorbon deflated with a heavy sigh. He shoved his hands in his trouser pockets before perching himself next to Sly by Kahled's knee.

Sly's mouth went dry. "Kahled's going home? The Harem's really taking him off Earth?"

He kept staring off into space, but Sly felt the doctor sway with a nod. "Yes. Thank the stars."

Sly flinched. His insides turned gelatinous and cold, and he spent a long moment whirling with unnamable emotion. Nothing made sense.

This was good news. Kahled didn't deserve to waste his final days on this despicable little planet. It shouldn't make Sly feel gutted, like the Harem's decision was no different from Kahled's questionable mortality. In fact, it felt like having fresh chunks carved out of the raw places in his heart so recently left behind by his father. It shouldn't feel like Sly was losing another piece of himself, but it did.

Phink stepped closer, his bulbous belly brushing Sly's knee. His words were hesitant but gruff with conviction. "You should go with him, Sly."

Sly frowned. "But I'm not under contract."

"So what?" Phink scoffed. "Even if you hadn't negotiated for your missed wages from Centrism beforehand, I have no doubt the crap ton of luggage you came back with would turn more than enough profit to cover a shuttle pass to Luna and then some. If it's not enough to get you all the way to Ethos, then…" Phink's face scrunched with involuntary distaste, but he gritted through his teeth, "Shit, kid. Blythe and I will pitch in for the rest."

"That won't be necessary," Gorbon interjected, patting Sly's shoulder. "The Harem will take care of you."

Phink frowned at Gorbon. "HEPP won't let him sign a Companion Contract. Not for a few more weeks, and definitely not if Kahled's unfit to consent."

As one, they all turned to stare at the unconscious vampire. Kahled was unchanged, as still and eerily human as the moment Sly first stepped through the curtain. Sly felt as though the scarce scales and fashionably shrunken fangs were mocking him.

He felt Gorbon lean on his back and murmur in his ear, "He'll be fine."

Sniffling, Sly nodded. "He better."

Blythe was waiting for him in the entrance hall with dinner. She wasn't alone.

"What's happening here?" Sly asked as he descended the stairway.

The place was crowded. Collapsible tables lined the far wall with large foil pans of unremarkable edibles. There was a single pot of something steaming, but everything else was room-temperature at best. Sly recognized some of the provisions from menial port markets, and the mental image of Kamari or Walters picking through a plate of preservatives gave him pause.

Blythe handed him one such meal as they met at the base of the stairs.

"The European Port," she explained, gesturing toward the throng of people around the tables and crossing to and from the hangar bay. "This is their humanitarian relief effort. Tilla's pretty sure Vauqeulin paid them off to get so many people and supplies out here so fast." She didn't meet his eye as she wondered, "Do you think any of them know about Kahled's condition?"

Sly watched a group of strangers in gray-green bodysuits casually chat around the makeshift buffet. He recognized a few members of Walters's staff nearby, but they were diligently sticking to themselves as they grabbed their food.

"I doubt it," Sly admitted. "No way the port found this many people willing to consciously hang around him. Not with so many unknowns."

Blythe nodded, her back stiff and arms folded as she watched along with him. "Tilla and I spoke with the Nocturni bodyguards. The two that survived, anyway. They helped your friend Walters clean up the bodies before aide arrived."

"That makes sense," Sly agreed, fiddling with the flimsy edge of his plate. "I should be starving right now. I'm not."

Blythe's shoulder bumped his as she shrugged. "Me neither, but I choked some down anyway. Come on. Eat. You'll need the fuel when your vampire wakes up."

His fingers tightened on the plate, but he didn't eat. "Is he still my vampire?"

Blythe took the plate from him and set it on the banister before tackling him with a hug. "Let's just get you fed and cleaned up. One thing at a time, Hun."

CHAPTER 28

Tilla's ship continued to accommodate, but its toilets were a sorry comparison to what the estate was known for. Between the manor staff and Kamari's men, it took several hours before Sly got his chance in one of the closet-sized showers. Fortunately, the port volunteers and HEPP agents championing the cleanup and recovery had their own facilities, so they weren't contributing to the inconvenience.

Sly's hair was still wet when his stomach had to decide whether it was going to reject the food Blythe forced on him or not. A distraction was precisely what he needed to settle things down.

"Sly!" Phink shouted, well before he appeared in the doorway of Tilla's cargo hold. His fur stood on end, his eyes wide enough to burst out of his skull.

Sly abandoned his plate on a storage container and hurried over, Blythe glued to his side.

"I think you better get back to the medical lounge," Phink panted, visibly out of breath.

"What happened?" Sly demanded even as he shifted to go around Phink.

Phink and Blythe came charging out of the garage with him, the former huffing along. "I don't know. Something about HEPP having their panties in a twist and threatening to involve the European Guardsmen. Oh. And your vampire's awake."

Sly stalled on the entrance hall stairs, turning to stare at Phink. "Kahled's awake?"

"Yeah!" Phink gestured for him to keep moving. "He's cognizant, talking, and everything. Gorbon says he's stabilizing, whatever that means."

Blythe smacked him on the shoulder. "You should have led with that, Phinkster!"

Sly's heart jumped. He ran up the remaining steps, spluttering over his shoulder at Phink, "That's good, right? He woke up in his right mind? That's great!"

"He's pissed off, that's what he is," Phink countered. "That old woman with the stick up her ass told me to get you for damage control. I'd say she was being hyperbolic, but considering the bloodbath he took yesterday…"

Sly picked up the pace, so Phink stopped talking to conserve his lung capacity for running. They flew past the residential quarters and Sly's long-abandoned guest room. Blythe hesitated when they approached the metal barrier that should have stopped them from reaching the medical suite; someone's claws had torn through it since the last time she saw it, but Sly had his chance to ogle the damage before his previous visit with Kahled. He didn't slow down.

They could hear shouting. The words were indistinct, but at least two male voices were ricocheting off the med bay's walls and echoing down the hall.

Blythe set a warning hand on Sly's shoulder, forcing him

to a standstill. "Are you sure you want to get involved? I don't smell blood, but that doesn't sound like any of our business, Sly."

Sly shrugged her off and pushed on. His friends followed, but Blythe was dragging her feet. She was several paces behind Sly and Phink when the bite of Kamari Vauqeulin's voice made them pull up short.

"Back off!"

An unfamiliar voice murmured, "Caution, Master—"

"You keep that thing away from him unless he's actively threatening me! Which he isn't."

Then, Kahled said, "You should listen to him."

Sly's breath caught in his throat, and he stumbled over thin air.

The medical suite's doors were wide open. From down the hall, he could see members of the staff loitering in the opening. The distance didn't stop Kahled's voice from ringing in Sly's ears like a bell.

He spoke in that mild, commanding tone that Sly doubted he would ever grow accustomed to. "Perhaps if you armed my mortal nannies with more than tranquilizers, we wouldn't be in this situation in the first place."

"I wasn't going to give anyone a convenient means to end their assignment early."

Kahled laughed, but it wasn't the laugh Sly knew. It was cold, loud, and damning. "What a marvelous Harem Leader you've become, Kamari. Truly. I'm so proud."

"What did you expect me to do, Kahled? The whole point of bringing you here was to prolong your life! I wasn't going to leave you to be shot in the head by your own Harem at the first convenient opportunity!"

"No. Instead, you decided to weigh my dwindling quality

of life against the safety and well-being of an entire household."

"You are my brother!"

"Yes, and you are my Harem Leader, which makes me a responsibility you shouldn't have mishandled. I was already dying before I came here, Kamari, but none of them were!"

"How in the cosmos," Kamari screamed quietly, "was I supposed to know a psychotic loner was going to wreck the building? How, Kahled?"

There was a collective gasp, and the staff in the doorway jerked back into the hall. Sly was close enough to hear Kahled hissing at his brother before the doors closed.

"*You*, Kamari, are the one who dumped a Cursed vampire on them in the first place. If you had the nerves to do what should have been done, none of this would have happened."

The doors shut.

The group of human servants cloistered in the hall, murmuring to each other. Sly recognized Felix among them, worry lines carved into his brow as he comforted one of his peers.

Sly, Phink, and Blythe reached them in the next moment.

"What's going on?" Sly demanded.

Glancing about, Sly counted half a dozen familiar faces. All but one of them glared at him and inched away, their expressions ranging from devastation to fury.

Felix, however, shoved his hands in his pockets and hung his head as he faced Sly. "Master Kahled's lucid. They don't know how long it will last, and HEPP's labeled him an unacceptable threat to humanity. I think they're kicking him off Earth."

Sly gaped from the blond to the doors and back. "So, that's decided, then? For sure?"

Felix shrugged. "I don't know what's going on, but

there's been a lot of talk. Madam Walters hasn't told us about any definitive plans, but she knows the Harem Elders want Master Vauqeulin to resolve the matter fast and clean."

Phink puffed up, arms crossing his chest. "What's that mean, exactly?"

Felix shrugged again, exaggerating the gesture needlessly.

"He's disbanding the estate!" an older man shouted at them from the nearby huddle of staff.

Sly stared at Felix, wide-eyed. "Seriously? Are you getting fired right now?"

Felix's jaw tightened. "Something like that."

"Don't worry." Phink hitched his pants up with a determined glower. "You won't be left to fend for yourselves. If the Harem doesn't step up and reassign you, HEPP will find you all jobs and probably browbeat the Harem into funding your relocation."

"Master Kahled already took care of it." Felix rolled his eyes as he grimaced in distaste. "First thing upon waking, he gave Master Vauqeulin a scolding and made him promise the surviving staff a handsome pension plan." He paused to pull a slip of paper from his pocket with a flourish, adding, "We have it in writing. Guaranteed with the Harem Scion's signature."

Sly eyed the dissatisfied set to Felix's shoulders. The blond caught him looking and glared back at him.

"None of us will have to work again, if we're content with life in the European Port."

Sly nodded in understanding. "And if you want to get out of here?"

"I'm sure I can find a job on Luna," Felix said offhand, but his jaw was still tight as he gave Sly a glacial once-over. "I'll have to part ways with Gorbon, though. I'm not you."

"What's that supposed to mean?" Blythe shouldered her

way in front of Sly. She was a head shorter than Felix, but he backpedaled anyway.

Before there could be any further comment or cause for a scene, the medical suite opened again. Walters stood in the doorway, hands folded in front of her hips and an unimpressed arch to her thin brow.

"Well, you certainly took your time, Mr. Phink." As Phink blustered at his side, Walters turned her attention on Sly, and her face softened. "Come along, Mr. Spurgeon. I need you to talk some sense into Kahled."

She turned on her heel and walked into the suite.

Phink pouted, pulling Blythe away as he nudged Sly forward. "I don't think we were invited."

Leaving them behind, Sly went after Walters. As he caught up to her, all he could discern was the click of her heels on the floor and the dull thud of his own. There was no shouting, no voices of any kind, raised or otherwise.

Half a step ahead of him, Walters reached the curtained partition between the doctor's office and Kahled's cot. She glanced at Sly with a tense, hopeful expression before yanking it back.

And there he was. Kahled Vauqeulin.

He sat on the cot, clad only in lounge pants with the legs rolled up to expose the bestial shape of his lower limbs. His upper body was bare, composed of so much warm tawny flesh and only the barest streaks of scales along his ribs and outer arms. The patterns were symmetrical on either side of his torso as well as the sides of his neck, where they crept along his collarbone like a gleaming torque.

Bright crystalline eyes grew wide as they landed on Sly.

"Sly?" he gasped, leaning forward as if drawn to a tether. "You're really here?"

Sly responded with a watery chuckle. "Did you seriously think you could get rid of me that easily?"

He wanted to launch himself at the vampire. He moved to do just that, but then Gorbon was in the way, his hand on Sly's chest. In his other hand, the doctor held a tranquilizer gun at the ready. It wasn't pointed at Kahled, but Gorbon's finger was poised near the trigger.

"Take it slow," Gorbon said, his calm at odds with the weapon in his hand. "Don't startle him, Sly. A perceived threat might kickstart another episode, and we don't know what that might look like right now."

Sly began nodding but stopped when Kahled spoke next.

"You shouldn't be here."

Sly huffed an awkward, stilted laugh. "I disagree, Maestro."

But Kahled was no longer fixated on his face. His eyes flashed a burning white as they darted all over Sly's person, inspecting and braced to discover grievous injuries. Upon spotting Sly's bandaged wrist, Kahled growled. His bared fangs grew an inch or more.

Sly gaped. "Kahled?"

"Easy, brother," Kamari warned from the sidelines, stepping between them.

In his periphery, Sly caught a vague motion as Kamari's remaining security members took aim with guns similar to Gorbon's.

"Hey!" Sly scurried forward to Kamari's side to catch Kahled's notice.

The blinding white flickered out, and Sly was left staring into wary gray eyes as the fangs receded back into his mouth.

"It's okay." Sly grinned through renewed tears. "I'm fine."

Kahled frowned. Unhampered by fangs, Sly found the

expression awkward on his handsome face. It was unsettling in the oddest way, like a fundamental part of Sly's mental image of the vampire had been replaced. The resulting visage was picturesque, the inhuman attributes adopted in a fashionable way that could be confused for an intentional aesthetic. He was recognizable, but altogether too different for Sly's peace of mind.

This Kahled eyed Sly's injury with none of his typical guilt and far too much possessive ire.

Sly waved his bandaged wrist, careful not to wince. "This is nothing. You already got the guy that hurt me anyway."

"I hurt you."

Sly winced.

"It was an accident," Gorbon interjected, but there was a weary edge to his voice, like he was getting tired of repeating himself.

Kamari gave an eager nod, his hand clamping down on Sly's shoulder. "We should have been monitoring your symptoms more closely."

"We can limit your contact with humans," Gorbon jumped forward. "No direct feedings or bedsharing until we're confident your mental and physical states have finished adapting."

"We'll take more precautions!" Kamari said in agreement, giving Sly a gentle shake. "Isn't that right, Sly?"

"Yeah." Sly nodded along, even as he strove to piece everything together while keeping his heart from leaping out of his throat. "We can play it safe till we know what we're dealing with."

"No." Kahled raised a hand to stop them, shaking his head. "Companionship was a bad idea in the first place. Get him out of here, Kamari."

"Oh, fuck you," Sly hissed.

He made a move toward the vampire, but Kamari and Gorbon held him back.

"You shouldn't have sent me away like that!" Sly scowled, struggling in their grip.

Kahled rose to his feet, and he was bigger than ever, towering over the rest of them with his pearly fangs bared. "I was trying to protect you, you idiot Earthling!"

"Great job, Kahled!" Sly spat, and the venom in his voice almost stunned Kamari into letting him go. "Did you see how well that worked out?"

Kahled snarled and tossed up his hands as he whirled away. As human as he seemed from the front, his back side appeared completely alien. From beneath the hair falling over the back of his neck to the waistband of his trousers, there was nothing but scales. Thick armor coated his muscles, stretching around his sides. They peppered the outermost curve of his shoulders and biceps, leaving tawny human flesh only on the vulnerable spots of his underarms and forearms.

He didn't look at anyone as he paced. His mutated legs crossed the full span of the room in four seamless strides. His chest and shoulders heaved with gritted breaths as he flexed his fingers. His nails stretched into claws, not unlike the unsheathing of a wildcat's talons, only to shrink back into the nailbed. He did it again and again, pacing all the while.

Everyone let him. Kamari's hand was tight on Sly's shoulder. Gorbon was stiff and his knuckles were white on the gun at his side. No one intruded on Kahled's frantic movement, and no one commented on the new trick he was pulling with his claws. With utmost care and economy of movement, Sly glanced around the room, but no one else seemed startled, so he bit his tongue and didn't argue when Walters took his hand and tugged him back a few steps. The Nocturni bodyguards positioned themselves closer to Kamari without word or signal, though neither raised their weapon toward Kahled yet.

They simply waited. Wordless and expectant, they watched Kahled pace, working his claws in and out and growling under his breath. His eyes remained gray.

Eventually, Kahled uttered a single irritated snarl and shuddered to a halt.

"Good," Gorbon murmured, inching forward. "You see, Kahled? See how easier it is to control?"

Sly poked Kamari in the side and nodded toward Kahled's de-clawed fingers. "He's doing that intentionally?"

Kamari shrugged. "More or less."

"Less," Kahled grunted, not looking at them.

"It's been a week," Gorbon said, his voice encouraging. "Only a few days, really, since we've been certain your intentions are influencing your physiology—"

Kahled cut him off with a growl. "That means nothing if my intention is murder."

"I don't think it was," Sly interjected, trying to weasel his way past Kamari to no avail. "Kahled, look at me. Please."

Kahled didn't.

"Do you remember coming to find me," Sly persisted, "after Le Vau was dead? Do you?"

Kahled didn't respond, didn't look at him, but he went still. Attentive. His posture was familiar, and Sly knew he was listening.

"You remember," Sly said, certainty growing with every breath. "You didn't go down to that basement with murder in mind. You were looking for me. You were trying to protect me."

"I had no control yesterday. I heard your voice over the speakers and I..." Kahled grimaced before starting over. "He was trespassing. Intruding. He was hunting my—" He cut himself off again, expression hardening.

"Don't you hear yourself, Kahled?" Kamari said. "You were conscious. Maybe you weren't completely in control, but you knew what was happening. That's nothing like what happened on Ethos."

Kahled's shoulders hunched. He didn't respond.

"You didn't hurt Sly," Kamari continued, "but you could have. You reached him well before we did. No one stopped you from going for his throat. You did that all on your own."

Kahled began shaking his head, slow and sad. The sight was intolerable.

Shameless, Sly tripped Kamari with a well-placed kick to his ankle and threw himself past Gorbon. Before anyone could react, he had his hands on Kahled's shoulders, his face tilted up and shoved into the vampire's line of sight.

"I love you," Sly said.

Kahled turned into rock under his touch, so still he couldn't possibly be breathing. His eyes were the cool gray of a clear sky Sly had never seen in person, right before a mellow rainfall that had nothing in common with his reality. It was a poor, clunky analogy, but accurate; Sly didn't have Kahled's gift for sentimental poetry, but the thought made him smile.

"I love you," he said, and this time, Sly took Kahled's face in his hands and drew him in. "I love you so fucking much, and if you think you're going to get off this planet without me, you're in for a fight."

Slowly, so awfully slowly, Kahled's hand found his hip, his thumb caressing Sly's side. "If you stay with me, I might kill you."

"And the planet might implode tomorrow and take me with it," Sly scoffed. "I'll take my chances, Maestro."

Kahled kissed him, and for one glorious moment, Sly let himself believe everything would be all right.

THE FOLLOWING DAY WAS CHAOS.

Under the Harem Elders' direction, Kamari officially decommissioned the Earthly estate. Of the few dozen surviving staff members, only four remained in the Harem's employ. Tilla was given another minor fortune to briefly upset their trade route while they transported Walters and two of her underlings to a smaller property on Luna. The rest of the humans took the considerable payout Kahled offered via his brother's pocket, and HEPP saw them all carted off to the European Port, safe and sound.

Doctor Gorbon was the only human from the manor permitted to travel with Kahled to Ethos.

"What does this mean, exactly?" Sly asked him late in the afternoon.

He joined Gorbon leaning against the polished bulkhead of Kamari Vauqeulin's personal transport. It wasn't the little land rover Kamari used to deliver Sly to the manor so many months ago. This one was larger, grander, and designed for space travel.

"Honestly?" Gorbon said, shooting him a side-eye as people carried packages and bundles past them. "I'm not sure yet. Kahled has his suspicions, but it'll take time, further testing, and observation before we can determine anything and plan accordingly."

They fell silent as they watched Walters direct a group of European volunteers around the Captain's Quarters. It was the largest and most secure space aboard the ship, making it the default option to harbor Kahled for the journey home. To no one's surprise, Kamari was quick to relinquish the spacious compartment to his brother the moment it was decided which Harem vehicle would be best to transport him in.

"They're really letting him come home?" Sly sounded dazed as he watched the manacled frame of Kahled's hospital bed roll by, closely followed by a volunteer holding the IV stand.

Gorbon nodded. "We'll leave some time after sunset and avoid the worst of the sunfire, hopefully."

Sly chewed on his bottom lip. "I've never been off-planet before."

"I know. You'll be fine." Gorbon shoved off the wall and gave Sly's arm a fond pat. "I knew the moment I met you we were going to make history together, Sly."

Sly snorted. "Yeah? Seems like your would-be cure is even further away now than it was six months ago, Doc."

"It looks that way, doesn't it?" Gorbon stared off in thought with a cautious smile quirking his lips. "I think this is the way things were supposed to work out. You and Kahled together. Maybe not whole, exactly, maybe not the way you hoped to be, but at least you're alive and well. You're getting off this rock with the one you love by your side."

Sly nodded, his throat tight.

Gorbon's voice softened. "You'll be all right, Sly. Both of you."

BLYTHE, TILLA, AND PHINK WERE WAITING FOR HIM IN THE garage, smack between Tilla's vessel and Kamari's. Blythe caught sight of him first, and her eyes overflowed with tears before she wrapped herself around him.

"Don't forget about me," she grumbled against his cheek before smacking him with a kiss.

"Impossible."

She leaned back far enough for Tilla to snag him in a one-armed hug.

"Earthlings," Phink scoffed. "Bunch of gossips with too much time and imagination on their hands. You haven't heard what they're saying, have you, Sly?"

"Do I care?" Sly said as he squeezed Tilla and Blythe with all his might.

"We've got five ships trying to load up and get out of here, and no one's focusing on the task," Phink fussed. "All anyone's talking about is your vampire."

Blythe ruffled Sly's hair and snickered. "Apparently, he's going home to fulfill his calling as the vampire messiah. The herald of a new dawn for Nocturni kind or some shit."

Sly cackled. "I don't know about that. It's going to be a while before anyone's willing to trust Kahled's in complete control of himself, and it'll take longer still for him to believe it. I don't even know if he wants that kind of responsibility again."

"Well, the old lady—"

"Walters," Blythe corrected, kicking Phink's shin

"Whatever," Phink scoffed as he swerved out of range. "She's going around telling people he'll be reinstated at the head of the Harem by the end of the decade."

Sly narrowed his eyes. "She is not. Walters isn't the type to spread unfounded rumors."

"No, she's not."

Phink cussed under his breath as he stepped aside to make room for the former Head of Household. Walters gave him a critical side-eye before she approached Sly with an outstretched hand. Sly had to untangle himself from Tilla and pry his arm from Blythe's grip to shake it.

"Thank you, Mr. Spurgeon."

"Seeing as I effectively got you fired, I think you should call me Sly now."

One brow arched in faint amusement, but Walters didn't comment otherwise. Respectable and direct as always, she continued, "If you ever find yourself on Luna, feel free to reach out."

"Sure," Sly nodded toward the bustling gangway to Kamari's aircraft. "But I don't see many chances for interplanetary travel in my future. Kahled and I are on a one-way track to Ethos."

She followed his gaze toward the ship and cracked a small smile. "We'll see, Mr. Spurgeon. From my perspective, you've already pulled off one miracle. If the Harem is ready to support their Cursed kin instead of condemning them, who knows what might happen."

"Madam Walters," he gawked at her, scandalized. "Don't you dare turn me into a liar and start gossiping now."

"Of course not." Her smile fell, and the stare she gave him was unnerving and grave. "You're giving Kahled an opportunity I never had the chance to give Tahliah. I don't know what the Harem will do with him, Mr. Spurgeon, but I'm sure he'll rise to the occasion. I imagine you'll be there helping him every step of the way."

She walked off in a swish of her skirts, leaving him staring after her.

Blythe sighed as she hung off his shoulder. "I want to be her when I grow up."

"Speaking of growing up," Sly shifted out from under her and dug into his pocket. He pulled out a nondescript key card and handed it to her. "I want you to have this."

Blythe eyed the card without taking it. "What is it?"

Phink piped up, "If she doesn't want it, I'll take it!"

Blythe snatched the key, glowering at them both. "I didn't say I didn't want it. I just want to know what it is first."

"Smart," Tilla said over her shoulder.

Sly brushed a stray curl back over his best friend's shoulder. His touch lingered on a few jaguar spots, and he was stunned to realize how well they suited her. "I'm not coming back. You know that, right?"

She went cold beneath his touch. "Yeah. Good for you, Sly. You deserve it."

"So do you. Back at Centrism, you said you needed to leave." Sly tapped the card in her hand. "That's the key to the station locker holding all the expensive crap the Harem gave me when Kahled terminated the contract. I want you to use it."

Blythe's lip trembled. "Are you sure about this?"

"I know what I'm doing," he lied unrepentantly. With more sincerity, he assured her, "You don't need to worry about me."

"Wish I could say the same," Blythe admitted with a grumpy look over her shoulder at Tilla.

Tilla was unfazed as they sent Sly a pointed look. "I offered to take her to Luna when I drop off Walters and her people. She hasn't given me a definitive answer."

"You could always come back to the port with me," Phink suggested with a forlorn sigh. "But I don't think anyone here likes that idea."

Blythe grimaced and shook her head as Sly commented, "Yeah, I'd rather you didn't go back to a doomed port known to harbor extremists with your name on their shit list."

"Agreed," Tilla said with a sage nod.

Blythe wagged the key card under his nose. "What about this, then?"

Phink reached for it. "I could take it off your hands."

Snorting, Blythe held it at arm's length in the opposite direction. Tilla stopped Phink from going after it with a stubborn hand planted on his forehead, their arm fully extended. Phink sputtered and swatted at the restricting grip, but Tilla was unmoved.

Phink in one hand and tossing a gold braid over their shoulder with the other, Tilla gave Sly a discerning stare. "What about the painting? If I'm taking teddy bear here back to America, want me to pack up Kahled's portrait of you and forward it to Ethos?"

Phink ceased his token struggles to stare at Sly, his expectant face matching the trader's.

Sly blushed and couldn't bring himself to meet their stares. "Thanks, but I think I'll let Phink keep it."

Phink grinned. "On your way out the door, and you're still doing me favors."

Sly rolled his eyes as Tilla gave Phink's furry head a rude shove.

Blythe wormed her way between them to reclaim center-stage in Sly's field of vision. "That painting's amazing, Sly. Are you sure you don't want it?"

Sly shrugged. "I've got the artist chained to a bed."

They all laughed, just as he hoped they would. Tilla's was quiet yet heartfelt while Phink's was reluctant and chuffed. Blythe's was high, maybe a little morose. They were familiar. Safe.

He was going to miss them fiercely.

❧

ONCE KAMARI'S PRIVATE SPACECRAFT WAS THE ONLY VESSEL that remained in the hangar, Gorbon and the Harem Scion escorted Kahled from the medical suite for the last time. In theory, Sly should have been with them, but he wasn't.

As his last act on Earth, Sly made one final trip to the master suite, heading straight for the bedroom. He deserved a moment or two to admire the cozy little nest that had sheltered them from so much worry over the last few months. That was the idea, anyway, but he hadn't expected to find something so sentimental stowed away among Kahled's rumpled bedding, crumpled and stuffed under a pillow like a dirty secret.

Sly was the last to board the transport as a result. The gangway reeled in with a mechanical hiss, and the portal closed behind him with a gentle snap that nevertheless made him jump. He was locked inside. There was no going back now.

As the surrounding walls began to subtly hum with liftoff, Sly made his way toward the Captain's Quarters. The princely medical cot and it's accoutrements had taken over the place, and Sly found Kahled safely tucked in, with Kamari perched on the edge of the bed. The two remaining security guards stood just inside the room's entrance, tranquilizers holstered beside their more lethal counterparts, but Sly barely spared them a glance on his way in.

Kamari saw him first, and his jaw dropped. "My stars, Sly. I didn't know you had it in you."

Sly blushed through his grin.

Kahled's face turned to him, and those gray eyes flashed crystalline and hot. He smiled. "Sly?"

With his usual lack of finesse, Sly spread his arms and attempted a twirl. It wasn't the smoothest move, but the skirt billowed out around his legs obediently anyway. The fanciful collage of blues and patterns fell just below his knees when he stopped moving, and he was fairly confident he hadn't just flashed his lover's baby brother a peek at his underwear. Cheekily, Sly ended with a rough imitation of a curtsy.

The vampires laughed at him. Kamari was suitably amused, but there was a note of something tearful and important in Kahled's voice.

"Good choice," Kamari said, nodding as he surveyed Sly's outfit. "You don't have the hips to fill it out properly but, otherwise, it suits you."

"It fits him fine," Kahled countered as he reached for Sly with five well-formed fingers tipped by neatly subdued claws. "Come here, you little menace."

Uninterested in anything else, Sly did just that. Kamari slipped off to the side as Sly approached, but instead of taking his seat, Sly found himself tugged into Kahled's lap. With a tremulous giggle, Sly wrapped his arms around Kahled's neck as he felt a heavy hand slide under the dress to graze his thigh.

"Is this really happening?" he asked.

"I hope so," Kahled replied as he nuzzled his nose against Sly's cheek.

"I'm still here, by the way," Kamari chimed.

"That sounds like a personal problem," Sly snipped without tearing his gaze from Kahled's.

Beyond his line of sight, Kamari scoffed and began muttering, "Last I checked, I'm still the leader of this Harem and owner of this ship. Who do you think you are to talk to me like that, Earthling?"

Kahled kissed him, and Sly promptly forgot to care about whatever Kamari was grumbling about.

"My Earthling," Kahled murmured against his lips. "My Companion."

ABOUT THE AUTHOR

K.R. Bady is a debut author, pro visual artist, and a general nerd. She comes from an eclectic background that criss-crosses the country, but she currently calls Colorado her home. Fantastical escapism was her first love, and she still harbors a deep and abiding passion for all things science fiction/fantasy and the supernatural.

As a queer woman who was raised in a religious American household, she aspires to write the sort of novels she wishes were more readily available to anyone who felt similarly disenfranchised. Since making a difference in the real world seems impossible at times, she happily indulges in her obsession of exercising change in fiction by envisioning worlds where people are free to be who they want to be.

Lightning Source UK Ltd.
Milton Keynes UK
UKHW020745090922
408600UK00009B/789